Anonymous

**Revival and Camp Meeting Minstrel**

Containing the Best Hymns and Spiritual Songs, Original and Selected

Anonymous

**Revival and Camp Meeting Minstrel**
*Containing the Best Hymns and Spiritual Songs, Original and Selected*

ISBN/EAN: 9783337081775

Printed in Europe, USA, Canada, Australia, Japan

Cover: Foto ©Andreas Hilbeck / pixelio.de

More available books at **www.hansebooks.com**

# REVIVAL

### AND

# CAMP MEETING MINSTREL.

#### CONTAINING THE BEST

## HYMNS AND SPIRITUAL SONGS,

## ORIGINAL AND SELECTED.

———●———

## PHILADELPHIA:
## PERKINPINE & HIGGINS,
### 56 N. FOURTH STREET.

Entered according to Act of Congress, in the year 1867, by

PERKINPINE & HIGGINS,

in the Clerk's Office of the District Court for the Eastern
District of Pennsylvania.

WESTCOTT & THOMSON,
Stereotypers, Philada.

CAXTON PRESS OF
SHERMAN & CO., PHILADELPHIA.

# PREFACE.

The principal design of the present work is to save to the Church the many soul-reviving and spiritual songs which were fast passing into forgetfulness, and which, by the blessing of God, have been of such remarkable benefit to the Church and the world.

The Hymns are such as are not found in the Church Hymn Book—the compilers being careful to give those which are more desirable for social and prayer-meetings.

Such as it is, the book is devoutly commended to the blessing of that God who "loveth the gates of Zion," and who has commanded us to "teach and admonish one another in psalms, and hymns, and spiritual songs, singing with grace in our hearts to the Lord."

3

# CONTENTS.

4

# REVIVAL

### AND

# CAMP MEETING MINSTREL.

---

## AWAKENING AND INVITING.

**1**

*C. M.*

HEAR the royal proclamation,
The glad tidings of salvation,
Published to every creature,
To the ruined sons of nature.

> *Jesus reigns, He reigns victorious!*
> *Over heaven and earth, most glorious,*
> *Jesus reigns.*

2 See the royal banners flying,
Hear the heralds loudly crying
Rebel sinners, royal favor
Now is offered by the Saviour.

3 There, ye sons of wrath and ruin,
Who have wrought your own undoing,
There is life and free salvation,
Offer'd to the whole creation.

4 'Twas for you that Jesus died,
For you he was crucified,
Conquered death and rose to heaven;
Through him life eternal's given.

5 Turn unto the Lord most holy;
Shun the path of vice and folly:
Turn or you are lost forever,
O now turn to Christ your Saviour.

6 There is wine, and milk, and honey,
Come and purchase without money,
Mercy like a flowing fountain,
Streaming from the holy mountain.

7 For this love let rocks and mountains,
Purling streams, and flowing fountains,
Roaring thunders, lightning blazes
Sing the great Messiah's praises.

8 Shout ye saints of every nation,
To the bounds of the creation;
Shout the praise of Judah's Lion,
The Almighty King of Zion.

9 Shout ye saints! make joyful mention;
Christ has purchas'd your redemption:
Angels tell the pleasing story,
Through the brightest worlds of glory.

### 2 *C. M.*

ATTEND, young friends, while I relate
The dangers you are in;
The evils that around you wait,
    While you remain in sin.
Although you flourish like the rose,
    Amid its branches green;
Your sparkling eyes in death must close,
    And never more be seen.

2 In silent shades must you lie down,
    Long in your graves to dwell;
Your friends will then stand weeping round,
    And take their long farewell.
How small this world will then appear,
    At the tremendous hour
When you Jehovah's voice shall hear,
    And feel his mighty power!

3 Departed days, the harvest past,
    In vain you then shall mourn;

Your golden hours are spent at last,
And never will return.
Oh, come this moment, seek the Lord;
Accept his offers now;
Yield to the mandate of his word,
And at his altar bow.

**3** *P. M.*

AH! guilty sinner, ruin'd by transgression,
What shall thy doom be when array'd in
terror,
God shall command thee, cover'd with pollution,
Up to the judgment?

2 Wilt thou escape from his omniscient notice,
Fly to the caverns, court.annihilation?
Vain thy presumption, justice still shall triumph
In thy destruction.

3 Stop, thoughtless sinner, stop awhile and ponder,
Ere death arrest thee, and the Judge, in ven-
geance,
Hurl from his presence thine affrighted spirit,
Swift to perdition.

4 Oft has he called thee, but thou wouldst not
hear him,
Mercies and judgments have alike been slighted;
Yet he is gracious, and with arms unfolded
Waits to embrace thee.

5 Come, then, poor sinner, come away this· mo-
ment,
Just as you are, come, filthy and polluted,
Come to the fountain open for uncleanness;
Jesus invites you.

6 But, if you trifle with his gracious message,
Cleave to the world and love its guilty pleasures,
Mercy, grown weary, shall in righteous judg-
ment,      Leave you forever.

7 Then you shall call, but he will not regard you,
Seek for his favor, yet shall never find it,
Cry to the rocks to hide you from his presence,
      Deep in their caverns.

8 Where the worm dies not, and the fire eternal,
Fills every soul with anguish and with terror,
There shall the sinner spend a long for ever,
      Dying unpardoned.

9 Oh! guilty sinner, hear the voice of warning;
Fly to the Saviour and embrace his pardon;
So shall your spirit meet with joy triumphant,
      Death and the judgment

**4**           *L. M.*

BEHOLD the Saviour at the door!
   He gently knocks, has knock'd before,
Has waited long, is waiting still;
You use no other friend so ill.

2 But will he prove a friend indeed?
He will—the very friend you need:
The man of Nazareth is he,
With garments dyed from Calvary.

3 O lovely attitude! he stands
With melting heart and open hands;
O matchless kindness! and he shows
That matchless kindness to his foes.

4 Rise, touch'd with gratitude divine,
Turn out his enemy and thine,
Turn out that hateful monster, sin,
And let the heavenly stranger in.

**5**           *P. M.*

COME ye poor and thirsty sinners,
   To the living waters, come;
Jesus bids you come and welcome,
   And declares he'll cast out none—

Give him credit!
He's Jehovah's faithful Son.

2 Hearken to the bride and Spirit,
　　Seize the promises divine;
Without money, price, or merit,
　　Buy of Jesus milk and wine—
　　　　His rich bounty
　　Freely take—he makes it thine.

3 Wherefore will you toil for nothing?
　　Spend your strength and treasure too?
Joyfully receive the blessing
　　Which his liberal hands bestow—
　　　　All his goodness
　　Let your souls delight to know.

4 Hearken, sinners, to your Saviour;
　　"Hear me, and your souls shall live;
You my covenant shall discover,
　　I will David's mercies give"—
　　　　As your witness,
　　And your leader, him receive.

# 6

COME to Jesus, trembling mourner,
　Come to Jesus, trembling mourner,

　　　　*Come to Jesus just now,*
　　　　*Just now, just now,*
　　　　*Come to Jesus just now.*

2 He will save you.
3 O, believe him.
4 He is able.
5 He is willing.
6 Flee to Jesus.
7 He'll receive you.

8 Call unto him.

9 He will hear you.

10 He'll have mercy.

11 He'll forgive you.

12 He will cleanse you.

13 He'll renew you.

14 Send the power.

15 Jesus loves you.

## 7

COME to the place of prayer,
  The day is past and gone,
And on the silent air,
  The voice of praise is borne:
Sweet is the hour of rest,
  Pleasant the heart's low sigh,
The glow within our breast,
  And the hope beyond the sky.

2 Yes! tuneful is the sound
    Of converts as they sing;
  Welcome the glory round,
    Shed from the Spirit's wing;
  But bliss more sweet and still
    Than aught on earth e'er gave,
  Our yearning souls shall fill
    In the world beyond the grave.

3 Earth with her dreams shall fade,
    And our bodies turn to dust;
  But our souls shall soar and sing
    In the mansions of the just;
  "So we lift our trusting eyes
    From the hills our fathers trod,
  To the quiet of the skies,
    To the Sabbath of our God."

**8**

COME—'tis Jesus' invitation—
  Now to mourning souls addressed;
Why, O why such hesitation?
  Mourners, he will give you rest.

2 Do ye fear your own unfitness,
    Burdened as ye are with sin?
  'Tis the Holy Spirit's witness—
    Christ invites you, enter in.

3 He will give—we ne'er can merit—
    Perfect peace and heavenly rest;
  What a treasure we inherit!
    How are contrite sinners blest!

**9**                    *C. M.*

COME, trembling sinner, from thy seat,
  And bow before the Lord:
Fall as a mourner at his feet,
  And hang upon his word.

2 Why should you stray and cease to strive,
    Or drive your fears away,
  Since you may come to Christ, and live
    In that eternal day?

3 Oh, why let sin allure your heart,
    Or fill your souls with pain?
  Can you with every blessing part,
    Eternal wo to gain?

4 Come, while you may, to Christ and live,
    For life will soon be done;
  Oh, come, and to the Saviour give
    That guilty heart of stone.

5 No longer vain excuses frame,
    But venture as you are:
  The dumb, the blind, the halt, the lame,
    May all his blessings share.

6 Come, if thou canst or canst not feel,
    Come, trusting in his grace;
He will the work of pardon seal,
    On all who seek his face.

7 Come, while the voice of Jesus calls,
    In accents full and clear;
And mercy's sweetest language falls
    Inviting on thine ear.

8 The Saviour stands, thy cause to plead,
    Before the throne above;
Come, in thine hour of greatest need,
    And feel his pardoning love.

## 10                    *L. M.*

COME, then, ye sinners, to your Lord,
    In Christ to paradise restored:
His proffer'd benefits embrace,
The plenitude of gospel grace.

2 A pardon written with his blood,
The favor and the peace of God;
The seeing eye, the feeling sense,
The mystic joys of penitence.

3 The godly fear, the pleasing smart,
The meltings of a broken heart;
The tears that tell your sins forgiven;
The sighs that waft your souls to heaven.

4 The guiltless shame, the sweet distress,
The unutterable tenderness;
The genuine, meek humility;
The wonder, "Why such love to me!"

5 Th' o'erwhelming power of saving grace,
The sight that veils the seraph's face;
The speechless awe that dares not move,
And all the silent heaven of love.

# 11

*Tune.—Oh! how he loves.*

COME, poor guilty, anxious mourner,
 Look to the cross;
Leave the proud, the gay, the scorner—
 Look to the cross;
Lift the eye of faith to Jesus,
He from sin's hard bondage frees us,
When we grieve, his grace can ease us,
 Look to the cross.

2 Bow in humble prayer before him—
 Look to the cross.
Now by faith and love adore him—
 Look to the cross;
Let thy guilt no more distress thee,
Peace and pardon soon shall·bless thee,
And the Saviour's love caress thee;
 Look to the cross.

3 Jesus waits to grant his favor,
 Look to the cross;
He's an all-sufficient Saviour,
 Look to the cross;
Though thy crimes reach high as heaven,
Thou 'gainst grace and truth hast striven,
Here the vilest are forgiven;
 Look to the cross.

4 Dost thou feel thy spirit harden?
 Look to the cross;
See repentance joined with pardon,
 Look to the cross;
Hear what words of grace are spoken,
Love presents her highest token,
Gaze till thy hard heart is broken;
 Look to the cross.

5 Wouldst thou hear thy Saviour claim thee?
 Look to the cross;

Wouldst thou feel his love inflame thee?
 Look to the cross;
Hark! he speaks, but not in thunder,
Hear, O earth, let angels wonder,
"I have snapp'd thy chains asunder;
 Look to my cross."

6 Thence flows full and free salvation,
 Look to the cross;
Bought for all of every nation,
 Look to the cross;
Life and 'joy for all the dying,
Come, 'tis offered without buying,
Dry thy tears and stay thy sighing;
 Look to the cross.

## 12     *P. M.*

COME, all ye mourning pilgrims now,
 The joyful news I'll tell;
The Lord hath sent salvation down,
 To save our souls from hell;
The angels brought the tidings down,
 To shepherds in the field,
That God to man is reconciled,
 His Son, to man reveal'd.

  *Sing glory, honor, to the Lamb,*
   *Salvation to our King ;*
  *Let all that's wash'd in Jesus' blood,*
   *His praises ever sing.*

2 Come, all ye poor despised souls,
 Unto his fold repair;
Where God his boundless love unfolds,
 And says he'll meet us there.
His glorious presence fills our souls
 With songs of loudest praise;
Let all that want a Saviour dear,
 Their hearts and voices raise.

3 There's glory, glory in my soul,
    It came from heaven above;
Which makes me praise my God so bold,
    And his dear children love.
I'll serve the bleeding Lamb of God,
    I love his ways so well;
Because his precious blood was shed
    To save our souls from hell.

## 13 *11s & 10s.*

DELAY not, delay not, O sinner draw near!
    The waters of life are now flowing for thee,
No price is demanded, the Saviour is here,
    Redemption is purchased, salvation is free.

2 Delay not, delay not, why longer abuse
    The love and compassion of Jesus, thy God?
A fountain is opened, how canst thou refuse
    To wash and be cleansed in his pardoning
      blood.

3 Delay not, delay not, O sinner, to come,
    For mercy still lingers, and calls thee to-day;
Her voice is not heard in the vale of the tomb,
    Her message, unheeded, will soon pass away.

4 Delay not, delay not, the Spirit of Grace,
    Long grieved and resisted, may take its sad
      flight;
And leave thee in darkness to finish thy race,
    To sink in the vale of eternity's night.

5 Delay not, delay not, the hour is at hand,
    The earth shall dissolve, and the heavens
      shall fade;
The dead, small and great, in the judgment
      shall stand;
    What power then, O sinner, shall lend thee
      its aid!

## 14

HARK! hark! the gospel trumpet sounds,
Through earth and heaven the echo bounds;
Pardon and peace by Jesus' blood!
Sinners are reconciled to God,
Sinners are reconciled to God,
By grace divine.

2 Come, sinners, hear the joyful news,
No longer dare the grace refuse;
Mercy and justice here combine,
Goodness and truth harmonious join,
Goodness and truth harmonious join,
To invite you near.

3 Ye saints in glory, strike the lyre;
Ye mortals, catch the sacred fire:
Let both the Saviour's love proclaim,
Forever worthy is the Lamb,
Forever worthy is the Lamb,
Of endless praise.

## 15
*8s & 7s.*

HARK! the Gospel trumpet's sounding!
Sinners, hear the joyful call;
Christ, in pardoning love abounding,
Offers liberty to all.

*Turn to the Lord and seek Salvation,*
*Through the precious Saviour's name,*
*Pardon, peace, and full redemption,*
*None that seek shall seek in vain.*

2 Tho' your crimes have reached to heaven,
And of deepest dye appear;
Ask, and they shall be forgiven,
Seek, and you shall find him near.

3 Though the sinful world reject you,
Guardian angels hovering round,

Ever ready to protect you,
Flaming ministers are found.

4 Cast your load of guilt behind you,
To the Lord for mercy flee;
Though the strongest fetters bind you,
His salvation makes you free.

5 Free from héll's eternal prison,
Unbelief's tormenting chain;
Endless wo, and sad perdition;
Free from everlasting pain.

6 Turn, poor sinners, turn to Jesus,
Now while he inviting stands;
See, the blessed, loving Saviour
Holds to you his wounded hands.

# 16

JESUS, dear name, how sweet the sound,
Replete with balm for every wound;
His word declares his grace is free—
Come, needy sinner, come and see;
Come, guilty sinner, come and see;

*Will you come?   Will you come?*

2 He left the shining courts on high,
Came to our world to bleed and die;
Jesus, the God, hung on the tree—
Come, helpless sinner, come and see;
Come, guilty sinner, come and see.

3 Your sins did pierce his bleeding heart,
Till death had done its dreadful part;
Yet his dear love still burns to thee—
Come, careless sinner, come and see;
Come, guilty sinner, come and see.

4 His blood can cleanse the foulest stain,
And make the filthy leper cleau;

2

His blood at once availed for me—
Come, anxious sinner, come and see;
Come, guilty sinner, come and see.

## 17                    *L. M.*

JUST as I am—without one plea,
  But that thy blood was shed for me,
And that thou bid'st me come to thee;
    O Lamb of God, I come, I come.

2 Just as I am—and waiting not
To rid my soul of one dark blot;
To thee, whose blood can cleanse each spot,
    O Lamb of God, I come, I come.

3 Just as I am—poor, wretched, blind;
Sight, riches, healing of the mind;
Yea, all I need, in thee I find;
    O Lamb of God, I come, I come.

4 Just as I am—though toss'd about,
With many a conflict, many a doubt;
Fightings within, and fears without—
    O Lamb of God, I come, I come.

5 Just as I am—thou wilt receive,
Wilt welcome, pardon, cleanse, relieve,
Because thy promise I believe—
    O Lamb of God, I come, I come.

6 Just as I am—thy love, unknown,
Has broken every barrier down;
Now to be thine, yea, thine alone,
    O Lamb of God, I come, I come.

## 18                    *L. M.*

JUST as thou art—without one trace
  Of love, or joy, or inward grace,
Or meetness for the heavenly place,
    O guilty sinner, come, O come!

2 Thy sins I bore on Calvary's tree:
  The stripes, thy due, were laid on me,
  That peace and pardon might be free—
    O wretched sinner, come, O come!

3 Come, hither bring thy boding fears,
  Thy aching heart, thy bursting tears;
  'Tis mercy's voice salutes thine ears:
    O trembling sinner, come, O come!

4 "The Spirit and the bride say, Come!"
  Rejoicing saints re-echo, Come!
  Who faints, who thirsts, who will, may come,
    Thy Saviour bids thee; come, O come!

# 19 *P. M.*

LISTED into the cause of sin,
  Why should a good be evil?
Music, alas, too long has been
  Pressed to obey the devil:
Drunken or lewd, or light, the lay
  Flows to the soul's undoing,
Widens and strews with flowers the way
  Down to eternal ruin.

2 Who on the part of God will rise?
    Innocent sounds recover;
  Fly on the prey, and seize the prize,
    Plunder the carnal lover;
  Strip him of every moving strain,
    Ev'ry melting measure;
  Music in virtue's cause retain,
    Rescue the holy pleasure.

3 Come, let us try if Jesus' love
    Will not as well inspire us;
  This is the theme of those above,
    This upon earth shall fire us:

Try if your hearts are tuned to sing,
  Is there a subject greater?
Harmony all its strains may bring,
  Jesus' name is sweeter.

4 Jesus the soul of music is,
    His is the noblest passion;
  Jesus' name is life and peace,
    Happiness and salvation;
  Jesus' name the dead can raise,
    Show us our sins forgiven;
  Fill us with all the life of grace,
    Carry us up to heaven.

5 Who have a right like us to sing?
    Us whom his mercy raises?
  Cheerful our hearts, for Christ is king,
    Joyful are all our faces.
  Who of his perfect love partakes,
    He evermore rejoices;
  Melody in our hearts we make,
    Melody with our voices.

6 He that a sprinkled conscience hath,
    He that in God is merry,
  Let him sing Psalms, the Spirit saith,
    Joyful and never weary;
  Offer the sacrifice of praise,
    In spirit never ceasing;
  Spiritual songs and anthems raise,
    Worship, and thanks, and blessing.

7 Then let us in his praises join,
    Triumph in his salvation;
  Glory ascribe to love divine,
    Worship and adoration.
  Heaven already is begun,
    Opened in each believer;
  Only believe, and then sing on,
    Heaven is ours forever.

**20** *8s & 7s.*

NOW the Saviour standeth pleading
At the sinner's bolted heart;
Now in heaven he's interceding,
Undertaking sinners' part.

*Sinner! can you hate this Saviour?*
*Will you thrust him from your arms?*
*Once he died for your behaviour,*
*Now he calls you to his charms.*

2 Sinner! hear your God and Saviour,
Hear his gracious voice to-day,
Turn from all your vain behaviour,
O repent, return and pray!

3 Now he's waiting to be gracious,
Now he stands and looks on thee:
See what kindness, love, and pity
Shine around on you and me.

4 Come, for all things now are ready,
Yet there's room for many more:
O ye blind, ye lame and needy,
Come to wisdom's boundless store!

**21** *11s.*

O TURN ye, O turn ye, for why will ye die?
When God in great mercy is coming so nigh;
Since Jesus invites you, the Spirit says, come,
And angels are waiting to welcome you home.

2 How vain the delusion, that while you delay,
Your hearts may grow better by staying away;
Come wretched, come starving, come just as
you be,
While streams of salvation are flowing so free.

3 And now Christ is ready your souls to receive,
O how can you question, if you will believe!

If sin is your-burden, why will you not come?
'Tis you he bids welcome; he bids you come
home.

4 Why will you be starving and feeding on air?
There's mercy in Jesus, enough and to spare;
If still you are doubting, make trial and see,
And prove that his mercy is boundless and free.

**22**          *P. M.*

O HEARKEN, sinners, we have cause
To warn you of your danger;
We pray be reconcil'd to him,
Who once lay in a manger.

> *Ho! every one that thirsts,*
> *Come ye to the waters,*
> *Freely drink and quench your thirst,*
> *Zion's sons and daughters.*

2 The awful God who made your soul,
And all the world around you,
Doth charge you with ten thousand crimes,
But hateth to confound you.

3 O seek the circumcising grace,
Be wise, do not refuse it,
For if you seek your life to save,
You will be sure to lose it.

4 The cross of Christ you have to bear,
Fearless of persecution,
Or groan you will when time shall cease,
In darkness and confusion.

5 Come all ye humble weeping souls,
Who long to be forgiv'n,
We bring glad tidings unto you,
From the good Lord of heav'n.

6 There is a fountain deep and wide,
For sin and all uncleanness,

Come drink and wash, and be made white,
 And prove the gospel fulness.

7 O! see the crowd that's trav'ling on,
 In paths of self-denial;
They march along the banks of love,
 And long for your arrival.

8 Shall unbelief debar you from
 The knowledge of your Saviour?
Believe, and you'll be justified:
 Believe and live forever.

9 My night of sin and grief is gone,
 My soul is filled with glory:
O! for a thousand tongues to tell
 Love's animating story.

10 Let heav'n and earth with me unite,
 And sing and shout hosanna;
The Lord has pardon'd all my sins,
 And fill'd my soul with manna.

**23**      *P. M.*

OH ye young, ye gay, ye proud,
 You must die and wear the shroud
Time will rob you of your bloom,
Death will drag you to the tomb;

  *Then you'll cry, and want to be*
  *Happy in eternity.*

2 Will you go to heaven? or hell?
One you must, and there to dwell:
Christ will come, and quickly too;
I must meet him, so must you.

3 The white throne will soon appear,
All the world must then draw near
Sinners will be driven down—
Saints will wear the starry crown.

**24** *P. M.*

POOR trembling sinner, tell me why
   Such floods of grief proceed from thee!
"My sins distress me," you reply;
   Then look to Christ on Calvary.

2 Behold his sacred hands stretch'd wide,
   Fast nail'd upon the fatal tree;
The cruel spear thrust in his side—
   O look by faith to Calvary.

3 See! streams of blood flow from his veins;
   How great must his distresses be!
Think on his agonizing pains,
   When you remember Calvary.

4 "'Tis finished," the Redeemer cried,
   And paid th' amazing price for thee;
Then bow'd his sacred head and died—
   O, sinner, look on Calvary!

5 Come fall with love at Jesus' feet,
   He suffer'd all the woes for thee;
Salvation's work he made complete,
   And still remembers Calvary.

6 He reigns a Prince exalted high,
   An ever-glorious Priest to be;
And will not trembling souls deny,
   The bliss which flows from Calvary.

**25** *5 6s & 3 5s.*

POOR, wildered, weeping heart
   What can relieve thee?
Come, sinful as thou art,
   Christ will receive thee:
Come, though with woes oppressed,
Soft is thy Saviour's breast,
There mayst thou sweetly rest,
   There naught can grieve thee.

2 Come, trembling, timid soul, ·
   Why this delaying?
Thunders that o'er thee roll,
   Fall on thee straying;
Turn from destruction's ways,
Turn to the throne of grace;
There seek thy Father's face,
   Weeping and praying.

3 Hence guilty fear and doubt,
   Leave me forever;
Lord, wilt thou cast me out?
   Never—oh, never:
From unbelief of mind;
From thoughts to sin inclined—
From flesh and hell combined
   Thou wilt deliver.

## 26       *P. M.*

PILGRIM, burden'd with thy sin,
   Come the way to Zion's gate;
There, till mercy speaks within,
   Knock and weep, and watch and wait.
Knock—he knows the sinner's cry,
   Weep—he loves the mourner's tears,
Watch—for saving grace is nigh,
   Wait—till heavenly grace appears.

2 Hark, it is thy Saviour's voice!
   "Welcome, pilgrim, to thy rest."
Now within the gate rejoice,
   Safe and own'd and bought and blest.
Safe—from all the lures of vice,
   Own'd—by joys the contrite know,
Bought—by love, and life the price,
   Blest—the mighty debt to owe!

3 Holy pilgrim! what for thee
   In a world like this remains?

From thy guarded breast shall flee
    Fear and shame, and doubt and pains.
Fear—the hope of heaven shall flee,
    Shame—from glory's view retire,
Doubt—in full belief shall die,
    Pain—in endless bliss expire.

**27**              *P. M.*

OH! turn, rebel souls, there's mercy to-day
    The Saviour invites you—and for you he is
        pleading;
Come, enter his service—no longer delay;
    Your Captain is waiting, with his wounds all
        fresh bleeding;
    And the full crimson tide,
    From his deep pierced side,
    Gives proof he'll protect you, whate'er may
        betide,
He has vanquish'd all hell, and triumphed o'er
    the grave:
Fear not doubting sinner—he is mighty to save.

2 In front of the fight, see the Conqueror stands,
    With the trophies of war, and new glories
        full beaming,
While onward he marches, subduing all lands
    By the blood of his cross as from Calvary
        streaming;
    From the field of the slain,
    Shall our Jesus again
    Return in full triumph, and strengthen his
        reign.
O! rejoice brother soldier, his banner's unfurl'd,
And his reign shall increase, and he'll conquer
    the world.

3 On Zion's high walls, let his watchmen all stand,
    To espy the dread foe—and the Gospel trump
        sounding,

To encourage to fight—Immanuel's band—
    And induce conquer'd sinners, their weapons
        now grounding,
      To look up for his grace,
      And repair to their place,
    In phalanx to stand, and his enemies face,
While his blood-stained banner in triumph is
      wav'd
O'er the hosts he's redeemed, and the thousands
    he's sav'd.

4 For soldiers I come, my commission I show,
    In the name of my Saviour, I now am re-
      cruiting,
I enlist old and young, not fearing the foe;
    For the conquest he'll gain, and the honors
      well suiting
      To the cause shall attend;
      For he's always a friend
In danger and loss, to the war's final end,
And when time is no more, still his banner
      shall wave,
To show to all worlds, that he is mighty to save.

5 The saints from all lands, who have faithfully
    stood
    In the patience of hope, through the war's
      desolation,
Array'd in the robes, which they wash'd in his
    blood,
    To Mount Zion shall come, and with high
      approbation,
      Shall rejoicingly stand,
      And await the command,
To turn to the right, and inherit the land
Prepar'd for his soldiers, where his banner shall
    wave,
O'er the ransom'd from hell, and the spoils of
    the grave.

6 In glory they rise from their mould'ring beds,
    Where with honors of war, they have long
        been reposing;
With palms in their hands, and bright crowns
    on their heads,
    All adorn'd with the light of a day—never
        closing!
    . See the glorious band,
        In Immanuel's land;
    Now honor'd of God, for they died sword in
        hand;
Through the blood of the Lamb, who is mighty
    to save,
They have conquer'd all hell, and escaped from
    the grave!

**28**            *7s & 5s.*

ROUSE ye at the Saviour's call,
    Sinners, rouse ye, one and all;
Wake, or soon your souls will fall—
    Fall in deep despair.
Wo to him who turns away;
Jesus kindly calls to-day:
Come, O sinner, while you may,
    Raise your soul in prayer.

2 Heard ye not the Saviour cry?
"Turn, O turn, why will you die?"
And in keenest agony.
    Mourn too late your doom!
Haste, for time is rushing on!
Soon the fleeting hour is gone,
The lifted arrow flies anon,
    To sink you in the tomb!

3 By the Saviour's bleeding love,
By the joys of heaven above,
Let these words your spirit move;
    Quick to Jesus fly!

Come and save your souls from death,
Haste! escape Jehovah's wrath;
Fly! for life's a fleeting breath,
  Soon, O soon you'll die.

## 29        *P. M.*

REMEMBER, sinful youth, you must die!
     you must die!
Remember, sinful youth, you must die!
Remember, sinful youth, who hate the way of
     truth,
And in your pleasures boast, you must die! you
     must die!
And in your pleasures boast, you must die.

2 Uncertain are your days here below, here below,
  Uncertain are your days here below,
  Uncertain are your days, for God hath many
     ways
  To bring you to your graves here below, here
     below,
  To bring you to your graves here below.

3 And if you travel down the broad road, the
     broad road,
  And if you travel down the broad road,
  And if you travel down, to darkness you are
     bound,
  Eternally around, the broad road, the broad road,
  Eternally around, the broad road.

4 To a dreadful judgment day you are bound, you
     are bound,
  To a dreadful judgment day you are bound,
  To a dreadful judgment day, be your thoughts
     whate'er they may;
  Nor can you it delay, you are bound, you are
     bound,
  Nor can you it delay, you are bound.

5 The God who built the sky, great I AM, great
　　I AM,
The God who built the sky, great I AM,
The God who built the sky, hath said (and can-
　　not lie),
Impenitents must die, and be lost. and be lost,
Impenitents must die, and be lost.

6 And O! my friends, don't you, I entreat, I entreat,
And O! my friends, don't you, I entreat,
And O! my friends, don't you your carnal mirth
　　pursue,
Your guilty souls undo, I entreat, I entreat,
Your guilty souls undo, I entreat.

7 Unto the Saviour flee, 'scape for life, 'scape for
　　life,
Unto the Saviour flee, 'scape for life,
Unto the Saviour flee, lest death eternal be,
Your final destiny, 'scape for life, 'scape for life,
Your final destiny, 'scape for life.

## 30

SINNERS, go, will you go,
　To the highlands of Heaven,
Where the storms never blow,
　And the long summer's given?
Where the bright blooming flowers,
　Are their odors emitting,
And the leaves of the bowers
　In the hedges are flitting.

2 Where the saints robed in white,
　Cleansed in life's flowing fountain,
Shining beauteous and bright,
　They inhabit the mountain
Where no sin nor dismay,
　Neither trouble nor sorrow,
Will be felt for a day,
　Nor be feared for the morrow.

3 He's prepared thee a home,
  Sinner, canst thou believe it?
And invites thee to come,
  Sinner, wilt thou receive it?
O come, sinner, come,
  For the tide is receding,
And the Saviour will soon
  And forever cease pleading.

**31**                    *8s, 7s & 4s.*

SINNERS, will you scorn the message
  Sent in mercy from above?
Every sentence—oh, how tender!
  Every line is full of love;
    Listen to it—
  Every line is full of love.

2 Hear the heralds of the Gospel,
  News from Zion's King proclaim,
To each rebel sinner—"Pardon,
  Free forgiveness in his name!"
    How important!
  Free forgiveness in his name!

3 Tempted souls, they bring you succor;
  Fearful hearts, they quell your fears;
And with news of consolation
  Chase away the falling tears;
    Tender heralds—
  Chase away the falling tears.

4 Who hath our report believed?
  Who received the joyful word?
Who embraced the news of pardon,
  Offered to you by the Lord?
    Can you slight it—
  Offered to you by the Lord?

5 Oh, ye angels, hovering round us,
  Waiting spirits, speed your way,

Hasten to the court of heaven,
  Tidings bear without delay:
    Rebel sinners
  Glad the message will obey.

**32**            *P. M.*

STOP, poor sinner! stop and think,
  Before you farther go!
Can you sport upon the brink
  Of everlasting wo?
Hell beneath is gaping wide,
  Vengeance waits the dread command;
Soon he'll stop your sport and pride,
  And sink you with the damn'd.

      *Then be entreated now to stop;*
        *For unless you warning take,*
      *Ere you are aware you'll drop*
        *Into a burning lake.*

2 Say, have you an arm like God,
  That you his will oppose?
Fear you not that iron rod
  With which he breaks his foes?
Can you stand in that great day
  When he judgment will proclaim?
When the earth shall melt away
  Like wax before the flame?

3 Ghastly death shall quickly come,
  And drag you to the bar;
Then to hear your awful doom
  Will fill you with despair;
All your sins around you'll crowd—
  Sins of a blood-crimson dye;
Each for vengeance crying loud;
  And what will you reply?

4 Though your heart be made of steel,
  Your forehead lined with brass,

God at length will make you feel,
   He will not let you pass;
Sinners then in vain will call,
   (Though they now despise his grace,)
"Rocks and mountains on us fall,
   And hide us from his face."

5 But as yet there is a hope
   You may his mercy know:
Though his arm is lifted up,
   He still forbears the blow:
'Twas for sinners Jesus died,
   Sinners he invites to come:
None that come shall be denied,
   He says, "There still is room."

**33**       *C. M.*

SINNERS, the city where you dwell
   Is doomed to fearful wo;
Those dark, impending clouds foretell
   The quick descending blow.

    *Sinners, the hiding-place is nigh,*
      *The Saviour calls—away;*
    *He is your only refuge—fly;*
      *There's danger in delay.*

2 Beneath you shall the trembling ground
   Quake with the wrath of God;
While all above you, and around,
   Shall roll the fiery flood.

3 Haste from your revels and your mirth,
   And all your carnal joys;
The day of wrath is bursting forth;
   Oh! hasten to be wise.

4 Fly to the mountain, quickly fly;
   Nor will your flight be vain;
'Tis God's own house, and heaven is nigh;
   Stay not in all the plain.
    3

5 Angels, sweet messengers of love,
 Lend them your rapid wing;
And thou, good Spirit from above,
 All needful succors bring.

6 Why do you tarry, trembling souls?
 Haste ere the lightning's blaze;
Fly ere the rumbling thunder calls;
 Fly to the hiding-place.

**34**       *8s, 7s & 4s.*

STOP, poor sinners, and look yonder,
 See your sins like mountains rise,
O astonishing the number,
 Higher mounting than the skies:
  Cry for mercy,
 Dread the death that never dies.

2 On the crumbling banks of ruin,
 How can you securely dwell?
Sinners, vengeance is pursuing,
 And will sweep you down to hell:
  Then to heaven
 Finally you'll bid farewell.

3 Doomed where sorrow after sorrow
 Follow on without control,
Floods of vengeance big with horror
 Without intermission roll;
  Wrath vindictive
 Overwhelms the guilty soul.

4 See yon sun how swift he hasteth
 Through the circuit of the skies;
How your golden moment wasteth,
 Sinners, pray at length be wise:
  O! he's setting,
 And may set no more to rise.

5 See how fast your time is flying,
 Will ye sinners yet delay?

One is gone, another's dying,
  O! to God for mercy pray:
    Time is precious;
  God may next call you away.

6 Now's the time for preparation,
  While the vital air you breathe;
God is offering you salvation,
  Calls you yet to turn and live;
    Boundless mercy—
  All who come he will receive.

7 See the precious blood of Jesus
  Streaming from th' accursed tree,
Will not this suffice to grieve us,
  Jesus spilt his blood for me;
    Come then, sinners,
  And his great salvation see.

**35**        *8s & 4s.*

SINNERS, come, let's fly to Jesus!
    Oh! how he loves!
From our thraldom he'll release us,
    Oh, how he loves!
Oh, how glad we are to hear him
Bid such sinful worms come near him,
Why should we distrust or fear him?
    Oh, how he loves!

2 It's life, eternal life to know him,
    Oh, how he loves!
Think, oh, think, how much we owe him,
    Oh, how he loves!
With his precious blood he bought us,
In the wilderness he sought us,
To his fold he kindly brought us,
    Oh, how he loves!

3 Come, and in his arms he'll take us,
    Oh, how he loves!

Never leave us, nor forsake us,
  Oh, how he loves!
Men may slight and disrespect us,
But their wrath shall not affect us,
Jesus will from harm protect us,
  Oh, how he loves!

4 When the spark of life is waning,
    Oh, how he loves!
  When the languid eye is straining,
    Oh, how he loves!
  When the feeble pulse is ceasing,
  Start not at its swift decreasing,
  'Tis the fettered soul releasing;
    Oh, how he loves!

5 When the pangs of death assail thee,
    Oh, how he loves!
  Christ is thine, he cannot fail thee,
    Oh, how he loves!
  Yes, though death and hell endeavor,
  From his love thy soul to sever,
  Jesus is thy strength forever;
    Oh, how he loves!

6 Soon in heaven we'll adore him,
    Oh, how he loves!
  Cast our glitt'ring crowns before him,
    Oh, how he loves!
  When the victory is completed,
  And around his throne we're seated,
  Then we'll sing and still repeat it;
    Oh, how he loves.

36                   *L. M.*

THOUGH in the outward church below,
  The wheat and tares together grow;
Jesus ere long will weed the crop,
And pluck the tares in anger up.

*For soon the reaping time will come,*
*And angels shout the harvest home.*

2 Will it relieve their horrors there,
To recollect their stations here;
How much they heard, how much they knew,
How much among the wheat they grew?

3 Oh! this will aggravate their case,
They perish'd under means of grace;
To them the word of life and faith
Became an instrument of death.

4 We seem alike when thus we meet,
Strangers might think we all were wheat;
But to the Lord's all-searching eyes,
Each heart appears without disguise.

5 The tares are spar'd for various ends,
Some for the sake of praying friends;
Others the Lord, against their will,
Employs his counsels to fulfil.

6 But tho' they grow so tall and strong,
His plan will not require them long;
In harvest when he saves his own,
The tares shall into hell be thrown.

7 Most awful thought, and is it so?
Must all mankind the harvest know?
Is every man a wheat or tare?
Me, for that harvest, Lord, prepare.

**37**    *P. M. 10 10, 11 11.*

THY faithfulness, Lord, each moment we find,
So true to thy word, so loving and kind:
Thy mercy so tender to all the lost race,
The vilest offender may turn and find grace.

2 The mercy I feel, to others I show,
I set to my seal that Jesus is true:

Ye all may find favor, who come at his call,
O come to my Saviour, his grace is for all.

3 To save what was lost from heaven he came;
Come, sinners, and trust in Jesus' name!
He offers you pardon; he bids you be free;
"If sin be your burden, O come unto me!"

4 O let me commend my Saviour to you;
The publican's friend, and advocate too:
For you he is pleading his merits and death;
With God interceding for sinners beneath.

5 Then let us submit his grace to receive:
Fall down at his feet, and gladly believe:
We all are forgiven for Jesus' sake:
Our title to heaven, his merits we take.

**38**                *Come to Me.*                *L. M.*

WITH tearful eyes I look around,
    Life seems a dark and stormy sea;
Yet 'midst the gloom, I hear a sound,
    A heavenly whisper, "Come to Me."

2 It tells me of a place of rest—
    It tells me where my soul may flee;
O! to the weary, faint, oppressed,
    How sweet the bidding, "Come to Me."

3 When nature shudders, loth to part
    From all I love, enjoy, and see;
When a faint chill steals o'er my heart,
    A sweet voice utters, "Come to Me."

4 Come, for all else must fail and die;
    . Earth is no resting-place for thee;
Heavenward direct thy weeping eye,
    I am thy portion, "Come to Me."

**39**                          *P. M.*

WE'RE traveling home to heaven above,
   Will you go? will you go?
To sing the Saviour's dying love,
   Will you go? will you go?
Millions have reach'd that blest abode,
Anointed kings and priests to God;
And millions more are on the road.
   Will you go? will you go?

2 We're going to walk the plains of light,
   Will you go? will you go?
Where perfect day excludes the night;
   Will you go? will you go?
Our sun will there no more go down,
In that blest world of great renown,
Our days of mourning past and gone;
   Will you go? will you go?

3 We're going to see the bleeding Lamb,
   Will you go? will you go?
In rapturous strains to praise his name,
   Will you go? will you go?
A crown of life we there shall wear,
The conqueror's palms our hands shall bear
And all the joys of heaven we'll share;
   Will you go? will you go?

4 We're going where tears will never flow,
   Will you go? will you go?
And sorrow we no more shall know,
   Will you go? will you go?
'Tis there the saints shall die no more,
But live with Christ in heaven secure,
Their God and Saviour to adore;
   Will you go? will you go?

5 We're going to join the heavenly choir,
   Will you go? will you go?

To raise our voice and tune the lyre,
      Will you go? will you go?
There saints and angels sweetly sing
Hosannas to their God and King,
And make the heavenly arches ring;
      Will you go? will you go?

6 Ye mourning, heavy laden souls,
      Will you go? will you go?
Where peace and joy forever roll,
      Will you go? will you go?
Jesus is ready to receive
If thou wilt on him now believe,
He'll give thy troubled conscience ease;
      Come believe! come believe!

7 Come, O backsliders! come away!
      Will you go? will you go?
Return again to Christ and say,
      I will go! I will go!
The Lord will thy backslidings heal,
His love again he will reveal,
And pardon on thy conscience seal;
      Will you go? will you go?

8 The way to heaven is free for all,
      Will you go? will you go?
For Jew and Gentile, great and small,
      Will you go? will you go?
Make up your mind, give God your heart,
With every sin and idol part,
And now for glory make a start;
      Will you go? will you go?

9 The way to heaven is straight and plain,
      Will you go? will you go?
Repent, believe, be born again,
      Will you go? will you go?
The Saviour cries aloud to thee,
Take up thy cross and follow me,

And thou shalt my salvation see;
    Come to me! come to me!

10 Oh! could I hear some sinner say,
    I will go! I will go!
I'll start this moment, clear the way,
    Let me go! let me go!
My old companions fare you well,
I will not go with you to hell,
I mean with Jesus Christ to dwell;
    Let me go! fare you well!

**40**            *P. M. 8s & 7s.*

WHAT could your Redeemer do,
    More than he hath done for you?
To procure your peace with God,
Could he more than shed his blood?
After all his flow of love,
All his drawings from above,
Why will ye your Lord deny?
Why will ye resolve to die?

2 Turn, he cries, ye sinners, turn:
By his life your God hath sworn,
He would have you turn and live,
He would all the world receive;
If your death were his delight,
Would he you to life invite?
Would he ask, beseech, and cry,
Why will ye resolve to die?

3 Sinners, turn, while God is near:
Dare not think him insincere:
Now, e'en now, your Saviour stands,
All day long he spreads his hands;
Cries, " Ye will not happy be;
No, ye will not come to me,—
Me, who life to none deny;
Why will ye resolve to die?"

4 Can ye doubt if God is love?
  If to all his bowels move?
  Will ye not his *word* receive?
  Will ye not his OATH believe?
  See, the suffering God appears;
  Jesus weeps, believe his tears!
  Mingled with his blood they cry,
"Why will ye resolve to die?"

**41**                    *C. M.*

*Pilgrim Band.*

WE'RE marching to the promised land,
  A land all fair and bright;
Come, join our happy pilgrim band,
  And seek the plains of light.

> *Oh! come, and join our Pilgrim band,*
>   *Our toils and triumphs share,*
> *We soon shall reach the promised land,*
>   *And rest forever there.*

2 The deep Red Sea already crossed,
    Safe on its banks we stood;
  And saw our foes, old Pharaoh's host,
    Plunged in the angry flood.

3 The Saviour feeds his little flock;
    His grace is richly given;
  The living water from the rock,
    And daily bread from heaven.

4 To Canaan's bounds he points the way,
    And guides our feet aright;
  A cloudy pillar leads by day;
    A fiery one by night.

5 "Come with us, we will do thee good;"
    Here is our heart and hand,
  To meet you over Jordan's flood,
    And share the promised land.

6 There in that land no tears are shed;
  Nor sigh escapes the heart;
To joy's full fountain all are led;
  And there they never part.

## 42

WHY wanderest thou so far from home?
        *Fly to Jesus:*
The vilest of the vile may come:
        *Fly to Jesus.*

  *To the Saviour fly—to his shielding breast;*
          *Fly to Jesus;*
  *Lay thy burden there—he will give thee rest;*
          *Fly to Jesus.*

2 The tempter whispers, "Yet delay;"
  Resist his wiles and come to-day.

3 To-day thy homeward pathway trace;
  Long hast thou toiled in folly's ways.

4 Thy toils have only brought thee woes;
  Oh, tarry not—the door may close.

5 Come feast on joys divinely pure:
  Come, and eternal life secure.

## 43                    *L. M.*

YOUNG people all, attention give,
    While I address you in God's name;
You who in sin and folly live,
    Come hear the counsel of a friend:
I sought for bliss in glitt'ring toys,
    And rang'd the luring scenes of vice,
But never found substantial joys,
    Until I heard my Saviour's voice.

2 He spake my sins at once forgiv'n,
    And wash'd my load of guilt away,

He gave me pardon, peace, and heaven,
 And thus I found the good old way:
And now with trembling sense I view,
 Huge billows roll beneath your feet,
For death eternal waits for you,
 Who slight the force of gospel truth.

3 Youth, like the spring, will soon be gone,
 By fleeting time, or conq'ring death;
Yon morning sun may set at noon,
 And leave you ever in the dark:
Your sparkling eyes and blooming cheeks
 Must wither, like the blasted rose,
The coffin, earth, and winding sheet,
 Will soon your active limbs enclose.

4 Ye heedless ones that widely stroll,
 The grave must soon become your bed;
Where silence reigns, and vapors roll,
 In solemn silence round your head:
Your friends may pass that lonesome place,
 And with a sigh move slowly on,
Still gazing on the spires of grass,
 With which your graves are overgrown.

5 But O, the soul! where vengeance reigns,
 It sinks with groans and ceaseless cries,
It rolls amidst the burning flames
 In endless wo and agonies:
There swallow'd up in darkest night,
 Where devils howl, and thunders roar,
To rage in keen despair and guilt,
 When thousand, thousand years are o'er.

6 O! fellow youth, this is the state
 Of all who do free grace refuse,
And soon with you 'twill be too late,
 The way of life in Christ to choose:
Come, lay your carnal weapons by,
 No longer fight against your God;

But with my mission now comply,
   And heaven shall be your great reward.

**44**           *P. M. 10 10, 11 11.*

YE thirsty for God, to Jesus give ear,
   And take, through his blood, a pow'r to
      draw near;
His kind invitation, ye sinners, embrace,
Accepting salvation, salvation by grace.

2 Send down from above, who governs the skies,
  In vehement love, to sinners he cries,
  "Drink unto my Spirit, who happy would be,
  And all things inherit, by coming to me."

3 O Saviour of all, thy word we believe,
  And come at thy call, thy grace to receive:
  The blessing is given wherever thou art:
  The earnest of heaven is love in the heart.

4 To us at thy feet the Comforter give,
  Who gasp to admit thy Spirit, and live;
  The weakest believers acknowledge for thine,
  And fill us with rivers of water divine!

**45**           *L. M.*

YE blooming youth, I pray give ear,
   A death-bed lamentation hear!
Ere death shall blast the opening flower,
O make your peace and calling sure.

2 In pride, and wealth, and pleasure's maze,
  I've spent the morning of my days;
  Did oft in gayest circles shine,
  Nor thought my sun would e'er decline.

3 My beauty, once my greatest pride,
  The cold and silent grave will hide;
  The rose so late in sweetest bloom,
  The hungry worm will soon consume.

4 Oft I've adorned this blooming face,
　My limbs have decked with sweetest grace;
　But though so lovely and so fair,
　The winding sheet I soon must wear.

5 In sinful pleasures I have spent
　The golden moments God hath lent;
　And now, beneath his awful frown,
　I soon shall sink in anguish down.

6 Oft I have heard the gospel call,
　But madly have rejected all;
　And now the day of grace is o'er,
　I sink, alas! to rise no more.

7 Oft I have felt the inward smart,
　And anguish keen has seized my heart,
　And oft, alone, resolved in tears,
　To seek the Lord in riper years.

8 But with conviction still I strove,
　Despised a Saviour's offered love,
　Refused with sinful joys to part,
　And grieved his Spirit from my heart.

9 Now soon with me shall time be o'er:
　My sun shall rise and set no more;
　But, sinking down in endless pain,
　Shall never, never rise again.

10 Ye blooming youth, a long farewell,
　O shun the path that leads to hell,
　Seek now your slighted Saviour's face,
　No more despise his offered grace.

11 No more his loving Spirit grieve,
　Lest he your precious soul should leave;
　O think, that ere to-morrow's sun
　You may forever be undone.

12 O Christian friends, a long adieu.
　I've been reproved and warned by you;

Oft have I heard your weeping cry,
"Turn, sinner, turn, why will you die?"

13 But mercy has forever fled,
I sink among the silent dead;
My life is o'er, my glass has run,
Farewell to all below the sun.

## SEEKING SALVATION.

**46**      *C. M.*

A FFLICTIONS, though they seem severe,
In mercy oft are sent;
They stopped the Prodigal's career,
And caused him to repent.

2 Although he no relentings felt
Till he had spent his store,
His stubborn heart began to melt
When famine pinched him sore.

3 "What have I gained by sin." he said,
"But hunger, shame, and fear?
My father's house abounds with bread,
While I am starving here.

4 "I'll go and tell him all I've done,
Fall down before his face:
Unworthy to be called his son,
I'll seek a servant's place."

5 His father saw him coming back:
He saw, and ran, and smiled;
Then threw his arms around the neck
Of his rebellious child.

6 "Father, I've sinned, but oh, forgive!"
"Enough," the father said:
"Rejoice, my house, my son's alive,
For whom I mourned as dead.

7 "Now let the fatted calf be slain,
　　Go spread the news around,—
My son was dead, but lives again;
　　Was lost, but now is found."

8 'Tis thus the Lord his love reveals,
　　To call poor sinners home;
More than a father's love he feels,
　　And welcomes all that come.

**47** P. M.

A WAKED by Sinai's awful sound,
　My soul in guilt and thrall I found,
　．I knew not what to do;
O'erwhelmed with guilt, with anguish slain,
The sinner must be born again,
　　Or sink in endless wo.

2 Amazed I stood, but could not tell
Which way to shun the gates of hell,
　　For death and hell drew near:
I strove indeed, but strove in vain;
The sinner must be born again,
　　Still sounded in my ear.

3 Then to the law I trembling fled,
It poured its curses on my head,
　　I no relief could find;
This fearful truth I found remain,
The sinner must be born again,
　　O'erwhelmed my troubled mind.

4 Again did Sinai's thunder roll,
And guilt lay heavy on my soul,
　　A vast unwieldy load:
Alas! I heard and found it plain,
The sinner must be born again,
　　Or drink the wrath of God.

5 The saints I heard with rapture tell
How Jesus conquered death and hell,

And broke the fowler's snare;
But when I found this truth remain,
The sinner must be born again,
 I sunk in deep despair.

6 While thus my soul in anguish lay,
Jesus of Naz'reth passed that way,
 I felt his pity move:
The sinner by his justice slain,
Now by his grace is born again,
 And sings redeeming love.

7 To heaven the joyful tidings flew,
The angels tuned their harps anew,
 And loftier sounds did raise:
All hail the Lamb that once was slain,
Unnumbered millions born again,
 Shall shout thy endless praise.

## 48    *6 8s.*

AWAKE! O guilty world, awake!
 Behold the earth's foundation shake!
 While the Redeemer bleeds for you:
His death proclaims to all our race
Free grace, free grace, free grace, free grace,
 To all the Jews and Gentiles too!

2 Come, guilty mortals, come and see
Your Saviour hanging on the tree!
 For you all drest in purple gore;
His weight of wo did veil the sun!
'Tis done, 'tis done, 'tis done, 'tis done,
 That man might live for evermore!

3 Behold the wounded Lamb of God,
Spreading his bleeding hands abroad!
 Come see him yielding up to death!
Behold him in his agonies!
He dies! he dies! he dies! he dies!
 And yields his last expiring breath.

4

4 He dies, and triumphs over death,
   To give the dead immortal breath,
      And spread the wonders of his name!
   Shout, brethren, shout with cheerful voice;
   Rejoice, rejoice, rejoice, rejoice,
      And give the glory to the Lamb.

**49**                    *4 8s, 4 7s.*

REVIEW the palsied sinner's case,
   Who sought for health in Jesus;
His friends conveyed him to the place
   Where he might meet with Jesus.
A multitude were thronging round
   To keep them back from Jesus;
But from the roof they let him down
   Before the face of Jesus.

2 Thus, brethren, help these friends of yours
   To find their way to Jesus;
His grace the worst diseases cures;
   Oh, help them on to Jesus.
The palsy's fearful stroke they feel:
   There's none can save but Jesus;
'Tis he alone their souls can heal:
   Oh, help them on to Jesus.

3 The fainting souls by sin diseased,
   There's none can save but Jesus;
With more than plague or palsy seized,
   Oh, help them on to Jesus.
The seeds of death are sown within;
   There's none can save but Jesus;
The worst disease on earth is sin,
   Oh, help them on to Jesus.

4 O Saviour, hear their mournful cry,
   And tell them thou art Jesus;
Oh, speak the word, or they must die,
   And bid farewell to Jesus:

Now let them hear thy voice declare,
  Thou all-sufficient Jesus,
That thou didst die to hear their prayer,
  And give them health in Jesus.

5 The great Physician now is near,
  The sympathizing Jesus;
He speaks the drooping heart to cheer,
  Oh, hear the voice of Jesus:
Your many sins are all forgiven,
  Oh, hear the voice of Jesus;
Go on your way in peace to heaven,
  And wear a crown with Jesus.

6 All glory to the dying Lamb!
  I now believe in Jesus,
I love my blessed Saviour's name,
  I love the name of Jesus:
His name dispels my guilt and fear,
  No other name but Jesus;
Oh. how my soul delights to hear
  The charming name of Jesus!

7 Come, brethren, help me sing his praise;
  Oh, praise the name of Jesus;
And sisters, all your voices raise;
  Oh, bless the name of Jesus:
And when to that bright world above
  We rise to see our Jesus,
We'll sing around the throne of love,
  The name, the name of Jesus.

## 50      *C. M.*

BLESSED Saviour! when my thoughts recall
  The wonders of thy grace,
Low at thy feet ashamed I fall,
  And hide this wretched face.

2 Shall love like thine be thus repaid?
  Ah, vile, ungrateful heart!

By earth's low cares detained—betrayed
From Jesus to depart.

3 From Jesus, who alone can give
True pleasure, peace, and rest:
When absent from my Lord, I live
Unsatisfied, unblest.

4 But he for his own mercy's sake
My wandering soul restores;
He bids the mourning heart partake
The pardon it implores.

5 Oh, while I breathe to thee, my Lord,
The penitential sigh,
Confirm the kind forgiving word
With pity in thine eye!

6 Then shall the mourner at thy feet
Rejoice to seek thy face;
And grateful own how kind, how sweet,
Thy condescending grace.

**51** *L. M.*

WITH melting heart and weeping eyes,
My guilty soul for mercy cries;
What shall I do, or whither flee,
T' escape that vengeance due to me?

2 Till now I saw no danger nigh;
I lived at ease, nor feared to die;
Wrapt up in self-deceit and pride,
"I shall have peace at last," I cried.

3 But when, Great God! thy light divine
Had shone on this dark soul of mine,
Then I beheld, with trembling awe,
The terrors of thy holy law.

4 How dreadful now my guilt appears,
In childhood, youth, and growing years!

Before thy pure, discerning eye,
Lord, what a filthy wretch am I!

5 Should vengeance still my soul pursue,
Death and destruction are my due;
Yet mercy can my guilt forgive,
And bid a dying sinner live.

6 Does not thy sacred word proclaim
Salvation free in Jesus' name?
To him I look, and humbly cry,
"O save a wretch condemned to die!"

## 52        *P. M. 8s & 7s.*

DROOPING soul, shake off thy fears;
  Fearful soul, be strong, be bold;
Tarry till thy Lord appears,
  Never, never quit thy hold!
Murmur not at his delay,
  Dare not set thy God a time:
Calmly for his coming stay,
  Leave it, leave it all to him.

2 Fainting soul, be bold, be strong;
  Wait the coming of thy Lord,
Though it seem to tarry long,
  True and faithful is his word;
On his word my soul I cast,
  (He cannot himself deny,)
Surely it shall speak at last:
  It shall speak, and shall not lie.

3 Every one that seeks shall find;
  Every one that asks shall have
Christ, the Saviour of mankind,
  Willing, able all to save;
I shall his salvation see;
  I in faith on Jesus call;
I from sin shall be set free,
  Perfectly set free from all.

4 Lord, my time is in thine hand,
    Weak and helpless as I am;
Surely thou canst make me stand;
    I believe in Jesus' name;
Saviour in temptation thou,
    Thou hast saved me heretofore;
Thou from sin dost save me now:
    Thou shalt save me evermore.

**53**                    *C. M.*

ENSLAVED to sense, to pleasure prone,
    Fond of created good:
Father, our helplessness we own,
    And trembling taste our food.

2 Trembling we taste; for ah! no more
    To thee the creatures lead;
Changed, they exert a baneful power,
    And poison while they feed.

3 Cursed for the sake of wretched man,
    They now engross him whole;
With pleasing force on earth detain,
    And sensualize his soul.

4 Grov'ling on earth, we still must lie
    Till Christ the curse repeal;
Till Christ, descending from on high,
    Infected nature heal.

5 Come then, our heavenly Adam, come,
    Thy healing influence give;
Hallow our food, reverse our doom,
    And bid us eat and live. .

6 The bondage of corruption break;
    For this our spirits groan:
Thy only will we fain would seek;
    O save us from our own:

7 Turn the full stream of nature's tide;
   Let all our actions tend
To thee, their source; thy love the guide,
   Thy glory be the end.

8 Earth then a scale to heaven shall be;
   Sense shall point out the road;
The creatures all shall lead to thee,
   And all we taste be God.

## 54 *C. M.*

JESUS, my advocate on high,
   I yield myself to thee;
While thou art sitting on thy throne
   O Lord! remember me.

> *Remember me, remember me,*
> *O Lord, remember me,*
> *Remember, Lord, thy dying groans,*
> *And then remember me.*

2 Jesus! thou art the sinner's friend,
   As such I look to thee;
Now in the bowels of thy love,
   Oh, Lord! remember me.

3 Remember thy pure word of grace,
   Remember Calvary;
Remember all thy dying groans,
   And then remember me.

4 Thou wondrous Advocate with God!
   I yield myself to thee;
While thou art sitting on thy throne,
   Oh, Lord! remember me.

5 I own I'm guilty, own I'm vile,
   Yet thy salvation's free;
Then, in thy all-abounding grace,
   Oh, Lord! remember me.

6 Howe'er forsaken or distressed,
   Howe'er oppressed I be,
Howe'er afflicted here on earth,
   Do thou remember me.

7 And when I close mine eyes in death,
   And creature helps all flee,
Then, oh, my great Redeemer, God!
   I pray, remember me.

**55**              *C. M.*

HARK! from the cross a gracious voice
   Salutes my ravish'd ears,
Rejoice, thou ransomed soul, rejoice,
   And dry those falling tears.

2 Amazed, I turn, grown strangely bold,
   This wondrous thing to see;
And there my dying Lord behold,
   Stretched on the bloody tree!

3 "Sinner," he cries, "behold the head
   This thorny wreath entwines;
Look on these wounded hands, and read
   Thy name in crimson lines.

4 "These wounds I bear, these pains I feel,
   This anguish rends my breast,
That I may save thy soul from hell,
   And give thee endless rest."

5 The power, the sweetness of that voice,
   My stony heart can move,
Make me in Christ, my Lord, rejoice,
   And melt my soul to love.

6 No more my harp neglected lies,
   With silent, broken strings;
From earth my soul has learned to rise,
   And mount on eagles' wings.

7 My dying Saviour's wondrous love
  On earth employs my tongue;
And when I walk in white above,
  That love shall be my song.

**56**                    *P. M.*

JESUS, save my dying soul,
    Make the broken spirit whole;
Humbled in the dust I lie,
Saviour, leave me not to die.

2 Jesus, full of every grace,
  Now reveal thy smiling face;
Grant the joy of saints forgiven,
Foretaste of the bliss of heaven.

3 All my guilt to thee is known;
  Thou art righteous, thou alone:
All my help is from thy cross,
All beside I count but loss.

4 Lord, in thee I now believe;
  Wilt thou, wilt thou not forgive?
Helpless at thy feet I lie,
Saviour, leave me not to die.      .

**57**                    *L. M.*

MY Lord, my Life, at last to thee,
    The sinner's Friend, for aid I flee;
No other help, nor hope have I;
Oh! wilt thou let the sinner die?

2 Thy name is love—to me make known
  The grace for which I pant and groan;
Thou only canst that grace supply;
Oh! wilt thou let the sinner die?

3 My guilt I own—'tis wholly mine,
  The power to save is only thine;

Canst thou that saving power deny?
Oh! wilt thou let the sinner die?

4 I weep, I mourn—but how can tears
Wash out the harden'd guilt of years?
I only on thy blood rely;
Oh! wilt thou let the sinner die?

5 To save my soul didst thou not bleed?
Dost thou not live to intercede?
My Friend, my Advocate on high,
Oh! wilt thou let the sinner die?

6 Oh no, oh no—my soul shall live,
And Christ shall all the praise receive,
Shall live, his grace to testify;
Thou wilt not let the sinner die.

## PRAYER.

**58** *P. M.*

BRETHREN, we have met to worship
And adore the Lord our God;
Will you pray with all your power,
While we try to preach the word?
All is vain unless the Spirit
Of the holy one comes down—
Brethren, pray, and holy manna
Will be shower'd all around.

2 Brethren, see poor sinners round you
Slumbering on the brink of woe,
Death is coming, hell is moving,
Can you bear to let them go?
See our fathers, and our mothers,
And our children sinking down;
Brethren, pray, and holy manna
Will be shower'd all around.

3 Brethren, here are poor backsliders,
    Who were once near heaven's door,
But they have betray'd their Saviour,
    And are worse than e'er before;
Yet the Saviour offers pardon,
    If they will lament their wound,
Brethren, pray, and holy manna
    Will be shower'd all around.

4 Sisters, will you join and help, as
    Moses' sister helped him,
While you see the trembling sinners
    Who are struggling hard with sin?
Tell them all about the Saviour,
    Tell them that he will be found;
Pray on, sisters, and the manna
    Will be shower'd all around.

5 Let us love our God supremely,
    Let us love each other too,
Let us love and pray for sinners,
    Till our God makes all things new:
Then he'll call us home to heav'n,
    At his table we'll sit down,
Christ will gird himself and serve us
    With sweet manna all around.

## 59 *8s & 7s.*

BRETHREN, here are mourners pleading
    For the mercy of the Lord:
Come, and for them, interceding,
    All your promised help afford.

    *Hear them, like Bartimeus crying,*
      *Who is this that passes by?*
    *Jesus! Jesus! Son of David!*
      *Mercy grant, or else I die.*

2 Have you not a prayer to offer?
    Can you not their sorrows feel?

Think on what their souls must suffer,
 Till the Lord their blindness heal.

3 They have come to Christ their Saviour,
 All their sins on him were laid :
While they supplicate his favor,
 Cheer them with your promised aid.

4 Cannot two be found agreeing,
 Touching what you seek from heaven ?
Hear ye not the Saviour saying,
 Ask in faith, it shall be given ?

*Hallelujah to the Saviour !*
 *Who has died that we may live ;*
*In his name we now find favor,*
 *And the blind their sight receive.*

5 Open now your eyes and view him ;
 Blind they are, but they shall see ;
Hark ! he bids you hasten to him ;
 Jesus says, "Come unto me."

6 Now we join our cheerful voices,
 And the loud hosanna raise ;
While the angel-throng rejoices,
 Loftier be our notes of praise.

*Hallelujah ! Judah's Lion*
 *Leads the conquering hosts along ;*
*Lo ! the pearly gates of Zion*
 *Rise in echo to our song.*

## 60

COME, Lord, dwell in my bosom !
 There, there hast thou thy throne ;
Thou, thou knowest I love thee,
 Deign, Lord, to call me thine own.

2 Sweet, sweet voice of my Jesus,
 Soft as music of heaven,

"Fear not, I have redeemed thee—
Fear not, thy sins are forgiven!"

3 O then, dwell in my bosom!
There, there reign on thy throne,
Thou, thou knowest I love thee,
Now I am ever thine own.

**61**       *P. M. 10 11, 10 11.*

COME, Lord, from above, the mountains re-
move,
O'erturn all that hinders the course of thy love;
My bosom inspire, enkindle the fire,
And wrap my whole soul in the flames of desire.

•2 I languish and pine for the comfort divine,
O when shall I say my beloved is mine!
I've chose the good part, my portion thou art:
O Love, let me find thee, O God, in my heart!

3 For this my heart sighs, nothing else can suffice;
How, Lord, can I purchase the pearl of great
price?
It cannot be bought, thou know'st I have nought,
Not an action, a word, or a truly good thought.

4 But I hear a voice say, without money you may
Receive it, whoever hath nothing to pay:
Who on Jesus relies, without money or price,
The pearl of forgiveness and holiness buys.

5 The blessing is free, so, Lord, let it be:
I yield that thy love should be given to me;
I freely receive what thou freely dost give,
And consent to thy love, in thine Eden to live.

6 The gift I embrace, the giver I praise,
And ascribe my salvation to Jesus' grace;
It came from above, the foretaste I prove,
And I soon shall receive all thy fulness of love.

**62**    *P. M.*

DEAR Jesus! here comes and knocks at thy door,
A beggar for crumbs, distressed and poor,
Blind, lame, and forsaken, all roll'd in his blood,
At last overtaken when running from God.

2 To ask children's bread I dare not presume,
But, Lord, to be fed with fragments I come;
Some crumbs from thy table O let me obtain,
For lo! thou art able my wants to sustain.

3 I own I deserve no favor to see,
So long did I swerve and wander from thee,
Till brought by affliction my follies to mourn;
Now under conviction to thee I return.

4 For since thou hast said, thou'lt cast away none
Who fly to thine aid as sinners undone;
Now, Lord, I am come as condemned to die,
And on this sweet promise I humbly rely.

5 I cannot depart, dear Jesus, nor yield,
Till my poor heart feels this promise fulfill'd;
That I may forever a monument be,
To praise the dear Saviour of sinners like me.

**63**    *P. M.*

ENCOURAGED by thy word
    Of promise to the poor,
Behold a beggar, Lord,
    Waits at thy mercy's door:
No hand, no heart, O Lord! but thine,
Can help or pity wants like mine.

2 The beggar's usual plea,
    Relief from men to gain,
If offer'd unto thee,
    I know thou would'st disdain:

But those which move thy gracious ear,
Are such as men would scorn to hear.

3 I have no right to say,
　　That though I now am poor,
Yet once there was a day
　　When I possessed more;
Thou knowest, from my very birth,
I've been the poorest wretch on earth.

4 Nor dare I to profess,
　　As beggars often do,
Though great is my distress,
　　My faults have been but few;
If thou shouldst leave my soul to starve,
It would be what I should deserve.

5 Nor dare I to pretend
　　I never begg'd before,
And if thou now befriend,
　　I'll trouble thee no more:
Thou often hast relieved my pain,
And often I must come again.

6 Though crumbs are much too good
　　For such a wretch as I,
No less than children's food,
　　My soul can satisfy:
O, do not frown and bid me go,
Until a blessing thou bestow.

7 Nor can I willing be,
　　Thy bounties to conceal
From others, who, like me,
　　.Their wants and hunger feel;
I'll tell them of thy mercy's store,
And try to send ten thousand more.

8 Thy ways, thou only wise,
　　Our ways and thoughts transcend,

Far as the arched skies
Above the earth extend:
Such pleas as mine men would not hear,
But God receives the beggar's prayer.

**64** *P. M.*

FATHER of mercies, God of love!
Oh, hear an humble suppliant's cry;
Bend from thy lofty seat above,
Thy throne of glorious majesty:
Oh, deign to listen to my voice,
And bid this drooping heart rejoice.

2 I urge no merits of my own,
For I, alas, am all that's vile;
No—when I bow before thy throne,
Dare to converse with God awhile,
Thy name, blest Jesus, is my plea,
That dearest, sweetest name to me.

3 Within this heart of mine, I feel
The weight of sin's oppressive load.
Oh, help! or else I sink to hell—
Crush'd by thine arm, avenging God!
Entomb'd within that dread abyss,
And exiled from the realms of bliss.

4 But ah! the thought alone is hell—
That prospect drives me to despair;
For who can 'mid those horrors dwell?
Or who those dreadful torments bear?
Where not a ray of hope appears,
Or beam of joy the bosom cheers!

5 Yet, mighty God! thy powerful arm
Can snatch me from that dread abode,
Can shield me from th' impending harm,
And ease me of my heavy load:
One pardoning word can make me whole,
And soothe the anguish of my soul.

6 Father of mercies, God of Love!
   Then, hear thy humble suppliant's cry;
Bend from thy lofty seat above,
   Thy throne of glorious majesty:
Oh! listen to a sufferer's voice,
Then shall this bleeding heart rejoice!

## 65         *7s.*

FATHER, at thy call I come!
   In thy bosom there is room
For a guilty soul to hide,
Pressed with grief on every side.

2 Here I'll make my piteous moan—
Thou canst understand a groan:
Here my sins and sorrows tell;
What I feel thou knowest well.

3 Ah, how foolish I have been,
To obey the voice of sin—
To forget thy love to me,
And to break my vows to thee.

4 Darkness fills my trembling soul;
Floods of sorrows o'er me roll;
Pity, Father, pity me;
All my hope's alone in thee.

## 66         *8s & 7s.*

FULL of trembling expectation,
   Feeling much, and fearing more,
Mighty God of my salvation,
   I thy timely aid implore:
Suffering Son of man, be near me,
   All my sufferings to sustain,
By thy sorer griefs to cheer me,
   By thy more than mortal pain.

2 Call to mind that unknown anguish
   In thy days of flesh below,

5

When thy troubled soul did languish
　Under a whole world of wo;
When thou didst our curse inherit,
　Groan beneath our guilty load,
Burden'd with a wounded spirit,
　Bruised by all the wrath of God.

3 By thy most severe temptation,
　In the dark Satanic hour;
By thy last mysterious passion,
　Screen me from the adverse power:
By thy fainting in the garden,
　By thy bloody sweat, I pray,
Write upon my heart the pardon,
　Take my sins and fears away.

4 By the travail of thy spirit
　By thine outcry on the tree,
By thine agonizing merit:
　In thy pangs remember me!
By thy death I thee conjure,
　A weak, dying soul befriend;
Make me patient to endure,
　Make me faithful to the end.

**67**　　　　　　　*8s, 7s & 4s.*

GENTLY, Lord, O, gently lead us
　Through this lonely vale of tears!
And, O Lord, in mercy give us
　Thy rich grace in all our fears.
　　O refresh us!
O, refresh us with thy grace!

2 Though ten thousand ills beset us
　From without and from within,
Jesus says he'll ne'er forget us,
　But will save from every sin.
　　Therefore praise him—
Praise the great Redeemer's name.

3 Though distresses now attend thee,
    And thou tread'st the thorny road,
His right hand shall still defend thee;
    Soon he'll bring thee home to God!
        Therefore praise him—
Praise the great Redeemer's name.

4 O, that I could now adore him,
    Like the heavenly hosts above,
Who forever bow before him,
    And unceasing sing his love!
        Happy songsters,
When shall I your chorus join.

## 68       *7s & 6s.*

GO, when the morning shineth,
    Go, when the noon is bright,
Go, when the eve declineth,
    Go, in the hush of night—
Go, with pure mind and feeling;
    Fling earthly care away,
And, in thy chamber kneeling,
    Do thou in secret pray.

2 Remember all who love thee,
    All who are loved by thee;
Pray, too, for those who hate thee,
    If any such there be;
Then for thyself, in meekness,
    A blessing humbly claim,
And link with each petition
    Thy great Redeemer's name.

3 Or if 'tis e'er denied thee
    In solitude to pray,
Should holy thoughts come o'er thee,
    When friends are round thy way,
E'en then the silent breathing
    Of thy spirit raised above,

Will reach his throne of glory,
  Who is Mercy, Truth, and Love.

**69**                    *8s & 7s.*

LET thy kingdom, blessed Saviour,
  Come, and bid our jarrings cease;
Come, O come, and reign forever,
  God of love and Prince of peace!
Visit now thy precious Zion,
  See thy people mourn and weep;
Day and night thy lambs are crying,
  Come, good Shepherd, feed thy sheep.

2 Lord, in us there is no merit,
    We've been sinners from our youth;
  Guide us, Lord, by thy good Spirit,
    That shall teach us all the truth.
  On the gospel word we'll venture,
    Till in death's cold arms we sleep;
  Love's our bond, and Christ our centre,
    Come, good Shepherd, feed thy sheep.

3 Christ alone our souls shall rest on,
    Taught by him we own his name;
  Sweetest of all names is Jesus,
    How it doth our hearts inflame
  Glory! Glory! give him glory,
    Strong is he his flock to keep;
  He will clear our way before us,
    Come, good Shepherd, feed thy sheep.

**70**                    *P. M.*

NEARER, my God, to thee,—
        Nearer to thee!
E'en though it be a cross
        That raiseth me
Still all my song shall be,
Nearer, my God, to thee,
        Nearer to thee!

2 Though like a wanderer,
　　　　The sun gone down,
Darkness comes over me,
　　　　My rest a stone,
Yet in my dreams I'd be
Nearer, my God, to thee.—
　　　　Nearer to thee!

3 There let my way appear
　　　　Steps unto heav'n;
All that thou sendest me
　　　　In mercy giv'n;
Angels to beckon me
Nearer, my God, to thee,—
　　　　Nearer to thee!

4 Then with my waking thoughts
　　　　Bright with thy praise,
Out of my stony griefs
　　　　Bethel I'll raise;
So by my woes to be
Nearer, my God, to thee,—
　　　　Nearer to thee!

5 And when on joyful wing,
　　　　Cleaving the sky;
Sun, moon, and stars forgot,
　　　　Upward I fly;
Still all my song shall be,
Nearer, my God, to thee,—
　　　　Nearer to thee!

**71**　　　　　　*P. M.*

NAY, I cannot let thee go,
　　Till a blessing thou bestow;
Do not turn away thy face,
Mine's an urgent pressing case.

2 Dost thou ask me who I am?
Ah! my Lord, thou know'st my name;

Yet the question gives a plea
To support my suit with thee.

3 Thou didst once a wretch behold,
In rebellion blindly bold,
Scorn thy grace, thy power defy;
That poor rebel, Lord, was I.

4 Once a sinner near despair
Sought thy mercy-seat by prayer;
Mercy heard, and set him free;
Lord, that mercy came to me.

5 Many years have passed since then,
Many changes I have seen,
Yet I've been upheld till now;
Who could hold me up but thou?

6 Thou hast helped in every need,
This emboldens me to plead;
After so much mercy past,
Canst thou let me sink at last?

7 No—I must maintain my hold,
'Tis thy goodness makes me bold;
I can no denial take,
When I plead for Jesus' sake.

## 72                    *7s, 6 lines.*

NOW in Jesus' name I pray,
Father, take my sins away;
Give me sight, I still am blind;
Give me all my Saviour's mind;
Let me enter into rest,
Bless me—for I will be blest.

2 Jesus is within the veil,
Still his groans thine ears assail;
Stronger pleadings have I none,
Hear me for his sake alone;

Let me enter into rest,
Bless me—for I will be blest.

3 My affections fix above,
Rooted, grounded in thy love!
Let me only Jesus see,
Let me only dwell in thee,
Let me enter into rest,
Bless me—for I will be blest.

4 Bruise in me the hateful foe;
Perfect me in love below;
Let me Adam's loss regain,
Wrestle, and the prize obtain,
Let me enter into rest,
Bless me—for I will be blest.

# 73

OH, in that day, grant that I may
Find mercy, Lord, with thee!
Through Him who kept thy holy law,
Without a blemish or a flaw,
Then died upon the tree.

2 Full, full of sin and guilt within,
No worthiness I plead;
If thou iniquity shouldst mark,
Dismal my prospects were and dark,
Hopeless my case indeed.

3 Of merit none call I my own,
But my demerits vast;
Think of the merits of thy Son,
What he hath suffered, he hath done,
And I am safe at last.

4 Vile, vile I am, but this blest Lamb
His precious blood has spilt;

That blood, thou hast been pleased to say,
Can wash the foulest stains away,
   And cancel all my guilt.

5 On Jesus I humbly rely,
   All other trust abjure;
Jesus! to thee alone I flee;
Th's hope shall like an anchor be,
   Forever firm and sure.

**74**     ·        *L. M.*

OH! mèet me at the throne of grace,
   At rosy eve and dewy morn,
And cherish hopes of sweet embrace,
   When I from toil to thee return.
I go, my Master's work to do,
   His truth to spread, his grace to show;
But while I wander, thoughts of you
   Shall ever in my bosom glow.

       *Oh! meet me at the throne of grace,*
        *At rosy eve and dewy morn,*
        *And cherish hopes of sweet embrace,*
        *When I from toil to thee return.*

2 'Tis duty's lofty voice I hear,
   And hearing must obey the sound;
For notes of love and friendship dear
   Are in the sovereign echo drowned.
I seek not fame nor glittering gold,
   Not these could tempt me hence to roam;
But, wandering sheep, strayed from the fold,
   I would to Christ and heaven bring home.

3 Go, stay that trusting heart on heaven,
   Let not those tears too freely flow:
And pray that to our love be given
   Yet other interviews below;
But if to hearts so intertwined,
   His will permit a stroke severe;

If thine the fall, I'll haste to find
    Thy rest in yonder happier sphere.

4 Or, if while roving far from thee,
    In quest of Israel's wandering sheep,
Shall come my hour of destiny,
    And lull me into death's cold sleep;
Then follow thou: oh, speed thy wing,
    And to my spirit-mansion come,
While I from heaven's bright walls shall sing,
    Come home, my love, come quickly home.

**75**           *D. L. M.*

SWEET hour of prayer! sweet hour of prayer!
    That calls me from a world of care,
And bids me, at my Father's throne,
Make all my wants and wishes known.
In seasons of distress and grief,
My soul has often found relief,
And oft escaped the tempter's snare,
By thy return, sweet hour of prayer!

2 Sweet hour of prayer! sweet hour of prayer!
Thy wings shall my petition bear
To Him whose truth and faithfulness
Engage the waiting soul to bless.
And since he bids me seek his face,
Believe his word, and trust his grace,
I'll cast on him my every care,
And wait for thee, sweet hour of prayer!

3 Sweet hour of prayer! sweet hour of prayer!
May I thy consolations share,
Till from Mount Pisgah's lofty height
I view my heaven, and at the sight
Put off this robe of flesh, and rise
To seize the everlasting prize;
Shouting, as I pass through the air,
Farewell! farewell! sweet hour of prayer!

**76**        *2 8s, 3 7s & 1 4.*

SAVIOUR, visit thy plantation!
    Grant us, Lord, a gracious rain!
All will come to desolation,
    Unless thou return again.

            *Lord, revive us !*
        *All our help must come from thee.*

2 Keep no longer at a distance,
      Shine upon us from on high!
  Lest for want of thine assistance,
      Every plant should droop and die.

3 Surely once thy garden flourished,
      Every part looked gay and green;
  Then thy word our spirits nourished,
      Happy seasons we have seen!

4 But a drought has since succeeded,
      And a sad decline we see;
  Lord, thy help is greatly needed,
      Help can only come from thee.

5 Where are those we counted leaders,
      Filled with zeal, and love, and truth?
  Old professors tall as cedars,
      Bright examples to our youth.

6 Some in whom we once delighted,
      We shall meet no more below;
  Some, alas, we fear are blighted,
      Scarce a single leaf they show.

7 Younger plants—the sight, how pleasant!
      Covered thick with blossoms stood;
  But they cost us grief at present,
      Frost has nipped them in the bud.

8 Dearest Saviour, hasten hither,
      Thou canst make them bloom again;

Oh, permit them not to wither,
  Let not all our hopes be vain.

9 Let our mutual love be fervent,
    Make us prevalent in prayer;
  Let each one, esteemed thy servant,
    Shun the world's bewitching snare.

10 Break the tempter's fatal power,
    Turn the stony heart to flesh;
  And begin, from this good hour,
    To revive thy work afresh.

## 77

TARRY with me, O my Saviour,
  For the day is passing by;
See, the shades of evening gather,
  And the night is drawing nigh.
Tarry with me, O my Saviour,
  Pass me not unheeded by.

2 Faithful mem'ry paints before me
    Ev'ry deed and thought of sin;
  Open thou the blood-filled fountain,
    Cleanse my guilty soul within.
  Tarry thou forgiving Saviour,
    Wash me wholly from my sin.

3 Many friends were gathered round me
    In the bright days of the past;
  But the grave has closed above them,
    And I linger here the last.
  I am lonely, tarry with me
    Till the dreary night is passed.

4 Deeper, deeper grow the shadows,
    Paler now the glowing west;
  Swift the night of death advances,
    Shall it be the night of rest?
  Tarry with me, O my Saviour,
    Lay my head upon thy breast.

**78** *P. M.*

WHEN gath'ring clouds around I view,
  And days are dark, and friends are few,
On him I lean, who, not in vain,
Experienced ev'ry human pain;
He feels my grief, and sees my fears,
And counts and treasures up my tears.

2 If aught should tempt my soul to stray
From heavenly wisdom's narrow way,
To fly the good I would pursue,
Or do the ill I would not do;
Still he, who felt temptation's pow'r,
Shall guard me in that dang'rous hour.

3 When vexing thoughts within me rise,
And, sore dismayed, my spirit dies,
Then he, who once vouchsafed to bear
The sick'ning anguish of despair,
Shall sweetly soothe, shall gently dry,
The throbbing heart, the streaming eye.

4 And, oh! when I have safely past
Through ev'ry conflict but the last,
Still, still unchanging, watch beside
My bed of death—for thou hast died:
Then point to realms of endless day,
And wipe the latest tear away.

**79**

WHILE wandering to and fro
  In this wide world of wo,
Where streams of sorrow flow,
      Give me Jesus!

> *Give me Jesus!*
> *Give me Jesus!*
> *You may have all the world!*
> *Give me Jesus!*

2 When tears o'erflow mine eye,
   When pressed by grief I sigh;
   Still this shall be my cry,
      Give me Jesus!

3 When to the mercy-seat
   I go my Lord to meet,
   My heart shall still repeat,
      Give me Jesus!

4 And when my faith is tried,
   In him will I confide,
   And all the storms outride:
      Give me Jesus!

5 Though strength and friends should fail,
   And foes my soul assail,
   Through him I shall prevail.
      Give me Jesus!

6 And when my toils are o'er,
   When nearing Jordan's shore,
   I'll sing as up I soar,
      Give me Jesus!

7 When at the judgment-seat
   I stand at Jesus' feet;
   When worlds on worlds shall meet,
      Give me Jesus!

8 When heaven and earth shall flee,
   When time shall cease to be,
   Through all eternity,
      Give me Jesus!

# 80

AIR.—*Sweet Home.*

WHEN torn is the bosom by sorrow or care,
   Be it ever so simple, there's nothing like
      prayer;

It eases, soothes, softens, subdues, yet sustains,
Gives vigor to hope, and puts passion in chains.

*Prayer, prayer, O sweet prayer,*
*Be it ever so simple, there's nothing like prayer.*

2 When far from the friends we hold dearest, we
    part,
What fond recollections still cling to the heart!
Past converse, past scenes, past enjoyments are
    there;
O how hurtfully pleasing till hallow'd by prayer!

3 When pleasure would woo us from piety's arms,
The siren sings sweetly, or silently charms;
We listen, love, loiter, are caught in the snare—
But, looking to Jesus, we conquer by prayer.

4 While strangers to prayer, we are strangers to
    bliss;
Heaven pours its full streams through no medium
    but this;
And till we the seraph's full ecstasy share,
Our chalice of joy must be guarded by prayer.

# 81

WHEN burdened is my breast,
    When friendless seems my lot,
When earth affords no rest,
    And refuge I have not:
Father! if thou wilt suffer me,
I will arise and come to thee.

2 When conscience thunders loud,
    When sins in dread array
Upon my memory crowd,
    And fill me with dismay;
Yet glancing once on Calvary,
Father! I'll rise and come to thee.

3 And if I am a child,
　　But have backslidden still,
And filled with projects wild,
　　Have followed my own will;
Yet penitent, resolved I'll be,
Father! to rise and come to thee.

4 And thou in love wilt turn
　　To thy poor rebel child;
Nor let thine anger burn,
　　Though sin my heart beguiled:
Thy voice shall greet me graciously,
"Arise! arise! and come to me."

**82** *P. M.*

WHEN through the torn sail the wild tem-
　　　　pest is streaming,
When o'er the dark waves the red lightning is
　　gleaming,
Nor hope lends a ray the poor seamen to
　　cherish;
We fly to our Maker; "Save, Lord! or we
　　perish!"

2 O Jesus, once rocked on the breast of the billow,
　Aroused by the shriek of despair from thy
　　pillow,
Now seated in glory, the mariner cherish,
Who cries in his anguish, "Save, Lord! or we
　　perish."

3 And O! when the whirlwind of passion is
　　raging,
· When sin in our hearts its wild warfare is
　　waging,
Then send down thy Spirit thy ransomed to
　　cherish,
Rebuke the destroyer; "Save, Lord! or we
　　perish!"

## 83

YES, there's *one* place like home—'tis God's
    holy shrine,
Where high thoughts are kindled, and feelings
    divine;
How the *Spirit's* sweet breathings calm peace
    can impart,
In the home of devotion—the home of the *heart.*

    *Home, home, sweet, sweet home,*
    *The home of devotion, the home of the heart.*

2 As weary and sad, through this lone "vale of
    tears,"
Our steps we pursue, filled with doubts and
    with fears;
On *Jesus'* kind breast we repose all our care,
In this home of devotion—this sweet home of
    prayer.

    *Home, home, sweet, sweet home,*
    *The home of devotion, the sweet home of prayer.*

3 As the Sabbath's calm hours we delightfully
    spend,
In holding high converse with Jesus, our
    Friend;
Though often our thoughts to our absent friends
    roam,
We feel that God's house is the Christian's own
    home.

    *Home, home, sweet, sweet home,*
    *We feel that God's house is the Christian's own*
    *home.*

4 And trusting in Jesus, almighty to save,
We rob death of its sting—of its victory the
    grave;

All honor, and glory, and praise shall be given,
While we swell the full song in that *better home*
—HEAVEN.

*Home, home, sweet, sweet home,*
*O when shall I dwell in my better home, heaven?*

## CHRISTIAN EXPERIENCE.

**84**      *D. L. M.*     \

A SOLDIER, Lord, thou hast me made,
  Thou art my captain, king, and head,
And under thee I mean to fight
The fight of faith with all my might.
The cross all stained with hallowed blood,
The ensign of our conquering Lord,
The Christian soldier's standard is,
And I will fight for King Jesus.

2 Grant me the arrows of thy word,
Thy Spirit's powerful two-edged sword,
To slay my foes where'er they be,
And own the victory won by thee;
That I a duteous child may be,
To stand and fight the enemy;
That when the alarm's to call, the Lord
May pass the word unto the guard.

3 Thou art my guard, keep me, I pray,
That I may walk the narrow way,
Nor from my duty e'er depart,
But live to Christ with all my heart;
Help me to keep my guardian dress,
And march to th' right in holiness;
O make me pure and spotless too,
And fit to stand the grand review.

4 And when our general he has come
With sound of trumpet—not with drum,

6

And when our well-dressed rank shall stand
In full review at God's right hand,
It's then the enemy he'll rout,
And make them wheel to the left about;
Then we'll march up the heavenly street,
And ground our arms at Jesus' feet.

5 The war is o'er, and we are free
To join the blood-washed company,
Our wages shall be crowns of gold,
And joys of heaven that can't be told.
There, like our glorious Lord, we'll shine,
In heavenly concert we shall join,
And praises on the highest key,
Shall be our theme eternally.

## 85                    *P. M.*

A ND are our joys so quickly fled?
We, who were filled with living bread,
    With calm delight and peace;
Constrained, into the ship we go,
And now the boist'rous vi'lence know
    Of these strong winds and seas.

2 To shipwreck our weak faith and hope,
Satan has raised a tempest up;
    Prince of the lower air,
The world he actuates and guides,
And in that troubled ocean rides,
    And reigns despotic there.

3 But lo! in our distress we see
The Saviour walking on the sea,
    Even now he passes by;
He silences our clam'rous fear,
And mildly says, " Be of good cheer,
    Be not afraid, 'tis I."

4 " 'Tis I, who bought you with my blood!
'Tis I, who bring you washed to God!

'Tis I, the sinner's friend!
'Tis I, in whom you pardon have!
Who speak the truth, mighty to save,
   And love you to the end."

5 Ah! Lord, if it be thou indeed,
So near us in the time of need,
   So good, so strong to save;
Stretch out thy hand and ask me, " Why,
. Why didst thou doubt or fear, when I,
   Thy Lord, had bid thee live?"

## 86 *P. M.*

A DIEU, my dear brethren, adieu,
   Reluctant I give you my hand,
No more to assemble with you,
   Till we on Mount Zion shall stand.
My heart swells with tender regret
   To leave your embraces so soon,
Though heaven my course must direct,
   And others succeed in my room.

2 Your acts of benevolence past,
   Your gentle, compassionate love,
Henceforth in my mem'ry shall last,
   Though far from your sight I remove,
While roving the wilds of the west,
   When through foreign regions I steer,
Still friendship inspiring my breast,
   Shall then drop her own native tear.

3 Our labors will shortly subside,
   For vigor and life must decay,
But wisdom and truth shall abide
   To pilot our souls on the way.
As time rolls his seasons around,
   And truth shall new teachers inspire,
O may we in love still abound,
   And after new conquests aspire.

4 Our seasons of converse are o'er,
   Till mortal commotions are past,
Till nature and time are no more,
   Or we are in Paradise blest,
Sweet comforting Spirit, draw near,
   And shed forth thy luminous rays,
My parting reflections to cheer,
   And change lamentation to praise.

5 O may we conform to his will,
   Aspiring for glory and peace,
Our covenant vows to fulfil,
   Till Jesus shall sign our release.
Till suddenly wafted above,   ·
   Where saints in sweet harmony meet,
To feel all the pleasures of love,
   And each happy conqueror greet.

## 87                 *8, 8, 6.*

HOW happy are the favored few,
   Who live below as angels do
      In blissful bowers above!
Serenely calm, with sweet content,
Their days, like days in heaven, are spent
      In holiness and love.

2 Say, what to them is pleasure's voice?
   Or glory's flame? or wealth's gay toys?
      Or all earth boasts besides?
This world is but their pilgrim rest:
And onward to their home they haste,
      Where Christ their Lord abides.

3 The ills that o'er their pathway cross,
   Disease, and poverty, and loss,
      Are servants in disguise;
Who aid them in the holy strife,
To seize the crown of endless life:—
      Bright heaven's enduring prize.

4 How peaceful their communings are,
  Who thus, with Christ, their Saviour, share
    The Father's boundless grace!
Assured of his unfailing love,
Their hopes, their joys are all above—
    In heaven their native place.

5 Let storm on storm in angry mood,
  And earthquake dire, and flame and flood,
    In all their fury rise:
Their steady hearts shall know no fear,
For lo! their Father. God, is near,
    Who rules both earth and skies.

6 Oh! let me with that radiant band
  Unite my trembling heart and hand;
    Nor thence again be riven:
In life, in death, oh! let me be
One of that goodly company,
    And shine with them in heaven.

## 88        *4 lines 11s.*

AN alien from God, and a stranger to grace,
  I wandered through earth, its gay pleasures
    to trace;
In the pathway of sin I continued to roam,
Unmindful, alas! that it led me from home.

  *Home, home, sweet, sweet home!*
  *O Saviour! direct me to heaven, my home.*

2 The pleasures of earth I have seen fade away,
They bloom for a season, but soon they decay;
But pleasures more lasting, in Jesus are given,
Salvation on earth, and a mansion in heaven.

  *Home, home, sweet, sweet home!*
  *The saints in those mansions are ever at home!*

3 Allure me no longer, ye false glowing charms!
The Saviour invites me, I'll go to his arms;

At the banquet of mercy, I hear there is room,
Oh, there may I feast with his children at home!

*Home, home, sweet, sweet home,*
*O Jesus, conduct me, to heaven my home!*

4 Farewell vain amusements, my follies adieu,
While Jesus, and heaven, and glory I view:
I feast on the pleasures that flow from his throne,
The foretaste of heaven, sweet heaven, my home.

*Home, home, sweet, sweet home!*
*Oh, when shall I share the fruition of home?*

5 The days of my exile are passing away,
The time is approaching when Jesus will say,
"Well done, faithful servant, sit down on my
    throne,
And dwell in my presence forever at home."

*Home, home, sweet, sweet home!*
*Oh, there I shall rest with the Saviour at home.*

6 Affliction, and sorrow, and death shall be o'er,
The saints shall unite to be parted no more;
There loud hallelujahs fill heaven's high dome,
They dwell with the Saviour forever at home.

*Home, home, sweet, sweet home!*
*They dwell with the Saviour forever at home.*

**89**                    *L. M.*

A POOR wayfaring man of grief
  Hath often crossed me on my way,
Who sued so humbly for relief,
  That I could never answer nay:
I had no power to ask his name,
Whither he went, or whence he came;
Yet there was something in his eye
That won my love, I knew not why.

2 Once, when my scanty meal was spread,
   He entered—not a word he spake;
Just perishing for want of bread;
   I gave him all—he blessed it, brake,
And ate, but gave me part again:
Mine was an angel's portion then;
And while I fed with eager haste,
The crust was manna to my taste.

3 I spied him where a fountain burst
   Clear from the rock,—his strength was gone
The heedless water mocked his thirst,
   He heard it, saw it hurrying on.
I ran and raised the sufferer up,
Thrice from the stream he drained my cup,
Dipped, and returned it running o'er:
I drank, and never thirsted more.

4 'Twas night; the floods were out; it blew
   A winter hurricane aloof;
I heard his voice abroad, and flew
   To bid him welcome to my roof:
I warmed, I clothed, and cheered my guest,
Laid him on my own couch to rest,
Then made the earth my bed, and seemed
In Eden's garden while I dreamed.

5 Stripped, wounded, beaten, nigh to death,
   I found him by the highway-side;
I roused his pulse, brought back his breath,
   Revived his spirit, and supplied
Wine, oil, refreshment; he was healed:
I had myself a wound concealed,
But from that hour forgot the smart,
And peace bound up my broken heart.

6 In prison I saw him next, condemned
   To meet a traitor's doom at morn;
The tide of lying tongues I stemmed,
   And honored him mid shame and scorn:

My friendship's utmost zeal to try,
He asked if I for him would die :
The flesh was weak, my blood ran chill,
But the free spirit cried, " I will !"

7 Then in a moment, to my view,
   The stranger darted from disguise;
The tokens in his hands I knew;
   My Saviour stood before my eyes!
He spake, and my poor name he named—
"Of me thou hast not been ashaméd;
These deeds shall thy memorial be;
Fear not, thou didst them unto me."

## 90        *P. M. 10 10, 11 11.*

ALL thanks to the Lamb, who gives us to meet:
  His love we proclaim, his praises repeat:
We own him our Jesus, continually near,
To pardon and bless us, and perfect us here.

2 In him we have peace, in him we have power,
Preserved by his grace throughout the dark
     hour :
In all our temptation he keeps us, to prove
His utmost salvation, his fulness of love.

3 Pronounce the glad word, and bid us be free;
Ah! hast thou not, Lord, a blessing for me?
The peace thou hast given this moment impart,
And open thy heaven, O love, in my heart.

## 91        *L. M.*

AFFLICTED saint! to Christ draw near;
  Thy Saviour's gracious promise hear:
His faithful word declares to thee,
That "as thy day, thy strength shall be."

2 Thy faith is weak, thy foes are strong;
And if the conflict should be long,

Thy Lord will make the tempter flee;
For "as thy day, thy strength shall be."

3 Should persecution rage and flame,
Still trust in thy Redeemer's name:
In fiery trials thou shalt see,
That "as thy day, thy strength shall be."

4 When call'd by Him to bear the cross,
Reproach, affliction, pain, or loss,
Or deep distress and poverty,
Still "as thy day, thy strength shall be."

5 When death at length appears in view,
Christ's presence shall thy fears subdue:
He'll come to set thy spirit free,
And "as thy day, thy strength shall be."

## 92 *P. M.*

BRIGHT scenes of glory strike my sense,
And all my passions capture,
Eternal beauties round me shine,
Infusing warmest rapture.
I dive in pleasures, deep and full
In swelling waves of glory,
And feel my Saviour in my soul,
And groan to tell my story.

2 I feast on honey, milk, and wine,
I drink perpetual sweetness;
Mount Zion's beauties round me shine,
While Christ unfolds his glory!
No mortal tongue can show my joys,
Nor can an angel tell them;
Ten thousand times surpassing all
Terrestrial worlds or emblems.

3 The bliss that rolls through those above,
Through those in glory seated,

Which causes them loud songs to sing,
  Ten thousand times repeated— •
Dart through my soul in radiant flame,
  Constraining loudest praises;
O'erwhelming all my powers with joy,
  While all within me blazes.

4 When earth and sea shall be no more,
  And all their glory perish;
When sun and moon shall cease to shine,
  And stars at midnight languish,
My joys refin'd shall higher shine
With heav'n's radiant glory,
And tell through one eternal day,
  Love's all immortal story.

**93** *P. M.*

BEGONE, unbelief! my Saviour is near,
  And for my relief will surely appear;
By prayer let me wrestle, and he will perform;
With Christ in the vessel, I smile at the storm.

2 Though dark be my way, since he is my guide,
'Tis mine to obey, 'tis his to provide;
Though cisterns be broken, and creatures all
      fail,
The word he has spoken shall surely prevail.

3 His love, in time past, forbids me to think
He'll leave me at last in trouble to sink;
Each sweet Ebenezer I have in review,
Confirms his good pleasure to help me quite
      through.

4 Determined to save, he watched o'er my path,
When, Satan's blind slave, I sported with death;
And can he have taught me to trust in his name,
And thus far have brought me to put me to
      shame?

5 Why should I complain of want or distress,
  Temptation or pain?—he told me no less;
  The heirs of salvation, I know from his word,
  Through much tribulation must follow their
    Lord.

6 How bitter that cup no heart can conceive,
  Which he drank quite up that sinners might
    live!
  His way was much rougher and darker than
    mine;
  Did Christ, my Lord, suffer, and shall I repine?

7 Since all that I meet shall work for my good,
  The bitter is sweet, the medicine is food;
  Though painful at present, 'twill cease before
    long,
  And then, O how pleasant the conqueror's song!

## 94 *P. M.*

COME, saints and sinners, hear me tell
  The wonders of Immanuel;
Who sav'd me from a burning hell
And brought my soul with him to dwell,
  And gave me heavenly union.

2 When Jesus saw me from on high,
  Beheld my soul in ruin lie,
  He look'd on me with pitying eye,
  And said to me as he pass'd by,
    With God you have no union.

3 Then I began to weep and pray,
  I look'd this way and that to fly,
  It grieved me sore that I must die,
  I sought salvation for to buy,
    But still I found no union.

4 But when I hated all my sins,
  My dear Redeemer took me in,

And with his blood he wash'd me clean,
And O what seasons I have seen
　　E'er since I felt this union.

5 I prais'd the Lord both night and day,
I went from house to house to pray,
And if I met one on the way,
I always found something to say,
　　About this heavenly union.

6 I wonder why old saints don't sing,
And praise the Lord upon the wing,
And make the heavenly arches ring,
With loud hosannas to our king,
　　Who brought our souls to union.

7 Come, poor backslider, come away,
And mind to do as well as say,
And learn to watch as well as pray,
And bear your cross from day to day,
　　And then you'll feel this union.

8 O! could I like an angel sound
Salvation through the earth around,
The devil's kingdom to confound,
I'd triumph on Immanuel's ground,
　　And spread this heavenly union.

9 Come, heaven and earth unite your lays,
And give to Jesus endless praise,
And thou, my soul, look on and gaze,
He weeps, he bleeds, thy debt he pays,
　　To give thee heavenly union.

10 We soon shall leave all things below,
And quit this vale of pain and wo,
And then we'll all to glory go,
And there we'll see, and hear, and know,
　　And feel a perfect union.

11 There we the glorious Lamb shall see,
Who groan'd and died upon the tree,
Who spill'd his blood to set us free,
That we might his salvation see,
    And feel a gracious union.

12 Almighty God, teach heart and tongue,
To thee to raise a grateful song,
All praises to thy name belong,
Let Zion sing, thy kingdom come,
    And fill the world with union.

**95**               *P. M.*

COME, my brethren, let us try, for a little
    season,
Every burden to lay by; come, and let us
    reason.
What is this that casts you down? what is this
    that grieves you?
Speak, and let the worst be known, speaking
    may relieve you.

2 Christ at times by faith I view, and it doth re-
    lieve me,
But my doubts return anew, they are those that
    grieve me.
Troubled like the restless sea, feeble, faint, and
    fearful,
Plagued with every sore disease, how can I be
    cheerful?

3 Think on what your Saviour bore in the gloomy
    garden,
Sweating blood at every pore to procure thy
    pardon;
View him nailed to the tree, bleeding, groaning,
    dying,
Since he suffered this for thee, therefore be be-
    lieving.

4 Joseph took his body down, shrouded it in linen,
   Laid it in the silent tomb, and returned
      mourning;
   Jesus rises from the tomb, angels tell the story:
   See what glory shines around, hallelujah, glory.

5 Brethren, don't you feel the flame? sisters, don't
      you love him?
   Let us join to praise his name, let us never
      grieve him;
   Soon we'll meet to part no more, soon we'll
      meet in heaven,
   There we'll join the saints above, and forever
      praise him.

## 96 *4 8s & 2 6s.*

COME, brethren dear, who know the Lord,
  And taste the sweetness of his word,
    In Jesus' ways go on:
  Our troubles and our trials here
  Will only make us richer there,
    When we arrive at home.

2 We feel that heaven is now begun,
  It issues from the sparkling throne,
    From Jesus' throne on high;
  It comes in floods we can't contain,
  We drink, and drink, and drink again,
    The fountain ne'er runs dry.

3 Oh, when we once shall dwell above,
  Around the dazzling throne of love,
    Where heavenly glory beams;
  Jesus will lead his people through
  The groves of bliss forever new—
    Watered with living streams.

4 Triumphantly we there shall sing
  The conquests of our Saviour king—

When all his saints get home:
Come, hasten on my brethren dear,
Soon we shall meet together there:
For Jesus bids us come.

5 Amen, amen, my soul replies,
I'm bound to meet you in the skies,
When all our toils are o'er;
Now here's my heart and here's my hand,
To meet you in that heavenly land,
Where we shall part no more.

**97** *8 lines, 7s & 9s.*

BRETHREN, hear the martial sound,
The gospel trumpet now is blowing;
Men in order 'listing round,
And soldiers to the standard flowing!
Bounty's offered—joy and peace—
To every soldier this is given;
When from toil and war they cease,
A mansion bright prepared in heaven.

2 Those who long in debt have laid,
And feel the hand of sore oppression,
Have their debts all freely paid,
And share at once a rich possession:
Lo! the sick, the blind, the dumb,
Leave all their maladies behind them!
See, the sinners, when they come,
Feel love's sweet bonds completely bind them.

3 Victory is not to the strong;
The burden's on our Captain's shoulder;
None so aged, none so young,
But he may 'list and be a soldier;
Those who cannot fight or fly—
Beneath this banner find protection;
None who on his name rely
Shall be reduced to base subjection.

4 Fear ye not, the cause is good;
    Come—who will to the crown aspire:
In this cause the martyrs stood,
    And shouted victory in the fire.
In this cause we'll follow on :
    And soon we'll tell the wondrous story,
How, by faith, we won the crown,
    And fought our way to life and glory.

5 Lo, the battle is begun,
    Behold the armies now in motion!
Some the fight have almost won,
    And grasp by faith their future portion!
Hark! the victors sing aloud;
    Immanuel's chariot wheels are rolling;
Mourners weeping through the crowd,.
    And Satan's throne like lightning falling.

6 Now, ye sinners, come, enlist.
    The officers are still recruiting;
Will you still in sin persist,
    And spend your time in vain disputing?
All your caviling is in vain;
    And if you do not sue for favor,
Down you'll sink to endless pain,
    To bear the wrath of God forever.

## 98           *P. M.*

COME, sisters and brothers, who love one
    another,
    And have done so for years that are gone,
How often we've met him, in sweet heavenly
    union,
    Who opens the way to God's throne;
While we run in the bright, shining way,
    With joy and thanksgiving we'll praise him
    who loved us,
Though we part here in body, we're bound for
    one glory,
    And bound for each other to pray.

2 There was Joshua and Joseph, Elias and Moses,
    Who prayed as they journeyed along;
There was Abra'm and Isaac, and Jacob and
    David,
    And Solomon, Stephen. and John :
There was Simeon and Anna, and I don't know
    how many,
    Who prayed, and God heard from his throne :
Some cast among lions, some bound with rough
    irons,
    Yet glory and praises they sung.

3 Some tell us that praying, and also that praising,
    Is labor that's all spent in vain :
But we have such witness that God hears with
    swiftness,
    From praying we will not refrain :
There was old father Noah, and ten thousand
    more,
    Who witnessed that God heard them pray;
There was Samuel and Hannah, Paul, Silas,
    and Peter,
    And Daniel and Jonah will say,

4 That God by his Spirit, or an angel doth visit,
    Our souls and our bodies while praying;
Shall we all go fainting, while they all go
    praising,
    And glorify God in the flame?
God grant us to inherit the same praying spirit,
    While onward we journey below,
So that when we cease praying, we may not
    cease praising,
    But around God's bright throne we may bow.

**99**        *1-9 & 11-9.*

COME away to the skies, my beloved arise,
    And rejoice in the day thou wast born:
  7

On this festival day come exulting away,
　　And with singing to Sion return.

2 We have laid up our love and our treasure above,
　　Though our bodies continue below:
　The redeemed of our Lord, we remember his
　　　word,
　　And with singing to paradise go.

3 With singing we praise the original grace,
　　By our heavenly Father bestowed;
　Our being receive from his bounty, and live
　　To the honor and glory of God.

4 For thy glory we are created to share
　　Both the nature and kingdom divine:
　Created again, that our souls may remain
　　In time and eternity thine.

5 With thanks we approve the design of thy love
　　Which hath joined us in Jesus' name;
　So united in heart that we never can part,
　　Till we meet at the feast of the Lamb.

6 There, there at his feet, we shall suddenly meet,
　　And be parted in body no more!
　We shall sing to our lyres with the heavenly
　　　choirs,
　　And our Saviour in glory adore.

7 Hallelujah we sing to our Father and king,
　　And his rapturous praises repeat;
　To the Lamb that was slain, hallelujah again,
　　Sing all heaven, and fall at his feet!

8 In assurance of hope, we to Jesus look up,
　　Till his banner unfurled in the air
　From our graves we shall see, and cry out, "It
　　　is he!"
　　And fly up to acknowledge him there.

**100**            *11s.*

FROM gloomy dejection my thoughts mount
    the sky,
And realms ever peaceful, transported descry;
There joys ever blooming enrapture the soul,
And rivers of pleasure incessantly roll.

2 If such be my portion, why should I complain?
Why cherish despondence, why sadness retain?
Is sorrow then meet for an heir of the skies,
Who shortly to blessings unbounded shall rise?

3 No longer I'll murmur, no longer repine,
But joy 'mid all troubles, since heaven is mine;
Then deep in oblivion be sunk every fear,
Be erased from my bosom each trace of despair.

4 How glorious the scheme that grace doth en-
    hance,
Our hopes to enliven, our bliss to advance!
It fills me with transport, my joys overflow,
Too big for expression, ecstatic they grow.

5 O aid me, ye angels, its wonders to tell,
Encompass the theme, in full symphony dwell;
But still it enlarges—no angel can scan
The scheme of redemption, the wonderful plan.

**101**            *C. M.*

FROM all that's mortal, all that's vain,
    And from this earthly clod,
Arise, my soul, and strive to gain
    Some fellowship with God.

2 Say, what is there below the sky,
    O'er all the paths thou'st trod,
Can suit thy wishes or thy joys,
    Like fellowship with God.

3 Not life, nor all the toys of art,
　　Nor pleasure's flow'ry road,
Can to my soul such bliss impart,
　　As fellowship with God.

4 Not health or friendship here below,
　　Nor wealth, that golden load,
Can such delights and comforts show,
　　As fellowship with God.

5 When I in love am made to bear
　　Affliction's needful rod,
Light, sweet, and kind the strokes appear,
　　Through fellowship with God.

6 In fierce temptation's fiery blast,
　　And dark distraction's road,
I'm happy, if I can but taste
　　Some fellowship with God.

7 And when the icy arms of death
　　Shall chill my flowing blood,
With joy I'll yield my latest breath
　　In fellowship with God.

8 When I at last to heaven ascend,
　　And join that blest abode—
There an eternity I'll spend
　　In fellowship with God.

**102**　　　　・　*6 lines, 8s.*

FOUNTAIN of life and all my joy,
　　Jesus, thy mercies I embrace;
The breath thou giv'st, for thee employ,
　　And wait to taste thy perfect grace;
No more forsaken and forlorn,
I bless the day that I was born!

2 Preserved through faith, by power divine,
　　A miracle of grace I stand!

I prove the strength of Jesus mine!
  Jesus, upheld by thy right hand,
Though in my flesh I feel the thorn,
I bless the day that I was born.

3 Weary of life, through inbred sin,
  I was, but now defy its power;
When as a flood the foe comes in,
  My soul is more than conqueror:
I tread him down with holy scorn,
And bless the day that I was born.

4 Come, Lord, and make me pure within,
  And let me now be filled with God!
Live to declare I'm saved from sin;
  And if I seal the truth with blood,
My soul, from out the body torn,
Shall bless the day that I was born!

# 103 P. M.

HOW firm a foundation, ye saints of the Lord,
  Is laid for your faith in his excellent word!
What more can he say than to you he hath said,
You who unto Jesus for refuge have fled?

2 In every condition, in sickness and health,
In poverty's vale, or abounding in wealth,
At home and abroad, on the land, on the sea,
As thy days may demand, shall thy strength
    ever be.

3 Fear not, I am with thee—O, be not dismay'd,
I, I am thy God, and will still give thee aid;
I'll strengthen thee, help thee, and cause thee
    to stand,
Upheld by my righteous, omnipotent hand.

4 When thro' the deep waters I call thee to go,
The rivers of woe shall not thee overflow;

For I will be with thee, thy troubles to bless,
And sanctify to thee thy deepest distress.

5 When thro' fiery trials thy pathway shall lie,
My grace all-sufficient shall be thy supply;
The flame shall not hurt thee, I only design
Thy dross to consume, and thy gold to refine.

6 Even down to old age, all my people shall prove,
My sov'reign, eternal, unchangeable love;
And when hoary hairs shall their temples adorn,
Like lambs they shall still in my bosom be
borne.

7 The soul that on Jesus doth lean for repose,
I will not, I will not desert to his foes;
That soul, tho' all hell should endeavor to shake
I'll never—no, never—no, never forsake.

## 104 *P. M.*

HOW lost was my condition
Till Jesus made me whole!
There is but one Physician
Can cure a sin-sick soul:
Next door to death he found me,
And snatch'd me from the grave,
To tell to all around me
His wondrous power to save.

*There's balm in Gilead:*
*To make the wounded whole,*
*There's power enough in Jesus,*
*To cure the sin-sick soul.*

2 The worst of all diseases
Is light, compared to sin;
On every part it seizes,
But rages most within:
'Tis palsy, plague, and fever
And madness all combined;

And none but a believer,
  The least relief can find.

3 From men great skill professing,
    I sought a cure to gain;
  But this proved more distressing,
    And added to my pain.
  Some said that nothing ail'd me,
    Some gave me up for lost;
  Thus every refuge fail'd me,
    And all my hopes were cross'd.

4 At length this great Physician
    (How matchless is his grace)
  Accepted my petition,
    And undertook my case:
  First gave me sight to view him,
    For sin mine eyes had seal'd;
  Then bade me look unto him;
    I look'd—and I was heal'd.

5 A dying, risen Jesus,
  ·   Seen by an eye of faith,
  At once from danger frees us,
    And saves the soul from death.
  Come, then, to this Physician,
    His help he'll freely give;
  He makes no hard condition—
    'Tis only, Look and live!

**105**            *4 8s and 2 6s.*

HOW happy are the new-born race,
    Partakers of adopting grace!
  How pure the bliss they share!
  Hid from the world, and all its eyes,
  Within their heart the blessing lies,
    And conscience feels it there.

2 The moment we believe, 'tis ours;
  And if we love, with all our powers,

The God from whom it came,
And if we swerve with heart sincere,
'Tis still discernible and clear,
An undisputed claim.

3 But, ah! if foul and wilful sin
Stain and dishonor us within,
   Farewell the joy we knew;
Again the slaves of nature's sway,
In lab'rinths of our own we stray,
   Without a guide or clue.

4 The chaste and pure, who fear to grieve
The gracious Spirit they receive,
   His work distinctly trace;
And strong in undissembling love,
Boldly assert and clearly prove
   Their hearts his dwelling-place.

## 106 *4 lines 11s.*

HOW sad are the moments when wandering
   from God,
And thorny and dark is the dangerous road!
But light is the pathway which leads to the
   tomb,
When cheered by the presence of Jesus, my
   home.

   *Home, home, sweet, sweet home!*
   *When cheered by the presence of Jesus, my home.*

2 Though fading the joys which earth can bestow,
And false is the light which illumes us below.
Though sorrows, like clouds, hang around us in
   gloom,
The beams of his love light me on my way
   home.

   *Home, home, sweet, sweet home!*
   *The beams of his love light me on my way home.*

3 When the tempest of life has sunk to repose,
And death shall the beauties of heaven disclose,
With all the redeemed I o'er it will roam,
And sing hallelujah to Jesus, my home.

*Home, home, sweet, sweet home!*
*And sing hallelujah to Jesus, my home.*

**107**  *8 lines 7s.*

HASTE, again, ye days of grace,
When, assembled in one place,
Signs and wonders marked the hour!
All were filled and spoke with power;
Hands uplifted, eyes o'erflowed,
Hearts enlarged, and self destroyed!
All things common, now we'll prove
All our common stock be love.

2 Jesus now his work revives,
Now his quick'ning Spirit strives,
Oh, let preachers, people, all
Listen to the glorious call,
Join the simple, lively throng,
Catch the fire, and swell the song;
Heart in heart, and hand in hand,
Spread the life through all the land.

3 Oh, that each may now prevail!
Act the faith that cannot fail;
Rise, and pull the blessing down,
Seize the kingdom for his own;
Fire our hearts with holy zeal;
Glowing still for Zion's weal;
Heaven open—blessings pour—
Spirit work this present hour!

4 Lo! the knife we boldly take,
Bind our Isaacs to the stake;
Freely part with all for thee:
Welcome, King of liberty!

Now we die to self and sin,
Nothing feel but love within,
May this faith in words abound,
Shine and burn to all around.

5 Pilgrims! soon the journey's done;
Warriors! soon the battle's won;
Where your doubts, your cares, your fears?
See! the glittering crown appears!
Hark! the angels shouting cry,
"Welcome! welcome to the sky!"
Jesus calls, and calls for thee;
"Faithful servant, come to me."

## 108     *C. M.*

HAPPY the man whose bliss supreme
   Flows from a source on high,
And flows in one perpetual stream,
   When earthly springs are dry.

2 If Providence their comforts shroud,
   And dark distresses lower,
Hope paints its rainbow on the cloud,
   And grace shines through the shower.

3 What troubles can their hearts o'erwhelm
   Who view a Saviour near?
Whose Father sits and guides the helm—
   Whose voice forbids their fear?

4 Let tempests rage, and billows rise,
   And mortal firmness shrink:
Their anchor fastens in the skies—
   Their bark no more can sink.

5 God is their joy and portion still,
   When earthly good retires;
And shall their hearts sustain and fill,
   When earth itself expires.

**109**                        *11s.*

HOW happy, how loving, how joyful I feel!
　I want to feel more love, yea more love
　　and zeal,
I want my love perfect, I want my love pure,
That all things with patience I well may en-
　dure.

2 I want to love wisdom that comes from above,
I want to be holy and fill'd with pure love,
I want my light clear that beholders may see
How faith and good works in sweet union agree.

3 My treasure in heaven I want to lay up,
　Where no moth nor rust can ever corrupt,
Where no thief nor robber will venture or dare:
My heart and my treasure I want to be there.

4 My union I want with the Father and Son,
I want that perfected which is begun,
That love and sweet union that soothes every
　care,
And with my dear brethren all burdens to
　bear.

5 Come all my dear brethren both aged and youth,
And all who are willing to walk in the truth,
Let us all join together in union and love,
And on our blest journey so joyful we'll move.

6 When time is no more, and from earth we re-
　move,
To dwell in the regions of peace, life and love,
With Jesus our Saviour, and all holy men,
We'll shout hallelujahs forever, Amen!

**110**

I HAVE sought round the verdant earth,
　　For unfading joy;
I have tried every source of mirth,
　　But all, all will cloy.

Lord, bestow on me
Grace to set my spirit free:
Thine the praise shall be,
    Mine, mine the joy.

2 I have wandered in mazes dark
    Of doubt and distress,
I have not had a kindling spark
    My spirit to bless.
Cheerless unbelief
Filled my laboring soul with grief,
What shall give relief?
    What shall give peace?

3 I then turned to thy gospel, Lord,
    From folly away,
I then trusted thy holy word,
    That taught me to pray.
Here I found release;
Weary spirit here found rest,
Hope of endless bliss—
    Eternal day.

4 I will praise now my heavenly King,
    I'll praise and adore;
The heart's richest tribute bring
    To thee, God of power;
And in heaven above,
Saved by thy redeeming love,
Loud the strains shall move
    For evermore.

5 When my life's fearful strife is done,
    Its sorrows all past,
Before my Redeemer's throne
    My crown I will cast:
There, where angels dwell,
Saints their highest rapture tell;
This my song shall swell,
    He died for me.

6 O come, then, ye weary ones,
  Who comfort ne'er know,
And here at the Saviour's throne
  In prayerfulness bow;
Guilt shall then remove,
Light shall cheer thee from above;
Come—come—share his love—
  Come, come-away.

## 111   *C. M.*

IN evil long I took delight,
  Unawed by shame or fear;
Till a new object struck my sight,
  And stopped my wild career.

2 I saw One hanging on a tree
  In agonies and blood;
Who fixed his languid eyes on me,
  As near his cross I stood.

3 Sure never to my latest breath
  Can I forget that look;
It seemed to charge me with his death,
  Though not a word he spoke.

4 My conscience felt, and owned the guilt,
  And plunged me in despair;
I saw my sins his blood had spilt,
  And helped to nail him there.

5 Alas! I knew not what I did;
  But now my tears are vain:
Where shall my trembling soul be hid?
  For I the Lord have slain.

6 A second look he gave, which said,
  "I freely all forgive;
This blood is for thy ransom paid,
  I'll die that thou may'st live."

7 Thus, while his death my sin displays
   In all its blackest hue;
(Such is the mystery of grace,)
   It seals my pardon too.

8 With pleasing grief and mournful joy
   My spirit now is filled,
That I should such a life destroy,
   Yet live by him I killed.

## 112       *P. M.*

IF 'tis sweet to mingle where
  Christians meet for social prayer;
If 'tis sweet with them to raise,
Songs of holy joy and praise—
Passing sweet that state must be
Where they meet eternally.

2 Saviour, may these meetings prove
Preparations for above;
While we worship in this place,
May we go from grace to grace;
Till we, each in his degree,
Fit for endless glory be.

## 113       *11s.*

I WOULD not live alway: I ask not to stay
  Where storm after storm rises dark o'er the
     way;
The few lurid mornings that dawn on us here
Are enough for life's woes, full enough for its
     cheer.

2 I would not live alway thus fettered by sin—
Temptation without, and corruption within:
E'en the rapture of pardon is mingled with
     fears,
And the cup of thanksgiving with penitent
     tears.

3 I would not live alway : no—welcome the tomb:
  Since Jesus hath lain there, I dread not its gloom.
  There sweet be my rest till he bid me arise
  To hail him in triumph descending the skies.

4 Who, who would live alway away from his God,
  Away from yon heaven, that blissful abode,
  Where the rivers of pleasure flow bright o'er
        the plains,
  And the noontide of glory eternally reigns?

5 Where the saints of all ages in harmony meet,
  Their Saviour and brethren transported to greet,
  While the anthems of rapture unceasingly roll,
  And the smile of the Lord is the feast of the soul.

## 114                    *S. M.*

I WAS a wandering sheep,
    I did not love the fold;
I did not love my Shepherd's voice,
    I would not be controlled.

2 I was a wayward child,
    I did not love my home;
  I did not love my Father's voice,
    I loved afar to roam.

3 The Shepherd sought his sheep,
    The Father sought his child;
  They followed me o'er vale and hill,
    O'er desert, waste, and wild.

4 They found me nigh to death,
    Famished, and faint, and lone;
  They bound me with the bands of love,
    They saved the wandering one.

5 They washed my filth away,
    They made me clean and fair;
  They brought me to my home in peace,
    The long-sought wanderer!

6 Jesus my Shepherd is,
　'Twas he that loved my soul,
'Twas he that washed me in his blood,
　'Twas he that made me whole.

7 'Twas he that sought the lost,
　That found the wandering sheep;
'Twas he that brought me to the fold,
　'Tis he that still doth keep.

8 I was a wandering sheep,
　I would not be controlled;
But now I love the Shepherd's voice,
　I love, I love the fold!

9 I was a wayward child,
　I once preferred to roam;
But now I love my Father's voice,
　I love, I love his home!

## 115 *P. M.*

I SEEK a place which is out of sight;
　A city high up in the skies;
There, there is my home, all pure and bright,
　And homeward my spirit still hies.

　　*I'm bound for home, for my blissful home,*
　　*The house and the city above;*
　　*And all who forsake their sins may come,*
　　*And dwell in that city of love.*

2 I seek a place where they heave no sigh;
　Where sorrow can never be known;
But where I shall drink from founts of joy,
　That gush ever bright from the throne.

3 I seek a place where they never die;
　Where beauty and youth never fade;
Where never is heard the mournful cry,
　"My friend, my beloved, is dead."

4 I seek a place where they sin no more;
  Where Satan my foe cannot lure;
  And oh! when I reach that blessed shore;
  My soul is forever secure.

5 I seek a place where the patriarchs shine;
  Apostles, and martyrs, and seers;
  Encircled in robes of light divine,
  Triumphant o'er sorrow and fears.

6 I seek a place where the Saviour reigns;
  That Jesus once nailed to the tree;
  He purchased that place with blood and pains,
  And went to prepare it for me.

## 116

I'LL sing my Saviour's grace, and his dear
    name I'll praise,
  While in this land of sorrow I remain;
My troubles soon will end, and my soul ascend,
  When freed from this dull clog of cumbrous
    clay.

2 A pilgrim here below, while in this vale of wo,
  I live in exile, mourning like a dove;
My days in sorrow roll, and my weary soul
  With earnest longings pants to mount above.

3 Tho' few my days have been, much trouble
    have I seen,
  And deep afflictions I have waded through;
For thorny is the way to eternal day,
  Yet forward will I press, and onward go.

4 Another day is gone, and yon declining sun
  Has veiled his radiant beams in sable shades,
While gloomy darkness reigns o'er the extensive
    plains,
  And awful silence closes up the scene.

8

5 Thus rapid flies away every succeeding day,
    And life's declining light draws to a close;
Thus life's short setting sun will soon in death
    go down,
    And lay my weary limbs in sweet repose.

6 On eagle wings of love, then I shall mount
    above,
    And find my passage safe to endless day;
Then happy, sweet surprise, what great new
    wonders rise!
    When freed from this dull clog of cumbrous
    clay.

7 Oh, what a glorious sight! and what supreme
    delight
    Will strike my raptured soul, when I be-
    hold—
When Salem's gates I see open wide to me,
    And streets of glittering, new, transparent
    gold!

8 But oh! and shall I then behold the Friend
    of men,
    The man who suffered, bled, and died for me?
Who bore my load of sin, sorrow, grief, and pain,
    To make me happy, and to set me free.

9 To living fountains then, and rich pastures
    green,
    To trees of paradise he leads his lambs;
While millions, falling down, prostrate all
    around,
    And at his footstool cast their glittering
    crowns.

10 Ye heavenly arches ring! sing hallelujah, sing,
    Hail holy, holy, holy, bleeding Lamb;
Once I was dead in sin, now I live again,
    And glory, glory, glory to his name!

## 117 *L. M.*

IF now I have acceptance found
　With thee, or favor in thy sight,
Still with thy grace and truth surround,
　And arm me with thy Spirit's might.

2 O may I hear thy warning voice,
　And timely fly from danger near,
With rev'rence unto thee rejoice,
　And love thee with a filial fear:

3 Still hold my soul in second life,
　And suffer not my feet to slide;
Support me in the glorious strife,
　And comfort me on every side.

4 O give me faith, and faith's increase;
　Finish the work begun in me.
Preserve my soul in perfect peace,
　And let me always rest on thee!

5 O let thy gracious Spirit guide
　And bring me to the promised land;
Where righteousness and peace reside,
　And all submit to love's command!

6 A land where milk and honey flow,
　And springs of pure delights arise,
Delights which I shall shortly know,
　When I regain my paradise.

## 118 *L. M.*

I LEFT the God of truth and light,
　I left the God who gave me breath,
To wander in the wilds of night,
　And perish in the snares of death.

2 Sweet was his service, and his yoke
　Was light and easy to be borne;

Through all his bonds of love I broke,
  I cast away his gifts with scorn.

3 I danced in folly's giddy maze,
  And drunk the sea, and chased the wind;
But falsehood lurked in all her ways,
  Her laughter left remorse behind.

4 I dreamed of bliss in pleasure's bowers,
  While pillowing roses stayed my head;
But serpents hissed amongst the flowers;
  I 'woke, and thorns were all my bed.

5 In riches when I sought for joy,
  And placed in sordid gains my trust,
I found that gold was all alloy,
  And worldly treasures fleeting dust.

6 I wooed ambition, climbed the pole,
  And shone among the stars;—but fell,
Headlong in all my pride of soul,
  Like Lucifer, from heaven to hell.

7 Heart-broken, friendless, poor, cast down,
  Where shall the chief of sinners fly,
Almighty vengeance, from thy frown?
  Eternal justice, from thine eye?

8 Lo, through the gloom of guilty fears,
  My faith discerns a dawn of grace;
The sun of righteousness appears
  In Jesus' reconciling face.

9 My suffering, slain, and risen Lord,
  In sore distress I turn to thee;
I claim acceptance on thy work,
  My God! my God! forsake not me.

10 Prostrate before the mercy-seat,
  I dare not, if I would, despair;
None ever perished at thy feet,
  And I will lie forever there.

**119**

JOYFULLY, joyfully, onward I move,
　Bound for the land of bright spirits above;
Angelic choristers sing as I come,
Joyfully, joyfully, haste to thy home.
Soon with my pilgrimage ended below,
Home to the land of bright spirits I'll go,
Pilgrim and stranger no more shall I roam;
Joyfully, joyfully, resting at home.

2 Friends fondly cherished have passed on before,
　Waiting, they watch me approaching that
　　shore;
Singing, to cheer me through death's chilling
　　gloom,
Joyfully, joyfully, haste to thy home.
Sounds of sweet melody fall on my ear,
Harps of the blessed, your voices I hear:
Rings with the harmony heaven's high dome,
Joyfully, joyfully, resting at home.

3 Death, with thy weapons of war lay me low;
　Strike, king of terrors, I fear not thy blow;
Jesus has broken the bars of the tomb,
Joyfully, joyfully, will I go home.
Bright will the morn of eternity dawn;
Death shall be banished, his sceptre be gone;
Joyfully then shall I witness his doom,
Joyfully, joyfully resting at home.

**120**　　　　*8s & 7s.*

JESUS, I my cross have taken,
　All to leave and follow thee;
Naked, poor, despised, forsaken—
　*Thou* henceforth my all shalt be!
Perish every fond ambition—
　All I've sought, or hoped, or known;

Yet how rich is my condition !
God and heaven are all my own.

2 Let the world despise and leave me—
They have left my Saviour too;
Human hopes and looks deceive me—
Thou art not, like them, untrue;
And while *thou* shalt smile upon me—
God of wisdom, love, and might,
Friends may hate, and foes may scorn me,
Show thy face, and all is right.

3 Go, then, earthly fame and treasure;
Come, disaster, scorn, and pain;
In thy service pain is pleasure,
With thy favor loss is gain.
I have called thee Abba, Father—
I have set my heart on thee;
Storms may howl, and clouds may gather,
All must work for good to me.

4 Soul, then know thy full salvation—
Rise o'er sin, and fear, and care;
Joy to find in every station
Something still to do or bear.
Think what spirit dwells within thee:
Think what heavenly bliss is thine;
Think that Jesus died to save thee—
Child of heaven, canst thou repine?

5 Haste thee on from grace to glory,
Armed by faith, and winged by prayer—
Heaven's eternal day's before thee—
God's own hand shall guide thee there;
Soon shall close thy earthly mission,
Soon shall pass thy pilgrim days;
Hope shall change to glad fruition,
Faith to sight, and prayer to praise.

**121**     *6 lines, 8s.*

JESUS, with kindest pity see
  The souls that would be one in thee!
If now accepted in thy sight,
Thou dost our upright hearts unite,
Allow us e'en on earth to prove
The noblest joys of heavenly love!

2 Before thy glorious eyes we spread
  The wish which doth from thee proceed:
Our love from earthly dross refine;
Holy, angelical, divine,
Thee, its great author, let it show,
And back to the pure fountain flow,

3 A drop of that unbounded sea,
  O Lord, resorb it into thee!
While all our souls. with restless strife,
Spring up into eternal life;
And lost in endless rapture prove
Thy whole immensity of love.

4 A spark of that ethereal fire
  Still let it to its source aspire;
To thee in every wish return,
Intensely for thy glory burn;
While all our souls fly up to thee,
And blaze through all eternity.

**122**     *P. M.*

LET others delight in the gambols of mirth,
  In pleasures of riot and glee;
But among all the places frequented on earth,
  The class room is sweetest to me.

    *Oh! the class room, the class room,*
    *Oh! the class room, the class room,*
    *No place like the class room to me.*

2 There kindred souls meet, and converse as of
          old,
    Their record on high is the same;
    But the Lord looketh down, and includes in his
          fold
    The faithful who think on his name.

3 There spirit meets spirit, and eye speaks to eye,
    And cords of sweet sympathy bind;
    And together they press to their home in the
          sky,
    Forgetting the sorrows behind.

4 There hope plumes her wings, and exultingly
          goes
    To bring from the land of the blest,
    Those sweet leaves from the tree that in Para-
          dise grows,
    To heal all the wounds of the breast.

5 Hope sings of a land where none ever shall die—
    Where friendships shall never be riven;
    Where the tears shall be wiped from each sor-
          rowing eye,
    And all shall be happy in heaven.

**123**                    *P. M.*

MY days, my weeks, my months, my years,
    Fly rapid as the whirling spheres
    Around the steady pole;
    Time, like the tide, its motion keeps,
    And I must launch through endless deeps,
    Where endless ages roll.

2 The grave is near the cradle seen,
    How swift the moments pass between,
    And whisper, as they fly,
    "Unthinking man, remember this,
    Though fond of sublunary bliss,
    That you must groan and die."

3 My soul, attend the solemn call,
  Thine earthly tent must shortly fall,
    And thou must take thy flight,
  Beyond the vast expansive blue
  To sing above as angels do,
    Or sink in endless night.

4 How great the bliss, how great the wo,
  Hangs on this inch of time below,
    On this precarious breath !
  The Lord of nature only knows
  Whether another year shall close,
    Ere I expire in death.

5 Long ere the sun shall run his round,
. I may be buried under ground,
    And there in silence rot:
  Alas! an hour may close the scene;
  And ere twelve months shall roll between,
    My name be quite forgot.

6 But will my soul be thus extinct,
  And cease to live, and cease to think?
    It cannot, cannot be;
  No. my immortal cannot die!
  What wilt thou do, or whither fly,
    When death shall set thee free?

7 Will mercy then her arms extend,
  Will Jesus be thy guardian friend,
    And heaven thy dwelling-place?
  Or shall insulting fiends appear,
  And drag thee down to dark despair
    Below the reach of grace?

8 A heaven or hell, and these alone,
  Beyond the present life are known;
    There is no middle state:
  To-day attend the call divine,
  To-morrow may be none of thine,
    Or it may be too late.

9 Oh, do not pass this as a dream,
   Vast is the change, whate'er it seem
     To poor unthinking man ;
   Lord, at thy footstool I would bow,
   Bid conscience plainly tell me now
     What it would tell me then.

10 If in destruction's road I stray,
   Help me to choose the better way
     That leads to joys on high ;
   Thy grace impart, my guilt forgive,
   Nor let me ever dare to live,
     So as I dare not die.

## 124                    *L. M.*

MY dearest friends, in bonds of love,
   Whose hearts the sweetest union prove ;
Your friendship's like the strongest band,
Yet we must take the parting hand.

2 Your company's sweet, your union dear,
  Your words delightful to the ear,
  And when I see that we must part,
  You draw like cords around my heart.

3 How sweet the hours have passed away
  Since we have met to sing and pray !
  How loth we are to leave the place
  Where Jesus shows his smiling face !

4 O could I stay with friends so kind,
  How would it cheer my fainting mind !
  But duty makes me understand
  That we must take the parting hand.

5 And since it is God's holy will
  That we be parted for a while,
  In sweet submission, all as one,
  We'll say our Father's will be done.

6 My dearest friends, both old and young,
  I hope you will in Christ go on;
  Fight on, and soon you'll win the prize,
  Those happy regions in the skies.

7 How oft I've seen your flowing tears,
  And heard you tell your hopes and fears!
  Your hearts with love have seemed to flame.
  Which makes me think we'll meet again.

8 A few more days and years at most,
  And we shall reach fair Canaan's coast,
  When in that holy, happy land,
  We'll clasp anew the immortal hand.

9 I hope you will remember me,
  If you no more my face should see;
  An interest in your prayers I crave,
  That we may meet beyond the grave.

10 O blessed day, O glorious hope,
  My soul leaps forward at the thought,
  When in that holy, happy land,
  We'll take no more the parting hand.

## 125 *P. M.*

MY soul is full of glory, inspiring my tongue,
  Could I meet with angels, I would sing
    them a song;
I would sing of my Jesus, and tell of his charms,
And beg them to bear me to his loving arms.

2 Methinks they're descending to hear what I
    sing;
  Well pleased to hear mortals praising their king:
  O angels, O angels! my soul's in a flame;
  I faint in sweet raptures at Jesus' name.

3 O Jesus! O Jesus! thou balm of my soul,
  'Twas thou, my dear Jesus, that made my heart
    whole:

O bring me to view thee, thou precious sweet
    King,
In oceans of glory thy praises to sing.

4 O heaven! sweet heaven! I long to be there,
To meet all my brethren, and Jesus my dear:
Come angels! come angels! I'm ready to fly; ·
Come, quickly convey me to God in the sky.

5 Sweet Spirit attend me, till Jesus shall come;
Protect and defend me till I am called home:
Though worms my poor body may claim as
    their prey,
'Twill outshine, when rising, the sun at noon-
    day.

6 The sun shall be darkened, the moon turned to
    blood;
The mountains all melt at the presence of God;
Red lightnings may flash, loud thunders may
    roar,
All this cannot daunt me on Canaan's blest
    shore.

7 A glimpse of bright glory surprises my soul;
I sink in sweet visions to view the bright goal:
My soul, while I'm singing, is leaping to go:
This moment for heaven I'd leave all below.

8 Farewell, my dear brethren, my Lord bids me
    come;
Farewell, my dear sisters. I'm now going home;
Bright angels are whispering so sweet in my
    ear,
Away to my Saviour my spirit they'll bear.

9 I'm going, I'm going, but what do I see?
'Tis Jesus in glory appears unto me!
I'm going, I'm going, I'm going, I'm gone!
O glory! O glory! 'tis done! it is done!

10 To the regions of glory the spirit is fled,
And left this poor body inactive and dead;
With angelic armies in glory to blaze,
On Jesus' beauties for ever to gaze.

11 When the six seals shall open, the trumpet
shall sound,
To awake God's dear children that sleep under
ground:
Their souls and their bodies shall then join in
one,
And each from their Saviour receive a bright
crown.

## 126 *P. M.*

'MID scenes of confusion and creature com-
plaints,
How sweet to my soul is communion with saints!
To find at the banquet of mercy there's room,
And feel in the presence of Jesus at home.

*Home, home, sweet, sweet home!*
*Prepare me, dear Saviour, for glory, my home.*

2 Sweet bonds that unite all the children of peace,
And their precious Jesus, whose love cannot
cease,
Though oft from thy presence in sadness I roam,
I long to behold thee in glory at home.

3 I sigh from this body of sin to be free;
Which hinders my joy and communion with
thee:
Though now my temptations like billows may
foam,
All, all will be peace when I'm with thee at
home.

4 While here in the valley of conflict I stay,
O give me submission and strength as my day;

In all my afflictions to thee would I come,
Rejoicing in hope of my glorious home.

5 Whate'er thou deniest, O give me thy grace!
The Spirit's sure witness, and smiles of thy face:
Indulge me with patience to wait at thy throne,
And find even now a sweet foretaste of home.

6 I long, dearest Lord, in thy beauties to shine,
No more as an exile in sorrow to pine,
And in thy dear image, arise from the tomb,
With glorified millions to praise thee at home.

# 127

MY soul is happy in its choice,
   With Christ's dear flock enrolled;
I hear my Shepherd's soothing voice,
   And rest within his fold.

2 He leads me through the pastures sweet
   Beside the flowing rills,
And all my longing wishes meets,
   And all my spirit fills.

3 Daily I find his love the same,
   And run at his command;
He knows and calls me by my name,
   And guides me with his hand.

4 Had I but dreamed how great the joys
   Of those who Jesus know,
I should have made his love my choice,
   And sought him years ago.

5 But vainly, madly did I stray,
   A stranger to his grace,
Far from the fold—from bliss away,
   In sin's wide wilderness.

6 When round me wolves with fury strove,
   The wanderer to destroy,

My Shepherd ran with haste and love,
   And brought me home with joy.

7 Now safe returned, my wanderings past,
   My soul adores his charms,
Who laid me on his pitying breast,
   And shields me with his arms.

8 Redeemer—Shepherd—guard my soul
   From every future ill :
While storms without and thunders roll,
   Be mine, my Saviour, still.

## 128

MY days are gliding swiftly by,
   And I, a pilgrim stranger,
Would not detain them as they fly,
   Those hours of toil and danger.

*For O! we stand on Jordan's strand,*
   *Our friends are passing over,*
*And just before, the shining shore*
   *We may almost discover.*

2 We'll gird our loins, my brethren dear,
   Our heavenly home discerning ;
Our absent Lord has left us word,
   Let every lamp be burning.

3 Should coming days be cold and dark,
   We need not cease our singing ;
That perfect rest naught can molest,
   Where golden harps are ringing.

4 Let sorrow's rudest tempest blow,
   Each chord on earth to sever ;
Our King says come, and there's our home,
   Forever, O forever !

**129** *C. M.*

MISTAKEN souls that dream of heaven,
    And make their empty boast
Of inward joys, and sins forgiven,
    While they are slaves to lust.

2 Vain are our fancies, airy flights,
    If faith be cold and dead;
None but a living power unites
    To Christ the living head.

3 'Tis faith that changes all the heart;
    'Tis faith that works by love,
That bids all sinful joys depart,
    And lifts the thoughts above.

4 'Tis faith that conquers earth and hell
    By a celestial power;
This is the grace that shall prevail
    In the decisive hour.

5 Faith must obey her Father's will,
    As well as trust his grace;
A pardoning God is jealous still
    For his own holiness.

6 When from the curse he sets us free,
    He makes our nature clean;
Nor would he send his Son to be
    The minister of sin.

**130** *C. M.*

OUR souls by love together knit,
    Cemented, mixed in one,
One hope, one heart, one mind, one voice,
    'Tis heaven on earth begun;
Our hearts have burned while Jesus spoke,
    And glowed with sacred fire;
He stopped, and talked, and fed, and blessed,
    And filled the enlarged desire.

*A Saviour! let creation sing!*
*A Saviour! let all heaven ring!*
*He's God with us, we feel him ours,*
*His fulness in our souls he pours,*
*'Tis almost done—'tis almost o'er,*
*We're joining those who're gone before,*
*We then shall meet to part no more.*

2 We're soldiers fighting for our God,
　Let trembling cowards fly;
We'll stand unshaken, firm, and fixed,
　With Christ to live and die:
Let devils rage, and hell assail,
　We'll force our passage through;
Let foes unite, and friends desert,
　We'll seize the crown, our due.

3 The little cloud increases still,
　The heavens are big with rain;
We haste to catch the teeming shower,
　And all its moisture drain:
A rill, a stream, a torrent flows;
　O pour the mighty flood;
And sweep the nations, shake the earth,
　Till all proclaim thee God.

4 When thou shalt make thy jewels up,
　And set thy starry crown;
When all thy sparkling gems shall shine,
　By thee proclaimed thine own;
May we, a little band of love,
　Be sinners saved by grace:
From glory into glory changed,
　Behold thee face to face.

**131**　　　　　　　*11s.*

O BLESSED Lord Jesus! I know thou art
　　mine!
For thee all the pleasures of sin I resign;
　9

Of objects most pleasing, I love thee the best;
Without thee I'm wretched, but with thee I'm
blessed.

2 Thy Spirit first taught me to know I was blind,
Then taught me the way of salvation to find;
For when I was sinking in gloomy despair,
Thy Spirit relieved me, and bid me not fear.

3 In vain I attempt to describe what I feel,
The language of mortals forever must fail;
My Jesus is precious, my soul's all on flame,
I'm raised into rapture while praising his name.

4 I find him in singing, I find him in prayer,
In sweet meditation he always is near;
My constant companion, O may we not part!
O glory to Jesus! he dwells in my heart!

5 If ever I loved, I love thee, my Lord,
I love all thy people, thy ways, and thy word;
With tender emotion I love sinners too,
For Jesus did die to save them from wo.

6 In Jesus confirmed, I'll praise his dear name,
Regardless of censure, of praise, or of blame;
When happy in Jesus I cannot forbear,
Though sinners despise me, his love to declare.

**132** *C. M.*

OH, let me sing of sins forgiven!
 The tranquil triumph of my soul;
Oh, let me sing a song of heaven,
 While streams of living comfort roll.
Adieu to every earthly toy,
 For nobler objects I am bound;
Since not one single drop of joy
 I ever yet from earth have found.

2 Its brightest beauties fade away,
 Its richest jewels are but dross;

Its honors scarcely live a day,
   And every gain has proved a loss.
But there's an honor that will live,
   A gem that never will decay;
There is a gain that can't deceive,
   A beauty fading not away.

3 This priceless boon I humbly claim,
   This speechless joy of sins forgiven,
The love of God, that, like a flame,
   Burns on and lights the soul to heaven.
By faith I have this treasure found,
   And gaze with wonder and surprise,
While in this dark, enchanted ground,
   "The day-spring opens" from the skies.

4 My home is in the distance seen,
   And gales come soft from Canaan's shore;
Though dark the wilderness between,
   My hopes are bright of passing o'er.
Oh, happiness! no transient dream!
   For glory's opened in my soul;
And love divine shall be my theme,
   Long as eternal ages roll.

# 133

OH, how can I forget the hour
   When love divine I found!
The place was filled with sacred power,
   And glory beamed around!
My soul, relieved from sorrow's load,
   From guilty bondage free,
Adored with joy the pardoning God,
   That showed such love to me!

2 For me the earth and skies rejoiced,
   That I no more was sad;
The thirsty land with dew was moist,
   The wilderness was glad:

The scenes of nature, then how bright!
  My eyes rejoiced to view;
I praised the Lord with warm delight,
  And thought they praised him too!

3 My darkness then to light gave place,
  My guilt to pardon free;
My rags of sin to robes of grace,
  My bonds to liberty:
I toiled no more a wandering child,
  In slavish base employ;
But safe at home, my Father smiled
  And feasted me with joy.

4 Nor did I then that bliss confine
  Within my bounding breast:
The friends who poured their tears with mine
  Were sharers in the feast;
And angels, on their watchful posts,
  With gladness hasted round,
To tell to all the heavenly hosts,
  "The long-lost child is found."

## 134          *L. M.*

WE are a band of brethren dear;
  We have a place in glory;
Our Jesus tells us not to fear,
  We have a home in glory.

  *For oh! there is glory,*
  *For oh! there is glory,*
  *For oh! there is glory,*
  *We have a home in glory.*

Or,

  *We're going on to glory,*
  *We're going on to glory,*
  *We're going on to glory,*
  *To find our friends in glory.*

2 A pilgrim and a stranger here,
I'll seek the home to pilgrims dear,
I'll leave the world and sin behind,
That better home in heaven to find.

3 Come, all ye souls by sin oppressed,
Ye restless wanderers after rest;
Come all the world, come sinner thou,
All things in Christ are ready now.

4 Come on, come on, my brethren dear,
We soon shall meet each other there;
If you get there before I do,
Look out for me, I'm coming too.

## 135 *L. M.*

OH! who will come and go with me?
I'm bound fair Canaan's land to see;
I'll join with those who've gone before,
Where sin and sorrow are no more.

*In the morning,*
*What a beautiful morning that will be,*
*When we all rise together in the morning!*

2 A few more days or years at most,
And I shall land on Canaan's coast;
There on the mount of sweet repose,
I'll bid farewell to all my woes.

3 Oh! may my soul march boldly on,
And ever sing the blessed song!
Oh! may I always persevere,
And never stop till I get there!

4 Oh! what a happy time 'twill be,
When we our friends in heaven shall see!
There we will tell our sufferings o'er,
When we shall reach that happy shore.

5 Oh! what a pleasant company!
    May we be there that sight to see,
And join in praise to Jesus' name,
    All glorious in Jerusalem.

6 Now here's my heart and here's my hand,
    To meet you in that heavenly land;
My hand again I give to thee,
    Hoping thy face in heaven to see.

## 136     *C. M.*

ONE evening pensive as I lay,
    Alone upon the ground,
As I to God began to pray,
    A light shone all around;
These words with power went through my heart,
    "I've come to set thee free,
Death, hell, nor grave, shall ever part,
    My love, my son, from thee."

2 My dungeon shook, my chains flew off,
    "Glory to God," I cried,
My soul was filled, I cried "enough,"
    For me the Saviour died.
The winter's past, the rain is gone,
    Sweet flowers now appear,
The morning brought a glorious sun,
    And banished every tear.

3 Hail, mighty Prince, eternal Lord,
    Who left the heav'nly throne,
Eternal truth attends thy word,
    Thou art the Father's Son.
When on the brink of hell I lay,
    Enclosed in blackest night,
Thou, Lord, didst hear the sinner pray,
    And brought my soul to light.

4 You who are grov'ling in your chains,
    Without one spark of hope,

Though inexpressible your pains,
  O still be looking up.
Tho' winds may blow, and storms may rise,
  A dark and gloomy night,
The morning sun will clear the skies
  With sweet prevailing light.

**137**       *7s, 6s & 8s.*

SINCE I've known a Saviour's name,
  And sin's strong fetters broke,
Careful without care I am,
  Nor feel my easy yoke:
Joyful now my faith to show,
  I find his service my reward;
All the work I do below
  Is light, for such a Lord.

2 To the desert or the cell,
  Let others blindly fly,
In this evil world I dwell,
  Nor fear its enmity:
Here I find a house of prayer,
  To which I inwardly retire;
Walking unconcerned in care,
  And unconsumed in fire.

3 O that all the world might know
  Of living, Lord, to thee,
Find their heaven begun below,
  And here thy goodness see;
Walk in all the works prepared
  By thee to exercise their grace,
Till they gain their full reward,
  And see thee face to face.

**138**      *8 lines, 9s, 10s & 1 10.*

RELIGION is a glorious treasure,
  Diffusion of the Saviour's love;

The Spirit's comfort without measure;
  It joins our souls to those above;
It calms our fears, it soothes our sorrows—
  It smooths our way o'er life's rough sea;
While endless ages are onward rolling,
  This heavenly portion ours shall be.

2 While journeying here through tribulations,
  In phalanx firm we'll march along:
Contentions may divide the nations,
  But Christ shall be our common song—
For pure religion knits together—
  It binds in love, but makes us free;
While endless ages are onward rolling,
  This heavenly portion ours shall be.

3 How vain! how frail! how transitory!
  This world, with all its pomp and show;
Its mighty names, renowned in story—
  We'll gladly leave them all below.
A brighter object now enraptures—
  In Christ alone we beauties see:
While endless ages are onward rolling,
  This heavenly portion ours shall be.

4 Our earthly house is fast dissolving,
  And mortal life will soon be o'er;
The cares within us now revolving
  Will soon afflict our hearts no more;
But pure religion lasts forever;
  In death our souls shall strengthened be;
While endless ages are onward rolling,
  This heavenly portion ours shall be.

## 139                    7s.

SWEET the time—exceeding sweet!
  When the saints together meet,
When the Saviour is the theme,
When they join to sing of him.

2 Sing we then eternal love,
Such as did the Father move:
He beheld the world undone,
Loved the world—and gave his Son.

3 Sing the Son's amazing love;
How he left the realms above,
Took our nature and our place,
Lived and died to save our race.

4 Sing we, too, the Spirit's love;
With our wretched hearts he strove,
Filled our minds with grief and fear,
Brought the precious Saviour near.

5 Sweet the place—exceeding sweet,
Where the saints in glory meet,
Where the Saviour's still the theme,
Where they see and sing of him.

## 140 *P. M.*

SOMETIMES a light surprises
The Christian while he sings;
It is the Lord who rises
  With healing in his wings;
When comforts are declining,
  He grants the soul again
A season of clear shining,
  To cheer it after rain.

2 In holy contemplation,
  We sweetly then pursue
The theme of God's salvation,
  And find it ever new;
Set free from present sorrow,
  We cheerfully can say,
E'en let th' unknown to-morrow
  Bring with it what it may.

3 It can bring with it nothing
    But he will bear us through;
Who gives the lilies clothing
    Will clothe his people too;
Beneath the spreading heavens,
    No creature but is fed;
Safe they feed upon the manna
    Which he gives them when they pray.

4 Blest inhabitants of Zion,
    Washed in the Redeemer's blood!
Jesus, whom their souls rely on,
    Makes them kings and priests to God;
'Tis his love his people raises
    Over self to reign as kings;
And, as priests, his solemn praises,
    Each for a thank-offering brings.

## 141        *P. M. 6 lines, 7s.*

SINCE the Son hath made me free,
  Let me taste my liberty!
Thee behold with open face,
Triumph in thy saving grace!
Thy great will delight to prove,
Glory in thy perfect love.

2 Abba, Father, hear thy child,
Late in Jesus reconciled;
Hear, and all the graces shower,
All the joy, and peace, and power;
All my Saviour asks above,
All the life and heaven of love.

3 Lord, I will not let thee go
Till the blessing thou bestow:
Hear my advocate divine!
Lo! to his my suit I join:
Joined to his, it cannot fail:
Bless me; for I *will* prevail.

4 Heavenly Father, life divine,
  Change my nature into thine!
  Move, and spread throughout my soul,
  Actuate, and fill the whole!
  Be it I no longer now
  Living in the flesh, but thou.

5 Holy Ghost, no more delay!
  Come, and in thy temples stay!
  Now thine inward witness bear,
  Strong, and permanent, and clear:
  Spring of life, thyself impart;
  Rise eternal in my heart!

# 142 *P. M.*

THE Lord's into his garden come,
  The spices yield a rich perfume,
    The lilies grow and thrive;
Refreshing showers of grace divine
From Jesus flow to every vine,
    And make the dead revive.

2 O how this dry and barren ground
  In springs of water shall abound,
    A fruitful soil become,
  The desert blossom as the rose;
  When Jesus conquers all his foes,
    And makes his people one.

3 The glorious time is coming on,
  The gracious work is now begun,
    My soul a witness is:
  I taste and see the pardon free
  For all mankind, as well as me,
    Who come to Christ, may live.

4 The worst of sinners here may find
  A Saviour merciful and kind,

Who will them all receive;
None are too vile who will repent,
Out of one sinner legions went,
The Lord did him relieve.

5 Come, brethren dear, who know the Lord,
And taste the sweetness of his word,
In Jesus' ways go on;
Our troubles and our trials here
Will only make us richer there,
When we arrive at home.

6 We feel that heaven is now begun,
It issues from the sparkling throne,
From Jesus' throne on high!
It comes in floods we can't contain,
We drink, and drink, and drink again,
And yet we still are dry.

7 But when we come to dwell above,
And all surround the throne of love,
We'll drink a full supply;
Jesus will lead his armies through
To living fountains where they flow,
That never will run dry.

8 'Tis there we'll reign, and shout, and sing,
And make the upper regions ring,
When all the saints get home:
Come on, come on, my brethren dear,
Soon we shall meet together there,
For Jesus bids us come.

9 Amen, amen, my soul replies,
I'm bound to meet you in the skies,
And claim my mansion there;
Now here's my heart, and here's my hand,
To meet you in that heavenly land,
Where we shall part no more.

**143** *P. M.*

TELL me no more of earthly toys,
  Of sinful mirth and carnal joys,
    The things I loved before;
Let me but view my Saviour's face,
And feel his animating grace,
    And I desire no more.

2 Tell me no more of praise and wealth,
  Tell me no more of ease and health,
    For these have all their snares;
Let me but know my sins forgiven,
But see my name enrolled in heaven,
    And I am free from cares.

3 Tell me no more of lofty towers,
  Delightful gardens, fragrant bowers,
    For these are trifling things:
The little room for me designed
Will suit as well my easy mind,
    As palaces of kings.

4 Tell me no more of crowding guests,
  Of sumptuous feasts and gaudy dress,
    Extravagance and waste:
My little table, only spread
With wholesome herbs and wholesome bread,
    Will better suit my taste.

5 Give me a Bible in my hand,
  A heart to read and understand,
    This sure unerring word:
I'd urge no company to stay,
But sit alone from day to day,
    And converse with the Lord.

**144** *P. M.*

'TIS a point I long to know,
  Oft it causes anxious thought:

Do I love the Lord or no?
　Am I his or am I not?

2 If I love, why am I thus?
　Why this dull and lifeless frame?
Hardly, sure, can they be worse,
　Who have never heard his name.

3 Could my heart so hard remain,
　Prayer a task and burden prove,
Every trifle give me pain;
　If I knew a Saviour's love?

4 When I turn mine eyes within,
　Oh, how dark, and vain, and wild!
Prone to unbelief and sin,
　Can I deem myself a child?

5 If I pray, or hear, or read,
　Faith is weak in all I do:
You that love the Lord indeed,
　Tell me, is it thus with you?

6 Yet I mourn my stubborn will,
　Find my sin a grief and thrall;
Should I grieve for what I feel,
　If I did not love at all?

7 Could I joy with saints to meet,
　Choose the ways I once abhorred,
Find at times the promise sweet,
　If I did not love the Lord?

8 Lord, decide the doubtful case,
　Thou who art thy people's sun;
Shine upon thy work of grace,
　If it be indeed begun.

9 Let me love thee more and more,
　If I love at all, I pray;
If I have not loved before,
　Help me to begin to-day.

## 145

THE specious world promiscuous flows,
  Enrapt in fancy's vision;
Allured by sound, beguiled by shows,
And empty dreams, nor scarcely knows
  There is a brighter heaven.

2 Fine gold will change, and diamonds fade,
  Swift wings to wealth be given,
All-varying time, our forms invade,
The seasons roll, light sink in shade,
  There's nothing lasts but heaven.

3 Creation's mighty fabric all
  Will be to atoms riven;
The sky consumed, the planets fall,
Convulsions rock this earthly ball,
  There's nothing firm but heaven.

4 This world, with all its wealth, is poor,
  And like a baseless vision,
Its lofty domes and brilliant ore,
Its gems and crowns, are vain and poor,
  There's nothing rich but heaven.

5 A stranger lonely here I roam,
  From place to place I'm driven;
My friends are gone, and I'm in gloom,
This earth is lonely as a tomb,
  I have no home but heaven.

6 The clouds disperse, the light appears,
  My sins are all forgiven;
Triumphant grace has quelled my fears;
Roll on, ye suns, fly swift, ye years,
  I'm on the wing for heaven.

7 And now I bid the world adieu,
  Let life's dull chains be riven;

The charms of Christ have caught my view,
The world of light I will pursue,
  To live with him in heaven.

## 146

TOGETHER let us sweetly live,
  *I am bound for the land of Canaan,*
In peace which none but Christ can give,
  *I'm bound for the land of Canaan.*

      *O Canaan, bright Canaan,*
      *I am bound for the land of Canaan ;*
      *O Canaan, it is my happy home,*
      *I am bound for the land of Canaan.*

2 There is my house, not made with hands,
  And there my Saviour waiting stands.

3 This sinful world is not my rest,
  I long to lean on Jesus' breast.

## 147          *C. M.*

UNITED in affection dear,
  With hearts on Jesus set;
We trust our God will meet us here,
  Who in his name are met:
Our minds from earthly cares set free,
  And fixed on joys above;
Each hope, each wish, each prayer shall be,
  To share a Saviour's love.

2 Oh, could we, Lord, make others know
    The pleasures which we feel;
  What comforts from thy goodness flow,
    A sinner's wounds to heal;
  Soon would the heedless, vain, and gay,
    Thy goodness strive to prove;
  Forsake their sins, and seek the way
    To find a Saviour's love.

3 If to reform their wicked ways
   All gentle means should fail,
The terrors which thy power displays
   Against them may prevail;
Proud sinners, humbled by thy wrath,
   Shall trembling kiss the rod;
Oh, sweep the nations, shake the earth,
   Till all proclaim thee God.

## 148                *P. M.*

### TUNE.—*Annie Laurie.*

THOUGH in a world of sickness,
   While on my Saviour's breast,
He strengthens all my weakness,
   And makes me truly blest.

> *Christ is all the world to me,*
> *And his glory I shall see,*
> *And before I'd leave my Saviour,*
> *I'd lay me down and die.*

2 He cheers my drooping spirit,
   And fills me with his love,
And soon I shall inherit
   Those shining realms above.

3 While on the banks of Jordan,
   I now would launch away;
But, oh! this earthly burden
   Still forces me to stay.

4 Could I but see my Jesus,
   And scale the mountain height,
How would I shout his praises
   In yonder realms of light!

5 Christian, be not faint-hearted,
   Though least among the flock,
      10

From Christ you'll ne'er be parted,
   While built upon the rock.

6 Let's mend our pace to glory,
   We soon shall meet above,
And sing the pleasing story
   Of his redeeming love.

## 149 *11s.*

THE Lord is my Shepherd, how happy am I!
   How tender and watchful my wants to
      supply!
He daily provides me with raiment and food,
Whate'er he denies me is meant for my good.

2 The Lord is my Shepherd, then must I obey
His gracious commandment, and walk in his
      way—
His fear he will teach me, my heart he'll renew,
And tho' I'm so sinful, my sins he'll subdue.

3 The Lord is my Shepherd, how happy am I;
I'm blest while I live, and I'm blest when I die,
In death's gloomy valley no evil I'll dread,
"For I will be with thee," my Shepherd has
      said.

4 "The Lord is my Shepherd," I'll sing with
      delight,
Till called to adore him in regions of light;
Then praise him, with angels, to bright harps
      of gold,
And ever and ever his glory behold.

## 150 *P. M.*

WHY stand you here idle, my friends, all
      the day?
Your moments so fleeting will soon pass away;
All things are provided for sinners undone,
And you are invited, and welcome to come.

*The market is open, the stores you may see ;*
*Then come, take and welcome, all things here*
*are free.*

2 Here's mercy and pardon, here's love and free
    grace ;
  Here's strong consolation, here's great joy and
    peace ;
  Here's hope for the hopeless,—the weary find
    rest ;
  Here's all things in plenty for poor souls dis-
    tressed.

3 Here's clothes for the naked—here all may be
    clad ;
  Here's bread for the hungry—here souls may
    be fed ;
  Here's manna from heaven, the food is divine ;
  Here's food full of marrow, and wine well re-
    fined.

4 Here's oil, milk, and honey, and plenty in store,
  Sufficient for thousands, yea, millions, and more ;
  Here's balm for the wounded—here's strength
    for the weak ;
  Here cordials divine are prepared for the sick.

5 Here medicines for healing are given out free ;
  Here's eye salve for eyes, that will make them
    to see,
  Here cripples are healed, the lame made to walk ;
  The deaf made to hear, and the dumb made to
    talk.

6 Here lepers are cleansed and purged from their
    sins ;
  Here sinners are pardoned, and souls are made
    clean ;
  Here all that are willing are eased of their pains ;
  Here thousands are ransomed and freed from
    their chains.

7 Here's armor and weapons for soldiers to wield,
  A breastplate, a helmet, a sword, and a shield;
  The poor receive riches, a crown for their head,
  Eternal salvation, and life from the dead.

8 O come all ye needy, ye poor and distressed;
  Come and receive plenty, and be ever blessed.
  O come, without money, to Jesus, and buy;
  Then love him, and praise him, forever on high.

## 151    *P. M.*

WHAT'S this that rises in my soul?
      Is it grace?   Is it grace?
That makes my life of sin look foul?
      Is it grace?   Is it grace?
This work that's in my soul begun,
It makes me strive all sin to shun,
It plants my soul beneath the throne,
      Where mercy's free—mercy's free!

2 Great God of Love! I can't but wonder,
      Mercy's free—mercy's free!
  Though I've no price at all to tender,
      Mercy's free—mercy's free!
  Though mercy's free, our God is just,
  And if a soul should e'er be lost,
  This will torment the sinner most,—
      Mercy's free—mercy's free!

3 Swell, swell, oh swell the heavenly chorus!
      Mercy's free—mercy's free!
  The devil's kingdom falls before us:
      Mercy's free—mercy's free!
  Sinner repent, inquire the road
  That leads to glory and to God,
  And wash in Christ's atoning blood—
      Mercy's free—mercy's free!

4 This truth through all our life shall cheer us,
      Mercy's free—mercy's free!

And through the vale of death shall bear us,
    Mercy's free—mercy's free!
And when to Jordan's brink we come,
And cross the raging billows' foam,
We'll sing, when safely landed home,
    Mercy's free—mercy's free!

## 152

WHEN converts first begin to sing,
    *Wonder, wonder, wonder,*
Their happy souls are on the wing,
    *Glory, Hallelujah.*
Their theme is all redeeming love,
    *Glory, Hallelujah.*
Fain would they be with Christ above,
    *Sing, Glory, Hallelujah.*

2 With admiration they behold,
The love of Christ that can't be told,
They long for Canaan's peaceful shore,
Where they shall doubt and sin no more.

3 Well! the good Shepherd waiting stands,
To guard and guide his tender lambs:
Jesus! we give them up to thee,
Keep them from sin and error free.

4 In all their weakness be thou near,
Their steps to guide, their hearts to cheer;
Then every snare and danger past,
Take them to dwell with thee at last.

## 153          *7s.*

WHEN this mortal life is fled,
    When the death-shades o'er thee spread,
Thou hast finished earth's career,
Sinner, where wilt thou appear?

2 When the world has passed away,
When draws near the judgment day,

When the awful trump shall sound,
Say, O where wilt thou be found?

3 When the Judge descends in light,
Clothed in majesty and might;
When the wicked quail with fear,
Where, O where wilt thou appear?

4 What shall soothe thy pained heart,
When the saints and thou must part?
When the good with joy are crowned,
Sinner, where wilt thou be found?

5 While the Holy Ghost is nigh,
Quickly to the Saviour fly;
Then shall peace thy spirit cheer,
Then in heaven shalt thou appear.

## 154 *C. M.*

WHEN God revealed his gracious name,
And changed my mournful state,
My rapture seemed a pleasing dream,
The grace appeared so great.

2 The world beheld the glorious change,
And did thy hand confess;
My tongue broke out in unknown strains,
And sang surprising grace.

3 "Great is the work," my neighbors cried,
And owned thy power divine;
"Great is the work," my heart replied,
"And be the glory thine."

4 The Lord can clear the darkest skies,
Can give us day for night,
Make drops of sacred sorrow rise
To rivers of delight.

5 Let those that sow in sadness wait
Till the fair harvest come;

They shall confess their sheaves are great,
  And shout the blessings home.

6 Though seed lie buried long in dust,
  It sha'n't deceive their hope;
The precious grain can ne'er be lost,
  For grace ensures the crop.

## 155      *P. M.*

WHEN I set out for heaven,
  But few were in the way;
But oftentimes together
  We met to praise and pray:
Our bosoms glowed with rapture,
  With love our hearts were fired;
We sang and talked of glory,
  We sang and never tired.

2 Those days were full of sweetness;
  I think upon them yet;
Their holy joy and gladness
  I never can forget:
We were a band of brothers,
  Of brothers fond and true;
We were a band of brothers,
  And loved as brothers do.

3 The world was all against us,
  What cared we for its frown?
A better world before us
  Contained a starry crown:
We trampled on earth's pleasures,
  Its riches were but dross;
Its glory all was tarnished;
  We gloried in the cross.

4 When one was called to leave us,
  And fly away to God,
We cheered him with our voices,
  While crossing Jordan's flood:

We sang the songs of Zion
  Around his dying bed,
And witnessed with what triumph
  The soul from sorrow fled.

5 Then with our friends departed,
  We seemed the earth to leave;
And soaring up like seraphs,
  Forgot to weep and grieve:
With patriarchs and prophets,
  And blood-washed throngs above,
We sang the loud hosanna—
  The song of heavenly love.

6 Ye friends of former seasons,
  Of happy youthful days,
All, all have gone before me,
  Ye all have run your race:
And mine will soon be finished;
  I haste to grasp your hand,
To join again my comrades,
  In that undying land.

## 156       *P. M.*

YE angels who mortals attend,
  And minister comfort in woe,
Come listen, ye heavenly friends,
  My happier story to know.
I sing of a theme most sublime,
  No sorrow my song can control;
I sing of the rapturous time
  When Jesus spoke peace to my soul.

  *Hosanna! hosanna! hosanna we'll raise!*
  *Hosanna, hallelujah to the Lamb for free grace!*

2 When guilt my poor heart did assail,
  Because I had wandered from God,
I strove my sad case to bewail,
  My sins were a cumbrous load.

O Saviour, have mercy! I cried;
  O pardon a wretch that's so vile!
Then quickly his blood was applied,
  And Jesus spoke peace to my soul.

3 My guilt, like the cloud of the morn,
  Was chased in a moment away;
The joy of my soul newly born
  Increased like the dawning of day.
My Saviour redeemed me from sin;
  He saves not in part, but in whole;
He writes his salvation within,
  For Oh! he spoke peace to my soul.

4 I now am so blessed with his love,
  I covet not earth's greatest store;
He visits me oft from above—
  I have him, I want nothing more:
Resigned to his pleasure I live,
  Till time's latest circle shall roll,
His utmost salvation receive,
  For Oh! he spoke peace to my soul.

5 Nor Satan nor sin can dismay,
  No danger my soul can affright,
While onward to mansions of day
  I go in Immanuel's might:
Though earth in convulsions shall rend
  From the centre quite through to each pole,
I'll smile, for I'm sure of a friend,
  Since Jesus spoke peace to my soul.

6 Ye angels who hear while I sing,
  Send your wings, and I'll quickly be gone;
I'll haste to my Saviour and King,
  To join with the heavenly throng;
'Tis there I'll eternally feast
  On the joys that enrapture the whole;
All heaven would welcome the guest,
  Since Jesus spoke peace to my soul.

7 Farewell to earth's glittering toys,
  Farewell to my friends and my foes;
I haste from these scenes to the skies,
  Where pleasure eternally flows:
He bids me leave all for his sake—
  I'll run till I reach the bless'd goal;
Then me to his arms he will take,
  Oh! there he'll speak peace to my soul.

**157**                    *P. M.*

YE jewels of my Master,
  Who shine with heavenly rays,
Amidst the beams of glory,
  Reflect immortal blaze.
Ye diamonds of beauty,
  With pleasing lustre crowned,
Of heavenly extraction,
  To Zion's city bound.

  *Oh, how charming, how charming is Jesus!*
  *He is my Redeemer, my friend, and my king.*

2 Ye lambs of my Redeemer,
  The purchase of his blood,
Who feed among the lilies,
  Beside the purple flood;
Go on, ye happy pilgrims,
  Your journey still pursue,   ·
And at a humble distance
  I'll sing and follow too.

3 When I beheld your order,
  And harmony of soul,
And heard divinest numbers
  In pure devotion roll,
And gems immortal glowing
  With such enlivening grace,
I viewed the Saviour's image
  Impressed on every face.

4 Speak often to each other,
   To cheer the fainting mind,
And often be your voices
   In pure devotion joined;
Though trials may await you,
   The crown before you lies,
Take courage, brother pilgrims,
   And soon you'll win the prize.

5 Ye shall be mine, says Jesus,
   In that auspicious day,
When I make up my jewels,
   Released from cumbrous clay.
He'll polish and refine you
   From worthless dross and tin,
And to his heavenly kingdom
   Will bid you enter in.

6 On that important morning,
   When bursting thunders sound,
And nimble lightnings waving,
   Shall wing the gloom profound,
Lift up your heads rejoicing,
   And clap your joyful hands,
Lo! you're redeemed forever
   From death's corrupted bands.

7 As Aaron, with his girdle,
   In shining jewels dressed,
Bore all the tribes of Israel
   Inscribed upon his breast,
So will the priests of Zion,
   Before the Father's throne,
Present the heirs of glory,
   And God their kindred own.

8 The golden bell shall echo
   Around the sacred hill,
And sweet immortal anthems,
   The vocal regions fill;

In everlasting beauty
  The shining millions stand,
Safe on the rock of ages,
  Amidst the promised land.

9 We'll range the wide dominion
  Of our Redeemer round,
And in dissolving raptures
  Be lost in love profound :
While all the flaming harpers
  Begin the lasting song,
With hallelujahs rolling,
  From the unnumbered throng.

## DESCRIBING CHRIST.

**158**       *P. M.*

AS near to Calvary I pass,
  Methinks I see a bloody cross,
    Where a poor victim hangs ;
His flesh with rugged irons tore,
His limbs all dressed in purple gore,
    Gasping in dying pangs.

2 Surprised the spectacle to see,
  I asked, Who can this victim be,
    In such exquisite pain ?
Why thus consigned to woes ? I cried ;
"'Tis I," the bleeding Lamb replied,
  "To save a world from sin."

3 A Christ for rebel mortal dies !
  How can it be ! my soul replies ;
    What ! Jesus died for me !
"Yes," saith the suffering Son of God,
"I give my life, I spill my blood,
  For thee, poor soul, for thee."

4 Lord, since thy life thou'st freely given,
To bring my wretched soul to heaven,
  And bless me with thy love;
Then at thy feet, O God, I'll fall,
Give thee my life, my soul, my all,
  To reign with thee above.

## 159 *C. M.*

AT Jacob's well a stranger sought
  His drooping frame to cheer;
Samaria's daughter little thought
  That Jacob's God was near.

2 This had she known, her fainting mind
  For richer draughts had sighed;
Nor had Messiah, good and kind,
  Those richer draughts denied.

3 The Man who came on earth to die,
  How few appear to know!
The Friend of sinners, passing by,
  Is still esteemed a foe.

4 The sinner must the Stranger know,
  Or soon his loss deplore;
Behold the living waters flow!
  Come, drink and thirst no more.

## 160

BY faith I view my Saviour dying,
  On the tree, on the tree;
To every nation he is crying,
  "Look to me, look to me!"
He bids the guilty now draw near,
Repent, believe, dismiss their fear—
Hark! hark! what precious words I hear!
  Mercy's free, mercy's free.

2 Did Christ, when I was sin pursuing,
  Pity me? pity me?

And did he snatch my soul from ruin,
    Can it be? can it be?
Oh yes, he did salvation bring,
He is my Prophet, Priest, and King;
And now my happy soul can sing,
    Mercy's free, mercy's free.

3 Jesus, the mighty God, hath spoken
    Peace to me, peace to me;
Now all my chains of sin are broken,
    I am free, I am free.
Soon as I in his name believed,
The Holy Spirit I received;
And Christ from death my soul retrieved:
    Mercy's free, mercy's free.

4 Jesus my weary soul refreshes—
    Mercy's free, mercy's free—
And every moment Christ is precious
    Unto me, unto me.
None can describe the bliss I prove,
While through this wilderness I rove;
All may enjoy the Saviour's love—
    Mercy's free, mercy's free.

5 This precious truth, ye sinners hear it—
    Mercy's free, mercy's free.
Ye ministers of God, declare it—
    Mercy's free, mercy's free.
Visit the heathen's dark abode,
Proclaim to all the love of God,
And spread the glorious news abroad—
    Mercy's free, mercy's free.

6 Long as I live I'll still be crying,
    Mercy's free, mercy's free;
And this shall be my theme when dying,
    Mercy's free, mercy's free;
And when the vale of death I've passed,
When lodged above the stormy blast,

I'll sing while endless ages last,
Mercy's free, mercy's free.

**161** *P. M.*

A FOUNTAIN in Jesus which runs always
free;
For washing and cleansing such sinners as we;
Our sins, though like crimson, made white as
the wool,
No lack in the fountain, but always is full.

2 All things are now ready, he invites us to come;
The supper is made by the Father and Son;
Rich bounties, rich dainties, here we may
receive
A living forever, if we will believe.

3 The guests which were bidden, refused the call,
For they were not ready nor willing at all,
To be stripped of their honor and part with
their store,
For a feast that was given and made for the
poor.

4 If they are not ready, and wish to delay,
My house shall be filled, the Father doth say:
The highways and hedges, the halt and the
blind,
Shall come and be welcome, the supper is mine.

5 He decks us with jewels and gems of rich kind,
A garment not woven, but richly refined:
Redeemed by Jesus, made heirs with the King,
A plan of the Father in glory to sing.

**162** *P. M.*

BEHOLD, behold the Lamb of God—on the
cross, on the cross;
For you he shed his precious blood—on the
cross, on the cross;

Now hear his all-important cry—"Eloi lama
    sabacthani;"
Draw near and see your Saviour die—on the
    cross, on the cross.

2 Behold his arms extended wide—on the cross,
    on the cross:
And see his wounded hands and side—on the
    cross, on the cross.
The sun withholds his rays of light, the heavens
    are wrapped in shades of night,
While Jesus doth with devils fight—on the
    cross, on the cross.

3 Come, sinners, see him lifted up—on the cross,
    on the cross;
For you he drinks the bitter cup—on the cross,
    on the cross.
The rocks do rend, the mountains quake, while
    Jesus doth atonement make;
While Jesus suffers for our sake—on the cross,
    on the cross.

4 And now the mighty deed is done—on the cross,
    on the cross;
The battle's fought and victory's won—on the
    cross, on the cross;
To heaven he turns his languid eyes: "'Tis
    finished now," the Conqueror cries,
Then bows his sacred head and dies—on the
    cross, on the cross.

5 Where'er I go I'll tell the story—of the cross,
    of the cross;
In nothing else my soul shall glory—save the
    cross, save the cross;
Yes, this my constant theme shall be, in time
    and through eternity,
That Jesus tasted death for me—on the cross,
    on the cross.

6 Let every mourner rise and cling—to the cross.
    to the cross ;
  And every Christian come and sing—round the
    cross, round the cross ;
  Here let the preacher take his stand, and, with
    the Bible in his hand,
  Declare the triumphs of the Lamb—on the
    cross, on the cross.

## 163        *P. M.*

BLISSFUL hours, when first I knew him—
  Jesus, friend of all our race ;
When my heart clung fondly to him,  '
  In delighted, firm embrace ;
In his saving arms he took me ;
  I reposed upon his breast.
Then no fear nor sorrow shook me,
  Of his boundless love possessed.

2 When the sky with morning brightened,.
  And the day came on apace,
He my rising sun enlightened,
  All my soul with beams of grace ;
Upward to my Saviour springing,
  On the wings of faith I flew ;
Hymns of grateful praises singing,
 ' Neither doubt nor care I knew.

3 When the light of day was waning,
  And the evening shadows fell ;
On his bosom safely leaning,
  I could warble, "All is well."
I was happy in his keeping,
  Happy through the shades of night ;
Angels watched around me sleeping,
  And I dreamed of heavenly light.

4 When the blessed Sabbath entered,
  With its still and holy air ;
   11

On his house my thoughts were centred,
    For I longed to meet him there.
There I met my glorious Saviour,
    There I feasted on his word;
Mine his promises and favor,
    Mine the everlasting Lord.

## 164         *P. M.*

DROOPING saints, no longer grieve,
    Heaven is propitious,
If on Christ you do believe,
    You will find him precious.
Jesus, who is passing by,
    Calls the mourners to him;
He has died for you and me,
    Now look up and view him.

2 From his hands, his feet, his side,
    Runs a healing fountain;
See the heart-consoling tide,
    Boundless as the ocean.
See the living waters move
    For the sick and dying;
Now resolve to gain his love,
    Or to perish trying.

3 Grace's store is always free,
    Drooping souls to gladden;
Jesus calls, "Come unto me,
    Weary, heavy laden."
Though your sins like mountains rise,
    Rise and reach to heaven;
Soon as you on him rely,
    "All shall be forgiven."

4 Now methinks I hear one say,
    I will go and prove him;
If he takes my sins away,
    Surely I shall love him.

Yes, I see the Father smile,
  Smiling move my burden;
All is grace, for I am vile,
  Yet he seals my pardon.

5 Streaming mercy, how it flows.
  Now I know, I feel it;
Half has never yet been told,
  Yet I want to tell it.
Jesus' blood has healed my wounds,
  Oh, the wondrous story;
I was lost, but now am found,
  Glory! Glory! Glory!

6 Glory to my Saviour's name,
  Saints are bound to love him
Mourners, you may do the same,
  Only come and prove him.
Hasten to the Saviour's blood, ·
  Feel it and declare it;
Oh, that I could sing so loud,
  That the world might hear it.

7 If no greater joys are known
  In the upper regions,
I will try to travel on
  In this pure religion.
Heaven's here, and heaven's there,
  Glory's here and yonder;
Brightest seraphs shout Amen,
  While the angels wonder.

## 165 *P. M.*

DON'T you see my Jesus coming?
  Don't you see him in yonder cloud,
With ten thousand angels round him?
  See how they do my Jesus crowd?

2 Don't you see his arms extended?
  Don't you hear his charming voice?

Each loving heart beats high for glory:
  Oh! my Jesus is my choice.

3 Don't you see the saints ascending?
    Hear them shouting through the air?
  Jesus smiling, trumpets sounding,
    Now his glory they shall·share.

4 Don't you see the heav'ns open,
    And the saints in glory there?
  Shouts of triumph bursting round you,
    Glory, glory, glory here!

5 Come, backsliders, though you've pierced him,
    And have caused his church to mourn;
  Yet you may regain free pardon,
    If you will to him return.

6 Now behold each loving spirit,
    Shout the praise of his dear name;
  View the smiles of their dear Jesus,
    While his presence feeds the flame.

7 There we'll range the fields of pleasure
    By our dear Redeemer's side;
  Shouting glory, glory, glory,
    While eternal ages glide.

## 166      *C. M.*

FROM Salem's gates advancing slow,
    What object meets my eyes,
  What means that majesty of wo,
    What mean those mingled cries?

2 Who is the man that groans beneath
    The pond'rous cross of wood,
  Whose soul's oppressed with pangs of death,
    And body bathed in blood?

3 Is this the man! can this be he
    The prophets have foretold,

Should with transgressors numbered be,
  And for my crimes be sold?

4 Ah, lovely sight! a heavenly form
  For sinful souls to see,
I'll creep beside him as a worm,
  And see him die·for me.

## 167        *P. M.*

HAIL! the blest morn when the great Me-
    diator
Down from the mansion of heaven did de-
    scend,
Shepherds, go worship the babe in a manger,
  Lo! for his guard the bright angels attend.
*Kindest and best of the sons of the morning,*
  *Dawn on our darkness and lend us thine aid;*
*Star in the east the horizon adorning,*
  *Guide where our infant Redeemer was laid.*

2 Cold on his cradle the dew drops were shining,
. Low lay his head with the beasts of the stall,
Angels adore him, in slumbers reclining,
  Maker, and Monarch, and Saviour, and all.

3 Say, shall we yield him a costly devotion,
  Odors of Eden, or offering divine;
Gems from the mountains, or pearls from the
    ocean,
  Myrrh from the forest, or gold from the mine?

4 Vainly we offer each ample oblation,
  All those can never his favor secure;
Richer by far the heart's adoration,
  Dearest to God are the prayers of the poor.

5 Low at his feet, we in humble prostration·
  Lose all our sorrow, and trouble, and strife;
There we receive his divine consolation,
  Flowing afresh from the fountain of life.

6 He is our friend in the midst of temptation,
　　Faithful supporter, whose love cannot fail,
Rock of our refuge and hope of salvation,
　　Light to direct us thro' death's gloomy vale.

7 Star of the morning, thy brightness declining,
　　Shortly must fade when the sun doth arise,
Beaming refulgent, his glory eternal,
　　Shines on the children of love in the skies.

## 168

HOW lovely the place where the Saviour ap-
　　pears,
　　To those who believe in his word;
His presence disperses my sorrows and fears,
　　And bids me rejoice in my Lord.

2 A day in his courts, than a thousand beside,
　　Is better and lovelier far—
My soul hates the tents where the wicked reside,
　　And all their delights I abhor.

3 Lord! give me a place with the humblest of
　　saints,
　　For low at thy feet I would lie:
I know that thou hearest my feeble complaints;
　　Thou hearest the young raven's cry.

4 Give strength to the souls that now wait upon
　　thee,
　　O come in thy chariot of love!
From earth's vain enchantments, O help us to
　　flee,
　　And to set our affections above!

## 169　　　　*P. M.*

HIS vestment of righteousness,
　　Who shall describe?

Its purity words would defile;
The heav'ns from his presence
    Fresh beauties imbibe,
And earth is made rich by his smile.

2 Such is my beloved,
    In excellence bright,
When pleased he looks down from above,
Like the morn when he breathes
    From the chambers of light,
And comforts his people with love.

3 But when armed with vengeance,
    In terror he comes,
The nation rebellious to tame,
The reins of omnipotent
    Power he assumes,
And rides in a chariot of flame,

4 A two-edged sword
    From his mouth issues forth,
Bright quivers of fire are his eyes,
He speaks, and black tempests
    Are seen in the north,
And storms from their caverns arise.

5 Ten thousand destructions
    That wait for his word,
And ride on the wings of his breath,
Fly swift as the wind
    At the nod of their Lord,
And deal out the arrows of death.

6 His cloud-bursting thunders
    Their voices resound,
Through all the vast regions on high;
Till from the deep centre
    Loud echoes rebound,
And meet the quick flame in the sky.

7 The portals of heaven
  At his bidding obey,
And expand ere his banner appear;
Earth trembles beneath,
  Till her mountains give way,
And hell shakes her fetters with fear.

8 When he treads on the clouds,
  As the dust of his feet,
And grasps the big storm in his hand,
What eye the fierce glance
  Of his anger shall meet,
Or who in his presence shall stand?

## 170 *L. M.*

HE lives, the great Redeemer lives;
  What joy the bless'd assurance gives!
And now before his Father God,
Pleads the full merits of his blood.

2 Repeated crimes awake our fears,
And justice, armed with frowns, appears;
But in the Saviour's lovely face,
Sweet mercy smiles, and all is peace.

3 Hence, then, ye black despairing thoughts!
Above our fears, above our faults;
His powerful intercessions rise,
And guilt recedes, and terror dies.

4 In every dark, distressful hour,
When sin and Satan join their power,
Let this firm hope repel the dart,
That Jesus bears us on his heart.

5 Great Advocate, almighty Friend!
On thee our humble hopes depend!
Our cause can never, never fail,
For Jesus pleads, and must prevail.

## 171

*P. M.*

I'M tired with visits, modes, and forms,
 And flatteries paid to fellow-worms;
  Their conversation cloys:
Their vain amours and empty stuff:
But I can ne'er enjoy enough
  Of thy best company, my Lord, thou life of
   all my joys.

2 When he begins to tell his love,
Through every vein my passions move,
  The captives of his tongue:
In midnight shades, on frosty ground,
I could attend the pleasing sound,
  Nor should I feel December cold, nor think
   the darkness long.

3 There while I hear my Saviour God,
Count o'er the sins (a heavy load)
  He bore upon the tree,
Inward I blush with secret shame,
And weep, and love, and bless the name,
  That knew no guilt nor grief his own, but
   bare it all for me.

4 Next he describes the thorns he wore,
And talks his bloody passion o'er,
  Till I am drowned in tears:
Yet with the sympathetic smart,
There's a strange joy beats round my heart!
  The cursed tree has blessings in't, my sweet-
   est balm it bears.

5 I hear the glorious sufferer tell,
How on the cross he vanquished hell,
  And all the powers beneath:
Transported and inspired, my tongue
Attempts his triumphs in a song:
  How has the serpent lost his sting, and where's
   thy victory, death?

6 But when he shows his hands and heart,
With those dear prints of dying smart,
　　He sets my soul on fire:
Not the beloved John could rest
With more delight upon that breast,
　.　Nor Thomas pry into those wounds with more
　　　intense desire.

7 Kindly he opes to me his ear,
And bids me pour my sorrows there,
　　And tell him all my pains:
Thus while I ease my burdened heart,
In every wo he bears a part,
　　His arms embrace me, and his hand my
　　　drooping head sustains.

## 172                              *11s.*

"I AM thy REDEEMER—for thee I must die;
　The cup is most bitter, but cannot pass by;
Thy sins, which are many, are laid upon me,
*And all this sore anguish I suffer for thee!*"

2 I heard, with deep sorrow, the tales of his wo,
While tears of repentance mine eyes did o'er-
　　　flow;
The cause of his sorrows to hear him repeat,
Pierced deeply my bosom—I fell at his feet.

3 In humble contrition I poured out my cry,
"Lord, save a poor sinner! O save, or I die!"
He smiled, when he saw me, and said to me,
　　"Live!"
"*Thy sins, which were many, I freely forgive!*"

4 How sweet was that sentence! it made me
　　rejoice!
His smiles, how consoling!　How *charming* his
　　voice!
I ran from the garden to spread it abroad,
And shouted—"*Salvation! O glory to God!*"

5 I'm now on my journey to mansions above—
  My soul's full of glory, of light, peace, and
      love;
  I think of the garden, the prayers and the tears
  *Of my blessed Jesus, who banished my fears.*

6 The day of bright glory is rolling around,
  When, GABRIEL descending, the trumpet will
      sound;
  My soul to the Saviour in raptures shall rise,
  *And see him forever,* with unclouded eyes.

**173**          *8s & 7s.*

I WILL never, never leave thee,
  I will never thee forsake,
I will guide, and save, and keep thee,
  For my name and mercy's sake.
    Fear no evil, fear no evil,
  Only all my counsel take;          .

    *For I'll never, never leave thee,*
    *I will never thee forsake.*

2 When the storm is raging round thee,
    Call on me in humble prayer;
  I will fold my arms about thee,
    Guard thee with the tenderest care.
      In the trial, in the trial,
    I will make thy pathway clear.

3 When thy sky above is glowing,
    And around thee all is bright,
  Pleasure, like a river, flowing,
    All things tending to delight,
      I'll be with thee,
    I will guide thy steps aright.

4 When thy soul is dark and clouded,
    Filled with doubt, and grief, and care,

Through the mists by which 'tis shrouded,
  I will make a light appear,
    And the banner
Of My love I will uprear.

5 Thou may'st leave my care and keeping,
  Thou may'st wander far from me;
Sorrow, then, and wo and weeping,
  Mercy must mete out to thee;
    To the righteous
My rich blessings all are free.

6 When thy feeble frame is dying,
  And thy soul about to soar
To that land where pain and sighing
  Shall be heard and known no more,
    I will teach thee
To rejoice that life is o'er.

## 174        *C. M.*

JESUS! thy love shall we forget,
  And never bring to mind
The grace that paid our hopeless debt,
  And bade us pardon find?

  *Our sorrows and our sins were laid*
    *On thee—alone on thee!*
  *Thy precious blood our ransom paid;*
    *Thine all the glory be.*

2 Shall we thy life of grief forget,
  Thy fasting and thy prayer;
Thy locks with mountain vapors wet,
  To save us from despair?

3 Gethsemane can we forget;
  Thy struggling agony—
When night lay dark on Olivet,
 -And none to watch with thee?

4 Can we the plaited crown forget,
   The buffeting and shame,
When hell thy sinking soul beset,
   And earth reviled thy name?

5 The nails—the spear—can we forget;
   The agonizing cry—
"My God! my Father! wilt thou let
   Thy Son forsaken die?"

6 Life's brightest joys we may forget—
   Our kindred cease to love;
But He who paid our hopeless debt,
   Our constancy shall prove.

## 175

ONE there is, above all others,
   Well deserves the name of Friend;
He is love beyond a brother's,
   Costly, free, and knows no end:
They who once his kindness prove,
Find it everlasting love!

2 Which, of all our friends, to save us,
   Could, or would have shed his blood?
But this Saviour died to have us
   Reconciled in him to God:
It was boundless love to bleed;
Jesus is a Friend indeed.

3 When he lived on earth abaséd,
   "Friend of sinners" was his name;
Now, above all glory raiséd,
   He rejoices in the same:
Still he calls them brethren, friends,
And to all their wants attends.

4 Oh! for grace our hearts to soften!
   Teach us, Lord, at length to love,

We, alas! forget, too often,
 What a Friend we have above:
When to heaven our souls are brought,
.We will love thee as we ought.

**176**     *76, 76, 77, 76.*

JESUS drinks the bitter cup,
 The wine-press treads alone:
Tears the graves and mountains up,
 By his expiring groan:
Lo, the powers of heaven he shakes,
 Nature in convulsion lies;
Earth's profoundest centre quakes,
 The great Jehovah dies!

2 O my God he dies for me!
 I feel the mortal smart!
See him hanging on the tree,
 A sight that breaks my heart!
O that all to thee might turn!
 Sinners, ye may love him too;
Look on him, ye pierced, and mourn
 For one who bled for you.

3 Weep o'er your desire and hope,
 With tears of humblest love!
Sing, for Jesus is gone up,
 And reigns enthroned above!
Lives our head to die no more,
 Power is all to Jesus given;
Worshipped as he was before,
 The immortal King of heaven.

4 Lord, we bless thee for thy grace
 And truth, which never fail;
Hastening to behold thy face
 Without a dimming veil;
We shall see our heavenly King,
 All thy glorious love proclaim,

Help the angel choirs to sing
Our bless'd triumphant Lamb.

**177** .          *11s.*

IN the house of king David a fountain did
        spring,
For sin and uncleanness, from Jesus our king,
This fountain flows sweetly whenever applied;
It sprang from the bowels of Christ when he
        died.

2 Come all that have bathed in the fountain of
        love,
And have felt the heavy burden of guilt to
        remove;
Let's praise our dear Saviour as long as we've
        breath,
And after we're laid in the dust of the earth.

3 There, there we shall sleep, but not always
        remain;
We look for the coming of Jesus again;
When waked by the trumpet we'll lay by our
        shrouds,
And rise to meet Jesus, our Lord, in the clouds.

4 How we shall be fashioned, he does not declare,
But we shall be like him when he doth appear;
And that happy moment we're longing to see,
When we shall be perfectly happy in thee.

5 Lord Jesus I love thee, thou knowest very well,
Assist me to conquer the powers of hell;
Though Satan he rages, and frightens me too,
Lord Jesus protect me, and bring me safe
        through.

**178**          *7s & 6s.*

I LAY my sins on Jesus,
  The spotless Lamb of God;

He bears them all, and frees us
From the accursed load.
I bring my guilt to Jesus,
To wash my crimson stains
White, in his blood most precious,
Till not a spot remains.

2 I lay my wants on Jesus;
All fullness dwells in him;
He heals all my diseases,
He doth my soul redeem.
I lay my griefs on Jesus,
My burdens and my cares;
He from them all releases,
He all my sorrow shares.

3 I rest my soul on Jesus,
This weary soul of mine;
His right hand me embraces,
I on his breast recline.
I love the name of Jesus,
Immanuel, Christ, the Lord;
Like fragrance on the breezes
His name abroad is poured.

4 I long to be like Jesus,
Meek, loving, lowly, mild;
I long to be like Jesus,
The Father's holy child.
I long to be with Jesus,
Amid the heavenly throng,
To sing with saints his praises,
To learn the angels' song.

## 179

KING Messiah, take the throne,
Reign unrivalled, reign alone;
Claim the kingdom for thine own,
Claim thy lawful right:

Bow the nations to thy sway;
Near at hand and far away,
Make the stubborn world obey;
   Put thy foes to flight.

2 King Messiah, wear the crown,
Reign in glory and renown,
Cast the heathen idols down,
   Make the nations yield.
Lo! the nations all are given
To Messiah, king of heaven—
Let his enemies be driven
   From the battle-field.

3 King Messiah, o'er the world
Be thy banner wide unfurled;
Be the prince of darkness hurled
   From his usurped throne:
Reign abroad in every part,
Reign at home, in every heart,
Reign, Almighty as thou art,
   Sovereign Lord alone.

4 King Messiah, be our king,
Thy salvation to us bring—
Then shall we thy triumphs sing
   In exalted strains:
Zion's joyful sons cry out,
Salem's happy daughters shout,
Jesus reigns the world throughout,
   King Messiah reigns.

**180**        *11s & 8s.*

O THOU in whose presence my soul takes
   delight,
  On whom in affliction I call—
My comfort by day, and my song in the night,
  My hope, my salvation, my all—
    12

Where dost thou at noontide resort with thy
  sheep,
To feed on the pastures of love?
For why in the valley of death should I weep,
Or alone in the wilderness rove?

2 Oh, why should I wander an alien from thee,
  And cry in the desert for bread?
My foes will rejoice when my sorrows they see,
  And smile at the tears I have shed.
Ye daughters of Zion, declare, have you seen
  The Star that on Israel shone?
Say, if in your tents my Beloved has been,
  And where with his flocks he has gone.

3 This is my Beloved, his form is divine,
  His vestments shed odors around;
The locks on his head are as grapes on the vine,
  When autumn with plenty is crowned.
The roses of Sharon, the lilies that grow
  In the vales on the banks of the streams,
On his cheeks in the beauty of excellence glow,
  And his eyes are as quivers of beams.

4 His voice, as the sound of the dulcimer sweet,
  Is heard through the shadows of death;
The cedars of Lebanon bow at his feet,
  The air is perfumed with his breath.
His lips as a fountain of righteousness flow,
  That waters the garden of grace;
From which their salvation the gentiles shall
  know,
And bask in the smiles of his face.

5 Love sits in his eyelids, and scatters delight
  Through all the bright mansions on high:
Their faces the cherubim veil in his sight,
  And tremble with fullness of joy.
He looks, and ten thousands of angels rejoice,
  And myriads wait for his word;

He speaks—and eternity, filled with his voice,
Re-echoes the praise of the Lord.

**181** *P. M.*

O HOW I have longed for the coming of God!
And sought him by praying and searching
his word;
With watching and fasting my soul was op-
pressed,
Nor would I give over till Jesus had blessed.

2 The tokens of mercy at length did appear;
According to promise, he answered my prayer;
And glory is opened in floods on my soul;
Salvation from Zion's beginning to roll.

3 The news of his mercy is spreading abroad,
And sinners come crying and weeping to God;
Their mourning and praying is heard very loud,
And all may find favor in Jesus' blood.

4 Here are more, my dear Saviour, who fall at
thy feet,
Oppressed by a burden enormously great,
Oh, raise them, my Jesus, to tell of thy love,
And shout hallelujahs with angels above.

5 I'll sing, and I'll shout, and I'll shout, and I'll
sing;
O God, make the nations in praises to ring
With loud acclamations of Jesus' love,
And carry us all to the city above.

6 We'll wait for thy chariot, it seems to draw
near,
Oh come, my dear Saviour, let glory appear;
We long to be singing and shouting above,
With angels o'erwhelmed in Jesus' love.

**182**                        *P. M.*

PRISONER of hope, to thee I turn,
    And, calmly confident, I mourn,
And pray, and weep for thee;
Tell me thy love, thy secret tell,
Thy mystic name in me reveal,
Reveal thyself in me!

2 Descend, pass by me, and proclaim,
    O Lord of hosts, thy glorious name,
    "The Lord, the gracious Lord;
Long-suffering, merciful, and kind,
The God who always bears in mind
    His everlasting word."

3 Plenteous he is in truth and grace;
    He wills that all the fallen race
    Should turn, repent, and live:
His pardoning grace for all is free:
Transgression, sin, iniquity,
    He freely doth forgive.

4 Mercy he doth for thousands keep;
    He goes and seeks the one lost sheep,
    And brings his wand'rer home;
And every soul that sheep might be;
Come then, my Lord, and gather me,
    My Jesus, quickly come.

5 Take me into thy people's rest,
    O come, and with my sole request,
    My one desire comply!
Make me partaker of my hope,
Then bid me get me quickly up,
    And on thy bosom die!

**183**                        *P. M.*

SEE the Lord of glory dying
 See him gasping, hear him crying;

See his burdened bosom heave;
Look, ye sinners, you that hung him,
Look how deep your stings have stung him;
   Dying sinners, look and live.

2 See the rocks and mountains quaking;
Earth unto her centre shaking;
   Nature's groans awake the dead,
Look on Phœbus struck with wonders,
While the peals of legal thunders
   Smite the dear Redeemer's head.

3 Heaven's bright melodious legions,
Chanting through the tuneful regions,
   Cease to thrill the quiv'ring strings;
Songs seraphic all suspended,
Till the mighty war was ended
   By the all-victorious King.

4 Hell and all the powers infernal
Vanquished by the King eternal,
   When he poured the vital flood;
· By his groans which shook creation,
Lo! we found a proclamation;
   Peace and pardon by his blood.

5 Shout, ye saints, with adoration—
Fill with songs the wide creation,
   Since he's risen from the grave;
Shout with joyful acclamation
To the rock of your salvation,
   Who alone has power to save.

6 Bear with patience tribulation,
Overcoming all temptation,
   Till the glorious jubilee;
Then he'll come with bursts of thunder,
Then shall we adore and wonder,
   Singing on the highest key.

## 184                    *P. M.*

SAW ye my Saviour! Saw ye my Saviour!
   Saw ye my Saviour and God?
Oh! he died on Calvary, to atone for you and
   me,
   And to purchase our pardon with blood.

2 He was extended! he was extended!
   Shamefully nailed to the cross;
Oh! he bowed his head and died! thus my Lord
   was crucified,
   To atone for a world that was lost.

3 Jesus hung bleeding! Jesus hung bleeding!
   Three dreadful hours in pain;
Oh! the sun refused to shine, when his majesty
   divine
   Was derided, insulted, and slain.

4 Darkness prevailed! darkness prevailed!
   Darkness prevailed o'er the land;
Oh! the solid rocks were rent, through creation's
   vast extent,
   When the Jews crucified the God-man.

5 When it was finished, when it was finished,
   And the atonement was made,
He was taken by the great, and embalmed in
   spices sweet,
   And in a new sepulchre laid.

6 Hail, mighty Saviour! hail, mighty Saviour!
   Prince and the author of peace;
Oh! he burst the bands of death, and triumph-
   ant through the east
   He ascended to mansions of bliss.

7 Now interceding! now interceding!
   Pleading that sinners may live;

Crying, Father, I have died! Oh, behold my
· hands and side,
To redeem them;—I pray thee forgive.

8 I will forgive them; I will forgive them,
If they'll repent and believe;
Let them now return to me, and be reconciled
to thee,
And salvation they all shall receive.

## 185 *P. M.*

THE Son of man they did betray,
He was condemned and led away,
Think, O my soul, on that dread day;
Look on Mount Calvary.
Behold him lamb-like led along,
Surrounded by a wicked throng,
Accused by each lying tongue,
And then the Lamb of God they hung
Upon the shameful tree.

2 'Twas thus the glorious sufferer stood,
With hands and feet nailed to the wood;
From every wound a stream of blood
Came flowing down amain.
His bitter groans all nature shook,
And at his voice the rocks were broke,
And sleeping saints their graves forsook,
While spiteful Jews around him mocked
And laughed at his pain.

3 Now hung between the earth and skies,
Behold, in agonies he dies;
O sinners! hear his mournful cries,
Come, see his tort'ring pain.
The morning sun withdrew his light,
Blushed, and refused to view the sight:
The azure clothed in robes of night,
All nature mourned and stood affright,
When Christ the Lord was slain.

4 Hark! men and angels, hear the Son;
  He cries for help, but O! there's none:
  He treads the wine-press all alone.
    His garments stained with blood.
  In lamentations hear him cry,
  "Eloi, lama sabacthani!"
  Though death may close his languid eyes,
  He soon will mount the upper skies,
    The conquering Son of God.

5 The Jews and Romans in a band,
  With hearts like steel around him stand,
  And mocking say, "Come, save the land,
    Come, try yourself to free."
  A soldier pierced him when he died,—
  Then healing streams came from his side,
  And thus my Lord was crucified,
  Stern justice now is satisfied,
    Sinners, for you and me.

6 Behold, he mounts the throne of state,
  He fills the mediatorial seat,
  While millions bowing at his feet,
    With loud hosannas tell,
  Though he endured exquisite pains,
  He led the monster death in chains;
  Ye seraphs, raise your highest strains,
  With music fill bright Eden's plains;
    He conquered death and hell.

7 'Tis done! the dreadful debt is paid,
  The great atonement now is made:
  Sinners, on him your guilt was laid,
    For you he spilt his blood;
  For you his tender soul did move,
  For you he left the courts above,
  That you the length and breadth might prove,
  And height and depth of perfect love,
    In Christ your smiling God.

8 All glory be to God on high,
Who reigns enthroned above the sky,
Who sent his Son to bleed and die,
   Glory to him be given;
While heaven above his praise resounds,
O Zion, sing—his grace abounds;
I hope to shout eternal rounds,
In flaming love that knows no bounds,
   When swallowed up in heaven.

## 186 *P. M.*

THOU sweet, gliding Kedron, by thy silver
  stream,
Our Saviour at midnight, when Cynthia's pale
    beam
Shone bright on thy waters, did frequently stray,
And lose in thy murmurs the toils of the day.

*Come, saints, and adore him, come, bow at his feet,*
*Oh, give him the glory, the praise that is meet;*
*Let joyful hosannas unceasing arise,*
*And join the loud anthem that gladdens the skies.*

2 How damp were the vapors that fell on his head,
How hard was his pillow, how humble his bed!
The angels, astonished, grew sad at the sight,
And followed their Master with silent delight.

3 O garden of Olivet—dear honored spot,
The fame of thy wonders shall ne'er be forgot;
The theme most transporting to seraphs above,
The wonder of joy and the wonder of love.

## 187 *8s & 4s.*

THERE'S a friend above all others,
    Oh, how he loves!
His is love beyond a brother's,
    Oh, how he loves!

Earthly friends may fail and leave us,
This day kind, to-morrow grieve us,
But this friend will ne'er deceive us,
    Oh, how he loves!

2 Blessed Jesus! wouldst thou know him?
    Oh, how he loves!
Give thyself e'en this day to him,
    Oh, how he loves!
Is it sin that pains and grieves thee?
Unbelief and trials tease thee?
Jesus can from all release thee,
    Oh, how he loves!

3 Love this friend who longs to save thee,
    Oh, how he loves!
Dost thou love?  He will not leave thee,
    Oh, how he loves!
Think no more then of to-morrow,
Take his easy yoke and follow,
Jesus carries all thy sorrow,
    Oh, how he loves!

4 All thy sins shall be forgiven,
    Oh, how he loves!
Backward all thy foes be driven,
    Oh, how he loves!
Best of blessings he'll provide thee,
Naught but good shall e'er betide thee,·
Safe to glory he will guide thee,
    Oh, how he loves!

5 Pause, my soul! adore and wonder,
    Oh, how he loves!
Naught can cleave this love asunder,
    Oh, how he loves!
Neither trial nor temptation,
Doubt, nor fear, nor tribulation,
Can bereave us of salvation—
    Oh, how he loves!

6 Let us still this love be viewing,
  Oh, how he loves!
And though faint, keep on pursuing,
  Oh, how he loves!
He will strengthen each endeavor,
And when passed o'er Jordan's river,
This shall be our song forever,
  Oh, how he loves!

## 188

'TWAS Jesus, my Saviour, who died on a tree,
 To open a fountain for sinners like me:
His blood is that fountain which pardon bestows,
And cleanses the foulest wherever it flows.

 *For the Lion of Judah shall break ev'ry chain,*
 *And give us the vict'ry again and again;*
 *For the Lion of Judah shall break ev'ry chain,*
 *And give us the vict'ry again and again.*

2 And when I was willing with all things to part,
He gave me my bounty, his love in my heart;
So now I am joined with the conquering band,
Who are marching to glory at Jesus' command.

3 Though round me the storms of adversity roll,
And the waves of destruction encompass my
  soul,
In vain this frail vessel the tempest shall toss,
My hopes rest secure on the blood of the cross.

4 And when the last trumpet of judgment shall
  sound,
And wake all the nations that sleep in the
  ground,
Then, when heaven and earth shall be melting
  away,
I'll sing of the blood of the cross in that day.

5 And when with the ransomed by Jesus my head,
From fountain to fountain I then shall be led;
I'll fall at his feet, and his mercy adore,
And sing of the blood of the cross evermore.

## 189    *C. M.*

THOU dear Redeemer, dying Lamb,
  I love to hear of thee;
No music's like thy charming name,
  Nor half so sweet can be.

2 Oh, may I ever hear thy voice
  In mercy to me speak;
In thee, my priest, will I rejoice,
  And thy salvation seek.

3 While Jesus shall be still my theme,
  While on this earth I stay,
I'll sing my Jesus' lovely name,
  When all things else decay.

4 When I appear in yonder cloud
  With all his favored throng,
Then will I sing more sweet, more loud,
  And Christ shall be my song.

## 190    *P. M.*

WHAT think you of Christ? is the test
  To try both your state and your scheme,
You cannot be right in the rest,
  Unless you think rightly of him.
As Jesus appears in our view,
  As he is beloved or not,
So God is disposed to you,
  And mercy or wrath is your lot.

2 Some take him a creature to be,
  A man, or an angel at most;
Sure these have not feelings like me,
  Nor know themselves wretched and lost.

So guilty, so helpless am I,
    I durst not confide in his blood,
Nor on his protection rely,
    Unless I was sure he was God.

3 Some call him a Saviour, in word,
    But mix their own works with his plan;
And hope he his help will afford,
    When they have done all that they can:
If doings prove rather too light,
    (A little, they own, they may fall,)
They purpose to make up full weight
    By casting his name in the scale.

4 Some style him the pearl of great price,
    And say he's the fountain of joys;
Yet feed upon folly and vice,
    And cleave to the world and its toys;
Like Judas, the Saviour they kiss,
    And while they salute him, betray,
Ah! what will profession like this
    Avail in his terrible day?

5 If asked what of Jesus I think?
    Though still my best thoughts are but poor,
I say he's my meat and my drink,
    My life, and my strength, and my store;
My Shepherd, my Husband, my Friend,
    My Saviour from sin and from thrall;
My hope from beginning to end,
    My portion, my Lord, and my All.

## 191 *L. M.*

WHEN marshalled on the nightly plain,
    The glittering host bestud the sky,
One star alone of all the train
    Can fix the sinner's wand'ring eye.

2 Hark! hark! to God the chorus breaks
    From every host, from every gem;

But one alone the Saviour speaks:
It is the Star of Bethlehem.

3 Once on the raging seas I rode,
　The storm was loud—the night was dark—
The ocean yawned—and rudely blowed
　The wind that tossed my found'ring bark.

4 Deep horror then my vitals froze,
　Death-struck, I ceased the tide to stem;
When suddenly a star arose:
　It was the Star of Bethlehem.

5 It was my guide, my light, my all,
　It bade my dark forebodings cease;
And through the storms and danger's thrall,
　It led me to the port of peace.

6 Now safely moored—my peril o'er,
　I'll sing, first in night's diadem,
Forever and for evermore,
　The Star!—the Star of Bethlehem!

## 192                 11s.

WHEN nature was sinking in stillness to rest,
　In deep meditation I wandered abroad,
The last beams of daylight shone dim in the
　　west,
The moon cast her paleness in lone solitude.

2 While passing a garden, I lingered to hear
A voice, faint and plaintive, from one kneeling
　　there;
The voice of the suppliant affected my heart,
While pleading, in anguish, the poor sinner's
　　part.

3 .In offering to heaven his pitying prayer,
　He spake of the torments the sinner must bear;
His life as a ransom he offered to give,
That sinners redeemed in glory might live.

4 I listened a moment, then turned to see
What man of compassion this stranger could be,
When lo! I discovered, knelt on the cold ground,
The loveliest being I ever had found.

5 His mantle was wet with the dews of the night,
His locks, by pale moonlight, were glistening
    and bright;    .
His eyes, mildly beaming, to heaven were raised,
While round him in grandeur stood angels,
    amazed.

6 So deep was his sorrow, so fervent his prayers,
That down o'er his bosom rolled blood, sweat,
    and tears!
I wept to behold him, and asked him his name,
He answered, "'Tis JESUS! From heaven I
    came."

# 193 *L. M.*

WHEN on the cross my Lord I see,
    Bleeding to death for wretched me,
Satan and sin no more can move,
For I am all transformed to love.

2 His thorns and nails pierce through my heart;
In every groan I bear a part;
I view his wounds with streaming eyes;
But see! he bows his head and dies!

3 Come, sinners, view the Lamb of God,
Wounded, and dead, and bathed in blood!
Behold his side, and venture near;
The well of endless life is here.

4 Here I forget my cares and pains;
I drink, yet still my thirst remains:
Only the Fountain Head above
Can satisfy the thirst of love.

5 Oh that I thus could always feel!
Lord, more and more thy love reveal;
Then my glad tongue shall loud proclaim
The grace and glory of thy name.

6 Thy name dispels my guilt and fear,
Revives my heart, and charms my ear;
Affords a balm for every wound,
And Satan trembles at the sound.

## 194

YE prisoners of hope, o'erwhelmed with grief,
    To Jesus look up for certain relief;
There's no condemnation in Jesus the Lord,
But strong consolation his grace doth afford.

2 Then dry up your tears, ye children of grief,
For Jesus appears to give you relief:
If you are returning to Jesus, your friend,
Your sighing and mourning in singing shall
    end.

3 "None will I cast out who come," saith the
    Lord,
Why, then, do you doubt? lay hold of his word;
Ye mourners of Zion, be bold to believe;
Forever rely on your Saviour, and live.

### PRAISE.

## 195     *C. M.*

AMAZING grace! (how sweet the sound!)
    That saved a wretch like me!
I once was lost, but now am found—
    Was blind, but now I see.

2 'Twas grace that taught my heart to fear,
    And grace my fears relieved;

How precious did that grace appear,
　The hour I first believed!

3 Through many dangers, toils, and snares,
　　I have already come;
　'Tis grace has brought me safe thus far,
　　And grace will lead me home.

4 The Lord has promised good to me,
　　His word my hope secures;
　He will my shield and portion be,
　　As long as life endures.

5 Yes, when this flesh and heart shall fail,
　　And mortal life shall cease;
　I shall possess within the veil
　　A life of joy and peace.

6 The earth shall soon dissolve like snow,
　　The sun forbear to shine;
　But God, who called me here below,
　　Will be forever mine.

# 196

A WAY, far beyond the rolling river,
　　Of death's dark sea,
There, there my heart is turning ever;
　There would I ever be.
There Zion, city of the faithful,
　Fair to behold:
Her streams are ever clear as crystal,
　Her streets are paved with gold.

　　*All the world to me is dreary,*
　　　*Here have I no rest;*
　　*My troubled spirit ever weary,*
　　　*Till I am ever bless'd.*

2 The pearly gates are ever open,
　　Both night and day;
　13

To think of thee my heart doth soften,
 Why then do I delay?
By faith I see the ransomed spirits
 Hard by the throne:
They all the love of Christ inherit
 Forever safe at home.

3 There saints and angels sing hosanna,
 Happy in God;
Praising the name of Christ forever,
 In that high abode,
Soon shall I join the happy millions,
 Safe forevermore;
Soon shall I hear the music thrilling,
 On Zion's happy shore.

# 197

CREATOR, Preserver, Redeemer of men,
 Divine Intercessor above,
Oh, where shall the song of thy praises begin,
 Or how shall I speak of thy love?
  Heaven is telling,
  And earth is revealing
What wonders thy mercy can prove.

2 And do I not love thee, O Saviour divine,
 The chief of ten thousands to me?
Yes, infinite beauty and glory are thine,
 Whose effulgence no mortal can see;
  Angels shall bless thee,
  And men shall confess thee,
And worlds shall acknowledge thy sway.

3 Thine, thine is the kingdom, the wisdom, and
  power,
 The glory and honor supreme;
Forever and ever my soul would adore
 The unspeakable worth of thy name:
  Forever and ever,

O glorious Saviour,
I'll dwell on the rapturous theme.

# 198

FOR what shall I praise thee, my God and
    my King?
For what blessings the tribute of gratitude
    bring?
Shall I praise thee for pleasure, for health, or
    for ease?
For the spring of delight and the sunshine of
    peace?

2 Shall I praise thee for flowers that bloomed on
    my breast?
For joys in prospective, and pleasures pos-
    sessed?
For the spirits that brightened my days of de-
    light?
And the slumbers that sat on my pillow by
    night?

3 For this should I praise thee : but only for this,
I should leave half untold the donation of bliss;
I thank thee for sickness, for sorrow, for care,
For the thorns I have gathered, the anguish I
    bear :

4 For nights of anxiety, watching, and tears,
A present of pain, a prospective of fears;
I praise thee, I bless thee, my King and my
    God,
For the good and the evil thy hand hath be-
    stowed.

5 The flowers were sweet, but their fragrance is
    flown;
They yielded no fruit, they are withered and
    gone!

The thorn it was poignant, but precious to me:
'Twas the message of mercy—it led me to thee!

### 199            *L. M.*

GREAT God, we sing that mighty hand,
  By which supported still we stand:
The opening year thy mercy shows,
Let mercy crown it till it close.

2 By day, by night, at home, abroad,
  Still we are guarded by our God;
  By his incessant bounty fed,
  By his unerring counsel led.

3 With grateful hearts the past we own;
  The future, all to us unknown,
  We to thy guardian care commit,
  And peaceful leave before thy feet.

4 In scenes exalted or depressed,
  Be thou our joy, and thou our rest;
  Thy goodness all our hopes shall raise,
  Adored through all our changing days.

5 When death shall interrupt these songs,
  And seal in silence mortal tongues;
  Our helper, God, in whom we trust,
  In better worlds our souls shall boast.

### 200            *4 6s & 2 8s.*

GIVE thanks to God most high,
  The universal Lord;
The sovereign King of kings;
  And be his grace adored.
Thy mercy, Lord, shall still endure,
And ever sure abides thy word.

2 How mighty is his hand!
  What wonders hath he done!

He formed the earth and seas,
  And spread the heavens alone.
His power and grace are still the same;
And let his name have endless praise.

3 He saw the nations lie,
  All perishing in sin,
And pitied the sad state
  The ruined world was in.
Thy mercy, Lord, shall still endure,
And ever sure abides thy word.

4 He sent his holy Son
  To save us from our wo,
From Satan, sin, and death,
  And every hurtful foe.
His power and grace are still the same;
And let his name have endless praise.

## 201 *P. M.*

HOSANNA to Jesus! I'm filled with his
  praises;
  Come, O my dear brethren, and help me to
    sing;
No theme is so charming, no love is so warming,
  It gives joy and gladness, and comfort within.

2 Hosanna is ringing; I'm happy while singing
  And shouting the praises of Jesus' name;
The angels in glory repeat the glad story
  Of Jesus' love, which is made known to men.

3 Hosanna to Jesus, who died to redeem us,
  I'll serve him and love him wherever I go;
He's now gone to heaven, the Spirit he's given
  To quicken and comfort his children below.

4 Hosanna forever! his grace, like a river,
  Is rising and spreading all over the land:

His love is unbounded, to all it's extended,
And sinners are feeling the heavenly flame.

5 Hosanna to Jesus! my soul how it pleases
To see sinners falling and crying to God;
Then shouting and praising, they cry, "'Tis
amazing,
We've found peace and pardon in Jesus'
blood."

6 Hosanna is ringing, hark how they are singing
"All glory to Jesus, we've tasted his love."
The kingdom of heaven to mortals is given,
And rolls through my soul from the mansions
above.

7 Hosanna to Jesus! my soul feels him precious;
In bright beams of glory, he comes from
above.
My heart is now glowing, I feel his love flowing:
I'm sure that my Jesus I really do love.

8 Hosanna is ringing, the saints now are singing,
And marching to glory in bright royal bands:
Come on, my dear brethren, let us press towards
heaven,
For Jesus invites us with crowns in his
hands.

9 Hosanna to Jesus! my soul sweetly rises,
I'll soon be transported to a happier clime,
Where I shall see Jesus, and dwell in his pres-
ence,
And with him in glory eternally shine.

## 202 *P. M.*

HEAR the gospel trumpet sounding
Louder than the ocean's roar!
Hear it from the hills resounding,

Break in music on the shore!
  Hear it, mourner;
Let thy sorrows flow no more.

2 Where the gothic altars solemn
  Fed a feeble, flickering flame,
Wesley, leaning on a column,
  Called on God, his Saviour's name;
    Then from heaven
  Fires of living glory came.

3 Brighter with his mission glowing,
  Earth grew sweet with Sharon's rose;
Songs, like those of Eden flowing,
  Broke the rubric's dull repose.
    Then in power,
  Banner, star, and cross arose.

4 See another angel flying
  O'er the broad Atlantic wave!
Asb'ry lifts his trumpet, crying
  "Jesus came the world to save."
    Happy tidings!
  Millions in the fountains lave.

5 Now a thousand trumpets thunder
  Deep along the vaulted sky;
Now they part the spheres asunder,
  While the lightning arrows fly—
    Deep conviction
  Fills with tears the sinner's eye.

6 O'er the silver Lake of Simcoe,
  Hear the Indian chorus swell!
Softly blending with night's echo,
  All these strains of Jesus tell;
    Precious music!
  Like the gush of Elim's well.

7 Blessed Jesus, reign forever!
  Seated high on victory's car;

Bend the nations to thy sceptre,
　　Wave thine ensigns from afar.
　　　Hallelujah!
　　Thou art Christ, the morning star.

**203**　　　　　　　　　*P. M.*

HAIL, thou everlasting Saviour!
　　Prince and God of earth and sky!
In thy blood we all find favor,
　　Through thy name salvation's free:
　　　E'en the vilest
　　May redemption find in thee.

2 Let the news of thy salvation
　　Reach the bound'ries of the world,
And in every land and nation
　　May thy banner be unfurled—
　　　In oblivion
　　Superstition shall be hurled.

3 While thy heralds cross the ocean,
　　Fearless of each dangerous wave;
Fill their hearts with sweet devotion,
　　Save them from a watery grave.
　　　Land them safely
　　Where the briny billows lave.

4 Be their fortress and their tower;
　　Be their shield and hiding-place:
And, in every trying hour,
　　Aid them with thy mighty grace;
　　　Be their Saviour
　　In each moment of distress.

5 While they preach the truths of heaven,
　　On each superstitious shore,
May the poor benighted heathen
　　Feel thy Spirit's quickening power—
　　　And confess thee,
　　And thy holy name adore.

6 May, from all the hills and mountains,
   From the valleys and the plains,
 Loud hosannas (like the fountains)
    Soon burst forth in ceaseless strains—
      Hallelujah!
    Lo! the great Messiah reigns!

## 204 *L. M.*

HARK! don't you hear the Turtle Dove,
   The tokens of redeeming love?
From hill to hill we hear the sound,
The neighboring valleys echo round!
O Zion! hear the Turtle Dove,
The tokens of redeeming love:
They're come the barren land to cheer,
And welcome in the jubil year.

2 The winter's past, the rain is o'er,
  We feel the chilling winds no more;
  Sweet spring is come, and summer too,
  All things appear divinely new;
  On Zion's mount the watchmen cry,
  The resurrection's drawing nigh;
  Behold, the nations from abroad
  Are flocking to the mount of God.

3 The trumpet sounds both far and nigh,
  "O sinners, turn! why will you die?"
  How can you stand the gospel charms?
  Enlist with Christ, gird on your arms:
  These are the days that were foretold
  In ancient times by prophets old;
  They longed to see this glorious light,
  But all have died without the sight.

4 The *latter days* have now come on,
  And fugitives are flocking home;
  Behold them crowd the gospel road,
  All pressing for the mount of God.

Oh yes, and I will join the band—
Oh here's my heart and here's my hand;
With Satan's bands no more I'll be,
But fight for Christ and liberty.

5 His banner soon shall be unfurled,
And he will come to judge the world;
On Zion's mountain we will stand,
' Surrounded by fair Canaan's land.
The sun and moon shall darkened be,
The flames consume the land and sea;
When worlds on worlds together blaze,
We'll shout, and loud hosannas raise.

## 205                    *L. M.*

I N God let all his saints rejoice,
   With thankful heart and cheerful voice,
Thus saith his word, so kind, so true,
"I, even I, will comfort you."

2 Sweet words! oh, let us bless his name,
And joyful all his praise proclaim;
These words shall foes and fears subdue,
"I, even I, will comfort you."

3 Are you in darkness and distress?
Does Satan roar and break your peace?
Fear not, but still the truth review,
"I, even I, will comfort you."

4 Do sore afflictions on you lay,
And pungent sorrow, day by day?
Look to this word, 'twill bear you through,
"I, even I, will comfort you."

5 If death in gloomy form appear,
And overwhelm your souls with fear,
Let this sweet word your faith renew,
"I, even I, will comfort you."

6 Thus while you sojourn here below,
As pilgrims in this world of wo,
Make this your song, your journey through,
" I, even I, will comfort you."

7 And when each happy soul attains
That blissful state where glory reigns,
This song shall all his powers employ,
" God is my comfort and my joy."

## 206 *P. M.*

I LOVE my blessed Saviour,
I feel I'm in his favor,
And I am his forever,
If I but faithful prove;
And now I'm bound for Canaan,
I feel my sins forgiv'n,
And soon shall get to heaven,
To sing of his love.

2 Poor sinners may deride me,
And unbelievers chide me,
But nothing shall divide me
From Jesus my friend:
Supported by his power,
I long to see the hour
That bids my spirit tower,
And all my troubles end.

3 The pleasing time is hast'ning,
My tott'ring frame is wasting,
While I'm engaged in praising,
Impelled by his love.
When yonder shining orders,
Who sing on Canaan's borders,
Shall bear me to their Lord, there
To praise him above.

4 My thirsty soul is panting,
 My body almost fainting,
 While praise and pray'r are venting
   From my feeble tongue.
 How ardent my desire!
 Lord Jesus, raise me higher,
 To join the holy choir
   In that immortal song.

5 Farewell, I'm bound for glory,
 How pleasing is the story!
 Those shining worlds before me
   Invite me to be gone.
 Had I angels' pinions,
 I'd range the bright dominions,
 And join the shining millions,
   Who're shouting round the throne.

6 The pleasing smile of Jesus
 The rapturous sound increases,
 And tunes the heavenly voices
   Throughout the ethereal plains.
 My flesh and spirit failing,
 My soul in transports hailing,
 Bright seraphs in their dwelling,
   I sing immortal strains.

## 207                    *P. M.*

I'M not surprised that saints do sing,
   Or angels shout and wonder,
 I would sing glory if I could,
   As 'loud as mighty thunder.

2 My night of sin and grief is gone,
   My soul is filled with glory,
 Oh! for a thousand tongues to tell
   Love's animating story.

3 Let heav'n and earth with me unite,
   And sing and shout hosanna;

The Lord has pardoned all my sins,
And filled my soul with manna.

4 Poor sinners often laugh and scoff,
Because I sing hosanna;
But they don't know what this doth mean,
My soul is eating manna.

5 My old companions think I'm lost
Because I sing hosanna,
But they would sing as loud as me,
If they had tasted manna.

6 The cold professors do detest
Such loud noise and hosannas;
And so did we before we sought,
And found this holy manna.

7 When on my dying bed I lay,
My soul shall sing hosanna,
With happy saints that shout around,
We'll have a feast of manna.

8 A glorious throng have gone before,
Who sing and shout hosanna,
They stand around the tree of life,
And always gather manna.

9 Come on, ye follow'rs of the Lamb,
Love God and sing hosanna;
We soon shall join that holy throng,
And always live on manna.

# 208

LORD, and am I yet alive,
Not in torments, not in hell!
Still doth thy good Spirit strive!—
With the chief of sinners dwell!

*Tell it unto sinncrs, tell,*
*I am, I am out of hɛll!*

2· Yes, I still lift up my eyes,
   Will not of thy love despair;
Still in spite of sin I rise,
   Still I bow to thee in prayer.

3 O the length and breadth of love!
   Jesus, Saviour, can it be!
All thy mercy's height I prove,
   All the depth is seen in me.

4 See a stone that hangs in air!
   See a spark in ocean live!
Kept alive with death so near,
   I to God the glory give.

## 209

L ET us love, and sing, and wonder,
   Let us praise the Saviour's name;
He has hushed the law's loud thunder,
   He has quenched Mount Sinai's flame,
He has washed us with his blood,
He has brought us nigh to God.

2 Let us love the Lord who bought us,
   Pitied us when enemies;
Called us by his grace, and taught us,
   Gave us ears, and gave us eyes:
He has washed us with his blood,
He presents our souls to God.

3 Let us sing, though fierce temptation
   Threaten hard to bear us down,
For the Lord, our strong salvation,
   Holds in view the conqueror's crown:
He who washed us with his blood,
Soon will bring us home to God.

4 Let us wonder: grace and justice
    Join, and point to mercy's store;
Christ hath died (in him our trust is),
    Justice smiles, and asks no more:
He who washed us with his blood
Hath secured our way to God.

5 Let us praise, and join the chorus
    Of the saints enthroned on high;
Here they trusted him before us,
    Now their praises fill the sky:
"Thou hast washed us with thy blood;
Thou art worthy, Lamb of God."

6 Hark! the name of Jesus sounded
    Loud from golden harps above;
Lord, we blush, and are confounded,
    Faint our praises, cold our love:
Wash our souls and songs with blood,
For by thee we come to God.

# 210 *P. M.*

LISTEN, O Sion! Jehovah hath spoken,
    The Lord, thy Redeemer, commands thee
        arise;
Far o'er the earth reigns darkness unbroken,
    Whilst heaven's bright day-star illumines
        thy skies.

*Listen, O Sion! Jehovah hath spoken,*
*The Lord, thy Redeemer, commands thee arise.*

2 Rise to their rescue! lo! error is stealing,
    O'er souls thy Redeemer has bought for his
        fold!
View Calvary's scenes! are they not appealing?
    The light thence enkindled, O bid them be-
        hold.

3 Christian, awaken! thy darkness hath vanished,
   Thy sky has been lit by its radiant glow;
 Joy that the shades that enwrapt thee are ban-
   ished,
   And hasten that all may thy blessedness
   know.

4 Rouse thee to action, thy Saviour is pleading,
   Look upward, the strength of the mighty is
   thine;
   Omnipotent faith through Christ interceding
   Will soon bid the world in God's image to
   shine.

## 211        *P. M.*

MY heart and my tongue shall unite in the
   praise
Of Jesus my Saviour for mercy and grace;
He purchased my pardon by shedding his blood,
And bids me inherit the peace of my God.

2 My lot may be lowly, my parentage mean,
   Yet born of my God there are glories unseen,
   Surpassing all joys among sinners on earth,
   Prepared for souls of a heavenly birth.

3 Redeemed from a thousand allurements to sin,
   I find in my cottage my heaven begin;
   And soon shall I lay all my poverty by,
   Then mansions of glory forever enjoy.

4 By the sweat of my brow now I labor for bread,
   Yet guarded by him, not an evil I dread;
   And while I'm possessed of all riches in thee,
   My poverty comes with a blessing to me.

5 My laboring dress I shall soon lay aside
   For a robe bright and splendid, a dress for a
   bride—

A bride that is married to Jesus the Lamb
Shall be clad in the robes which are ever the
same.

6 If my fare should be scant while I travel below.
Yet a feast that's eternal shall Jesus bestow;
No sorrow, no sighing shall ever annoy
The heavenly banquet I there shall enjoy.

7 If my laboring body goes weary to rest,
Yet saved by the mercy of Jesus I'm blest:
Fresh strength for my labor on earth he bestows,
And above I shall bask in eternal repose.

212                    *7s & 6s.*

NOW be the gospel banner
    In every land unfurled;
And be the shout, hosanna,
    Re-echoed through the world;
Till every isle and nation,
    Till every tribe and tongue,
Receive the great salvation,
    And join the happy throng.

2 What though the embattled legions
    Of earth and hell combine—
His arm, throughout their legions,
    Shall soon resplendent shine:
Ride on, O Lord, victorious!
    Immanuel, Prince of Peace!
Thy triumph shall be glorious,
    Thy empire still increase.

3 Yes, thou shalt reign forever,
    O Jesus, King of kings!
Thy light, thy love, thy favor,
    Each ransomed captive sings:
The isles for thee are waiting,
    The deserts learn thy praise,
    14

The hills and valleys, greeting.
The song responsive raise.

**213**                          *7s.*

NOW begin the heavenly theme,
Sing aloud in Jesus' name!
Ye who his salvation prove,
Triumph in redeeming love.

2 Ye who see the Father's grace
Beaming in the Saviour's face,
As to Canaan on ye move,
Praise and bless redeeming love.

3 Mourning souls, dry up your tears,
Banish all your guilty fears;
See your guilt and curse remove,
Canceled by redeeming love.

4 Ye, alas! who long have been
Willing slaves to death and sin,
Now from bliss no longer rove,
Stop, and taste redeeming love.

5 Welcome all, by sin opprest,
Welcome to his sacred rest;
Nothing brought him from above,
Nothing but redeeming love.

6 Hither, then, your music bring,
Strike aloud each cheerful string;
Mortals, join the host above,
Join to praise redeeming love.

**214**                          *P. M.*

O JESUS, my Saviour, to thee I submit,
With love and thanksgiving I fall at thy
feet;
The sacrifice offer, my soul, flesh, and blood,
To thee, my Redeemer, my Lord, and my God.

2 I love thee, I love thee, I love thee, my Lord!
 I love thee, my Saviour, I love thee, my God!
 I love thee, I love thee, and that thou dost know,
 But how much I love thee I never can show:

3 All human expressions are empty and vain;
 They cannot unriddle the heavenly flame;
 I'm sure if the tongue of an angel I had,
 I could not the myst'ry completely describe.

4 I'm happy, I'm happy, oh wondrous account!
 My joys are immortal—I stand on the mount;
 I gaze on my treasure, and long to be there,
 With Jesus my Saviour, the kingdom to share.

5 O Jesus, my Saviour, in thee I am blest!
 My life and my treasure, my joy and my rest;
 Thy grace be my theme, and thy name be my
      song,
 Thy love doth inspire my heart and my tongue.

6 Oh, who is like Jesus! he's Salem's bright King;
 He smiles, and he loves me, and taught me to
      sing;
 I'll praise him, I'll praise him, and bow to his
      will,
 While rivers of pleasure my spirit do fill.

## 215

O JESUS, my Saviour! I know thou art mine;
   For thee all the pleasure of earth I resign;
 Of objects most pleasing, I love thee the best;
 Without thee I'm wretched, but with thee I'm
      blest.

2 Thou art my rich treasure, my joy and my love,
 (None richer possessed by the angels above);
 For thee all the pleasures of sense I forego,
 And wander a pilgrim despised below.

3 Thy Spirit first taught me to know I was blind,
And taught me the way of salvation to find;
For when I was sinking in dreadful despair,
My Jesus relieved me and bid me not fear.

4 In vain I attempt to describe what I feel:
The language of mortals forever must fail;
My Jesus is precious, my soul's in a flame;
I'm raised into raptures while praising his name.

5 Though weak and despised, by faith I now stand,
Preserved and defended by heav'n's kind hand;
By Jesus supported, I'll praise his dear name,
Regardless of danger, of praise or of blame.

6 I find him in singing, I find him in prayer;
In sweet meditation he always is near:
My constant companion, oh, may we not part!
All glory to Jesus, who dwells in my heart.

7 If ever I loved, sure I love thee, my Lord,
I love thy dear people, thy ways, and thy word;
I love all my brethren, I love sinners too,
Since Jesus has died to redeem them from wo.

8 When happy in Jesus, I regard not the proud,
Tho' sinners despise me for shouting so loud;
For death will soon call me, and then I shall
fly,
To praise my dear Jesus in mansions on high.

9 Through millions of ages sweet notes I'll employ
In praising my Jesus, my hope and my joy.:
The glorified spirits and angels around
Shall all be delighted to join the glad sound.

## 216

YES we'll meet beyond the river,
When our conflicts all are o'er;
And we'll spend the blest forever
On that bright celestial shore.

2 Yes we'll meet, in yonder mansions,
  Where our wand'rings all shall cease,
There we'll meet our dear companions
  And be crown'd with perfect peace.

3 Yes we'll meet where bliss immortal
  Sweeter far than rest can be,
And before the throne eternal
  All our earthly triumphs see.

4 We shall meet where all is onward,
  Every change new glories bring,
And the host still moving forward,
  Glorify our heav'nly King.

5 We shall meet, O! weary brother,
  When the burden we lay down;
We shall change our cross of anguish
  For a bright unfading crown.

## 217                    *P. M.*

O HOW charming, O how charming,
  Is the radiant band of music, music, music,
    music,
O how charming is the radiant band
Of music playing through the air:
Angelic armies tune their harps,
Angelic armies tune their harps,
Enraptured spirits play their parts,
Angelic armies tune their harps,
  Shout, shout! the great Messiah is come to
    reign.

2 Gabriel descending, Gabriel descending,
  Brings the joyful news, O joyful, joyful, joyful,
    joyful,
Brings the joyful news of our Redeemer's birth,
The great Messiah's come to earth:
Good will to men I now proclaim,
Good will to men I now proclaim,

The Saviour's born in Bethlehem,
Good will to men I now proclaim,
   Shout, shout! the King of glory is come to
   reign.

3 See his star arising, see his star arising,
  In the eastern sky, now rising, rising, rising,
    rising,
  See his star arising in the eastern sky,
  The day-spring opening from on high:
  The types and shadows flee away,
  The types and shadows flee away,
  And now begins the gospel day,
  The types and shadows flee away,
    Shout, shout! the King of glory is come to
    reign.

4 Shepherds adore him, wise men have found him,
  Glory be to God, O glory, glory, glory, glory,
  Wise men have found him by the rising star,
  And come to worship him afar:
  Their golden gifts they now present,
  Their golden gifts they now present,
  And spices of the sweetest scent,
  Their golden gifts they now present,
    Shout, shout! the King of glory is come to
    reign.

5 The Jews and Gentiles join in concert,
  To praise their infant King: O praise him, praise
    him, praise him, praise him,
  Jews and Gentiles praise their infant King,
  And loud hosannas sweetly sing:
  With Gabriel and the shining host,
  With Gabriel and the shining host,
  Praise Father, Son, and Holy Ghost,
  With Gabriel and the shining host,
    Shout, shout! the King of glory is come to
    reign.

6 I am happy, I am happy,
  Glory be to God, O glory, glory, glory, glory,
 · I am happy, glory be to God;
  My soul's on flame for the realms above:
  I feel the bliss his wounds impart,
  I feel the bliss his wounds impart,
  I find my Saviour in my heart,
  I feel the bliss his wounds impart,
     Shout, shout! the King of glory is come to
        reign.

7 Reign, reign, sweet Jesus, reign within and
        round us,
  By the Holy Spirit, holy, holy, holy, holy,
  By the Holy Spirit keep us in the way,
  That we may shout as we sing and pray:
  With all the saints that have gone home,
  With all the saints that have gone home,
  Unite to sing redeeming love,
  With all the saints that have gone home,
     To sing, to sing hallelujahs around the throne.

## 218 *P. M.*

REJOICE, my friends, the Lord is King,
  Let all prepare to take him in;
Let Jacob rise, and Zion sing,
And all the world with praises ring,
     And give to Jesus glory.

2 I long to see the Christians join
  In union sweet, and peace divine,
  When every church with grace shall shine,
  And grow to Christ the living vine,
     And give to Jesus glory.

3 Come, parents, children, bond and free,
  Come, will you go to heaven with me,
  That glorious land of rest to see,
  And shout with me eternally,
     And give to Jesus glory?

4 My soul feels happy while I sing:
  I feel that I am on the wing;
  I'll shout salvation to my king,
  Till I to heaven my trophies bring,
    And there we'll give him glory.

5 A few more days of pain and wo,
  A few more suffering scenes below,
  And then to Jesus we shall go,
  ·Where everlasting pleasures flow,
    And there we'll give him glory.

6 The awful trumpet soon will sound,
  And shake the vast creation round,
  And call the nations under ground;
  And all the saints shall then be crowned,
    And give to Jesus glory.

7 Ten thousand thunders then shall roll, ·
  And shake the globe from pole to pole;
  How dreadful to the guilty soul!
  But nothing shall the saints control,
    They'll give to Jesus glory.

8 Then tears shall all be wiped away;
  Then Christians ne'er shall go astray;
  When we are freed from cumbrous clay,
  We'll praise the Lord in endless day,
    And give to Jesus glory.

9 There all the saints shall join in one,
  And sing with Moses round the throne;
  Their troubles are forever gone,
  They'll shine with God's eternal Son,
    And give to Jesus glory.

## 219                *S. M.*

SERENE I laid me down,
  Beneath his guardian care;

I slept, and I awoke, and found
My kind Preserver near.

2 Thus does thine arm support
This weak, defenceless frame;
But whence these favors, Lord, to me,·
All worthless as I am?

3 O, how shall I repay
The bounties of my God?
This feeble spirit pants beneath
The pleasing, painful load.

4 My life I would anew,
Devote, O Lord, to thee;
And in thy service I would spend
A long eternity.

**220.** *P. M.*

REJOICE evermore with angels above,
In Jesus' power, in Jesus' love:
With glad exultation your triumph proclaim,
Ascribing salvation to God and the Lamb.

2 Thou, Lord, our relief in trouble hast been;
Hast saved us from grief, hast saved us from sin;
The power of thy Spirit hath set our hearts free,
And now we inherit all fullness in thee.

3 All fullness of peace, all fullness of joy,
And spiritual bliss that never shall cloy;
To us it is given in Jesus to know,
A kingdom of heaven, a heaven below.

4 No longer we join, while sinners invite,
Nor envy the swine their brutish delight;
Their joy is all sadness, their mirth is all vain,
Their laughter is madness, their pleasure is
pain.

5 O might they at last with sorrow return,
The pleasure to taste for which they were born:
Our Jesus receiving, our happiness prove,
The joy of believing, the heaven of love.

## 221

TO thee, O my Saviour, to thee will I cling,
For thou art my Lord, my Redeemer, and
King;
And feeling thy blessing, my spirit shall know
Thy mercy is with me wherever I go.          .

2 Farewell to the anguish of doubt and despair,
And welcome the rapture of praise and of
prayer;
Since, meekly confiding, in faith I rejoice,
To hear the sweet tones of thy comforting voice.

3 Around me there shineth the heavenly ray
Which scattereth clouds and their shadows
away,
And melteth my soul in devotional glow—
For mercy is with me wherever I go.

4 Farewell to the pleasures which time can afford,
Since thou art my glory, my Saviour and Lord;
Nor fear I the darkness of death and the tomb,
Since thou art my Light in the midst of the
gloom.

5 Before me there gloweth, around and above,
The pledges of favor, the tokens of love;
And gratitude teacheth my spirit to know,
Thy mercy is with me wherever I go.

## 222

THY mercy, my God, is the theme of my song,
The joy of my heart and the boast of my
tongue;

Thy free grace alone, from the first to the last,
Hath won my affections and bound my soul
fast.

2 Without thy sweet mercy I could not live here;
Sin soon would reduce me to utter despair;
But through thy free goodness my spirits revive,
And He that first made me still keeps me alive.

3 Thy mercy is more than a match for my heart,
Which wonders to feel its own hardness depart;
Dissolved by thy goodness, I fall to the ground,
And weep to the praise of the mercy I found.

4 The door of thy mercy stands open all day
To the poor and the needy, who knock by the
way:
No sinner shall ever be empty sent back,
Who comes seeking mercy for Jesus' sake.

5 Thy mercy in Jesus exempts me from hell:
Its glories I'll sing, and its wonders I'll tell.
'Twas Jesus my friend, when he hung on the
tree,
Who opened the channel of mercy for me.

6 Great Father of mercies! thy goodness I own,
And the covenant love of thy crucified Son:
All praise to the Spirit, whose whisper divine
Seals mercy, and pardon, and righteousness
mine.

**223**      *L. M.*

'TIS grace that quickens me when dead,
Grace can my soul to Jesus lead;
Grace brings me pardon for my sin—
'Tis grace subdues my lusts within.

2 'Tis grace that sweetens every cross,
'Tis grace supports in every loss;

Lord, in thy grace my soul is strong—
Grace is my hope, and Christ my song.

3 'Tis grace defends when danger's near;
By grace alone I persevere;
'Tis grace constrains my soul to love—
Free grace is all they sing above.

4 Thus 'tis alone of grace I boast,
And 'tis in grace alone I trust;
For all that's past, grace is my theme—
For what's to come 'tis still the same.

5 Through endless years, of grace I'll sing,
Adore and bless my heavenly King;
I'll cast my crown before his throne,
And shout free grace to him alone.

## 224      *P. M.*

THEE will I love, my strength, my tower;
Thee will I love, my joy, my crown;
Thee will I love with all my power,
In all thy works, and thee alone:
Thee will I love, till the pure fire
Fill my whole soul with chaste desire.

2 Ah! why did I so late thee know,
Thee, lovelier than the sons of men!
Ah! why did I no sooner go
To thee, the only ease in pain!
Ashamed I sigh, and inly mourn,
That I so late to thee did turn.

3 In darkness willingly I strayed:
I sought thee, yet from thee I roved:
Far wide my wandering thoughts were spread;
Thy creatures more than thee I loved;
And now, if more at length I see,
'Tis through thy light, and comes from thee.

4 I thank thee, uncreated sun,
    That thy bright beams on me have shined;
I thank thee who hast overthrown
    My foes, and healed my wounded mind.
I thank thee, whose enlivening voice
Bids my freed heart in thee rejoice.

5 Uphold me in the doubtful race,
    Nor suffer me again to stray;
Strengthen my feet, with steady pace
    Still to press forward in thy way;
My soul and flesh, O Lord of might,
Fill, satiate with thy heavenly light.

6 Give to mine eyes refreshing tears;
    Give to my heart chaste, hallowed fires;
Give to my soul, with filial fears,
    The love that all heaven's host inspires;
That all my powers, with all their might,
In thy sole glory may unite.

7 Thee will I love, my joy, my crown,
    Thee will I love, my Lord, my God;
Thee will I love, beneath thy frown,
    Or smile, thy sceptre, or thy rod;
What though my flesh and heart decay;
Thee shall I love in endless day!

## 225     *C. M.*

THROUGH all the changing scenes of life,
    In trouble and in joy,
The praises of my God shall still
    My heart and tongue employ.

2 Of his deliverance I will boast,
    Till all who are distressed
From my example comfort take,
    And charm their griefs to rest.

3 The hosts of God encamp around
　　The dwellings of the just:
Deliverance he affords to all
　　Who on his succor trust.

4 O make but trial of his love—
　　Experience will decide
How blest they are, and only they,
　　Who in his truth confide.

5 Fear him, ye saints; and you will then
　　Have nothing else to fear:
Make you his service your delight—
　　He'll make your wants his care.

**226**　　　*L. M.*

WHAT love, what pleasure, what surprise
　　Shall fill the enraptured heirs of heaven,
The day the Saviour meets their eyes,
　　The day the promised rest is given!

2 Their love is kindled here below,
　　The Author of their hope they love;
A purer, brighter flame will glow
　　In yonder glorious world above.

3 Of pleasure too they taste below,
　　But pleasure not unmixed with pain;
In yonder world 'twill not be so,
　　For there no sorrow will remain.

4 And if obscure and transient views
　　Of heavenly things yield such surprise,
What wonder must the sight produce,
　　When God appears before their eyes!

5 O joyful sight! O glorious day!
　　When God the Saviour shall be seen,
When earthly things shall pass away,
　　And heaven's unchanging state begin!

**227**      *P. M.*

WHAT wondrous love is this, O my soul! O
. my soul!
What wondrous love is this, O my soul!
What wondrous love is this that caused the
Lord of bliss
To send this precious peace to my soul, to my
soul,
To send this precious peace to my soul.

2 When I was sinking down, O my soul! O my
soul!
When I was sinking down, O my soul!
When I was sinking down beneath God's
righteous frown,
Christ laid aside his crown for my soul, for my
soul,
Christ laid aside his crown for my soul.

3 Ye winged seraphs fly, bear the news, bear the
news,
Ye winged seraphs fly, bear the news,
Ye winged seraphs fly, like comets through the
sky,
Fill vast eternity with the news, with the news,
Fill vast eternity with the news.

4 Ye friends of Zion's King, join his praise, join
his praise,
Ye friends of Zion's King, join his praise,
Ye friends of Zion's King with hearts and
voices sing,
And strike each tuneful string in his praise, in
his praise,
And strike each tuneful string in his praise.

5 To God and to the Lamb I will sing, I will sing,
To God and to the Lamb I will sing,

To God and to the Lamb, who is the great I
  AM!
While millions join the theme, I will sing, I
  will sing!
While millions join the theme, I will sing.

6 And when from death I'm free, I'll sing, I'll
    sing,
  And when from death I'm free, I'll sing,
  And when from death I'm free, I'll sing and
    joyful be;
  And through eternity I'll sing on, I'll sing on,
  And through eternity I'll sing on.

## 228 *P. M.*

YE heavens, rejoice in Jesus' grace,
  Let earth make a noise, and echo his praise:
Our all-loving Saviour hath pacified God,
And paid for his favor the price of his blood.

2 Ye mountains and vales, in praises abound,
  Ye hills and ye dales, continue the sound;
  Break forth into singing, ye trees of the wood,
  For Jesus is bringing lost sinners to God.

3 Atonement he made for every one,
  The debt he hath paid, the work he hath done;
  Shout, all the creation, below and above,
  Ascribing salvation to Jesus' love.

4 His mercy has brought salvation to all,
  Who take it unbought, he frees them from
    thrall,
  Throughout the believer his glory displays,
  And perfects forever the vessels of grace.

## 229 *P. M.*

YE servants of God, your Master proclaim,
  And publish abroad his wonderful name,

The name all victorious of Jesus extol ;
His kingdom is glorious, and rules over all.

2 God ruleth on high, almighty to save,
And still he is nigh, his presence we have :
The great congregation his triumphs shall sing,
Ascribing salvation to Jesus our King.

3 Salvation to God who sits on the throne,
Let all cry aloud, and honor the Son :
Our Jesus' praises the angels proclaim,
Fall down on their faces, and worship the Lamb.

4 Then let us adore, and give him his right;
All glory, and power, and wisdom, and might.
All honor and blessing, with angels above;
And thanks never ceasing, and infinite love.

## CHRISTIAN PILGRIMAGE AND WARFARE.

**230** *P. M.*

A FEW more days on earth to spend,
And all my toils and cares shall end,
Then I shall see my God and friend,
   And praise his name on high.
There's no more sighs, and no more tears,
There's no more pains, and no more fears,
But God, and Christ, and heaven appears,
   Unto the ravished eye.

2 Then O my soul, despond no more !
The storm of life will soon be o'er,
And I shall find the peaceful shore
   Of everlasting rest.
O happy day! O joyful hour,
When, freed from earth, my soul shall tower
Beyond the reach of Satan's power,
   To be forever bless'd.

15

3 My soul anticipates the day,
I'd joyfully the call obey,
Which summons thee, my soul, away,
　To seats prepared above.
There I shall see my Saviour's face,
And dwell in his beloved embrace,
And taste the fullness of his grace,
　And sing redeeming love.

4 Though dire afflictions press me sore,
And death's black billows roll before,
Yet still by faith I see the shore,
　Beyond the rolling flood;
The heavenly Canaan sweet and fair,
Before my ravished eyes appear;
It makes me almost think I'm there,
　In yonder bright abode.

5 To earthly cares I'd say farewell,
And triumph over death and hell,
And go where saints and angels dwell,
　To praise the eternal Three.
I'll join with them who're gone before,
Who sing and shout, their sufferings o'er,
Where pain and parting are no more,
　To all eternity.

6 Adieu, ye scenes of noise and show,
And all this region here below,
Where nought but disappointments grow,
　A better world's in view.
My Saviour calls! I haste away,
I would not here forever stay:
Hail! ye bright realms of endless day,
　Vain world, once more, adieu.

231　　　　　　　　　　P. M.

OH! that I had some humble place,
　Where I might hide from sorrow;

Where I might see my Saviour's face,
  And there be freed from terror.
Oh, had I wings like Noah's dove,
  I'd leave this world and Satan,
And fly away to realms above,
  Where Jesus stands inviting.

2 My heart is often made to mourn,
  Because I'm faint and feeble;
And when my Saviour seems to frown,
  My soul is filled with trouble.
But when he doth again return,
  And I repent my folly;
'Tis then I after glory run,
  And still my Jesus follow.

3 I have my bitter and my sweet,
  While through this world I travel;
Sometimes I shout, and often weep,
  Which makes my foes to marvel.
But let them think, and think again,
  I feel I'm bound for heaven;
I know I shall with Jesus reign,
  I therefore still will praise him.

4 I want to live a Christian here;
  I want to die while shouting;
I want to feel my Saviour near,
  When soul and body's parting;
I want to see bright angels stand,
  And waiting to receive me;
To bear my soul to Canaan's land,
  Where Christ is gone before me.

**232**          *4 6s & 2 8s.*

A WAKE our drowsy souls;
  Shake off each slothful band;
The wonders of this day,
  Our noblest songs demand;

Auspicious morn! thy blissful rays
Bright seraphs hail in songs of praise.

2 At thy approaching dawn,
　　Reluctant death resigned
The glorious Prince of life,
　　In dark domains confined!
The angelic host around him bends;
And, 'midst their shouts, the God ascends.

3 All hail, triumphant Lord!
　　Heaven with hosannas rings;
While earth, in humbler strains,
　　Thy praise responsive sings:
"Worthy art thou who once was slain,
Through endless years to live and reign."

4 Gird on, great God, thy sword,
　　Ascend thy conquering car;
While justice, truth, and love
　　Maintain the glorious war.
· Victorious, thou thy foes shalt tread,
And sin and hell in triumph lead.

**233**　　　　　　　*P. M.*

ZION! the marvellous story be telling,
　　The Son of the Highest, how lowly his
　　　birth!
The brightest archangel in glory excelling,
　　He stoops to redeem thee, he reigns upon
　　　earth.

*Shout the glad tidings, exultingly sing,*
*Jerusalem triumphs, Messiah is King.*

2 Tell.how he cometh, from nation to nation.
　　The heart-cheering news let the earth echo
　　　round;
How free to the faithful he offers salvation!
　　How his people with joy everlasting are
　　　crowned!

3 Mortals your homage be gratefully bringing,
   And sweet let the gladsome hosanna arise;
Ye angels! the full hallelujah be singing,
   One chorus resound through the earth and
     the skies.

**224**                    *P. M.*

O ZION, afflicted with wave upon wave,
  Whom no man can comfort, whom no man
    save,
Surrounded with troubles, with terror dismayed,
With toiling and rowing thy strength is decayed,
Loud roaring, the billows now high thee o'er-
    whelm,
But skillful the pilot that sits at the helm;
His wisdom conducts thee, his power shall de-
    fend,
'Tis he all victorious, thy warfare shall stand.

2 O fearful, O faithless, in mercy he cries,
  What though high the surges t' affright thee
    arise;
  Still, still I am with thee, my promise shall
    stand,
  Through tossings and tempests I'll bring thee
    to land.
  Forget thee I will not, I care for thy name,
  Engraved on my heart, it shall ever remain;
  The palms of my hands, when I look on, I see
  The wounds I received when I suffered for thee.

3 The fearful, the faithless, the weak are my care,
  The helpless, the hopeless, I hear their sad
    prayer;
  Through great tribulation my people I bring,
  And when they reach heaven the louder they'll
    sing.

I feel at my heart all thy sighs and thy groans!
For thou art most nigh me, my flesh and my
    bones:
In all my afflictions, though great is my pain,
They all are most needful, not one is in vain.

4 The day of eternal salvation draws near,
When Jesus our leader will dry every tear,
Our bodies and souls shall his glory partake,
When the trumpet shall sound, and the nations
    awake.
Fight on, ye old soldiers, you'll soon be dis-
    charged,
The war will be ended, your treasure enlarged;
With singing and shouting, though Jordan may
    roar,
We'll enter fair Canaan, and stand on the shore.

## 235    *C. M.*

A STRANGER and a pilgrim here, happy,
    happy, happy,
I seek the home to pilgrims dear, happy in the
    Lord.

*We'll cross the river of Jordan, happy, happy,
    happy,
We'll cross the river of Jordan, happy in the
    Lord.*

2 I leave a world of sin behind, happy, happy,
    happy,
A purer home in heaven to find, happy in
    the Lord;
Fair lands are here, and houses fair, happy,
    happy, happy,
But fairer is my home up there, happy in the
    Lord.

3 When death doth come, my soul shall fly, happy,
  happy, happy,
On wings of angels through the sky, happy in
  the Lord;
What though I weep a while below, happy,
  happy, happy,
In heaven my tears will cease to flow, happy
  in the Lord.

4 In that fair clime of endless day, happy, happy,
  happy,
The Lord shall wipe all tears away, happy in
  the Lord;
To living founts, through verdant meads, happy,
  happy, happy,
The Lamb his ransomed followers leads, happy
  in the Lord.

5 The fruits and flowers of Paradise, happy, happy,
  happy,
In plenteous showers round them rise, happy
  in the Lord;
No death shall visit them again, happy, happy,
  happy,
No sickness there, no touch of pain, happy in
  the Lord.

6 Farewell! vain world, I'm going home, happy,
  happy, happy,
My Saviour smiles, and bids me come, happy
  in the Lord;
No mourning there, no funeral gloom, happy,
  happy, happy,
But health and youth forever bloom, happy in
  the Lord.

**236**                    *P. M.*

O WHEN shall I see Jesus,
  And dwell with him above,

To drink the flowing fountains
  Of everlasting love?
When shall I be delivered
  From this vain world of sin,
And with my blessed Jesus
  Drink endless pleasures in?

2 But now I am a soldier,
  My captain's gone before,
He's given me my orders,
  And tells me not to fear,
And if I hold out faithful,
  A crown of life he'll give,
And all his valiant soldiers
  Eternal life shall have.

3 Through grace I am determined
  To conquer, though I die,
And then away to Jesus
  On wings of love I'll fly;
Farewell to sin and sorrow,
  I bid them all adieu;
And you my friends prove faithful,
  And on your way pursue.

4 And if you meet with troubles
  And trials on the way,
Then cast your care on Jesus,
  And don't forget to pray.
Gird on the heavenly armor
  Of faith, and hope, and love,
And when your race is ended,
  You'll reign with him above.

5 Oh, do not be discouraged,
  For Jesus is your friend;
And if you lack for knowledge,
  He'll not refuse to lend;
Neither will he upbraid you,
  Though often you request,

He'll give you grace to conquer,
And take you home to rest.

**237**                    *P. M.*

BROTHER soldier, still fight on,
     Till the battle thou hast won;
The great Captain thou didst choose
Never did a battle lose.

*We his soldiers sure shall be*
*Happy in eternity.*

2 Advocates for sin do say
   We can never win the day,
   Would discourage all the host;
   Meanly yield—the battle's lost.

3 They that do his host defy
   Shall before his presence fly;
   If we on our Captain call,
   They like Jericho shall fall.

4 Still fight on, and you shall see
   All the sons of Anak flee,
   Fear them not, tho' they be tall,
   Our great Captain conquers all.

*More than conqu'rors we shall be*
*Happy thro' eternity.*

**238**

OUT on an ocean all boundless we ride,
          We're homeward bound;
Tossed on the waves of a rough, restless tide,
          We're homeward bound;
Far from the safe, quiet harbor we've rode,
Seeking our Father's celestial abode,
Promise of which on us each he bestowed,
          We're homeward bound.

2 Wildly the storm sweeps us on as it roars,
        We're homeward bound;
  Look! yonder lie the bright heavenly shores,
        We're homeward bound;
  Steady, O pilot! stand firm at the wheel,
  Steady! we soon shall outweather the gale,
  O how we fly 'neath the loud creaking sail,
        We're homeward bound.

3 We'll tell the world as we journey along,
        We're homeward bound;
, Try to persuade them to enter our throng,
        We're homeward bound;
  Come, trembling sinner, forlorn and oppressed,
  Join in our number, O come and be blest;
  Journey with us to the mansions of rest,
        We're homeward bound.

4 Into the harbor of heaven now we glide,
        We're home at last;
  Softly we drift on its bright silver tide,
        We're home at last;
  Glory to God! all our dangers are o'er;
  We stand secure on the glorified shore,
  Glory to God! we will shout evermore,
        We're home at last.

**239**                   *P. M.*

BE still, my heart! those anxious cares
  To thee are burdens, thorns, and snares;
They cast dishonor on thy Lord,
And contradict his gracious word,

2 Brought safely by his hand thus far,
  Why wilt thou now give place to fear?
  How canst thou want if he provide,
  Or lose thy way with such a Guide?

3 Did ever trouble yet befall,
  And he refuse to hear thy call?

And has he not his promise past,
That thou shalt overcome at last?

4 He who has helped me hitherto
Will help me all my journey through,
And give me daily cause to raise
New trophies to his endless praise.

5 Though rough and thorny be the road,
It leads thee home, apace, to God;
Then count thy present trials small,
For heaven will make amends for all.

## 240

PILGRIMS on the burning sand,
 Look away, yes, look away;
Yonder is the promised land,
 Look, look away.
Jesus bids his followers come,
There you'll find a happy home.

*Look away, look away,*
*Look for the promised land.*

2 If the way seems dark and drear,
 Look away, yes, look away;
Jesus calls thee, never fear,
 Look, look away.
By the eye of faith you'll see
Mansions there prepared for thee.

3ᵃ Should your lot be hard to bear,
 Look away, yes, look away;
Jesus will your burdens share,
 Look, look away.
With each trial grace is given,
Grace which points thee up to heav'n.

4 When the tempest's most severe,
 Look away, yes, look away;

Jesus comes thy heart to cheer,
 Look, look away.
Pearly gates you'll soon behold,
Streets all paved with shining gold.

## 241

SHALL we meet beyond the river,
 Where the surges ne'er shall roll,
Where in all the bright forever
 Sorrow ne'er shall press the soul?

* Shall we meet, shall we meet, shall we meet,*
* Shall we meet beyond the river,*
* Where the surges ne'er shall roll?*

2 Shall we meet in that blest harbor,
 When our stormy voyage is o'er;
Shall we meet and cast our anchor
 By the fair celestial shore?

3 Shall we meet in yonder city,
 Where the towers of crystal shine;
Where the walls are all of jasper,
 Built by workmanship divine?

4 Where the music of the ransomed
 Rolls its harmony around;
And creation swells the chorus
 With its sweet melodious sound.

5 Shall we meet with many a loved one,
 That was torn from our embrace?
Shall we listen to their voices,
 And behold them face to face?

6 Shall we meet with Christ our Saviour,
 When he comes to claim his own?
Shall we know his blessed favor,
 And sit down upon his throne?

## 242

BREAST the wave, Christian,
  When it is strongest;
Watch for day, Christian,
  When the night's longest.

*    Onward and upward*    •
*     Still be thy endeavor,*
*    The rest that remaineth*
*     Shall be forever.*

2 Fight the fight, Christian,
  Jesus is o'er thee;
Run the race, Christian,
  Heav'n is before thee.

3 Bear the cross, Christian,
  Follow thy Master;
Bright the crown, Christian,
  Haste thee on faster.

4 Lift the eye, Christian,
  Just as it closeth;
Raise the heart, Christian,
  Ere it reposeth.

## 243          *P. M.*

THERE is a land of pleasure,
  Where streams of joy forever roll,
'Tis there I have my treasure,
  And there I long to rest my soul.
Long darkness dwelt around me,
  With scarcely once a cheering ray;
But since my Saviour found me,
  A lamp has shone along my way.

2 My way is full of danger;
  But 'tis the path that leads to God:

Then, like a valiant soldier,
　I'll dauntless keep the heavenly road.
Now I must gird my sword on,
　My breast-plate, helmet, and my shield;
And fight the hosts of Satan,
　Until I reach the heavenly field.

3 I'm on my way to Canaan,
　Still guided by my Saviour's hand;
Oh come along, dear sinners,
　And see Immanuel's happy land:
To all who stay behind me,
　I bid a long, a long farewell;
Oh come, or you'll repent it
　When you do reach the gates of hell.

4 The vale of tears surrounds me,
　And Jordan's current rolls before;
Oh how I stand and tremble
　To hear the dismal waters roar!
Whose hand shall then support me,
　And keep my soul from sinking there?
From sinking down to darkness,
　And to the regions of despair?

5 The stream shall not affright me,
　Although 'tis deeper than the grave;
If Jesus will be with me,
　I'll calmly ride on Jordan's wave:
His word has calmed the ocean,
　His lamp has cheered the gloomy vale,
Oh may this friend be with me
　While through the gates of death I sail!

6 Then come, thou king of terrors,
　And with thy weapon lay me low—
I soon shall reach those regions
　Where everlasting pleasures flow.
Then, Christian, I must leave you,
　A few more days to suffer here;

Through grace I soon shall meet you,
My soul exults, I'm almost there.

7 Soon the archangel's trumpet
Shall shake the globe from pole to pole,
And all the wheels of nature
Shall in a moment cease to roll;
Then I shall see my Saviour,
With shining ranks of angels come
To execute his vengeance,
And take his faithful servants home.

## 244 *L. M.*

COME, ye that love the Lord indeed,
Who are from sin and bondage freed,
Submit to all the ways of God,
And walk the narrow happy road.

*We're all united, heart and hand,*
*Joined in one band completely;*
*We're marching through Immanuel's land,*
*Where the waters flow most sweetly.*

2 Great tribulation you shall meet,
But soon shall walk the golden street,
Though hell may rage and vent her spite,
Yet Christ will save his heart's delight.

3 That happy day will soon appear,
When Gabriel's trumpet you shall hear
Sound through the earth, and down to hell,
To call the nations great and small.

4 Behold the earth in burning flames,
The trumpet louder still proclaims:
The earth must hear and know her doom,
The day of separation's come.

5 Behold the righteous marching home,
And all the angels bid them come;

When Christ himself these words proclaims,
"Here are my saints, I know their names."

6 "Ye everlasting gates, fly wide,
Make ready to receive my bride;
Ye harps of heaven, sound aloud,
Here comes the purchase of my blood!"

7 In grandeur see the royal line
In glittering robes the sun outshine:
See saints and angels join in one,
And march in splendor to the throne.

8 They stand in wonder and look on,
They join in one eternal song,
The great Redeemer to admire,
While rapture sweeps the golden lyre.

9 They've fought the fight, their race is run,
Their joys are now in heaven begun;
Their tears are gone, their sorrows flee,
No more afflicted now, like me.

## 245          *4 lines 8s & 7s.*

WHITHER goest thou, pilgrim stranger,
Passing through this darksome vale?
Knowest thou not 'tis full of danger,
And will not thy courage fail?

*I'm bound for the kingdom,*
*Will you go to glory with me?*
*Hallelujah! praise ye the Lord!*

2 Pilgrim, thou dost justly call me,
Wandering o'er this waste so wide;
Yet no harm will e'er befall me,
While I'm blessed with such a guide.

3 Such a guide!—No guide attends thee,
Hence for thee my fears arise;

If some guardian power befriends thee,
    'Tis unseen by mortal eyes.

4 Yes, unseen—but still believe me,
    Such a guide my steps attends;
He'll in every strait relieve me—
    He from every harm defends.

5 Pilgrim! see that stream before thee,
    Darkly winding through the vale;
Should its deadly waves roll o'er thee,
    Would not then thy courage fail?

6 No: that stream has nothing frightful,
    To its brink my steps I bend;
There to plunge will be delightful,
    There my pilgrimage will end.

7 While I gazed—with speed surprising
    Down the stream she plunged from sight;
Gazing still, I saw her rising
    Like an angel, clothed with light.

## 246

CHRISTIAN! walk carefully—danger is near:
    Work out thy journey with trembling and
        fear;
Snares from without, and temptations within,
Seek to entice thee again into sin.

2 Christian! walk humbly—exult not in pride;
All that thou hast is by Jesus supplied;
He holdeth thee up, he directeth thy ways,
To him be the glory—to him be the praise.

3 Christian! walk cheerfully, though the dark
        storm
Fill the bright sky with the clouds of alarm:
Soon will the clouds and the tempest be past,
And thou shalt dwell with thy Saviour at last.

16

4 Christian! walk steadfastly, while it is light;
Swift are approaching the shades of the night:
All that thy Master hath bidden thee do,
Haste to perform, for the moments are few.

5 Christian! walk prayferfully—oft wilt thou fall,
If thou forget on thy Saviour to call:
Safe shalt thou walk through each trial and
care,
If thou art clad in the armor of prayer.

247                              P. M.

THE people called Christians how many
things they tell,
About the land of Canaan, where saints and
angels dwell;
But sin, that dreadful ocean, compasses them
around,
While its tide still divides them from Canaan's
happy ground.

2 Thousands have been impatient to find their
passage through,
And, with united vigor, have tried what they
could do;
But vessels built by human skill have never
sailed afar,
Till they're found, run aground, on some dreadful sandy bar.

3 The Gospel, it is launched into the deep at last;
Behold her sail suspended around her towering
mast;
Around her decks, in order, the joyful sailors
stand,
Crying, O! here we go to Immanuel's happy
land!

4 To those who are spectators, what sorrow must
ensue,

To have their old companions bid them a long
    adieu!
The pleasures of a paradise no longer them
    invite:
They may rail while we sail, but we'll soon be
    out of sight.

5 We're now on the wide ocean, we bid them all
    farewell,
But where we shall cast anchor no mortal
    tongue can tell:
About our future happiness there need be no
    debate,
While we ride on the tide, with our Captain
    and his Mate.

6 We're passengers united, with harmony and
    love!
The wind's all in our favor, how joyfully we
    move!
Though troubles may surround us, and raging
    billows roar,
We will sweep through the deep till we land
    on Canaan's shore.

## 248 *P. M.*

COME all ye wandering pilgrims dear
    That's bound for Canaan's land;
Take courage and fight valiantly,
    Stand forth with sword in hand.
Our Captain's gone before us,
    The Father's only Son;
Then pilgrims dear, pray do not fear,
    But let us follow on.

2 We've a dark and howling wilderness
    'Twixt this and Canaan's shore,
A land of droughts, and pits, and snares,
    Where hideous dangers roar.

But Jesus will attend us,
    And guard us in the way;
If enemies examine us,
    He'll teach us what to say.

3 "Good morning, brother traveller,
    Pray tell me what's your name;
And where is it you're going to,
    Also from whence you came?"
"My name it is Bold Pilgrim,
    To Canaan I am bound;
I'm from the howling wilderness,
    From that enchanted ground."

4 "Pray what is that upon your head,
    That shines so clear and bright?
Likewise the covering of your breast,
    That's dazzling to my sight?
What kind of shoes are those you wear,
    On which you boldly stand?
Likewise that shining instrument,
    You bear in your right hand?"

5 "'Tis glorious hope upon my head,
    And on my breast a shield;
With this bright sword I mean to fight
    Until I win the field;
My feet are shod with gospel peace,
    On which I boldly stand,
And I'm resolved to fight till death,
    And win fair Canaan's land."

6 "You'd better stay with me, Pilgrim,
    And give your journey o'er;
Your Captain, he is out of sight,
    His face you'll see no more:
My name it is Apollyon,
    This land belongs to me,
And for your arms and pilgrim dress
    I'll give it all to thee."

7 "Oh no!" says the bold pilgrim; "sir,
  Your offer I disdain;
For a glittering crown of glory bright
  I shortly shall obtain.
If I but hold out faithful
  To my dear Lord's command,
I jointly shall be heir with him
  In Canaan's happy land.

8 "'Tis true, indeed, I am not freed
  From enemies as yet;
But by the grace of God I stand,
  With them beneath my feet:
Now I rejoice with a loud voice
  In hope of victory:
And to God's grace I'll give the praise
  To all eternity."

## 249

TO see a pilgrim as he dies,
  With glory in his view,
To heaven he lifts his longing eyes,
  And bids the world adieu;
While friends are weeping all around,
  And loth to let him go,
He shouts with his expiring breath,
  And leaves them all below!

2 O Christians! are you ready now
  To cross the swelling flood?
On Canaan's happy shore behold,
  And see your smiling God:
The dazzling charms of that bright world
  Attract my soul above;
My tongue shall shout redeeming grace,
  When perfected in love.

3 Go on, my brethren in the Lord,
  I'm bound to meet you there;

Although we tread enchanted ground,
  Be bold, and never fear:
Fight on, fight on, ye valiant souls,
  (Your Captain is in view):
And when I gain fair Canaan's land,
  I hope to meet with you.

4 Salvation through our conquering King,
    Now let the echo fly;
  While they repeat the song above,
    Through armies in the sky.
  O Christians! help me praise the Lamb,
    Who died for you and me!
  We'll sing his praises as we go,
    And shout eternally.

5 Go on, my brethren in the Lord,
    Until we meet again,
  Perhaps in time, or as we rise
    Above the fiery main,
  We'll join the heavenly armies bright,
    In presence of the Lamb,
  And tune our harps and sing free grace,
    In love's eternal flame.

## 250                        *P. M.*

CEASE, fond nature, cease this clinging
  To the objects dear below;
Hark! the voice of angels singing
  Bids me leave this vale of wo.

2 Stream of death, I'll soon be o'er thee—
    Soon I'll cross thy heaving flood:
  Jesus passed this sea before me,
    Lo! the waves are tinged with blood.

3 Blood divine! its power assuaging
    Lulls the foaming sea to sleep—
  Calms its surging, soothes its raging,
    Holds enchained the mighty deep.

4 Safely I will ride its billow,
  Safely reach the other shore;
Jesus' breast will be my pillow,
  While I pass its dangers o'er.

5 Jesus in the vessel with me:
  What can harm, or what assail?
Arms of love around, beneath me—
  Screened from all the powers of hell.

6 Hallelujah! homeward speeding;
  Friends behind, adieu, adieu:
Follow ye the Spirit's leading:
  Homeward ye are tending too.

## 251 *P. M.*

CHILD of sorrow, child of care,
  Wouldst thou learn thy griefs to bear,
And escape from every snare,
  Trust in God alone!
Human strength is weak and vain,
Let not sin its power gain;
Humbly ask, and help obtain
  From thy Father's throne.

2 Knowest thou not this vale of tears,
Gloomy doubts, distracting fears?
Painful months and sorrowing years?
  To the Saviour fly!
He that drank the bitter cup,
Bids thee in his mercy hope;
Let thy prayer be lifted up
  To the throne on high.

## 252 *10s & 11s.*

THOUGH troubles assail, and dangers affright,
  Though friends should all fail, and foes all
    unite,
Yet one thing secures us, whatever betide,
The promise assures us, The Lord will provide.

2 The birds, without barn or storehouse, are fed;
From them let us learn to trust for our bread:
His saints what is fitting shall ne'er be denied,
So long as 'tis written, The Lord will provide.

3 We all may, like ships, by tempests be tossed
On perilous deeps, but need not be lost;
Though Satan enrages the wind and the tide,
Yet Scripture engages, The Lord will provide.

4 His call we obey, like Abrah'm of old:
We know not the way, but faith makes us bold;
For though we are strangers, we have a sure
    guide,
And trust in all dangers, The Lord will provide.

5 When Satan appears to stop up our path,
And fills us with fears, we triumph by faith,
He cannot take from us (though oft he has
    tried)
The heart-cheering promise, The Lord will
    provide.

6 He tells us we're weak, our hope is in vain,
The good that we seek we ne'er shall obtain:
But when such suggestions, our graces have
    tried,
This answers all questions, The Lord will pro-
    vide.

7 No strength of our own, nor goodness we claim:
Our trust is all thrown on Jesus' name;
In this our strong tower for safety we hide:
The Lord is our tower, The Lord will provide.

8 When life sinks apace, and death is in view,
The word of his grace shall comfort us through:
Not fearing or doubting, with Christ on our
    side,
We hope to die shouting, The Lord will provide.

253 *P. M.*

DARK and thorny is the desert
  Through which pilgrims make their way;
Yet beyond this vale of sorrow,
  Lie the fields of endless day;
Fiends loud howling through the desert,
  Make them tremble as they go,
And the fiery darts of Satan
  Often bring their courage low.

2 O young soldiers, are you weary
  Of the roughness of the way?
Does your strength begin to fail you,
  And your vigor to decay?
Jesus, Jesus, will go with you,
  He will lead you to his throne,
He who dyed his garments for you,
  And the wine-press trod alone.

3 He whose thunder shakes creation,
  He who bids the planets roll;
He who rides upon the tempest,
  And whose sceptre sways the whole;
Round him are ten thousand angels,
  Ready to obey command,
They are always hov'ring round you,
  Till you reach the heav'nly land.

4 There on flow'ry hills of pleasure,
  Lie the fields of endless rest;
Love and joy, and peace forever
  Reign and triumph in your breast:
Who can paint the scenes of glory,
  Where the ransomed dwell on high;
They on golden harps forever
  Sound redemption through the sky.

5 Millions there of flaming seraphs
  Fly across the heav'nly plain,

There they sing immortal praises,
　Glory, glory is their strain.
But methinks a sweeter concert
　Makes the heavenly arches ring,
And the song is heard in Zion,
　Which the angels cannot sing.

6 O their crowns! how bright they sparkle,
　Such as monarchs never wore;
They are gone to richer pastures,
　Jesus is their shepherd there.
Hail! ye happy, happy spirits,
　Death no more shall make you fear,
Grief or sorrow, pain or anguish,
　Shall no more distress you there.

## 254

THE road that many travel
　Is not the road for me;
It leads to death and sorrow,
　In it I would not be.
But there's a road that leads to God,
It's marked by Christ's most precious blood.

　　　*The passage here is free,*
　　　*Oh, that's the road for me, &c.*

2 The pearl that worldlings covet
　Is not the pearl for me;
Its beauty fades as quickly
　As sunshine on the sea.
But there's a pearl sought by the wise,
It's called the pearl of greatest price.

　　　*Though few its value see,*
　　　*Oh, that's the pearl for me, &c.*

3 The hope that sinners cherish
　Is not the hope for me;

Most surely will they perish,
  Unless from sin made free.
But there's a hope that's fixed in God,
It leads the soul to keep his word.

      *And sinful pleasures flee,*
      *Oh, that's the hope for me, &c.*

4 The crown that decks the monarch
  Is not the crown for me;
It dazzles but a moment,
  Its brightness soon will flee.
But there's a crown prepared above
For those who walk in humble love.

      *Forever bright 'twill be,*
      *Oh, that's the crown for me, &c.*

## 255

FIRMLY, brethren, firmly stand,
  All united, heart and hand,
One unbroken, valiant band,
  Dauntless, brave, and true.

      *Die in the field of battle,*
      *Die in the field of battle,*
      *Die in the field of battle,*
      *Glory in your view.*

2 Lift your standard, lift it high,
  Raise the Christian battle-cry,
Christ, your glorious leader, nigh,
  Calls aloud to you.

3 Once our father freemen cried,
  "Victory *or* death" betide;
But with Jesus on our side,
  Death *and* vict'ry too.

4 There to die, the battle won,
  There to fall, the warfare done,

Glory brighter than the sun,
　　Then our promised due.

5 Glorious thus for Christ to die,
　And with Christ to reign on high;
　There with victor hosts to cry,
　　Christ hath brought us through.

6 Christ, our Captain's name, we boast,
　Quells the dark Satanic host;
　Fall we then, each at his post—
　　Fall as Christians do.

**256** From "GOLDEN CHAIN."
[By permission of W. B. BRADBURY.]

THE gospel ship is sailing,
　　Sailing, sailing,
The gospel ship is sailing,
　Bound for Canaan's happy shore;
All who would ship for glory,
　　Glory, glory,
All who would ship for glory,
　Come and welcome, rich and poor.

　　*Glory, hallelujah!*
　　　*All on board are sweetly singing,*
　　*Glory, hallelujah,*
　　　*Hallelujah to the Lamb!*

2 She has landed many thousands,
　　Thousands, thousands,
She has landed many thousands,
　On fair Canaan's happy shore;
And thousands now are sailing,
　　Sailing, sailing,
And thousands now are sailing,
　Yet there's room for thousands more.

3 Sails filled with heavenly breezes,
　　Breezes, breezes,
Sails filled with heavenly breezes,

Swiftly glides the ship along;
Her company are singing,
   Singing, singing,
Her company are singing,
  Glory, glory is their song.

4 Take passage now for glory,
   Glory, glory,
Take passage now for glory,
  Sailing o'er life's troubled sea;
With us you shall be happy,
   Happy, happy,
With us you shall be happy,
  Happy through eternity.

## 257

HERE o'er the earth as a stranger I roam;
  Here is no rest—is no rest;
Here as a pilgrim I wander alone,
  Yet I am blest—I am blest,
For I look forward to that glorious day,
When sin and sorrow shall vanish away,
My heart doth leap while I hear Jesus say,
  There, there is rest—there is rest.

2 Here fierce temptations beset me around;
  Here is no rest—is no rest;
Here I am grieved while my foes me surround,
  Yet I am blest—I am blest:
Let them revile me and scoff at my name,
Laugh at my weeping, endeavor to shame,
I will go forward, for this is my theme,
  There, there is rest—there is rest.

3 Here are afflictions and trials severe,
  Here is no rest—is no rest;
Here I must part with the friends I hold dear,
  Yet I am blest—I am blest:

Sweet is the promise I read in his word,
Blessed are they who have died in the Lord;
They have been called to receive their reward,
  There, there is rest—there is rest.

4 This world of care is a wilderness state,
      Here is no rest—is no rest;
  Here I must bear from the world all its hate,
      Yet I am blest—I am blest;
  Soon shall I be from the wicked released,
  Soon shall the weary forever be blest,
  Soon shall I lean upon Jesus' breast,
      There, there is rest—there is rest.

## 258

WHEN for eternal worlds I steer,
  And seas are calm and skies are clear,
And faith in lively exercise,
And distant hills of Canaan rise,
My soul for joy then claps her wings,
And loud her lovely sonnet sings,
      I'm going home.

2. With cheerful heart her eyes explore
  Each landmark on the distant shore,
  The tree of life, the pastures green,
  The pearly gates, the crystal stream,
  Again for joy she claps her wings,
  And loud her lovely sonnet sings,
      I'm almost home.

3 The nearer still she draws to land,
  Each moment all her powers expand;
  With steady helm and free bent sail,
  Her anchor drops within the veil,
  With holy joy she folds her wings,
  And her celestial sonnet sings,
      I'm safe at home.

**259** From "GOLDEN CHAIN."
[By permission of W. B. BRADBURY.]

THE soldiers are gathering from near and
    from far,
The trumpet is sounding the call for the war,
The conflict is raging, 'twill be fearful and long,
We'll gird on our armor and be marching along.

*Marching along, we are marching along,*
*Gird on the armor and be marching along,*
*The conflict is raging, 'twill be fearful and long,*
*Then gird on the armor and be marching along.*

2 The foe is before us in battle array,
But let us not waver nor turn from the way,
The Lord is our strength, be this ever our song,
With courage and faith we are marching along.

3 We've 'listed for life, and will camp on the field,
With Christ as our Captain we never will yield;
The "sword of the Spirit" both trusty and strong,
We'll hold in our hands as we're marching along.

4 Through conflicts and trials our crowns we must
    win,
For here we contend against temptation and sin;
But one thing assures us, we cannot go wrong
If trusting our Saviour while marching along.

**260** *P. M.*

I'M on my way to Canaan,
    I bid this world farewell;
Come on, my old companions,
    In spite of earth or hell.
Lo! Satan's army rages,
    And all his hosts combine!
Yet Scripture doth engage us,
    The strength of grace divine.

2 I'll blow the silver trumpet,
    And on the nations call;
 For Christ hath me commissioned
    To say he died for all.
Come try his grace, and prove him,
    You shall the gift obtain; .
He will not send you empty,
    Nor let you come in vain.

3 And if you want a witness,
    Here are some just at hand,
Who've lately felt the sweetness
    Now flowing from that land:
It comes in copious showers,
    Our bodies can't contain;
It fills our ransomed powers—
    And now we drink again!

4 The glories of that kingdom
    My soul cannot describe;
I feel it is within me,
    I feel the blood applied.
Oh, come unto the Saviour's arms,
    And you shall feel his love,
'Tis sweeter than all other charms,
    It comes from heaven above.

5 The glories of that heavenly place
    I've ofttimes felt before.
But what I've felt is but a taste,
    Which makes me long for more.
Had l the pinions of a dove,
    I'd fly and be at rest;
Then would I soar to worlds above,
    And be forever blest.

6 My soul looks up, and sees him smile,
    And then the blessing send,   .
And I am thinking all the while,
    When will this journey end?

I contemplate it can't be long
  Till he will come again,
Then I shall join the heav'nly throng,
  And in his kingdom reign.

7 Oh, could I join that heavenly throng,
  And ne'er return again,
I would not think the season long
  That I had suffered pain;
When Zion's sons are marching home
  Along the heavenly street,
Then I would march along with them,
  And bow before his feet.

8 The tallest of those heav'nly ones
  Would fail for to describe
The brightness which the Saviour puts
  Upon his lovely bride.
Ten thousand years around may roll,
  We have but just begun
To wear our robes and glitt'ring crowns,
  Bright shining as the sun.

## 261 *P. M.*

TO heaven I'm bound with prosperous gales,
  My bark by grace doth safely steer,
And going under Gospel sails,
  Celestial prospects bright appear.
To sound her ground my faith now springs,
And to her *Author* thus she sings,
    " *Thy will be done.*"

2 As bearing up to gain the port,
  A blood-stained cross and heav'n in view,
A Saviour's wounds my harbor—fort—
  The beacon—to my vessel true;
Again my faith her soundings tries,
And to my soul's sure pilot cries,
    "A blessed hope."

17

3 Now as the blissful shore draws near,
   With transports I behold the place
Where dwells my friend, my Saviour dear,
   And long with joy to see his face.
Once more my faith now tries her ground,
And thus re-echoes back the sound,
      "Christ is my rock."

4 When to her berth my bark draws nigh,
   And I have done with sails and tide,
"Strong is my cable," then I'll cry,
   My Anchor's sure—I safely ride;
No more my soul need try her ground,
Safe at her moorings she is found,
      And "all is well."

## 262      *P. M.*

IN the floods of tribulation,
   While the billows o'er me roll,
Jesus whispers consolation,
   And supports my fainting soul;
      Sweet affliction,
   That brings Jesus to my soul.

2 Thus the lion yields me honey,
   From the eater food is given;
Strengthened thus I still press forward,
   Singing as I wade to heaven,
      Sweet affliction,
   And my sins are all forgiven.

3 So, in darkest dispensations,
   Doth my faithful Lord appear
With his richest consolations,
   To re-animate and cheer:
      Sweet affliction,
   Thus to bring my Saviour near.

4 Floods of tribulation heighten,
    Billows still around me roar;
Those who know not Christ they frighten,
    But my soul defies their power:
       Sweet affliction,
    Thus to bring my Saviour near.

5 In the sacred page recorded,
    Thus his word securely stands;
"Fear not, I'm in trouble near thee,
    Naught shall pluck thee from my hands."
       Sweet affliction,
    Every word my love demands.

6 All I meet I find assists me
    In my path to heavenly joy,
Where, though trials now attend me,
    Trials never more annoy;
       Sweet affliction,
    Every promise gives me joy.

7 Wearing there a weight of glory,
    Still the path I'll ne'er forget,
But exulting cry, it led me
    To my blessed Saviour's feet:
       Sweet affliction,
    Which has brought me to his feet.

**263**        *P. M.*

WHY should I be affrighted at pestilence or
    war,
The fiercer be the tempest, the sooner it is o'er;
With Jesus in the vessel, the billows rise in
    vain,
They only will convey me to yon elysian plain.

2 This is a land of dangers, and foes they press
    me hard,
But Jesus he has promised that he will be my
    guard,

Then I shall not be tempted above what I can
 bear,
When fighting's done, escorted his kingdom
 then to share.

3 Although my flesh is mortal, immortal is my
 hope;
I'll try, like holy Moses, to gain the mountain
 top.
There, at Jehovah's bidding, with cheerfulness
 to die—
And then ascend to heaven to reign above the
 sky.

4 From him I have my orders, and while I do
 obey,
I find his Holy Spirit illuminates my way,
The way is so delightful I wish to travel on,
Till I am called away to receive a starry crown.

5 I feel that Jesus loves me, but why, I do not
 know,
To him I'm so unfaithful in what I have to do,
I grieve to see my failings, but he does all
 forgive,
Which makes me love him more, and by faith
 in him I live.

6 Though sinners do despise me, and laugh at
 what I say,
I find a little number walk with me in the way,
Come on, come on, my brethren, they laugh at
 Jesus too,
The crown appears before me, and heaven is in
 my view.

7 We soon shall gain fair Canaan, and on that
 happy shore,
Beyond the reach of sorrow, we'll shout for
 evermore;

There walk the golden pavement, and blood-
  washed garments wear,
And to increase our pleasure, our Jesus will be
  there.

## 264

I AM weary of straying—O fain would I rest
  In the far distant land of the pure and the
  blest,
Where sin can no longer her blandishments
  spread,
And tears and temptations forever are fled.

2 I am weary of hoping where hope is untrue;
As fair but as fleeting as morning's bright dew,
I long for that land whose blest promise alone
Is changeless and sure as eternity's throne.

3 I am weary of sighing o'er sorrows of earth,
O'er joy's glowing visions, that fade at their
  birth,
O'er the pangs of the loved, which we cannot
  assuage,
O'er the blightings of youth and the weakness
  of age.

4 I am weary of loving what passes away;
The sweetest, the dearest, alas, may not stay!
I long for that land where those partings are
  o'er,
And death and the tomb can divide hearts no
  more.

5 I am weary, my Saviour, of grieving thy love;
Oh, when shall I rest in thy presence above!
I am weary—but oh, never let me repine,
While thy word, and thy love, and thy promise
  are mine.

## 265　　　　*L. M.*

THE billows swell, the winds are high,
Clouds overcast my wintry sky;
Out of the depths to thee I call,
My fears are great, my strength is small.

2 O Lord, the pilot's part perform,
And guide and guard me through the storm;
Defend me through each threat'ning ill,
Control the waves, say, " Peace, be still."

3 Amidst the roaring of the sea,
My soul still hangs her hope on thee;
Thy constant love, thy faithful care,
Is all that saves me from despair.

4 Dangers of every shape and name
Attend the followers of the Lamb,
Who leave the world's deceitful shore,
And leave it to return no more.

5 Though tempest tossed and half a wreck,
My Saviour through the floods I seek;
Let neither winds nor stormy main
Force back my shattered bark again.

## 266

I AM a stranger here, heaven is my home,
Earth is a desert drear, heaven is my home;
Dangers and sorrows stand
Round me on every hand;
Heaven is my Father's land, heaven is my
home.

*Oh ! Hallelujah, glory, Hallelujah,*
*Oh ! Hallelujah, heaven is my home.*

2 What tho' the tempest rage, heaven is my home,
Short is my pilgrimage, heaven is my home,

For life's wild, wintry blast
Soon will be overpast.
I shall reach home at last, heaven is my home.

3 There at my Saviour's side, heaven is my home,
I shall be glorified, heaven is my home;
There are the good and blest,
Those I loved most and best,
And there I soon shall rest, heaven is my home.

4 Therefore I murmur not, heaven is my home,
Whate'er my earthly lot, heaven is my home,
For I shall surely stand
There at my Lord's right hand,
Heaven is my Father's land, heaven is my
home.

## 267

WE are pilgrims robed and ready,
Zion's pilgrims, Zion bound;
Earth affords no sure abiding;
Rest is found on Canaan's ground.

*Zion's pilgrims, robed and ready,*
*Pilgrims for the father land;*
*Soon with all the saved forever*
*By the throne we'll joyous stand.*

2 We are pilgrims robed and ready,
All arrayed by Christ our Lord;
Washed in God's all cleansing fountain,
We are kept by his sure word.

3 We are pilgrims robed and ready,
Ready for the cross or crown,
Ready now to do or suffer,
Ready for the saints' dear home.

4 We are pilgrims robed and ready,
Robed for all the journey through,

Robed for toiling or for glory
That awaits the pilgrim true.

5 We are pilgrims, though the Master
May have burdens we should bear;
Crowns will only be the brighter;
Higher glory we shall share.

6 We are pilgrims robed and ready,
Duty's call our great delight,
Cheering saints and winning sinners,
Till we gain the mansions bright.

7 We are pilgrims robed and ready;
Through the valley we'll press on,
Till the Master cries, "'Tis finished!
All thy work is done, well done."

# 268

I'M travelling through the wilderness,
I'm oft assailed by sore temptation;
In the world I find no peace,
But in Christ, sweet consolation.
When first for heaven I set out,
I thought the road was fair and even;
Sweet peace I had, and not a doubt
But that my sins were all forgiven.

2 I did not think that I so soon
Should meet with trials so afflicting,
That I should be so soon cast down,
By flesh and spirit so conflicting;
I soon found out, if I would gain-
Eternal life and joy forever,
If I would with my Saviour reign,
I must lay down my armor never.

3 I asked old soldiers in the way,
If they had been so troubled ever!

Oh yes, we often have, said they,
    But Christ as often did deliver;
So put you the whole armor on,
    And fight against the sore temptation,
And watch, and pray, and follow Christ,
    The corner-stone of your foundation.

4 I then resolved I would go up
    And gain the land beyond the river;
No more on this side Jordan stop,
    But trust in Jesus to deliver.
I'm sometimes in the valley low,
    I'm sometimes high upon the mountain,
I often travel very slow,
    Until I reach some cooling fountain.

# 269

IN seasons of grief, to my God I'll repair,
    When my heart is o'erwhelméd with sorrow
        and care;
From the ends of the earth unto thee will I cry,
Lead me to the Rock that is higher than I.

2 When Satan, my foe, comes in like a flood,
To drive my poor soul from the fountain of good,
I'll pray to the Saviour who kindly did die,
Lead me to the Rock that is higher than I.

3 And when I have ended my pilgrimage here,
In Jesus' pure righteousness let me appear,
In the swellings of Jordan on thee I'll rely,
And look to the Rock that is higher than I.

4 And when the last trumpet shall sound through
       the skies,
When the dead from the dust of the earth shall
       arise,
With millions I'll join, far above yonder sky,
To praise the dear Rock that is higher than I.

5 When my soul is distressed, and my comforts
    are flown,
To my Saviour I'll go, and my sorrows make
    known;
In secret devotion, to him will I cry,
Lead me to the Rock that is higher than I.

6 Though my friends may forsake me, and foes
    all unite
To hedge up my pathway, and fears to excite,
On the strength of Jehovah I'll firmly rely,
Still screened by the Rock that is higher than I.

7 Should sickness o'ertake me, and pain be severe,
And none be about me my spirit to cheer;
I'll hang on my Saviour until I shall die,
Sustained by the Rock that is higher than I.

8 And when I have finished my labor and care,
Bright angels my soul on their pinions shall
    bear,
To my home in the kingdom of glory on high,
To dwell by the Rock that is higher than I.

**270**          *S. M.*

WAKE, Christian soldiers, wake;
    Prepare for glorious strife;
Your heavenly armor quickly take,
    Contend for endless life.

2 Rally round the cross,
    Lift up your faithful eye,
And hail the symbol of your cause—
    Your banner in the sky.

3 By this invincible,
    Victoriously withstand
The legions from the gates of hell—
    Apollyon's veteran band.

4 Well trained to war are they,
     And fight with wild despair:
   To arms! to arms! and win the day,
     And drive them to their lair.

5 Your captain leads the van;
     Hark to his cheering words!
   Yours is the cause of God and man:
     Salvation is the Lord's.

6 Be firm, be bold, be true,
     Nor ever fly the field;
   Your God will bring you conquerors through:
     Your enemies must yield.

7 Your armor comes from heaven,
     To heaven it clears the way;
   And brighter crowns shall there be given,
     And palms of victory.

8 Courage, ye blood-washed host;
     Look to the Lord alone;
   And soon eternal triumphs boast,
     Through God's eternal Son.

## 271                    *L. M.*

I'VE listed in the holy war,
       *Sing glory, glory, hallelujah.*
Content to suffer soldiers' fare;
       *Sing glory, glory, hallelujah.*
The banner over me is love,
       *Sing glory, glory, hallelujah.*
I draw my rations from above,
       *Sing glory, glory, hallelujah.*

2 I've fought through many a battle sore,
   And I must fight through many more;
   I'll take my breastplate, sword, and shield,
   And boldly march into the field.

3 I've listed, and I mean to fight,
  Till all my foes are put to flight;
  And when the victory I have won,
  I'll give the praise to God alone.

4 Come, Christian heroes, go with me;
  Come, face the foe, and never flee;
  The heavenly battle is begun,
  Come, take the field and wear the crown.

5 With 'listing orders I am come—
  Come rich, come poor, come old and young;
  Here's bounty money Christ has given,
  And glorious crowns laid up in heaven.

6 Our General he is gone before,
  And you may draw on grace's store;
  But if you will not 'list and fight,
  You'll sink into eternal night.

**272**                        *P. M.*

WHEN I set out for glory,
    I left the world behind,
Determined for a city,
    That's out of sight, to find.
      *And to glory I will go—*
      *And to glory I will go—I'll go, I'll go,*
      *And to glory I will go.*

2 I left my worldly honor—
    I left my worldly fame—
  I left my young companions,
    And with them my good name.

3 Some said I'd better tarry—
    They thought I was too young
  For to prepare for dying,
    But that was all my theme.

4 Come, all my loving brethren,
    And listen to my cry;

All you that are backsliders
Must shortly beg or die.

*And to begging I will go—*
*And to begging I will go—will go, will go,*
*And to begging I will go.*

5 The Lord he loves the beggar,
Who truly begs indeed;
He always will relieve him
Whene'er he stands in need.

6 I do not beg for riches,
Nor to be dressed fine:
The garment Jesus gives me,
The sun it will outshine.

7 I'm not ashamed to beg
While here on earth I stay;
I'm not ashamed to watch—
And I'm not ashamed to pray.

8 The richest man I ever saw
Was one that begged the most;
His soul was filled with Jesus,
And with the Holy Ghost.

9 And now we are encouraged,
Come let us travel on,
Until we join the angels,
And sing the holy song.

## 273

TUNE—*On, on the boys are marching.*

HERE we meet to part,
For our meetings they are short,
But there we will meet to part no more;
In that world that's free from sin,
With our Saviour we shall sing,
When we meet on Canaan's happy, happy
shore.

*On, on, on, ye saints, go marching,*
  *Soon your Saviour's face you'll see;*
*And you'll wear a starry crown,*
*By your Father's side sit down,*
  *In the land where the pilgrims are set free.*

2 Here we're tossed about
With many a fear and doubt,
  But there a fear can never enter in;
But on Canaan's happy shore
We'll rejoice forevermore,
  As we march around the New Jerusalem.

3 Then let us courage take
For our dear Redeemer's sake,
  And gird the glorious gospel armor on;
Let us not give up the field
Until every foe shall yield,
  Then we'll sing, "The glorious victory is
    won."

**274**                    *P. M.*

IN time of tribulation,
  Hear, Lord, my feeble cries;
With humble supplication,
  To thee my spirit flies;
My heart with grief is breaking,
  Scarce can my voice complain;
Mine eyes with tears kept waking,
  Still watch and weep in vain.

2 The days of old, in vision,
  Bring vanished bliss to view;
The years of lost fruition
  Their joys in pangs renew:
Remembered songs of gladness,
  Through night's lone silence brought;
Strike notes of deeper sadness,
  And stir desponding thought.

3 Hath God cast off forever?
  Can time his truth impair?
His tender mercy never
  Shall I presume to share?
Hath he his loving-kindness
  Shut up in endless wrath?
No;—this is mine own blindness,
  That cannot see his path.

4 I call to recollection
  The years of his right hand;
And, strong in his protection,
  Again through faith I stand;
Thy deeds, O Lord, are wonder;
  Holy are all thy ways;
The secret place of thunder
  Shall utter forth thy praise.

5 Thee, with the tribes assembled,
  O God, the billows saw!
They saw thee, and they trembled,
  Turned, and stood still, with awe;
The clouds shot hail—they lightened;
  The earth reeled to and fro;
The fiery pillar brightened
  The gulf of gloom below.

6 Thy way is in great waters,
  Thy footsteps are not known;
Let Adam's sons and daughters
  Confide in thee alone:
Through the wild sea thou leddest
  Thy chosen flocks of yore;
Still on the waves thou treadest,
  And thy redeemed pass o'er.

# 275

YE soldiers of the cross, in the army of the
  Lord;
March to the city of the new Jerusalem;

Jesus is your Captain, he's given you the word,
To press with vigor on.

*Glory, glory hallelujah !*
*Glory, glory hallelujah !*
*Glory, glory hallelujah !*
*Jesus leads us on.*

2 Gird on the gospel armor, the battle ne'er give
o'er;
March till the pearly.gates of heaven do appear;
Rest not by the way till you've gained that
blissful shore,
Where your great Captain's gone.

3 Oh, watch, and fight, and pray, ever keep your
armor bright;
March on in duty to that glorious world of
. light;
There in crowns of splendor and beauteous
robes of white,
You'll shout the victory.

4 Ne'er think the victory won, nor lay the armor
down;
Fight on in faith till you get a starry crown;
When the war is over, and the battle you have
won,
Jesus will say, Well done!

# 276

I AM a poor wayfaring stranger,
A journeying through this world of wo,
Through sickness, sorrow, toil, and danger,
To that bright world to which I go.

*I am going there to see my mother,*
*I'm going there no more to roam,*
*I'm just going over Jordan,*
*I'm just going over home.*

2 I know dark clouds may gather round me ;
   I know my path is rough and steep ;
But beauteous fields lie just before me,
   Where God's redeemed their vigils keep.

> *I'm going there to see my father,*
>    *I'm going there no more to roam,*
> *I'm just going over Jordan,*
>    *I'm just going over home.*

3 I want to sing salvation's story
   In concert with the blood-washed band ;
I want to wear a crown of glory
   When I get home to that good land.

> *I'm going there to see my children,*
>    *I know they are near my Father's throne ;*
> *I'm just going over Jordan,*
>    *I'm just going over home.*

4 I feel my sins are all forgiven ;
   My thoughts are fixed on things above ;
I'm going away to that bright heaven
   Where all is joy, and peace, and love.

> *I'm going there to see my classmates,*
>    *They have gone before me one by one,*
> *I'm just going over Jordan,*
>    *I'm just going over home.*

5 I'll soon be free from every trial ;
   My body will sleep in the old church-yard ;
I'll drop the cross of self-denial,
   And enter on my great reward.

> *I'm going there to see my Saviour,*
>    *I'm going there no more to roam ;*
> *I'm just going over Jordan,*
>    *I'm just going over home.*

**277**          *P. M.*

LUKEWARM souls, the foe grows stronger,
   See what hosts your camp surround—

Arm to battle, lag no longer,
  Hark! the silver trumpets sound!
Wake, ye sleepers, wake! what mean you?
  Sin besets you round about;
Up and search, the world's within you,
  .Slay, or chase the traitor out.

2 What enchants you, sloth or pleasure?
  Pluck right eyes—with right hands part!
Ask your conscience, where's your treasure?
  For be certain, there's your heart:
Give the fawning foe no credit,
  See the bloody flag unfurled;
That base heart, the truth hath said it,
  Loves not God that loves the world.

3 God and mammon! Oh, be wiser!
  Serve them both! it cannot be;
Ease and warfare, saint and miser,
  These can never well agree:
Shun the shame of basely falling,
  Cumbered captives, clogged with clay,
Prove your faith, make sure your calling,
  Wield the sword, and win the day.

4 Onward press toward perfection,
  Watch and pray, and all things prove;
Seek to know your own election,
  Set your hearts on things above:
Shun backsliding, scorn dissembling,
  Lo! salvation's near in view!
Work it out with fear and trembling;
  'Tis your God that works in you.

**278**                     *P. M.*

YE soldiers of Jesus, pray stand to your arms,
  Prepare for the battle, the gospel alarms,
The trumpets are sounding, come soldiers and
    see
The standard and colors of sweet liberty.

2 Though Satan's black trumpet is .sounding so
  near,
 Take courage, brave soldiers, his armies we
  dare:
 In the strength of King Jesus we dare him to
  fight,
 We'll put his black armies of aliens to flight.

3 In the mount of salvation, in Christ's armory,
 There's swords, shields, and breast-plates, and
  helmets for thee;
 Be not faint-heart, though he roars like a flood,
 He'll not stand before the bright armies of God.

4 To battle, to battle, the trumpets doth sound;
 The watchmen are crying fair Zion around:
 The signal for victory! hark! hark! from the
  sky;
 Shout, shout, ye brave armies, the watchmen
  all cry.

5 As the great Goliath, Apollyon shall fall;
 With the sword of the Spirit we'll conquer them
  all;
 We'll leave no opposers alive in the field,
 By the strength of Jehovah we'll force them to
  yield.

6 Through Jesus, our wisdom, we'll baffle his
  rage;
 My heart beats for conquest, come soldiers engage;
 The trumpets are sounding—the armies appear,
 We'll not leave one standing from front to the
  rear.

7 King Jesus is riding the white horse before,
 The watchmen close after, the trumpet doth
  roar;

Some shouting, some singing, salvation they
    cry ;
In the strength of King Jesus all hell we defy.

8 Fair Zion's a shouting to her conquering King,
  Salvation to Jesus, the armies doth sing :
  Apollyon we've conquered and sunk in the
    flood :
  Oh, who can withstand the bright armies of
    God ?

9 Behold all the armies are now marching home,
  God's trumpet is sounding, and bids them to
    come ;
  All Zion's fair armies together doth meet,
  And lay down their armor at Jesus feet.

10 The angelic army with Zion combines ;
  In robes of bright glory eternally shines ;
  All shouting and singing on Canaan's bright
    shore,
  Where wars and commotions can reach them
    no more.

11 Cheer up, ye dear pilgrims, the time's draw-
    ing nigh,
  When we shall meet Jesus' bright host in the
    sky,
  Our friends and relations in Jesus so dear,
  Both preachers and people shall then meet us
    there.

12 We'll join the bright harpers in anthems
    divine,
  Whose crowns with bright diamonds the sun
    doth outshine :
  To the praise of King Jesus we'll tune our
    harps then :
  Salvation and glory to Jesus, Amen.

**279**　　　　　　　*L. M.*

LIFT up your hearts, Immanuel's friends,
　　　　*Oh halle, halle, hallelujah,*
And taste the pleasure Jesus sends;
　　　　*Oh halle, halle, hallelujah.*
Let nothing cause you to delay,
　　　　*Oh halle, halle, hallelujah,*
But hasten on the good old way,
　　　　*Oh halle, halle, hallelujah.*

2 Our conflicts here, though great they be,
Shall not prevent our victory,
If we but strive, and watch, and pray,
Like soldiers in the good old way.

3 Oh, good old way! how sweet thou art!
May none of us from thee depart;
But may our actions always say
We're marching in the good old way.

4 Though Satan may his powers employ,
Our happiness for to destroy;
Yet never fear, we'll gain the day,
And shout and sing the good old way.

5 The good old way is safe by night;
No mortal foe our souls shall fright,
If all along throughout the day
We're walking in the good old way.

6 Ye valiant soldiers of the cross,
Who count all earthly things but loss;
Continue still to watch and pray,
And hasten on the good old way.

7 The pillar and the cloud before!
The watchmen cry, the trumpets roar!
Tall sons of Anak we will slay,
And shout along the good old way.

8 The promised land is just in view,
And I'm resolved to go with you:
Press on, my soul, and win the day
By running in the good old way.

9 Then when on Pisgah's top we stand,
And view by faith that happy land;
Our God will wipe all tears away,
When we have run the good old way.

10 Then far beyond this mortal shore,
We'll meet with those who're gone before,
And shout to think we've gained the day
By marching in the good old way.

## 280 *C. M.*

LET worldly minds the world pursue,
It has no charms for me;
Once I admired its trifles too,
But grace has set me free.

2 Its pleasures now no longer please,
No more content afford;
Far from my heart be joys like these,
Now I have known the Lord.

3 As by the light of opening day
The stars are all concealed,
So earthly pleasures fade away,
When Jesus is revealed.

4 Creatures no more divide my choice,
I bid them all depart;
His name, and love, and gracious voice
Have fixed my roving heart.

5 Now, Lord, I would be thine alone,
And wholly live to thee;
But may I hope that thou wilt own
A worthless worm like me!

**281** *P. M.*

YE children of Zion, who're aiming for glory,
Enlisted with Jesus to fight against hell,
New Canaan's bright borders are now just before
you,
Though Jordan's proud billows its banks over-
swell.
Ten thousands have crossed it, and are now in
glory,
A shouting and telling the triumphant story,
And Jesus our Saviour will bring us all over,
In the land of sweet Canaan forever to dwell.

2 This makes my heart joyful, it fills me with
pleasure,
That suff'ring and toiling will one day be o'er,
At the feet of my Saviour I'll there count my
treasure,
Where sin, pain, and sorrow can reach me no
more.
Be bold and courageous, and fear not the devil,
Though he should speak of you all manner of
evil,
For tho' Satan rages, yet Jesus engages
To bring us all shouting to Canaan's bright
shore.

3 Like ships on the ocean we're tossed by com-
motion,
But Christ is the pilot, and he's a sure guide;
If sick and afflicted, kind love has a lotion
Which flows in abundance from Jesus' side.
Though Satan's wild whirlwinds like deluges
roaring,
And floods of temptation as hail are down
pouring,
Though devils should haunt you, yet let them
not daunt you,
For Jesus rules over the wind and the tide.

4 I feel his love blazing, my spirits are rising,
  Had I angels' pinions, away I would go,
And see that bright city, and hear angels
      praising,
  And all the enjoyment of glory to know.
.To our great Father, that shines throughout
      heaven,
  All glory from saints and from angels be given;
My heart's all on fire, my Jesus draws nigher,
  His love, like an ocean, all through me doth
      flow.

5 His love so constrains me, this earth can't con-
      tain me,
  My soul is so joyful, I'm filled with new wine,
'Tis grace that supports me, and glory awaits
      me,
  While beams from sweet heaven all round
      me do shine.
Bright angels attend me where'er I am going,
Sweet Jesus directs me, whatever I'm doing;
A subject of wonder, on which angels ponder,
  That beggars are raised to a life so divine.

## 282        *6s & 8s.*

JESUS, at thy command
  I launch into the deep,
And leave my native land,
  Where sin lulls all asleep:
For thee I fain would all resign,
And sail to heaven with thee and thine.

2 What though the seas are broad?
  What though the waves are strong?
What though tempestuous winds
  Distress me all along?
Yet what are seas or stormy wind
Compared to Christ, the sinner's friend?

3 Christ is my pilot wise,
  My compass is his word;
My soul each storm defies,
  While I have such a Lord:
I trust his faithfulness and power
To save me in the trying hour.

4 Though rocks and quicksands deep
  Through all my passage lie,
Yet Christ will safely keep
  And guide me with his eye!
How can I sink with such a prop,
That bears the world and all things up?

5 By faith I see the land,
  Haven of endless rest:
My soul, thy wings expand,
  And fly to Jesus' breast.
Oh, may I reach the heavenly shore,
Where winds and seas distress no more!

6 Whene'er becalmed I lie,
  And all my storms subside,
Then to my succor fly,
  And keep me near thy side;
For more the treacherous calm I dread
Than tempests bursting o'er my head.

7 Come, heavenly wind, and blow
  A prosperous gale of grace,
And waft me from below
  To heaven, my destined place;
Then in full sail my port I'll find,
And leave the world and sin behind.

**283** *P. M.*

YE sons of war, I pray, draw near,
  And 'list as generous volunteers,
Become our royal brothers here,
  I mean as valiant soldiers;

You'll enter into present pay,
And feasting live from day to day,
Turn right about and march away,
     And Jesus will support you.

2 Ye careless sons of Adam's race,
Who long have trod in folly's ways,
Oh, turn about to Zion's face,
     And meet Apollyon's forces;
Gird on your sword and glitt'ring shield,
And with your helmet take the field,
And fight your way and never yield,
     And Jesus will support you.

3 The bounty you shall have in hand,
If you will 'list in Jesus' band,
Your Captain in the front will stand,
     And beat your foes before you;
Come, throw your carnal weapons down,
And seek for honor and renown,
And you shall wear a starry crown,
     For Jesus will support you.

4 You long have been the slaves of sin,
With dire corruption deep within;
The Christian warfare now begin,
     And face Apollyon's forces;
The breast-plate take of righteousness,
Your feet be shod with gospel peace,
Be daily at the throne of grace,
     And Jesus will support you.

5 Desert the cause of Heaven's foe,
Before you plunge in endless wo;
Now courage take, to Jesus go,
     And he will now receive you;
From sin and Satan you'll get free,
And happy seasons you shall see,
And gain the Christian's liberty,
     For Jesus will support you.

6 No more in Satan's ranks appear,
But to our banner pray draw near,
We'll win the day, you need not fear,
Though earth and hell oppose us;
Our Captain he is always brave,
And able still his men to save,
He conquered death, hell, and the grave,
And he will still support you.

7 Let not sinners you affright,
Altho' they rage and vent their spite,
Wear but the Christian's armor right,
And none can stand before you;
Altho' your parents should oppose,
Your dearest friends become your foes,
Yet sweetly with the gospel close,
And Jesus will support you.

8 And when the war is at an end,
Our Captain still will be our friend,
We'll wing our way and up ascend,
To reign with him in glory;
Then shall our tears be wiped away,
Our night be turned to endless day,
And on our golden harps we'll play
The joyful song of heaven.

**284** *P. M.*

MY brethren all, on you I call,
Arise, and look around you,
How many foes, bound to oppose,
Are waiting to confound you;
The trumpet calls on Zion's walls—
Shake off your sleep and slumber;
Arise and pray, we'll win the day,
Though we are few in number.

2 To God we'll cry, and hell defy,
Though Satan roars like thunder;

The voice of prayer makes sinners stare,
　While filled with awe and wonder;
While music sweet makes some retreat,
　Our Jesus still draws nigher;
His precious name lights up the flame
　That sets our souls on fire.

3 While grace divine in others shines,
　With such we are delighted;
With them we crowd, and sing so loud,
　Poor sinners are affrighted.
The sweetest joys our powers employ,
　To see the cause advancing,
Though some go off, and boldly scoff,
　And say that we are dancing.

4 Some mournfully for mercy cry,
　And stubborn hearts are bended!
If we but smile, some say we're wild,
　And so go off offended;
· If souls are born, we'll bear the scorn,
　Let sinners tell this story;
For Jesus' name we'll bear the blame,
　And give him all the glory.

5 But as we fly, we'll always cry
　To God for their salvation—
O God of love, send from above,
　And save the wicked nation.
Thy Spirit send, their hearts to bend,
　Arrest them by thy thunder!
Let sweetest songs employ our tongues,
　While filled with joy and wonder.

6 The outward blaze sometimes decays,
　Some Christians seem contented;
The world is sure their work is o'er,
　They'll be no more tormented.
Some are afraid the Spirit's fled,
　While others are offended:

But never fear, let's persevere,
The warfare is not ended.

7 To men unknown, the seed is grown,
We've overcome temptation;
The cross we'll bear, and not despair,
We'll joy in tribulation.
The noisy scene comes on again!
The shouting trump is sounded!
We find at length we're gaining strength,
Our foes will be confounded.

## 285 *C. M.*

WHAT if our bark, o'er life's rough wave,
By adverse winds be driven,
And howling tempests round us rave—
There are no tears in heaven.

2 What though affliction be our lot,
Our hearts with anguish riven,
Still let it never be forgot—
There are no tears in heaven.

3 Our sweetest joys here banish all,
And fade like hues at even;
Our brightest hopes like meteors fall—
There are no tears in heaven.

4 The mourner sad, who, drowned in grief,
Hath long in sorrow striven,
Shall find at last a sweet relief—
Tears wiped away in heaven.

5 Thou, God, our joy and rest shall be,
And sorrow far be driven;
And sin and death forever flee—
There are no tears in heaven.

6 There from the blooming tree of life
The healing fruit is given;

There, there shall cease the painful strife—
There are no tears in heaven.

## 286

MY brethren, I have found
A land which doth abound
With food as sweet as manna,
The more I eat I find.
The more I am inclined
To shout and sing Hosanna.

*My soul doth long to go*
*Where it shall fully know*
*The beauties of my Saviour,*
*And as we march along,*
*We'll sing the Christian song,*
*We hope to live forever.*

2 What must the fountain be
From which grace flows so free?
It yields both peace and pleasure;
There's no terrestrial bliss
Could ever equal this.
A foretaste of my Saviour.

3 Perhaps you think I am wild
And simple as a child;
I am a child of glory,
My joy is from above.
My heart is filled with love,
I long to tell the story.

4 Now, brethren, can you say
That you are on the way,
Are on your way to glory?
I care not for your name,
Religion is the same,
Come, tell the pleasing story.

5 My soul doth set and sing,
And practices her wings,
   And contemplates the hour
When the messenger shall say,
Come, quit this house of clay,
   And with bright angels tower.


## REJOICING IN HOPE.

**287**                      *L. M.*

ASLEEP in Jesus! blessed sleep!
   From which none ever wakes to weep;
A calm and undisturbed repose,
Unbroken by the last of foes.

2 Asleep in Jesus! O how sweet
To be for such a slumber meet;
With holy confidence to sing,
That death has lost his venomed sting!

3 Asleep in Jesus! peaceful rest,
Whose waking is supremely bless'd:
No fear, no woe, shall dim that hour,
That so displays the Saviour's power.

4 Asleep in Jesus! O for me
May such a blissful refuge be!
Securely shall my ashes lie,
Waiting the summons from on high!

5 Asleep in Jesus! time nor space
Debars this precious "hiding-place;"
On Indian plains, on Lapland snows,
Believers find the same repose.

6 Asleep in Jesus! far from thee,
Thy kindred and their graves may be;
But thine is still a blessed sleep,
From which none ever wakes to weep.

288                         *P. M.*

A HOME in heaven! what a joyful thought,
   As the poor man toils in his weary lot!
His heart oppressed, and with anguish driven,
From his home below to his home in heaven.

2 A home in heaven! as the sufferer lies
On his bed of pain, and uplifts his eyes
To that bright home; what a joy is given
With the blessed thought of his home in
      heaven.

3 A home in heaven! when our pleasures fade,
And our wealth and fame in the dust are laid;
And strength decays, and out health is riven,
We are happy still with our home in heaven.

4 A home in heaven! when the faint heart bleeds,
By the Spirit's stroke, for its evil deeds;
Oh! then what bliss in that heart forgiven,
Does the hope inspire of a home in heaven!

5 A home in heaven! when our friends are fled
To the cheerless gloom of the mouldering dead;
We wait in hope on the promise given;
We will meet up there in our home in heaven.

6 A home in heaven! when the wheel is broke,
And the golden bowl by the terror-stroke;
When life's bright sun sinks in death's dark
      even,
We will then fly up to our home in heaven.

7 Our home in heaven! oh, the glorious home,
And the Spirit, joined with the bride, says
      "Come!"
Come, seek his face, and your sins forgiven,
And rejoice in hope of your home in heaven.

**289** From "GOLDEN CENSER."
[By permission of W. B. BRADBURY.] *P. M.*

A H, my heart is void and chill,
'Mid earth's noisy thronging;
For my Father's mansions still
Earnestly 'tis longing.

*Looking home, looking home,*
*Towards the heavenly mansions*
*Jesus hath prepared for me*
*In his Father's kingdom.*

2 Soon the glorious day will dawn,
Heavenly pleasures bringing;
Night will be exchanged for morn,
Sighs give place to singing.

3 Oh to be at home again,
All for which we're sighing,
From all earthly want and pain
To be swiftly flying.

4 Blessed home, O blessed home,
All for which we're sighing;
Soon our Lord will bid us come
To our Father's kingdom.

**290** From "GOLDEN CENSER."
[By permission of W. B. BRADBURY.] *L. M.*

A BEAUTIFUL land by faith I see,
A land of rest, from sorrow free,
The home of the ransomed, bright, and fair,
And beautiful angels, too, are there.

*Will you go? will you go?*
*Go to that beautiful land with me?*
*Will you go? will you go?*
*Go to that beautiful land?*

2 That beautiful land, the city of light,
It ne'er has known the shades of night;
.The glory of God, the light of day
Hath driven the darkness far away.

19

3 In vision I see its streets of gold,
  Its beautiful gates I too behold,
  The river of life, the crystal sea,
  The ambrosial fruit of life's fair tree.

4 The heavenly throng arrayed in white,
  In rapture range the plains of light;
  And in one harmonious choir they praise
  Their glorious Saviour's matchless grace.

## 291

A RISE, my soul, to Pisgah's height,
  And view the promised land,
And see by faith the glorious sight,
  Our heritage at hand.

  *We'll stem the storm, it won't be long,*
    *The heavenly port is nigh;*
  *We'll stem the storm, it won't be long,*
    *We'll anchor by and by.*

2 There endless springs of pleasure flow,
  At my Redeemer's side,
For all who live by faith below,
  And in their Lord confide.

3 Fair Salem's dazzling gates are seen,
  Just o'er the narrow flood,
And fields adorned in living green,
  The residence of God.

4 My conflicts here will soon be past,
  Where wild distraction reigns;
Through toil and death I'll reach at last
  Fair Canaan's happy plains.

5 Oh, could I cross rough Jordan's wave,
  No danger would I fear;
My bark would every tempest brave,
  For Oh! my Captain's near.

**292**                      *P. M.*

A WAY with our fears! the glad morning ap-
    pears,
  When an heir of salvation was born!
From Jehováh I came, for his glory I am,
  And to him I with singing return.

2 Thee, Jesus, alone, the fountain I own,
    Of my life and felicity here:
  And cheerfully sing my Redeemer and king,
    Till his sign in the heavens appear.

3 I sing of thy grace, from my earliest days,
    Ever near to allure and defend;
  Hitherto hast thou been my preserver from sin,
    And I trust thou wilt save to the end.

4 O the infinite cares, and temptations, and
    snares,
  Thy hand hath conducted me through!
Oh, the blessings bestowed by a bountiful God,
    And the mercies eternally new!

5 What a mercy is this! what a heaven of bliss!
    How unspeakably happy am I!
Gathered into thy fold, with thy people en-
    rolled,
  With thy people to live and to die!

6 Oh the goodness of God, in employing a clod,
    His tribute of glory to raise;
  His standard to bear, and with triumph declare,
    His unspeakable riches of grace!

7 O the fathomless love that has deigned to ap-
    prove,
  And prosper the work of my hands!
With my pastoral crook, I went over the brook,
    And behold I am spread into bands.

8 Who, I ask in amaze, hath begotten me
  these?
  And inquire from what quarter they came;
  My full heart it replies, They are born from
  the skies,
  And gives glory to God and the Lamb.

9 All honor and praise to the Father of grace,
  To the Spirit and Son, I return!
  The business pursue he hath made me to do,
  And rejoice that I ever was born.

10 In a rapture of joy my life I employ,
   The God of my life to proclaim;
   'Tis worth living for this, to administer bliss,
   And salvation in Jesus' name.

11 My remnant of days I spend in his praise,
   Who died the whole world to redeem:
   Be they many or few, my days are his due,
   And they all are devoted to him.

## 293                    *P. M.*

A HOPE of heaven, a precious treasure,
  The richest boon that man can crave;
For it affords unfading pleasure,
  A hope of heaven beyond the grave:
This hope has been my stay and comfort
  Through many a dark and gloomy hour;
Of it the world can never rob me,
  Long as I trust Almighty power.

2 When sorrow, death, and wo surround me,
  And all about me's filled with gloom,
My mind is peaceful, calm, and even—
  I have a hope beyond the tomb:
Strong ties by death long since were riven,
  And those I loved I see no more,
Nor will, until we meet in heaven—
  There we shall meet to part no more.

3 When friends are few, and the world alluring,
  And through temptation I'm cast down,
My way is dark, and nothing cheering,
  A hope of heaven still cheers me on.
Though prospects fade, and friends should fail
    me,
  And all seems cheerless on the road,
And though the powers of hell assail me,
  I'll hope for heaven, and trust in God.

4 And when I pass through death's dark valley,
  A light shall shine around my way—
His rod and staff shall then support me,
  He'll bring me through to endless day.
Until that hour still let me cherish
  A hope of heaven and all its joy,
Well grounded on my Saviour's merits,
  Whose praises shall my tongue employ.

## 294

FAR beyond this world of sorrow,
  Where the ransomed millions rest,
There's a glorious endless morrow
  In the mansions of the bless'd.
Shall we know them there,
  In that land far away?
They the same smile wear
  In that land far away?
Shall we meet and know each other
  *In that happy land far away?*

2 There 'neath bowers of endless glory,
  Every heart with peace possessed,
Sweetly chant redemption's story
  In the mansions of the bless'd.
Shall we know their voice
  In that land far away?
And with them rejoice
  In that land far away?

Shall we meet and know each other
*In that happy land far away?*

3 There are those I've loved and cherished,
 Leaning on the Saviour's breast;
They're at home, not dead nor perished,
 In the mansions of the bless'd.
We shall know them still
 In that land far away,
Where no partings chill
 In that land far away.
We shall meet and know each other
 *In that happy land far away.*

4 There the day knows no declining,
 Neither shade nor twilight rest,
But an endless brightness shining,
 In the mansions of the bless'd.
That's our Father's home
 In that land far way;
'Neath his smile we'll roam
 In that land far away.
We shall meet and live forever
 *In that happy land far away.*

## 295      *P. M.*

BURST, ye emerald gates, and bring,
 To my enraptured vision,
All the ecstatic joys that spring
 Around the bright elysian.
Lo! we lift our longing eyes,
Break, ye intervening skies;
Sons of righteousness, arise,
Ope the gates of paradise.

2 Floods of everlasting light,
 Freely flash before him;
Myriads, with supreme delight,
 Instantly adore him;

Angelic trumps resound his fame;
Lutes of lucid gold proclaim
All the music of his name;
Heaven echoing the theme.

3 Four and twenty elders rise
    From their princely station;
Shout the glorious victories,
    Sing the great salvation;
Cást their crowns before his throne,
Cry in reverential tone,
 Glory be to God alone,
Holy! Holy! Holy One!

4 Hark! the thrilling symphonies,
    Seem methinks to seize us;
Join we too the holy lays—
    Jesus—Jesus—Jesus!—
Sweetest sound in seraph's song,
Sweetest note on mortal's tongue,
Sweetest carol ever sung—
Jesus—Jesus—flows along.

## 296      *P. M.*

BRETHREN, see my Jesus coming,
    Don't you see him in yonder cloud,
With ten thousand angels round him?
    See how they do my Jesus crowd.
I'll arise and go and meet him;
    He'll embrace me in his arms;
In the arms of my dear Jesus,
    O there are ten thousand charms.

2 Death shall not destroy my comfort,
    Christ shall guide me through the gloom,
Down he'll send some heavenly convoy,
    To escort my spirit home:
Jordan's streams shall ne'er o'erflow me,
    While my Saviour's by my side:

Canaan, Canaan lies before me,
   Rise and cross the swelling tide.

3 See the happy spirits waiting,
   On the bank beyond the stream,
Sweet responses still repeating,
   Jesus, Jesus is their theme:
See, they whisper! hark! they call me,
   Sister spirit come away!
Lo, I come! earth can't contain me:
   Hail! ye realms of endless day.

4 Worlds of light and crowns of glory,
   Far above yon azure sky,
Though by faith I now explore ye,
   I'll enjoy you soon on high:
Soon I'll gain a full possession,
   Faith and hope shall henceforth cease,
Lost in love's exhaustless ocean,
   Love, that sweetest, brightest grace.

5 Swiftly roll ye lingering hours,
   Seraphs lend your glittering wings,
Love absorbs my ransomed powers,
   Heavenly sound around me rings.
Worlds above are bright and glorious,
   All beneath are dark and void;
Conquest gained, I'll shout victorious
   In the praises of my God.

6 Smiling angels now surround me,
   Troops resplendent fill the skies,
Glory shining all around me,
   While my towering spirit flies:
Jesus clad in dazzling splendor,
   Now methinks appears in view;
Brethren, could you see my Jesus,
   You would serve and love him too.

**297**

From "GOLDEN SHOWER."
[By permission of W. B. BRADBURY.]

BEAUTIFUL Zion, built above,
Beautiful city that I love!
Beautiful gates of pearly white,
Beautiful temple—God its light!
He who was slain on Calvary,
Opens those pearly gates to me.

2 Beautiful heaven, where all is light,
Beautiful angels, clothed in white;
Beautiful strains that never tire,
Beautiful harps through all the choir.
There shall I join the chorus sweet,
Worshipping at the Saviour's feet.

3 Beautiful crowns on every brow,
Beautiful palms the conquerors show;
Beautiful robes the ransomed wear;
Beautiful all who enter there.
Thither I press with eager feet,
There shall my rest be long and sweet.

4 Beautiful throne for Christ our King,
Beautiful songs the angels sing:
Beautiful rest—all wanderings cease,
Beautiful home of perfect peace.
There shall my eyes the Saviour see,
Haste to this heavenly home with me.

**298** *P. M.*

COME brethren and sisters, that love my dear
Lord,
I pray give attention and ear to my word;
What a wonder of mercy! behold now I see
What a tender kind Saviour has done for poor
me.

*Jesus, my Jesus, my own loving Saviour,*
*He's pardoned my sins, and set my soul free;*

And now through life's journey I'll tell the glad
 story
What Jesus has done for a sinner like me.

2 I was led by the devil, till lost and distressed;
 I thought that in torments I soon should be
 cast;
No peace to my conscience, but all misery,
Till by faith I saw Jesus hang bleeding for me.

3 O sinner, said Jesus, for you I have died;
All glory to Jesus, my soul then replied;
The guilt was removed, my soul did rejoice,
The blood was applied, the witness and voice.

4 On my low bended knees before God I did fall,
And glory to Jesus, for he's all in all;
The heart of his rebel was bursting in twain,
To see my dear Jesus on Calvary slain.

5 There was peace now in heaven, and peace
 upon earth,
The angels rejoice at a poor sinner's birth;
Your sins are forgiven, my Saviour did say,
Oh, witness kind heaven, on this my birthday!

6 My soul it was humbled, I fell to the ground;
The time of refreshing at length I have found;
O Lord, thou hast ravished my soul with thy
 charms,
Let me die like old Simeon, with Christ in my
 arms.

## 299

CHILDREN of Zion! what harp-notes are
 stealing
So soft o'er our senses, so soothingly sweet?
'Tis the music of angels, their raptures revealing,
That you have been brought to the Holy
 One's feet.

*Children of Zion ! we join in their welcome,*
*'Tis sweet to lie low at that blessed retreat.*

2 Children of Zion ! no longer in sadness
  Refrain from the feast that your Saviour hath
      given,
  Come, taste of the cup of salvation with glad-
      ness,
  And think of the banquet still sweeter in
      heaven.

3 Children of Zion ! we joyfully hail you
  Who've entered the sheepfold through Jesus
      the door,
  While pilgrims on earth, though the foe may
      assail you,
  Press forward, and soon will the conflict be
      o'er.

*Children of Zion ! O ! welcome, thrice welcome !*
*Till we meet where the foe shall oppress you no*
*   more.*

# 300

CHRISTIAN, the morn breaks sweetly o'er
      thee,
  And all the midnight shadows flee ;
Tinged are the distant skies with glory,
  A beacon light hangs out for thee.

*Arise, arise, the light breaks o'er thee ;*
*   Thy name is graven on his hands ;*
*Thy home is in those worlds of glory*
*   Where thy Redeemer reigns alone.*

2 Thy God is ever kind and gracious,
    He will direct thy course above,
  For thou art in his sight most precious,
    The object of his special love.

3 Though in the proud, dark waves of ocean,
　　O'erwhelmed thou need not, shalt not be;
'Midst the fierce tempest's dread commotion,
　　Thy God will still remember thee.

4 Tossed on time's rude, relentless surges,
　　Calmly composed, and dauntless stand,
For lo! beyond those seas emerges,
　　The height that bounds the promised land.

5 Christian, behold the land is nearing,
　　Where the wild sea-storm's rage is o'er;
Hark how the heavenly hosts are cheering,
　　See, in what throngs they range the shore!

## 301                    *P. M.*

COME and taste along with me,
　Consolation running free,
From our Father's wealthy throne,
Sweeter than the honeycomb.

　　*I'll praise God, and you'll praise God,*
　　　*And we'll all praise God together,*
　　*We'll praise the Lord for the work that he has*
　　　*done;*
　　　*Glory be to God forever.*

2 Wherefore should I feast alone?
Two are better still than one;
The more comes in with a free, good will,
Makes the banquet sweeter still.

3 Now I go to heaven's door,
Asking for a little more!
Jesus gives a double share,
Calling me his chosen heir.

4 Goodness running like a stream,
Through the New Jerusalem.
And by a constant breaking forth,
Sweetens earth and heaven both.

5 Saints in glory, sing aloud,
　For to see an heir of God!
　Coming in at heaven's door,
　Making of the number more.

6 Now my body doth its best,
　For to keep me back from Christ;
　But a treasure coming in,
　Doth oppose my inbred sin.

7 Sinful nature hatching vice,
　Cannot stop the force of grace;
　Whilst there is a God to give,
　And a sinner to receive.

8 Heaven's here, and heaven's there,
　Comfort's flowing everywhere!
　This I boldly do profess,
　That my soul hath got a taste.

9 Now I go rejoicing home,
　From the banquet of perfume!
　Finding manna on the road,
　Dropping from the mount of God.

# 302

PILGRIMS, we are to Canaan bound,
　Our journey lies along this road;
This wilderness we travel round,
　To reach the city of our God.

　　*O happy pilgrims, spotless fair,*
　　*What makes your robes so white appear?*
　　*Our robes are washed in Jesus' blood,*
　　*And we are trav'ling home to God.*

2 A few more days, or weeks, or years,
　In this dark desert to complain;
A few more sighs, a few more tears,
　And we shall bid adieu to pain.

3 O blessed land! O happy land!
   When shall we reach thy golden shore?
And one redeemed, unbroken band
   United be for evermore.

4 And if our robes are pure and white,
   May we all reach that blest abode?
Oh, yes, they all shall dwell in light
   Whose robes are washed in Jesus' blood.

5 We all shall reach that golden shore
   If here we watch, and fight, and pray;
Straight is the way, and straight the door,
   And none but pilgrims find the way.

6 Oh, may we meet at last above,
   Amid the holy blood-washed throng,
And sing forever Jesus' love,
   While saints and angels join the song.

## 303

COME, sing to me of heaven,
   When I'm about to die,
Sing songs of holy ecstacy,
   To waft my soul on high!

      *There'll be no sorrow there,*
      *There'll be no sorrow there,*
      *In heaven above, where all is love,*
      *There'll be no sorrow there.*

2 When cold and sluggish drops
   Roll off my marble brow,
Break forth in songs of joyfulness,—
   Let heaven begin below.

3 When the last moments come,
   Oh, watch my dying face,
To catch the bright seraphic glow,
   Which in each feature plays.

4 Then to my raptured ear
    Let one sweet song be given;
Let music charm me last on earth,
    And greet me first in heaven.

5 Then close my sightless eyes,
    And lay me down to rest,
And clasp my cold and icy hands
    Upon my lifeless breast.

6 When round my senseless clay,
    Assemble those I love—
Then sing of heav'n, delightful heav'n,
    My glorious home above.

# 304

OH, I have roamed through many lands,
    A stranger to delight;
Nor friendship's hopes nor love's sweet smiles
    Could make my pathway bright,
Till on the sky a Star arose,
    And lit night's sable dome,
Oh! steer my bark by that sweet Star,
    For Eden is my home.

2 Oh! Eden is my place of rest,
    I long to reach its shore,
To shake these troubles from my breast,
    And weep and sigh no more.
To that fair land my spirit flies,
    And angels bid me come!
Oh! steer my bark o'er Jordan's wave,
    For Eden is my home!

3 Oh! take me from this world of wo
    To my sweet home above,
Where tears of sorrow never flow,
    And all the air is love.

My sister spirits wait for me,
  And Jesus bids me come :
Oh ! steer my bark to that bright land,
  For Eden is my home.

## 305          *C. M.*

THERE is a land, surpassing fair,
  By holy pleasure owned ;
Nor hate nor strife approaches there,
  For love is there enthroned.

2 Nor hearts are there to gloom a prey,
    Nor sorrows e'er annoy ;
  The darkness yields to shining day,
    And pain to perfect joy.

3 No lamentations there are known,
    But songs alone are heard ;
  Nor lust of power itself has shown,
    Nor envy ever stirred.

4 Sweet gratulations there abound,
    Each welcomes each to heaven ;
  Their better portions all have found,
    Their griefless mansions given.

5 God's glowing glories all adorn
    With bliss-inspiring rays ;
  And blooms one endless vernal morn,
    Hallowed with endless praise.

6 The pilgrim, worn with toil below,
    This holy rest attains,
  And changes then his notes of wo
    To heaven's enchanting strains.

7 Oh when, delightsome land of God,
    Shall I thy plains survey ?
  How long, full weary on the road,
    Must I the sight delay !

8 Glad would I yield each earthly toy—
 Lay off my fleshy load—
And fly to thee, my rest, my joy,
 Delightsome land of God.

## 306

MEET again! when life is o'er,
 Meet again! to part no more;
How it cheers the drooping heart,
When from friends we're called to part.

2 Meet again! where endless joy,
 We shall taste without alloy;
Meet where songs shall ne'er grow old,
Sweetly tuned to harps of gold.

3 Meet again! how passing sweet,
 Friends long lost again to meet;
Careworn souls by tempest driven,
Oh, how sweet to meet in heaven.

## 307

COME, brethren, don't grow weary,
 But let us journey on;
The moments will not tarry,
 This life will soon be gone:
The passing scenes all tell us
 That death will surely come;
These bodies soon will moulder
 In the dark and dreary tomb.

2 Loved ones have gone before us,
 They beckon us away,
O'er aerial plains they're soaring,
 Blest in eternal day;
But we are in the army,
 And dare not leave our post;
We'll fight until we conquer
 The foe's most mighty host.
 20

3 Our Captain's gone before us,
   He kindly calls us home
To yonder world of glory,
   And sweetly bids us come.
The world, the flesh, and Satan
   Will strive to hedge our way,
But we'll o'ercome these powers—
   And hourly watch and pray.

4 And Jesus will be with us,
   E'en to our journey's end,
In every sore affliction
   His present help to lend.
He never will grow weary,
   Though often we request,
He'll give us grace to conquer,
   And take us home to rest.

# 308     *P. M.*

I SHALL rest, I shall rest,
   When the Christian's race is run;
I shall rest, I shall rest,
   When the glorious crown is won;
I shall rest on Zion's mountain,
I shall rest by life's pure fountain;
I shall rest, and rest in glory,
With my Lord who's gone before me;
I shall rest, I shall rest,
   When my faith and hope are tried;
I shall rest, I shall rest,
   By the crystal river side.

2 I shall rest, I shall rest,
   When life's conflicts are all o'er,
I shall rest, I shall rest,
   Where the tempted weep no more;
I shall rest from all temptation,
I shall share the great salvation;

I shall rest with Christ my Saviour,
Rest in peace, and rest forever.
I shall rest, I shall rest,
   When the saints are glorified,
I shall rest, I shall rest,
   By my conquering Saviour's side.

3 I shall rest, I shall rest,
   When time's tempests all are o'er,
I shall rest, I shall rest,
   When I reach the heavenly shore;
I shall rest from wo and sorrow
In that bright eternal morrow,
I shall rest from tears and sighing,
I shall rest from pain and dying.
I shall rest, I shall rest,
   When all mortal toils are past,
I shall rest, I shall rest,
   With the ransomed host at last.

## 309                    *P. M.*

WHEN pulse beats low, and cheeks grow pale,
   And storms of life are fiercely driven;
When fairest prospects quickly fail,
   How sweet to have *a hope in heaven!*

2 When friends that seemed most near and dear
   Are from our bosoms swiftly riven,
And life's bright joys in gloom appear,
   How sweet to have *a hope in heaven!*

3 When lone and wand'ring far from home,
   No kind relief to us is given,
Oh, what would then of us become,
   If we had not *a hope in heaven?*

4 And when the end is drawing nigh,
   Of life, through which we long have striven,
And we at last must droop and die,
   *How sweet to have a home in heaven!*

## 310

FLY away to thy long-sought home on high!
  Fly away to thy promised shore!
Where the Eden fields in glory lie,
  And the humble shall weep no more.
I long have thought on your scenes sublime,
  And dreamed of your temple of light;
I have wept while I mused on your sunlit clime,
  Borne on with ecstatic delight.

2 Fly away to the living streams of joy!
  Fly away to the garden of love!
Where the tempter again shall never destroy,
  Nor mar the bright beauties above;
But awhile I must stay in my prison of clay,
  Or roam on this desolate shore;
I must wait for the dawn of the opening day,
  When death and the curse are no more.

3 I must wait for the word of the Prince of Peace,
  I must wait for the guardian bands,
I must wait till the message brings release,
  That's signed by Immanuel's hands.
Then away from this desert, with joy I'll rise,
  Then away from my prison I'll fly;
My pinion I'll dip in the clear bright skies,
  And fly away to my home on high.

## 311        *C. M.*

O LAND of rest, for thee I sigh,
  When will the moment come,
When shall I lay my armor by,
  And dwell in peace at home?

2 No tranquil joys on earth I know,
  No peaceful sheltering dome,
This world's a wilderness of wo,
  This world is not my home.

3 To Jesus Christ I fled for rest;
    He bade me cease to roam,
And lean for succor on his breast,
    And he'd conduct me home.

4 I should at once have quit this field,
    Where foes with fury foam;
But ah! my passport was not sealed—
    I could not yet go home.

5 When by affliction sharply tried,
    I view the gaping tomb;
Although I dread death's chilling tide,
    Yet still I sigh for home.

6 Weary of wandering round and round
    This vale of sin and gloom,
I long to quit th' unhallowed ground,
    And dwell with Christ at home.

# 312

FLY up, my soul, and view the plains
    Where everlasting beauty reigns.

        *There's a better day a-coming!*
        *Glory, hallelujah!*

2 No sickness there—no grief—no sigh—
For there the dwellers never die.

3 While here, we groan with toil and care,
But we shall shine in glory there;

4 Shall range along the river side,
And drink the cool and living tide;

5 Shall stand the trees of life below,
And pluck the fruits that on them grow;

6 Shall pluck the fruits and pluck the flowers,
And dwell at ease in angel bowers.

7 Our huts below are poor and old,
Our mansions there are bright with gold.

8 Our robes shall all be purest white,
Our crowns more dazzling than the light.

9 Our conquering palms shall wave around,
Our harps like David's harp shall sound.

10 Our songs about the throne shall rise,
Our shouts shall echo through the skies.

11 Roll on, bright day, in glory roll,
Arise to meet it, O my soul.

## 313 *P. M.*

GAY pleasures and palaces, mention them not,
'Tis only in heaven that pain is forgot,
'Tis only in mansions prepared for the blest
That souls of believers can ever find rest.

*Home, home, sweet, sweet home,*
*There's no place like home, there's no place like*
*home.*

2 Poor exiles from heaven, we seek but in vain
For pleasures, which only in Christ we obtain;
Temptations beset us, afflictions pursue,
And all that supports us is heaven in view.

3 Oh, soon may this wearisome pilgrimage cease,
Oh, soon may we rest in the mansions of peace,
And soon may the Saviour our welcome pro-
claim,
To a home in the skies, which he died to obtain.

## 314

HOME is sweet, home is sweet, on Canaan's
happy shore,
And oh! 'twill fill my soul with joy to meet my
friends once more,

Here I dropt the parting tear, and I was left
alone,
But soon I'll meet again with those who'll kindly
greet me home.

2 Happy day, happy day, when Jesus I shall see,
And with the friends I've loved in youth shall
eat of life's fair tree;
But if my guide should be my fate that bids
me longer roam,
I know that death will soon release, and I shall
find my home.

3 Music sweet, music soft, that lingers on my ear,
And oh! I hear the word of Christ, that bids
me never fear,
Then give me but my Saviour's love, I'll ask no
higher boon,
For I shall meet with those I loved, and dwell
with them at home.

**315**                    *P. M.*

HOW sweet to reflect on those joys that await
me
In yon blissful region, the haven of rest,
Where glorified spirits with welcome shall greet
me,
And lead me to mansions prepared for the
blest;
Encircled in light and with glory enshrouded,
My happiness perfect, my mind's sky un-
clouded,
I'll bathe in the ocean of pleasure unbounded,
And range with delight through the *Eden of
Love.*

2. While angelic legions, with harps tuned celestial,
Harmoniously join in the concert of praise,

The saints, as they flock from the regions ter-
      restrial,
In loud hallelujahs their voices will raise:
The song of redemption shall echo through
      heaven,
My soul will respond, to Immanuel be given
All glory, all honor, all might and dominion.
    Who brought us thro' grace to the *Eden of
    Love.*

3 Hail! blessed estate! Hail, ye songsters of
      glory!
  Ye harpers of bliss, soon I'll meet you above!
  And join your full choir in rehearsing the story,
    "Salvation from sorrow through Jesus' love."
  Though prisoned in earth, yet by anticipation
  Already my soul feels a sweet prelibation
  Of joys that await me when freed from pro-
      bation:
    My heart's now in heaven, the *Eden of Love.*

# 316

HAVE you heard, have you heard of that sun-
      bright clime,
Undimmed by sorrow, unhurt by time,
Where age hath no power o'er the fadeless
      frame—
Where the eye is fire, and the heart is flame?
Have you heard of that sun-bright clime?

2 A river of water gushes there,
  'Mid flowers of beauty strangely fair,
  And a thousand wings are hovering o'er
  The dazzling wave and the golden shore,
    That are seen in that sun-bright clime.

3 Millions of forms, all clothed in light,
  And garments of beauty, clear and white—

They dwell in their own immortal bowers,
'Mid fadeless hues of countless flowers,
   That bloom in that sun-bright clime.

4 Ear hath not heard, and eye hath not seen,
Their swelling notes and their changeless sheen,
Their ensigns are waving and banners unfurl,
O'er the jasper walls and gates of pearl
   That are reared in that sun-bright clime.

5 But far, far away is that sinless clime,
Undimmed by sorrow, unhurt by time;
Where amid all things that's fair is given
The home of the saints—and its name is heaven,
   The name of that sun-bright clime.

**317**         *L. M.*

THE heavenly home is bright and fair,
  Nor death nor sighing visit there;
Its glittering towers the sun outshine—
That heavenly mansion shall be mine.

    *Will you go? will you go?*   *&c.*

2 My Father's house is built on high,
Above the arched and starry sky;
When from this earthly prison free,
That heavenly mansion mine shall be.

3 While here, a stranger far from home,
Affliction's waves may round me foam,
Although, like Lazarus, sick and poor,
My heavenly mansion is secure.

4 I envy not the rich and great
Their pomp of wealth and pride of state;
My Father is a richer King—
That heavenly mansion still I sing.

5 Let others seek a home below,
Which flames devour, or waves o'erflow;

Be mine the happier lot to own
A heavenly mansion near the throne.

6 Then, fail this earth, let stars decline,
And sun and moon refuse to shine,
All nature sink and cease to be,
That heavenly mansion stands for me.

## 318

JERUSALEM! thy mansions fair,
Ignoble souls may never share;
For all who walk thy streets of gold
Are in the book of life enrolled.

2 Whoso from earth would thither go
Must wash his robes as white as snow;
In Jesus' blood, the fount of grace,
Find pure, unspotted righteousness.

3 O Lamb of God, my heart prepare
To enter with the holy there;
Within thy book my name enroll,
And write thine own upon my soul.

4 To him that loves and trusts the Lord,
And keeps with patient hope his word,
The Spirit with his spirit bears
Sweet witness to his answered prayers.

5 Whoever has this seal of love,
His title reads to seats above;
And looking upward as he runs,
The soil of sinful pleasure shuns.

6 Jesus, fulfill my long desire,
To stand with thee in pure attire,
And find at last a place and name
Within the new Jerusalem.

**319** *L. M.*

HOW blessed the place where Jesus is !
The fountain-head of life and bliss ;
Celestial bands, assist my flight,
And bear me to those realms of light.
On high, above yon vault of blue,
That happier land appears in view ;
Oh, were I once from earth away !
Through all its blissful groves to stray.

2 Those blissful groves, so green and fair,
Perennial fruit and blossoms bear ;
And angel forms, of various grade,
Enjoy their ever-peaceful shade.
The seraph tall, with ardor bright,
Beloved among the sons of light,
And cherub grave, of thoughtful mien,
Stray o'er those hills of evergreen.

3 But oh, to my fond heart more dear,
Those whom I loved and cherished here,
In white and spotless robes I see,
From pain and death forever free.
Their harps of gold are tuned to sing
The triumphs of their Saviour King ;
And heavenly hill, and grove, and stream
Are vocal with the joyful theme.

4 When, through the strength of saving grace,
I finish my appointed race,
On that immortal, brighter plain,
I'll meet those kindred souls again.
Then speed your flight, ye passing years,
Till God shall wipe these falling tears,
And bid my exiled spirit come,
To dwell in that eternal home.

## 320

THERE is a place where my hopes are stayed,
My heart and my treasure are there;
Where verdure and blossoms never fade,
And fields are eternally fair. .

*That blissful place is my father-land,*
*By faith its delights I explore;*
*Come, favor my flight, angelic band,*
*And waft me in peace to the shore.*

2 There is a place where the angels dwell,
A pure and a peaceful abode;
The joys of that place no tongue can tell—
But there is the palace of God!

3 There is a place where my friends are gone,
Who suffered and worshipped with me;
Exalted with Christ, high on his throne,
The King in his beauty they see.

4 There is a place where I hope to live,
When life and its labors are o'er;
A place which the Lord to me will give,
And then I shall sorrow no more.

## 321

HERE we suffer grief and pain,
Here we meet to part again,
In heaven we part no more.

*Oh! that will be joyful!*
*Joyful, joyful, joyful,*
*Oh! that will be joyful!*
*When we meet to part no more.*

2 All who love the Lord below,
When they die to heaven will go,
And sing with saints above.

3 *Little children* will be there,
  Who have sought the Lord by prayer,
    From *every* Sunday-school.

4 *Teachers*, too, shall meet above,
  And our *pastors*, whom we love,
  ·  Shall meet to part no more.

5 Oh! how happy we shall be!
  For our Saviour we shall see,
    Exalted on his throne!

6 There we all shall sing with joy,
  And eternity employ
    In praising Christ the Lord.

## 322 *L. M.*

I'M glad that I am born to die,
  From grief and wo my soul shall fly;
Bright angels shall convey me home,
Away to New Jerusalem.

2 I'll praise him while he lends me breath,
  I hope to praise him after death,
  I hope to praise him when I die,
  And shout salvation as I fly.

3 Farewell, vain world, I'm going home,
  My Saviour smiles, and bids me come;
  Sweet angels beckon me away,
  To sing God's praise in endless day.

4 I soon shall pass the vale of death,
  And in his arms I'll lose my breath;
  And then my happy soul shall tell,
  My Jesus has done all things well.

5 I soon shall hear the awful sound,
  Awake, ye nations under ground;

Arise and drop your dying shrouds,
And meet king Jesus in the clouds.

6 When to that blessed world I rise,
And join the anthems in the skies,
This note above the rest shall swell,
My Jesus has done all things well.

7 Then shall I see my blessed God,
And praise him in his bright abode;
My theme through all eternity
Shall glory, glory, glory be.

**323**                 *5 6s & 1 7s.*

OUR bondage here shall end,
By and by—by and by;
Our griefs shall vanish then,
With our threescore years and ten,
And bright glory crown the day
By and by—by and by.

2 When our Deliverer comes,
By and by—by and by,
From Egypt's yoke set free,
We will hail the jubilee,
And to Canaan all return
By and by—by and by.

3 Though strong our foes appear,
We'll go on—we'll go on;
Our hearts shall know no fear,
For Israel's God is near—
While the fiery pillar moves
We'll go on—we'll go on.

4 By Marah's bitter streams
We'll go on—we'll go on;
Though Baca's vale be dry,
The Rock shall yield supply.

To a land of corn and wine
  We'll go on—we'll go on.

5 And when to Jordan's flood
  We are come—we are come;
Jehovah rules the tide,
And the waters will divide,
While the ransomed host shall shout,
  "We are come—we are come."

6 There friends shall meet again,
  Who have loved—who have loved;
Our embraces shall be sweet,
When we each other greet,
At our great Redeemer's feet,
  Who have loved—who have loved.

7 There, with the happy throng,
  We'll rejoice—we'll rejoice;
Shouting "Glory to our King,"
Till the dome of heaven shall ring,
And through all eternity
  We'll rejoice—we'll rejoice.

## 324

I AM fading away to the land of the bless'd,
  Like the last lingering hues of the even;
Reclining my head on my Saviour's breast,
  I soar to my own native heaven;
My warfare is finished, the battle is won,
  To a crown and a throne I aspire:
My coursers are swifter than steeds of the sun,
  I mount in a chariot of fire.

2 The world is fast sinking away from my sight,
  A trifle appears all its treasures!
I see them from hence by eternity's light:
  How vanish its pomp and its pleasures!

How faint are the notes of the trumpet of fame,
   Refreshing its soul-flattering story !
How tarnished the lustre of each noble name!
   A meteor flash is its glory.

3 But there is a spot—one beautiful spot
   My heart lingers o'er with emotion;
Its peaceful enjoyments shall ne'er be forgot;
   'Tis the place of my former devotion.
I see it, "outstretched in its loveliness," lie,
   Like a garden of lilies and roses;
More charming to me, as it fades from the eye,
   Than the valleys of Canaan to Moses.

4 Lo! upward I gaze, and the glory supreme,
   That illumines the height of elysian,
Shines down through the veil—there is life in
     each beam—
   It renders immortal my vision;
The notes of soft melody fall on my ear;
   Harmonious the cadence and measure;
'Tis the voice of the harpers on Zion I hear;
   Full high swells their chorus of pleasure.

5 Lo! there are the towers of my future abode,
   The city on high and eternal!
See, there is the Eden—the river of God!
   And the trees ever bearing and vernal:
Haste, haste with me onward, companion and
     guide,
   Let me join in that heavenly matin;
Fly wide, ye bright gates! swiftly through
     them I ride,
   Triumphant o'er sin, death, and Satan.

## 325

I HEAR thee speak of a better land;
  Thou call'st its children a happy band;

Mother, oh, where is that distant shore?
Shall we not seek it, sigh no more?
Is it where the flower of the orange blows,
And the fireflies dance in the myrtle boughs?
   Not there, not there, my child;
   Not there, not there, my child.

2 Is it far away in some region old,
Where rivers wander o'er sands of gold,
And the bright rays of the valleys shine,
And the diamond lights up the secret mine;
And the pearl glows forth from the coral
      strand—
Is it there, sweet mother, that better land?
   Not there, not there, my child;
   Not there, not there, my child.

3 Eye hath not seen it, my gentle boy,
Ear hath not heard its deep songs of joy;
Dreams cannot picture a world so fair;
Sorrow and death may not enter there;
Time may not breathe on its faultless bloom,
Far beyond the clouds and beyond the tomb.
   'Tis there, 'tis there, my child;
   'Tis there, 'tis there, my child.

# 326

I HAVE a home beyond the sky,
   Where saints in glory never die;
A home all fair and bright as noon,
Where sin and sorrow never come.

   *I'm going home, &c.*

2 In that fair land there still is room,
Where weary pilgrims may get home;
And join with angels in the song
Of praises to our God the Lamb.
   21

3 When done with earth; its follies past,
I'll reach my fatherland at last;
To sit and sing around the throne,
Glory to God! I'm safe at home.

4 When safe at home in that fair land,
I'll join the happy, sinless band;
And sing with rapture near the throne,
Vain world, adieu! I'm safe at home.

**327**     From "Golden Chain."     8s & 7s.
[By permission of W. B. Bradbury.]

IN the Christian's home in glory,
There remains a land of rest,
There my Saviour's gone before me,
To fulfill my soul's request.

*There is rest for the weary,*
*There is rest for the weary.*
*There is rest for you*
*On the other side of Jordan,*
*In the sweet fields of Eden,*
*Where the tree of life is blooming,*
*There is rest for you.*

2 He is fitting up my mansion,
Which eternally shall stand,
For my stay shall not be transient
In that holy, happy land.

3 Pain nor sickness ne'er shall enter,
Grief nor wo my lot shall share,
But in that celestial centre,
I a crown of life shall wear.

4 Death itself shall then be vanquished,
And his sting shall be withdrawn;
Shout for gladness, O ye ransomed,
Hail with joy the rising morn.

5 Sing, O sing, ye heirs of glory;
    Shout your triumph as you go.;
Zion's gates will open for you,
    You shall find an entrance through.

**328**          *C. M.*

JESUS, the visions of thy face
    Have overpowering charms;
Scarce shall I feel death's cold embrace,
    If Christ be in my arms.

2 Then, while you hear my heart-strings break,
    How sweet the minutes roll!
A mortal paleness on my cheek,
    But glory in my soul.

3 Death cannot make my soul afraid,
    If God be with me there;
Soft is the passage through the shade,
    And all the prospect fair.

4 When shall my happy soul arise
    To that bright world above,
And view with unbeclouded eyes,
    The Canaan which I love?

5 Clasped in my heavenly Father's arms,
    I would forget to breathe,
And lose my life amid the charms
    Of so divine a death.

**329**          *2 8s and 4 7s.*

LET me go, the day is breaking,
    Dear companions, let me go:
We have spent a night of waking
    In the wilderness below:
Upward now I bend my way,
Part we here at break of day.

2 Let me go, I may not tarry,
    Wrestling thus with doubts and fears;
Angels wait my soul to carry
    Where my risen Lord appears:
Friends and kindred, weep not so,
If you love me, let me go.

3 We have travelled long together,
    Hand in hand, and heart in heart,
Both through fair and stormy weather,
    And 'tis hard—'tis hard to part:
While I sigh "Farewell" to you:
Answer, one and all, "Adieu."

4 'Tis not darkness gathering round me
    That withdraws me from your sight:
Walls of earth no more can bound me,
    But, translated into light,
Like the lark on mounting wing,
Though unseen, you hear me sing.

5 Heaven's broad day hath o'er me broken,
    Far beyond earth's span of sky:
Am I dead?  Nay, by this token,
    Know that I have ceased to die:
Would you solve the mystery?
Come up hither—come and see.

# 330

MY rest is in heaven, my rest is not here,
    Then why should I tremble when trials
        are near?
Be hushed, my sad spirit, the worst that can
        come
But shortens thy journey, and hastens thee
        home.

2 It is not for me to be seeking my bliss,
    Or building my hopes in a region like this;

I look for a city that hands have not piled,
I pant for a country by sin undefiled.

3 The thorn and the thistle around me may grow,
I would not lie down upon roses below;
I ask not my portion, I seek not my rest,
Till I find them forever on Jesus' breast.

4 Afflictions may press me, they cannot destroy—
One glimpse of his love turns them all into
joy;
And the bitterest tears, if he smile but on
them,
Like dew in the sunshine, grow diamond and
gem.

5 Let doubt, then, and danger my progress op-
pose,
They only make heaven more sweet at its
close;
Come joy, or come sorrow, whate'er may befall,
An hour with my Saviour will make up for all.

6 A scrip on my back, and a staff in my hand,
I march on in haste, through an enemy's land;
The road may be rough, but it cannot be long,
And I'll smooth it with hope, and I'll cheer it
with song.

**331** *10 11, 10 11.*

O TELL me no more of this world's vain store,
The time for such trifles with me now is
o'er;
A country I've found where true joys abound,
To dwell I'm determined on that happy ground.

*Hallelujah, hallelujah, hallelujah to God!*
*We will praise him forever and ever. Amen.*

2 The souls that believe in Paradise live,
And me in that number will Jesus receive:
My soul, don't delay—he calls thee away,
Rise, follow thy Saviour, and bless the glad day.

3 No mortal doth know what he can bestow,
What light, strength, and comfort—go after
him, go;
Lo, onward I move to a city above;
None guesses how wondrous my journey will
prove.

4 Great spoils I shall win from death, hell, and
sin;
'Midst outward afflictions shall feel Christ
within:
And when I'm to die, receive me, I'll cry,
For Jesus hath loved me, I cannot tell why.

5 But this I do find, we two are so joined,
He'll not live in glory, and leave me behind:
So this is the race I'm running through grace,
Henceforth—till admitted to see my Lord's
face.

6 And now I'm in care, my neighbors may share
These blessings; to seek them, will none of you
dare?
In bondage, O why, and death will you lie,
When one here assures you free grace is so
nigh?

## 332

OH come, come away, from labor now re-
posing,
Let anxious care awhile forbear,
Oh come, come away.
Oh come, our sacred joys renew,

And here where faith will strengthen you,
And Christ will welcome you—
   Oh come, come away.

2 From toil and cares on which the day is
      closing,
  The hour of eve brings sweet reprieve,
   Oh come, come away.
O come, where God will smile on thee,
And in our hearts will rapture be,
And time pass happily—
   Oh come, come away.

3 While tuned to God's love, the angel harps are
      ringing,
  And sound his praise through endless days,
   Oh come, come away.
In answering songs of sympathy,
We'll sing in tuneful harmony
From earth's temptation free,
   Oh come, come away.

4 The bright day is gone, the moon and stars ap-
      pearing,
  With silver light illume the night,
   Oh come, come away.
Come join your prayers with ours—address
Kind Heaven, our meetings here to bless
With peace, hope, happiness—
   Oh come, come away.

**333**              *P. M.*

SOON will our suffering time be o'er,
  When we shall weep and sigh no more.

   *Roll on, roll on, sweet moments, roll on,*
   *And let these poor pilgrims go home, go home.*

2 Jesus himself shall guide our way,
  Till safe we rest in endless day.

3 A few more rolling years at most,
Will land us safe on Canaan's coast.

4 From sleeping clay and beds of dust,
Our Jesus will call home the just.

5 Our ransomed souls shall soar away,
To praise our God in endless day.

6 When landed on the heavenly shore,
Death and the curse shall be no more.

7 And when we Christ in glory meet,
Our thrilling hopes will be complete.

8 Then shall we sing the song of grace,
Safe in our glorious hiding-place.

9 Each soul shall feel what glories shine
In our Immanuel all divine.

10 Filled with his light, and life, and joy,
Praise shall our every hour employ.

## 334

SEE, Christian, see how time steals on;
Soon will sink life's setting sun;
Like the gleams of closing day,
Fade these fleeting hours away:
Then up, let us toil till our toilings are o'er,
Till we shall be borne to eternity's shore:
Our final summons having come,
How sweet the Christian's welcome home!
Home, home, home, the Christian's welcome
home,
Welcome home, welcome home.

2 See how the shades of death come nigh;
Blissful shades when Christians die:
They mark the path our Saviour trod,
Dying saints to waft to God:

Then up, fellow-Christian, let mourning be o'er;
Rejoice in the Saviour, rejoice evermore:
Our final summons having come,
How sweet the Christian's welcome home!
Home, home, home, the Christian's welcome
    home,
Welcome home, welcome home.

## 335

SHED not a tear o'er your friend's early bier;
  When I am gone—when I am gone;
Smile when the slow-tolling bell you shall
    hear—
  When I am gone—I am gone.
Weep not for me when you stand round my
    grave;
Think who has died His beloved to save;
Think of the crown all the ransomed shall
    have;
  When I am gone—I am gone.

2 Plant ye a tree that may wave over me,
  When I am gone—when I am gone;
Sing ye a song when my grave ye shall see,
  When I am gone—I am gone;
Come at the close of a bright summer's day;
Come when the sun sheds his last lingering
    ray;
Come and rejoice that I thus passed away;
  When I am gone—I am gone.

3 Shed not a tear when you stand round my
    grave,
  When I am gone—when I am gone;
Sing a sweet song unto Him who doth save,
  When I am gone—I am gone;
Sing to the Lamb who on earth once was slain,
Sing to the Lamb who in heaven doth reign,

Sing till the world shall be filled with his
name;
When I am gone—I am gone.

4 Plant ye a rose that may bloom o'er my bed,
When I am gone—when I am gone;
Breathe not a sigh for the blessed early dead,
When I am gone—I am gone;
Praise ye the Lord that I'm freed from all care;
Serve ye the Lord, that my bliss ye may share;
Look ye on high and believe I am there;
When I am gone—I am gone.

**336**          From "Golden Chain."
[By permission of W. B. Bradbury.]

SHALL we sing in heaven forever—
  Shall we sing?
Shall we sing in heaven forever,
  In that happy land?
Yes! O yes! in that land, that happy land,
  They that meet shall sing forever,
  Far beyond the rolling river,
  Meet to sing and love forever,
  In that happy land!

2 Shall we know each other ever
  In that land?
Shall we know each other ever
  In that happy land?
Yes! O yes! in that land, that happy land,
  They that meet shall know each other,
  Far beyond the rolling river,
  Meet to sing and love forever
  In that happy land!

3 Shall we sing with holy angels
  In that land?
Shall we sing with holy angels
  In that happy land?
Yes! O yes! in that land, that happy land,

Saints and angels sing forever,
Far beyond the rolling river,
Meet to sing and love forever
   In that happy land!

4 Shall we rest from care and sorrow
   In that land?
Shall we rest from care and sorrow
   In that happy land?
Yes! O yes! in that land, that happy land,
   They that meet shall rest forever,
   Far beyond the rolling river,
   Meet to sing and love forever,
     In that happy land!

# 337

SHOULD sorrow o'er thy brow,
  Its darkened shadows fling—
And hopes that cheer thee now,
  Die in their early spring;
Should pleasure at its birth,
  Fade like the hues of even,
Turn thou away from earth,
  There's rest for thee in heaven.

2 If ever life should seem
  To thee a toilsome way,
And gladness cease to beam
  Upon its clouded day;
If like the weary dove,
  O'er shoreless oceans driven;
Raise thou thine eyes above,
  There's rest for thee in heaven.

3 But O! if thornless flowers
  Throughout thy pathway bloom—
And gaily fleet the hours,
  Unstained by earthly gloom;

Still, let not every thought
    To this poor world be given;
Nor always be forgot,
    Thy better rest in heaven.

4 When sickness pales thy cheek,
    And dims thy lustrous eye,
And pulses low and weak,
    Tell of a time to die;
Sweet hope will whisper then,
    Though thou from earth be riven,
There's bliss beyond the ken,
    There's rest for thee in heaven.

### 338 *L. M.*

THERE is a heaven above the skies,
    A heaven where pleasure never dies;
A heaven I sometimes hope to see,
Yet often fear 'tis not for me.

*But Jesus, Jesus is my friend, oh, hallelujah;*
*Hallelujah, Jesus, Jesus is my friend.*

2 The way is difficult and straight,
    And narrow is the gospel gate;
Ten thousand dangers are therein,
Ten thousand snares to take me in.

3 I travel through a world of foes,
    Through conflicts sore my spirit goes;
The tempter cries, I ne'er shall stand,
Nor reach fair Canaan's happy land.

4 Through glimm'ring hopes and gloomy fears
    Dimly the heavenly way appears;
But in this way methinks I see
The track of him who died for me.

5 I trace the footsteps of my God,
    Who on the cross sustained my load;

'Twas on that dark and doleful day,
In streaming blood he passed this way.

6 Come life, come death, come then what will,
His footsteps I will follow still;
Through dangers thick and hell's alarms,
I shall be safe in his dear arms.

7 Then oh, my soul, arise and sing;
Behold thy Saviour, Friend, and King!
With pleasing smiles he now looks down,
And cries, "Press on, and take the crown."

8 "Prove faithful then a few more days,
Fight the good fight, and win the race;
And then thy soul with me shall reign,
Thy head a crown of glory gain."

9 My flesh shall slumber in the ground,
Till the last trumpet's joyful sound;
Then burst the tomb with sweet surprise,
And in my Saviour's image rise.

## 339 *P. M.*

THERE shall we reign with Jesus on that delightful shore,
And shout with the redeemed, our trials being
o'er;
The wicked cease from troubling, the weary
are at rest,
And we shall reign with Jesus, eternal ages
blest.

2 We shall be like the angels in that immortal
throng,
And shouting his salvation will be our lasting
song;

They sing creating goodness, and we redeeming love,
And this shall be our business in the bright worlds above.

3 This love so freely flowing, it animates our heart,
This love is still abounding in every place and part;
This love can ne'er be ended, though faith and hope should cease,
This love can ne'er be bounded, but ever will increase.

4 This love through endless ages, it ever is the same,
'Tis this our heart engages to love and serve the Lamb,
Unites us all together, and makes us of one soul:
It is the balm of Gilead, it makes the wounded whole. ^

# 340

THERE is a happy land, far, far away,
Where saints in glory stand, bright, bright as day;
Oh! how they sweetly sing, "Worthy is our Saviour King;"
Loud let his praises ring; praise, praise for aye.

2 Come to that happy land, come, come away;
Why will ye doubting stand, why still delay?
Oh, we shall happy be, when from sin and sorrow free;
Lord, we shall live for thee, blest, blest for aye.

3 Bright in that happy land beams every eye,
Kept by a Father's hand, love cannot die;

Oh, then to glory run; be a crown and kingdom
    won,
And bright above the sun, we reign for aye.

## 341

THROUGH the love of God our Saviour,
    All will be well;
Free and changeless is his favor,
    All, all is well.
Precious is the blood that healed us;
Perfect is the grace that sealed us,
Strong the hand stretched out to shield us,
    All must be well.

2 Though we pass through tribulation,
    All will be well;
Ours is such a full salvation,
    All, all is well.
Happy, still to God confiding,
Fruitful, if in Christ abiding,
Holy through the Spirit's guiding,
    All must be well.

3 We expect a bright to-morrow,
    All will be well;
Faith can sing through days of sorrow,
    All, all is well.
On our Father's love relying,
Jesus every need supplying,
Or in living or in dying,
    All must be well.

## 342

TO Jordan's banks our hosts are come,
    And shout to view their long-sought home.

    *And we're passing safely over*
    *To the other side of Jordan;*

*And we're passing safely over*
*To the land of endless rest.*

2 There in that beauteous, wealthy land,
  Bright streams "roll down their golden sand."

3 There trees of life, forever green,
  Along the river banks are seen.

4 There "never-withering flowers" appear,
  And spring and autumn rule the year.

5 Those lofty hills—I look on them,
  For there is New Jerusalem.

6 Its pearly gates, its golden streets,
  My longing heart with rapture greets.

7 The God of glory there displays
  The beamings of his smiling face.

8 O Zion! I have longed to be
  A happy citizen of thee.

9 No more to war, no more to roam,
  But dwell in peace and joy at home.

## 343

THE gloomy night of sadness
  Begins to flee away;
The glowing tinge of morning
  Proclaims the rising day:
The welcome day of promise,
  When Christ shall claim his right,
And on the world in darkness
  Pour forth a flood of light.

2 Now truth, unveiled, is shining
  With beams of sacred light;
And men, emerged from darkness,
  Behold the glorious sight;

Their glowing hearts in rapture
　　Are filled with joy divine;
And clad in borrowed lustre,
　　To Jesus' praise they shine.

3 Let us begin the anthems,
　　And join the choir above;
Exalt our great Redeemer,
　　And praise the God we love:
All honor, praise, and glory,
　　Salvation to our God;
Hosanna to the Saviour,
　　Who washed us in his blood.

4 The courts of heaven are ringing
　　With songs of highest strains,
And ceaseless praise is rolling
　　Along the flowery plains:
Oh! could we rise triumphant,
　　And join with those above,
To shout and sing forever
　　The Saviour's dying love.

## 344

THERE is a beautiful world
　　Where saints and angels sing,
A world where peace and pleasure reigns,
　　And heavenly praises ring.

　　　　*We'll be there, we'll be there;*
　　　　　*Palms of vict'ry, crowns of glory,*
　　　　*We shall wear*
　　　　　*In that beautiful world on high.*

2 There is a beautiful world,
　　Unseen to mortal sight;
And darkness never enters there:
　　That home is fair and bright.
　　22

3 There is a beautiful world
    Of harmony and love;
  Oh, may we safely enter there,
    And dwell with God above.

## 345                    *12s & 11s.*

WE'RE bound for the land of the pure and
        the holy,
  The home of the happy—the kingdom of love;
. Ye wanderers from God in the broad road of
        folly,
    Oh, say, will you go to the Eden above?

      *Will you go? will you go?*
      *Oh, say, will you go to the Eden above?*

2 In that blessed land neither sighing nor anguish
    Can breathe in the fields where the glorified
        rove;
  Ye heart-burdened ones who in misery lan-
        guish,
    Oh, say, will you go to the Eden above?

3 Nor fraud, nor deceit, nor the hand of op-
        pression,
    Can injure the dwellers in that holy grove;
  No wickedness there—not a shade of trans-
        gression,
    Oh, say, will you go to the Eden above?

4 No poverty there;—no, the saints are all
        wealthy,—
    The heirs of his glory whose nature is love;
  Nor sickness can reach them—that country is
        healthy;
    Oh, say, will you go to the Eden above?

5 Each saint has a mansion prepared and all
        furnished,
    Ere from this clay house he is summoned to
        move;

Its gates and its towers with glory are bur-
  nished;
Oh, say, will you go to the Eden above?

6 March on, happy pilgrims, that land is before
  you,
  And soon its ten thousand delights we shall
    prove;
Yes, soon we shall walk o'er the hills of bright
    glory,
  And drink the pure joys of the Eden above.

7 And yet, guilty sinner, we would not forsake
    thee,
  ·We halt yet a moment, as onward we move;
Oh! come to thy Lord—in his arms he will
    take thee,
  And bear thee along to the Eden above.

8 Methinks thou art now in thy wretchedness
    saying,
  Oh! who can this guilt from my conscience
    remove?
No other but Jesus; then come to him praying,
  Prepare me, O Lord, for the Eden above.

## 346    ·    *C. M.*

WHAT is there here to court my stay,
    To hold me back from home,
While angels beckon me away,
    And Jesus bids me come?
Shall I regret my parted friends,
    Still in the vale confined?
Nay, but whene'er my soul ascends,
    They will not stay behind.

2 The race we all are running now;
    And if I first attain,
They too their willing heads shall bow,
    They too the prize shall gain;

Now on the brink of death we stand,
And if I pass before,
They all shall soon escape to land,
And hail me on that shore.

3 Then if I suddenly remove
That hidden life to share,
I shall not lose my friends above,
But more enjoy them there:
There we in Jesus' praise shall join,
His boundless love proclaim,
And solemnize in songs divine .
The marriage of the Lamb.

**347**      From "GOLDEN CHAIN."     *8s & 7s.*
[By permission of W. B. BRADBURY.]

WE are out on the ocean sailing,
Homeward bound we sweetly glide;
We are out on the ocean sailing
To a home beyond the tide.

*All the storms will soon be over,*
*Then we'll anchor in the harbor;*
*We are out on the ocean sailing*
*To a home beyond the tide.*

2 Millions now are safely landed
Over on the golden shore;
Millions more are on their journey,
Yet there's room for millions more.

3 You have kindred over yonder,
On that bright and happy shore;
By and by we'll swell the number,
When the toils of life are o'er.

4 Spread your sails, while heavenly breezes
Gently waft our vessel on;

All on board are sweetly singing—
Free salvation is the song.

5 When we all are safely anchored,
We will shout—our trials o'er—
We will walk about the city,
And we'll sing for evermore.

## 348

WHEN I think of that city of light,
And of crowns which the glorified wear,
And of garments so pure and so white,
Then I long, oh, I long to be there.

*Oh, I long with the saints in light*
*To be clothed in the garments so white,*
*And in songs with the angels unite,*
*Singing glory, hallelujah, to the Lamb.*

2 It is not that I'm weary of pain,
Or impatient in trials and cares,
For I know that to die would be gain,
And I long, oh, I long to be there.

3 To that city my Saviour has gone,
A rich mansion and crowns to prepare,
For the hosts that are following on,
And I long, oh, I long to be there.

4 When I read of the saints gathered home,
To that city of jewels most rare;
I with joy hail the message to "come,"
For I long, oh, I long to be there.

## 349

WHITHER, pilgrims, are you going,
Each one on his way?
We are on our heavenly journey,
All of us to-day.

> *Going, going,*
> *To our heavenly home;*
> *Singing, singing,*
> *Singing as we go.*

2 Fear ye not the way so lonely,
　You a feeble band?
No, for friends unseen are near us,
　Angels round us stand.

3 Tell me, pilgrims, what you hope for
　In that better land?
Spotless robes and crowns of glory
　From our Saviour's hand.

4 Will you let me journey with you
　To that better land?
Come along, we bid you welcome
　To our happy band.

# 350

WE are going, going, going,
　To a land of light;
Where are flowing, flowing, flowing,
　Waters pure and bright.

> *Going, going,*
> *To our heavenly home;*
> *Singing, singing,*
> *Singing as we go.*

2 We are singing, singing, singing,
　As we pass along;
Hear the ringing, ringing, ringing,
　Of triumphant song.

3 Jesus, Saviour, leave us never,
　May we faithful prove;
Then at home with thee forever,
　Gathered be above.

## DEATH, JUDGMENT AND RESURRECTION.

**351**                              *P. M.*

COME, ghastly death, and lay me low,
  For I long to see that day;
I tremble not to meet thy blow,
  For I long to see that day.

> *Crying victory! victory!*
> *Victory over death!*
> *Crying victory! victory!*
> *I long to see that day.*

2 My Saviour's hand hath drawn thy sting,
  When I shall vict'ry, vict'ry sing!

3 The grave to me more pleasant seems,
  Than downy beds to weary limbs.

4 I there shall lay me down to sleep,
  And Christ my dust shall safely keep.

5 But oh! a brighter day shall rise,
  Shall blaze o'er earth, and sea, and skies.

6 That last great day of doom and dread,
  For which all other days were made.

7 Then Christ shall come, and I shall fly,
  In triumph to his throne on high.

8 His powerful voice shall rend my tomb,
  And starting I shall quit its gloom.

9 Then shall I join the ransomed throng,
  And vict'ry still shall be my song.

10 The long white robe we all shall wear,
  And palms of vict'ry each shall bear.

11 With harps in hand the host shall move
  Up to Jerusalem above.

12 Her pearly gates shall then unfold,
  When we shall walk her streets of gold.

13 These eyes at length shall weep no more,
    All sufferings past, all sorrows o'er.

14 The throne of light we then shall see,
    And shout eternal victory.

## 352 *4 lines, 8s.*

WE speak of the realms of the blest,
    That country so bright and so fair,
And oft are its glories confessed—
    But what must it be to be there?

2 We speak of its pathways of gold,
    Its walls decked with jewels so rare,
Its wonders and pleasures untold—
    But what must it be to be there?

3 We speak of its freedom from sin,
    From sorrow, temptation, and care;
From trials without and within—
    But what must it be to be there?

4 We speak of its service of love,
    The robes which the glorified wear,
The church of the first-born above—
    But what must it be to be there?

5 Do thou, Lord, 'midst pleasure or wo,
    For heaven our spirits prepare,
And shortly we also shall know,
    Shall feel what it is to be there.

## 353 *P. M.*

DAY of Judgment, day of wonders!
    Hark! the trumpet's awful sound,
Louder than ten thousand thunders,
    Shakes the vast creation round!
        How the summons
    Will the sinner's heart confound!

2 See the Judge our nature wearing,
    Clothed in majesty divine!
You who long for his appearing,
    Then shall say, "This God is mine."
        Gracious Saviour!
    Own me on that day for thine.

3 At his call the dead awaken,
    Rise to life from earth and sea;
All the powers of nature, shaken
    By his looks, prepare to flee:
        Careless sinner,
    What will then become of thee?

4 Horrors past imagination
    Will surprise your trembling heart,
When you hear your condemnation,
    "Hence, accursed wretch, depart!
        Thou with Satan
    And his angels have thy part!"

5 But to those who have confessed,
    Saved and served your Lord below,
He will say, "Come in, ye blessed,
    See the kingdom I bestow:
        You forever
    Shall my love in glory know."

6 Under sorrows and reproaches
    Let this thought our courage raise;
Swiftly God's great day approaches,
    Sighs shall then be turned to praise:
        May we triumph
    When this world is in a blaze.

## 354

GONE, gone from earth's wearisome trials and
    wo;
    The contest is over at length;
We selfishly sought to detain her below,

But the angels excelled us in strength,—
Excelled us poor mortals in strength.

2 Commissioned to bear from our bosoms away
The prize of our heart's fondest love,
They left in our grasp but the vesture of clay,
And lodged the pure spirit above;
They lodged it with Jesus above.

3 By prayer unremitting we struggled full long
The cohorts of mercy to foil;
Till, tuning their harps to the voice of sweet
song,
They vanquished, and bore off the spoil;
Triumphantly bore off the spoil.

4 What marvel the spirit accustomed to sighs,
Allured by soft melody's tone,
Should plume her white pinions, and mount to
the skies,
Where sighing is nevermore known;
Is never—can never be known?

5 Ah! wherefore the pious, the pure and the true,
Thus snatched from our sin-flooded shore.
Where saints, greatly needed, are feeble and
few,
And sinners in number are more;
Where sinners are stronger and more?

6 Be silent the cavil that whispers within:
Death comes as the mandate of love,
Removing the pious from suffering and sin,
Because they are needed above;
More needed for angels above.

7 They need them to strengthen the minist'ring
throng,
To whom the sweet office is given
To visit us wand'rers with harp and with song,

And win our affections to heaven;
  Our friends—our affections to heaven.

**355**      *8 lines, 8s & 7s.*

HAIL! ye sighing sons of sorrow,
  Learn with me your certain doom;
Learn with me your fate to-morrow;
  Dead, perhaps laid in the tomb.
See all nature fading, dying,
  Silent all things seem to mourn,
Life from vegetation flying,
  Calls to mind the mouldering urn.

2 Lo! in yonder forest standing
  Lofty cedars, how they nod!
Scenes of nature, how surprising!
  Read in nature nature's God:
While the annual frosts are cropping
  Leaves and tendrils from the trees,
So our friends are yearly dropping,
  We are like to one of these.

3 Hollow winds about me roaring,
  Noisy waters round me rise,
While I sit my fate deploring,
  Tears fast streaming from my eyes:
What to me is autumn's treasure,
  Since I know no earthly joy;
Long I've lost all youthful pleasure,
  Time will health and youth destroy.

4 Former friends, how oft I've sought them
  Just to cheer a troubled mind,
Now they're gone, like leaves of autumn,
  Driven before the dreary wind:
When a few more days are wasted,
  And a few more scenes are o'er,
When a few more griefs I've tasted,
  I shall fall to rise no more.

5 Fast my sun of life's declining,
 Soon 'twill set in endless night,
But my hopes, pure and reviving,
 Rise to fairer worlds of light.
Cease this trembling, mourning, sighing,
 Death shall burst this sullen gloom,
Then, my spirit, fluttering, flying,
 Shall be borne beyond the tomb.

## 356

HAPPY the spirit released from its clay;
 Happy the soul that goes bounding away;
Singing, as upward it hastes to the skies,
Victory! victory! homeward I rise.

2 Many the toils it has passed through below,
Many the seasons of trial and wo;
Many the doubtings it never should sing
Victory! victory! thus on the wing.

3 There lies the wearisome body at rest;
Closed are its eyelids, and quiet its breast;
But the glad spirit, on pinions of light,
Victory! victory! sings in its flight.

4 While we are weeping our friends gone from
  earth,
Angels are singing their heavenly birth:
Welcome, oh welcome to our happy shore;
Victory! victory! weep ye no more.

5 How can we wish them recalled from their
  home,
Longer in sorrowing exile to roam?
Safely they passed from their troubles beneath,
Victory! victory! shouting in death.

6 Thus let them slumber, till Christ from the
  skies,
Bids them in glorified bodies arise;

Singing, as upward they spring from the tomb,
Victory! victory! Jesus hath come!

**357** *C. M.*

HEAR what the voice from heaven proclaims
For all the pious dead:
Sweet is the savor of their name,
And soft their sleeping bed.

2 They die in Jesus, and are blest;
How kind their slumbers are!
From sufferings and from sin released,
And freed from every snare.

3 Far from this world of toil and strife,
They're present with the Lord;
The labors of their mortal life
End in a large reward.

**358** *P. M.*

HASTE, haste, the clouds arise;
Stay not in danger's path;
They gather up the frowning skies
Like messengers of wrath.
Behold the ark of safety near,
Be warned of God, be moved by fear.

2 See how the lightnings leap,
Exulting thunders shout,
Rebellious man from earth to sweep,
The foes of God to rout:
The door of mercy yet is wide,
Go, sinner, in the ark abide.

3 Behold the darkening gloom,
The skies send out a sound,
Unthinking man, the signs of doom
Are gathering thick around;
Go, seek for safety while you may,
The ark is waiting—come away.

4 Already streams descend
   Of condemnation dread;
Oh! who will thee from wrath defend?
   Who screen thy guilty head?
The ark, the ark alone can save
Poor sinking souls from death's dark wave.

5 Haste, haste to seek its door,
   The storm is coming fast;
To-day a refuge there secure:
   To-day may be the last;
Brave not the fury of the flood,
But rest thee in the ark of God.

6 That ark will bear thee up,
   O'er sin and danger's sea,
And land at last on Zion's top,
   Where dangers cease to be:
Come in, bewildered soul, come in;
Be safe from fear, and cease to sin.

7 Here rest thee, weary soul—
   Let torrents from the skies
Adown the sinking mountains roll,
   Let oceans foaming rise:
The ark, the ark will pass them o'er,
And land thee safe on Canaan's shore.

# 359

IF I, "in thy likeness," O Lord, may awake,
   And shine a pure image of thee,
Then "I shall be satisfied" when I can break
   These fetters of flesh, and be free.
I know this stained table must first be washed
     white,
   To let thy bright features be drawn;
I know I must suffer the darkness of night,
   To welcome the rising of morn.

2 Then "I shall be satisfied" when I can cast
   These shadows of nature all by;
When this cold dreary world from my vision
     shall pass,
   And let my soul open her eye;
I gladly shall see the bless'd morn drawing
     near,
   When time's dreary fancies shall fade,
If then, "in thy likeness," I may but appear,
   And rise in thy beauty arrayed.

3 To see thee in glory, O Lord, as thou art,
   From this mortal and perishing clay,
The spirit, immortal, in peace would depart,
   And joyous, mount up her high way;
When on thine own image in me thou hast
     smiled,
   Within thy bless'd mansions; and when
The arms of my Father encircle his child,
   Oh, " I shall be satisfied" then.

# 360         *8, 7, 4.*

LO! he cometh! countless trumpets
   Blow, to raise the sleeping dead;
'Midst ten thousand saints and angels
   See their great exalted Head.
     Hallelujah !
Welcome, welcome; Son of God.

2 Now his merit, by the harpers,
   Through the eternal deep resounds,
Now resplendent shine his nail-prints;
   Every eye shall see his wounds:
     They who pierced him
Shall at his appearance wail.

3 Full of joyful expectation,
   Saints behold the Judge appear:

Truth and justice go before him,
   Now the joyful sentence hear.
     Hallelujah!
Welcome, welcome, Judge divine.

4 "Come, ye blessed of my Father,
   Enter into life and joy;
Banish all your fears and sorrows,
   Endless praise be your employ."
     Hallelujah!
Welcome, welcome to the skies.

5 Now at once they rise to glory,
   Jesus brings them to the King.
There, with all the hosts of heaven,
   They eternal anthems sing.
     Hallelujah!
Boundless glory to the Lamb.

## 361        *C. M.*

MY thoughts on awful subjects roll,
   Damnation and the dead!
What horrors seize the guilty soul
   Upon a dying bed!
Lingering about these mortal shores,
   She makes a long delay;
Till, like a flood, with rapid force,
   Death sweeps the wretch away.

2 Then swift and dreadful she descends
   Down to the fiery coast,
Among abominable fiends,
   Herself a frighted ghost.
There endless crowds of sinners lie,
   And darkness makes their chains;
Tortured with keen despair, they cry,
   Yet wait for fiercer pains.

3 Not all their anguish and their blood,
   For their own guilt atones,

Nor the compassion of a God
  Shall hearken to their groans
Amazing grace, that kept my breath,
  Nor bid my soul remove,
Till I had learned my Saviour's death,
  And well insured his love.

# 362

O THERE will be mourning, mourning,
  mourning, mourning!
O there will be mourning at the judgment-seat
  of Christ.

*Parents and children there will part,*
*Parents and children there will part,*
*Parents and children there will part,*
  *Will part to meet no more.*

2 O there will be mourning, &c.

*Wives and husbands there will part, &c.*

3 O there will be mourning, &c.

*Brothers and sisters there will part, &c.*

4 O there will be mourning, &c.

*Friends and neighbors there will part, &c.*

5 O there will be mourning, &c.

*Pastors and people there will part, &c.*

6 O there will be mourning, &c.

*Devils and sinners there will meet, &c.*

7 O there will be shouting, shouting, shouting,
  shouting!
O there will be shouting at the judgment-seat
  of Christ.

*Saints and angels there will meet, &c.*
  23

## 363

RIVER of death, thy stream I see,
Between the bright city of rest and me;
Fearless thy sable surge I'll brave,
For sweet is the prospect o'er thy wave.

*Waft me, O waft me safely o'er,*
*And land me, dear Saviour, on Canaan's shore.*

2 Why should I fear to stem thy tide,
With him who has loved me, as guard and
guide?
Wisdom and power control thy flood,
While faith says my passage was paid with
blood.

3 What is it gilds thy darksome foam?
'Tis light shining forth from my happy home,
Music that thrills my soul to hear,
Seems floating me o'er thy surface drear.

4 Help me! I feel the waters rise,
Yet visions of glory still glad my eyes;
Saviour, I come; I soon shall be
Among the bless'd purchase of Calvary.

## 364                     *L. M.*

SEE the eternal Judge descending,
Seated on his Father's throne;
Now, poor sinner, Christ will show thee
That he's with the Father one:
Trumpets call thee,
Stand and hear thy awful doom.

2 Hear the sinner now lamenting,
At the sight of fiercer pain:
Cries and tears he now is venting,

But he weeps and cries in vain:
　　Greatly mourning
That he ne'er was born again.

3 Yonder sits my slighted Saviour,
　　With the marks of dying love:
O that I had sought his favor
　　When I felt the Spirit move!
　　　Doomed I'm justly,
　　For I have against him strove.

4 All his wooing I have slighted,
　　While he daily sought my soul;
If my vows to him I plighted,
　　Yet for sin I broke them all:
　　　Golden moments,
　　How neglected did they roll!

5 There I see my godly neighbors,
　　Who were once despised by me,
Now they're clad in dazzling splendor,
　　Waiting my sad fate to see;
　　　Farewell, neighbors—
　　Dismal gulf, I'm bound for thee.

6 Hail! ye ghosts that dwell in darkness,
　　Groaning, rattling of your chains!
Christ has now announced my sentence,
　　I'm to dwell in endless pains;
　　　Down I'm rolling,
　　Never to return again.

7 Now experience vainly shows me,
　　Hell is not a fabled thing,
Now I see my friends in glory,
　　Round the throne they ever sing.
　　　I'm tormented
　　With an everlasting sting.

## 365

SOON we shall see the glorious morning;
   Saints arise, saints arise;
Sinners, attend the notes of warning;
      Saints arise, saints arise:
   The resurrection day draws near,
   The King of saints shall soon appear,
   And high unfurl his banners here;
      Saints arise, saints arise.

2 Hear ye the trump of God resounding;
      Saints arise, saints arise;
Through death's dark vaults its notes rebound-
      ing;
      Saints arise, saints arise;
   To meet the bridegroom, haste prepare;
   Put on your bridal garments fair,
   And hail your Saviour in the air;
      Saints arise, saints arise.

3 The saints who sleep with joy awaken,
      All arise, all arise:
Their clay cold beds are quick forsaken;
      All arise, all arise:
   Not one, of all the faithful few,
   Who here on earth the Saviour knew,
   But starts, with bliss, his Lord to view:
      All arise, all arise.

4 Pursue them on their pathway glorious;
      All arise, all arise;
Led by their King, o'er death victorious;
      All arise, all arise;
   On Zion's hill secure they stand,
   With palms of victory in their hand;
   To that long-sought and peaceful land,
      All arise, all arise.

5 Fast by the throne of God, behold them;
    Blissful scene, blissful scene;
And in his arms the Saviour folds them,
    Blissful scene, blissful scene;
  With wreaths of glory round their head,
  No tears of sorrow now are shed,
  To joy's full fountain all are led;
    All is bliss, all is bliss.

## 366

•SEE the shadows thickly stealing   •
 O'er the sunny brow of day!
Hark! the bell's deep solemn pealing
    In the air has died away!
      Come, ere sleep unnerve our vigor,
    Let us for protection pray!

2 From the robber, from the madness
    Of the all-devouring fire,
From a troubled spirit's sadness,
    From the plague's unpitying ire,
      Save us, Lord! Good Lord, deliver!
    Thou whose mercies never tire!

3 Jesus! Saviour! lowly bending
    At the footstool of thy might,
Let thy love, our darkness ending,
    Robe us in thy garb of light!
      Guide us here, and then forever,
    Place us on thy glory's height.

## 367              *10s.*

" THOU must go with me," said the terror-
             king,
To a pale young man in the blooming spring;
" I must quench the light in thy brilliant eye,
And drain life's fountains of crimson dry."

2 "Is this death? is this death?" the young hero
  replied,
"With thy weapons of fear, and thine accents
  of pride?
Thou hast met me, indeed, at an early hour,
But I tremble not now as I face thy power!

3 "Ah! knowest thou not when my Master died,
Thy sting was lost in his wounded side;
And thy gates of steel and thy bars of brass
Gave way that the King of glory might pass?

4 "As the friend of him in his power complete,
The foe which he foiled I can fearlessly meet;
Thou may'st rob what I prize, and to flames
  may'st fling,
But more that I prize from the ashes shall
  spring.

5 "Though dear be the friends that my death
  may bereave,
Far better the circle I *join* than I *leave;*
Its numbers like drops in the ocean's abyss,
And such love in *that* world, as we know not in
  *this!*

6 "When God hath more work for his servant in
  heaven
Than he has on the earth, let the summons be
  given;
I will go; and my joy, but a *fountain* before,
Shall spread like a *sea* without sounding or
  shore."

**368**    *P. M.*

THE Lord shall come! the earth shall quake!
 The mountains to their centre shake!
And, withering from the vault of night,
The stars shed pale their feeble light.

2 The Lord shall come! but not the same
As once in lowliness he came;
A silent Lamb before his foes,
A weary man, and full of woes.

3 The Lord shall come, a dreadful form!
With rainbow wreath and robes of storm!
On cherub-wings, and wings of wind,
Appointed Judge of all mankind.

4 Can this be he, who wont to stray
As pilgrim on the world's highway,  ◀
Oppressed by power, and mocked by pride,
The Nazarene—the crucified?

5 While sinners in despair shall call,
" Rocks, hide us; mountains, on us fall!"
The saints, ascending from the tomb,
Shall joyful sing, "The Lord is come!"

## 369  *L. M.*

THERE comes a day, a fearful day,
When earth and heaven shall flee away,
When, flaming on his great white throne,
Naught shall be seen but God alone:
The myriad crowds from every clime,
Shall gaze upon that throne sublime;
The great and small, the quick and dead,
Shall shout for joy, or quake with dread.

2 Oh! how shall I, a sinner born,
Lift up my head on that dread morn,
When glory, brightening to excess,
Proclaims the God of holiness?
The triune God, the lofty Lord,
Who, by his own omnific word,
Made thousand thousand worlds to be;
He speaks again; and lo! they flee.

3 When orbs on orbs affrighted fly,
  In lawless terror through the sky;
  When thrones and powers celestial fall,
  Before the glorious ALL IN ALL;
  Oh! how shall I, of baser birth,
  A sinful man, a worm of earth,
  Presume to meet the burning gaze,
  That wraps the heavens in sheets of blaze?

4 Father Eternal! God of love!
  Look down from mercy's seat above;
  Through Jesus now be reconciled
  To me, a wayward, wandering child:
  Be thou, O Christ, my stay, my trust,
  And when I moulder into dust,
  And when I rise from dust again,
  Be mine, my God—amen—amen.

# 370

WHAT'S this that steals, that steals upon my
      frame?
    Is it death? is it death?
That soon will quench, will quench this vital
      flame;
    Is it death? is it death?
If this be death, I soon shall be
From every pain and sorrow free,
I shall the King of glory see—
    All is well—all is well.

2 Weep not, my friends, my friends, weep not for
      me,
    All is well—all is well.
My sins are pardoned, pardoned, I am free,
    All is well—all is well.
There's not a cloud that doth arise,
To hide my Saviour from my eyes.

I soon shall mount the upper skies.
  All is well—all is well.

3 Tune, tune your harps, your harps, ye saints in
      glory,
  All is well—all is well.
I will rehearse, rehearse the pleasing story,
  All is well—all is well.
Bright angels are from glory come;
They're round my bed—they're in my room:
They wait to waft my spirit home.
  All is well—all is well.

4 Hark! hark! my Lord, my Lord and Master
      calls me,
  All is well—all is well.
I soon shall see, shall see his face in glory,
  All is well—all is well.
Farewell, my friends, adieu, adieu,
 I can no longer stay with you,
My glittering crown appears in view.
  All is well—all is well.

5 Hail, hail, all hail, all hail ye blood-washed
      throng,
  Saved by grace—saved by grace.
I come to join, to join your rapturous song,
  Saved by grace—saved by grace.
All, all is peace, and joy divine,
And heaven and glory now are mine,
All hallelujah to the Lamb,
  All is well—all is well.

**371**                    *C. M.*

WHEN blooming youth is snatched away,
    By death's resistless hand,
Our hearts the mournful tribute pay;
  Which pity must demand.

2 While pity prompts the rising sigh,
   O may this truth—impress'd
With awful power—I too must die!
   Sink deep in every breast.

3 Let this vain world engage no more:
   Behold the gaping tomb!
It bids us seize the present hour,
   To-morrow death may come.

4 The voice of this alarming scene,
   May every heart obey:
Nor be the heavenly warning vain,
   Which calls to watch and pray.

5 O let us fly, to Jesus fly,
   Whose powerful arm can save;
Then shall our hopes ascend on high,
   And triumph o'er the grave.

6 Great God, thy sovereign grace impart,
   With cleansing, healing power;
This only can prepare the heart
   For death's all solemn hour.

## 372

WHEN the spark of life is waning,
   Weep not for me.
When the languid eye is straining,
   Weep not for me.
When the feeble pulse is ceasing,
Start not at its swift decreasing;
'Tis the fettered soul's releasing;
   Weep not for me.

2 When the pangs of death assail me,
   Weep not for me.
Christ is mine—he cannot fail me,
   Weep not for me.

Yes, though sin and doubt endeavor,
From his love my soul to sever,
Jesus is my strength forever!
    Weep not for me.

**373**          *P. M.*

WHY shrinks my weak nature? ah! what
    can it mean?
Why flutters my heart, which till now was
    serene?
Why lingering and trembling, while glory's so
    near?
Or whence the enchantment that fetters me
    here?

2 Thou world of illusions, forever adieu!
Your phantoms unhallowed recede from my
    view;
New worlds and new wonders my passions
    invite,
And glories ineffable dawn on my sight.

3 Hail, visions celestial, and thou divine Source
Of life, hope, and glory; if e'er in my course,
Thy grace hath renewed and made perfect my
    heart,
Now let me in peace and in triumph depart.

4 'Tis done; lo, they come! bright celestials
    descend;
Saints, angels, and seraphs, their symphonies
    lend:
The spheres are all vocal, the raptures draw
    near,
Impartial vibrations resound in my ear.

5 Cease! cease then, fond nature! O cease then
    thy strife!
And let me now languish and die into life:

Bless'd powers, receive me; I mount on your
    wing;
O grave, where's thy victory? O death, where's
    thy sting?

## 374. *P. M.*

WHAT sound is this salutes mine ear?
    Methinks 'tis Jubal's trump I hear,
Long looked for now has come;
It shakes the heavens, the earth, the sea,
Proclaims the year of jubilee,
    Return, ye exiles, home.

2 Behold the new Jerusalem,
    Illuminated by the Lamb,
      In glory doth appear;
Fair Zion rising from the tomb,
To meet the bridegroom now he's come,
    And hail the jubilee year.

3 King Jesus takes her to his arms—
    Transported with his glorious charms,
      She thus begins to sing;
From tears, and sighs, and groans, and pains,
She soars where joy immortal reigns,
    To view the rosy spring.

4 As larks and linnets sweetly sing,
    While hills and valleys round them ring,
      'Scaped from the fowler's snare,
One thousand years she here shall dwell,
While Satan is chained down in hell,
    Which ends the jubilee year.

5 The dragon is let loose once more,
    And round the earth his trumpets roar,
      He's now for war again;

But he that sits upon the throne
Drives Satan and his legions down
   Into the fiery main.

6 The seventh trumpet you shall hear,
  A great white throne shall then appear,
    Ten thousand angels round;
  An angel turns the moon to blood,
  Puts out the sun, consumes the flood,
    And burns the solid ground.

7 Arise, ye nations, and come forth,
  From east and west and north and south,
    Behold, the Judge is come;
  What horror fills the guilty breast,
  Compelled to stand the solemn test,
    And hear the awful doom.

8 Depart, ye cursed, down to hell,
  With howling fiends forever dwell,
    No more to see my face;
  My glorious gospel you've withstood,
  And set at naught my precious blood,
    And scoffed at sovereign grace.

9 See parents and their children part,
  Some shout for joy, some bleed in heart,
    Never to meet again;
  In fiery chariots Zion flies,
  And quickly gains the upper skies
    On Canaan's happy plain.

**375**           *P. M.*

YONDER! see the Lord descending,
  Hark! his chariot's drawing near;
Starry worlds before him rending,
  Flaming troops do now appear—

Heaven shaking, earth a quaking,
    Mountains fly before his face,
The dead their dusty beds forsaking,
    Nature sinking in a blaze.

*Hallelujah! hallelujah!*
    *Hark! the herald angels sing,*
*Join us, Christians!   Join us, Christians!*
    *Join to praise our new-born King.*

2 Now behold each shining conqueror,
    Rising from their dusty beds,
Fly to meet their blessed Saviour,
    Glittering crowns upon their heads;
Hear them tell their pleasing story
    To their smiling, lovely King,
Glory, glory, glory, glory,
    Glory is the song they sing.

3 Once an infant in a manger,
    . There the Lord of glory lay;
No place to lay that little stranger
    But upon the oxen's hay;
  Now he's crowned with a rainbow
    Brighter than a sardine stone;
He comes, he comes, the Christian sees him,
    Seated on his great white throne.

4 Jesus saves us from temptation,
    Sin and Satan, death and hell,
And he bought our great salvation:
    Glory to Immanuel.
Once a dying on a mountain,
    There his precious blood did run;
Now he's brought us to the fountain,
    Springing from his Father's throne.

*Give him glory, give him glory,*
    *Let all heaven begin to sing,*

*Glory, glory, glory, glory,*
  *Through eternal ages ring.*

## MISCELLANEOUS.

**376**                     *11s & 12s.*

A WAY from his home and the friends of his
      youth,
He hasted, the herald of mercy and truth:
For the love of his Lord, and to seek for the
      lost;
Soon, alas! was his fall—but he died at his
      post.

2 The stranger's eye wept, that, in life's brightest
      bloom,
One gifted so highly should sink to the tomb;
For in ardor he led in the van of the host,
And he fell like a soldier—he died at his post.

3 He wept not himself that his warfare was
      done;—
The battle was fought, and the victory won:
But he whispered of those whom his heart
      clung to most,
"Tell my brethren, for me, that I died at my
      post."

4 He asked not a stone to be sculptured with
      verse;
He asked not that fame should his merits re-
      hearse;
But he asked as a boon, when he gave up the
      ghost,
That his brethren might know that he died at
      his post.

5 Victorious his fall—for he rose as he fell,
  With Jesus, his Master, in glòry to dwell;
He has passed o'er the stream, and has reached
    the bright coast,
For he fell like a martyr—he died at his post.

6 And can we the words of his exit forget?
  Oh, no, they are fresh in our memory yet;
An example so brilliant shall never be lost,
We will fall in the work—we will die at our
    post.

**377**                 *P. M.*

ARISE and shine, O Zion fair,
  Behold thy light is come;
Thy glorious conquering king is near,
  To take his exiles home:
The trumpet sounding through the sky,
  To set poor sinners free;
The day of wonder now is nigh;
  The year of jubilee.

2 Ye heralds, blow your trumpets loud,
  The earth must know her doom;
Go spread the news from pole to pole,
  Behold, the Judge is come:
Blow out the sun! burn up the earth!
  Consume the rolling flood!
While every star shall disappear,
  Go turn the moon to blood!

3 Arise, ye nations under ground,
  Before the Judge appear;
All tongues and languages shall come,
  Their final doom to hear!
King Jesus on his dazzling throne,
  Ten thousand angels round,
And Gabriel with a silver trump,
  Echoes the awful sound.

4 The glorious news of gospel grace
    To sinners now is o'er;
The trump in Zion now is still,
    And to be heard no more!
The watchmen all have left their walls,
    And with their flocks above,
On Canaan's peaceful shore they sing, ,
    And shout redeeming love.

## 378 *C. M.*

*TUNE.—Should old acquaintance be forgot?*

BY cool Siloam's shady rill,
    How sweet the lily grows!
How sweet the breath beneath the hill
    Of Sharon's dewy rose!
And such the child whose early feet
    The paths of peace have trod,
Whose secret heart with influence sweet
    Is upward drawn to God.

2 By cool Siloam's shady rill
    The lily must decay;
The rose that blooms beneath the hill
    Must shortly fade away;
And soon, too soon, the wintry hour
    Of man's maturer age
May shake the soul with sorrow's power,
    And stormy passion's rage.

3 O thou, whose infancy was found
    With heavenly rays to shine,
Whose years, with changeless virtue crowned,
    Were all alike divine:
Dependent on thy bounteous breath,
    We seek thy grace alone;
In childhood, manhood, and in death,
    To keep us still thy own.
        24

**379**                    *12s & 8s.*

WHEN the harvest is past, and the summer
    is gone,
  And sermons and prayers shall be o'er,
When the beams cease to break of the sweet
    Sabbath morn,.
  And Jesus invites thee no more;
When the rich gales of mercy no longer shall
    blow,
  The gospel no message declare,
Sinner, how canst thou bear the deep wailings
    of wo!
  How suffer the night of despair!

2 When the holy have gone to the regions of
    peace,
  To dwell in the mansions above,
When their harmony wakes in the fullness of
    bliss,
  Their song to the Saviour they love;
Say, O sinner, that livest at rest and secure,
  Who fearest no trouble to come,
Can thy spirit the swellings of sorrow endure,
  Or bear the impenitent's doom?

**380**                    *P. M.*

BE KIND to thy father—for when thou wert
    young,
  Who loved thee so fondly as he?
He caught the first accents that fell from thy
    tongue,
  And joined in thine innocent glee.
Be kind to thy father—for now he is old,
  His locks intermingled with gray,
His footsteps are feeble, once fearless and bold,
  Thy father is passing away.

2 Be kind to thy mother—for lo! on her brow
    May traces of sorrow be seen ;
 Oh, well may'st thou cherish and comfort her
      now ;
    For loving and kind hath she been.
  Remember thy mother—for thee will she pray,
    As long as God giveth her breath—
  With accents of kindness, then, cheer her lone
      way,
    E'en to the dark valley of death.

3 Be kind to thy brother—his heart will have
      dearth,
    If the smile of thy joy be withdrawn ;
  The flowers of feeling will fade at their birth,
    If the dew of affection be gone.
  Be kind to thy brother—wherever you are,
    The love of a brother shall be
  An ornament purer and richer by far
    Than pearls from the depth of the sea.

4 Be kind to thy sister—not many may know
    The depth of true sisterly love,
 . The wealth of the ocean lies fathoms below
    The surface that sparkles above.
  Thy kindness shall bring to thee many sweet
      hours,
    And blessings thy pathway to crown,
  Affection shall weave thee a garland of flowers
    More precious than wealth or renown.

**381**       *8s & 6s.*

CAMP meetings with success are crowned,
  The wilderness and barren ground
    Now blossoms as the rose ;
The spices yield a rich perfume,
The rising lilies kindly bloom,
    And heavenly wisdom grows.

2 The num'rous praying, preaching host,
  Baptized with the Holy Ghost,
    The heavenly standard raise;
  They preach, and pray, and sweetly sing,
  And hills, and fields, and valleys ring
    With the Creator's praise.

3 Now sinners turning to the Lord,
  And falling down beneath the word,
    For mercy loudly cry;
  But when they taste his pard'ning love,
  And feel the witness from above,
    They rise and shout for joy.

4 To him who does our hearts inspire,
  Baptizes all our souls with fire,
    And makes us meet for heaven—
  To Christ the Lord, who reigns on high,
  Who rulès the ocean, earth, and sky,
    Be endless praises given.

## 382

C OME, tell of your vessel, and what is her
    name?
    Oh! happy Christian sailors!
Say, who is your captain, and what is his fame?
    Oh! happy Christian sailors!

    *She's the " Old ship of Zion,"*
      *Hallelujah!*
    *And her captain's Judah's Lion,*
      *Hallelujah!*

2 Say, who are on board, and from whence do
    they come?
    Oh! tell me, happy sailors!
And why do you bear them away from their
    home?
    Oh! tell me, happy sailors!

*They are chosen, called, and holy,*
*Hallelujah!*
*And have left the land of folly,*
*Hallelujah!*

3 Say, is her keel sound, and her larder well
stored?
Oh! tell me, happy sailors!
And will you receive other comrades on board?
Oh! tell me, happy sailors!

*Come on board the vessel, stranger;*
*, Hallelujah!*
*For we dread no want nor danger,*
*Hallelujah!*

**383** *P. M.*

DAUGHTER of Zion! awake from thy sadness,
Awake, for thy foes shall oppress thee no
more;
Bright o'er thy hills dawns the day-star of gladness;
Arise, for the night of thy sorrows is o'er.

2 Strong were thy foes; but the arm that subdued
them,
And scattered their legions, was mightier far:
They fled like the chaff from the scourge that
pursued them;
How vain were their steeds and their chariots
of war.

3 Daughter of Zion! the power that hath saved
thee,
Extolled with the harp and the timbrel shall
be:
Shout, for the foe is destroyed that enslaved
thee,
The oppressor is vanquished, and Zion is free.

384 *P. M.*

FAREWELL, my dear brethren, the time is
at hand
That we must be parted from this social band;
Our several engagements now call us away;
Our parting is needful, and we must obey.

2 Farewell, my dear brethren, farewell for awhile,
We'll soon meet again if kind Providence smile;
But when we are parted, and scattered abroad,
Let us pray for each other, and wrestle with
God.

3 Farewell, faithful soldiers, you'll soon be dis-
charged;
The war will be ended, your treasures enlarged;
With shouting and singing, though Jordan may
roar,
We'll enter fair Canaan, and rest evermore.

4 Farewell, ye young converts, who are 'listed for
war,
Some trials await you, but Jesus is near;
Although you must travel the dark wilderness,
Your Captain's before you, he'll lead you in
peace.

5 The world, and the devil, and hell all unite,
And bold persecution will try you to fright;
But Jesus is for you, who's stronger than they;
Let this animate you to march on your way.

6 Farewell, seeking mourners, with sad broken
heart,
Oh, hasten to Jesus, and choose the good part;
He's full of compassion, and mighty to save;
His arms are extended your souls to receive.

7 Farewell, faithful Christians, farewell all
    around,
Perhaps we'll not meet till the trumpet shall
    sound;
To meet you in glory I give you my hand,
Our Saviour to praise in the heavenly land.

8 Oh, glory, oh, glory, oh, glory to God!
Redemption we have through our Jesus' blood;
I long to be gone to meet him above,
To gaze on his glory, and feast on his love.

**385**           *12s & 11s.*

FROM the regions of love, lo! an angel de-
    scended,
And told the strange news, how the babe was
    attended;
Go, shepherds, and visit this wonderful stranger,
See yonder bright star—there's your Lord in
    the manger.

    *Hallelujah to the Lamb, who has purchased our*
      *pardon,*
    *We will praise him again when we pass over*
      *Jordan.*

2 Glad tidings I bring unto you and each nation,
Glad tidings of joy, now behold your salvation!
Then suddenly multitudes raise their glad
    voices,
And shout the Redeemer, while heaven rejoices.

3 Now glory to God in the highest is given,
Now glory to God is re-echoed through heaven,
Around the whole earth let us tell the glad story,
And sing of his love, his salvation, and glory.

4 Enraptured I burn, with delight and desire,
Such love, so divine, sets my soul all on fire;

Around the bright throne hosannas are ringing,
Oh, when shall I join them, and ever be singing?

5 Triumphantly ride in thy chariot victorious,·
And conquer with love, O Jesus, all glorious;
Thy banners unfurl!—let the nations surrender,
And own thee their Saviour, their God and De-
fender.

## 386     *L. M.*

FAREWELL, dear friends, I must be gone,
   I have no home or stay with you;
I'll take my staff and travel on,
   Till I a better world do view.

> *Farewell, farewell, farewell,*
> *My loving friends, farewell!*

2 Farewell, my friends, time rolls along,
   Nor waits for mortals, care, or bliss,
I leave you here, and travel on,
   Till I arrive where Jesus is.

.3 Farewell, my brethren in the Lord,
   To you I'm bound in cords of love,
Yet we believe his gracious word,
   That we shall all soon meet above.

4 Farewell, old soldier of the cross,
   You've struggled long and hard for heav'n;
You've counted all things here but dross,
   Fight on, the crown shall soon be given.

.5 Farewell, ye blooming sons of God,
   Sore conflicts yet await for you;
Yet dauntless keep the heavenly road,
   Till Canaan's happy land you view.

> *Fight on, fight on, fight on,*
> *The crown shall soon be given.*

6 Farewell, poor careless sinners too,
  It grieves my heart to leave you here,
Eternal vengeance waits for you ;
  O turn, and find salvation near.

> *O turn, O turn, O turn,*
> *And find salvation near.*

**387**                    *P. M.*

FAREWELL, my dear brethren, I bid you
    farewell,
I'm going to travel the way to excel ;
I'm going to travel the wilderness through,
Therefore, my dear brethren, I. bid you adieu.

2 The thoughts of our parting doth cause me to
    grieve,
  So well do I love you, but you I must leave ;
  My Jesus commands, and I must obey,
  Therefore, my dear brethren, don't grieve after
    me.

3 May heaven protect you, be Jesus your guide,
  On the walls of our Zion may you ever abide ;
  Though we live at a distance, and you I ne'er
    see,
  On the banks of sweet Canaan acquainted we'll
    be.

4 There all things are plenty, and the leaves
    growing green,
  And the parting of Christians no more to be
    seen ;
  No sorrow, no trouble shall enter that place,
  But there we shall join in a song of free grace.

5 And when we meet Jesus in the mansion above,
  Where saints and bright angels are feasting on
    love,

O then we shall look for each mourner that's
  here,
How glad we shall be to meet each other there!

6 Farewell to all sorrows, temptation, and pain,
I'm going where Jesus forever doth reign;
I'm going to Jesus, his goodness to prove,
Where saints and bright angels are feasting on
  love.

## 388

FADING, still fading, the last beam is shining,
  Father in heaven! the day is declining,
Safety and innocence fly with the light,
Temptation and danger walk forth with the
  night;
From the fall of the shade till the morning
  bells chime,
Shield me from danger, save me from crime,
  Father, have mercy, through Jesus Christ our
  Lord, Amen.

2 Father in heaven, O hear when we call;
Hear, for Christ's sake, who is Saviour of all;
Feeble and fainting we trust in thy might,
In doubting and darkness thy love be our light;
Let us sleep on thy breast while the night taper
  burns,
Wake in thy arms when morning returns.
  Father, have mercy, through Jesus Christ our
  Lord, Amen.

## 389 *C. M.*

TUNE.—*Auld Lang Syne.*

HAIL, sweetest, dearest tie that binds
  Our glowing hearts in one:
Hail! sacred hope, that tunes our minds,
  To joys before unknown.

*It is the hope, the blissful hope,*
*Which Jesus' grace has given :*
*The hope, when days and years are past,*
*We all shall meet in heaven.*

2 What though the northern winter-blast
  May howl around my cot;
What though beneath a southern sun
  Be cast thy distant lot.

  *For there we share the blissful hope, &c.*

3 From Burmah's shore, from Afric's strand,
  From India's burning plain;
From Europe and Columbia's land,
  We hope to meet again.

  *It is the hope, the blissful hope, &c.*

4 Nor lingering look, nor parting sigh
  Our future home shall know;
There love shall beam from every eye,
  And hope immortal grow.

  *Oh, sacred hope, oh, blissful hope, &c.*

# 390

HOW painfully pleasing the fond recollection
  Of youthful emotions and innocent joy,
When blessed with parental advice and affec-
    tion,
  Surrounded with mercies, with peace from
    on high!
I still view the chair of my father and mother,
  The seats of their offspring as ranged on each
    hand,
And that richest book which excels every other,
  The family Bible which lay on the stand.

  *The old-fashioned Bible, the dear blessed Bible,*
  *The family Bible that lay on the stand.*

2 That Bible, the volume of God's inspiration,
 At morn and at evening could yield us de-
 light;
'The prayer of our sire was a sweet invocation♥
 For mercy by day and for safety through
 night.
Our hymns of thanksgiving with harmony
 swelling,
All warm from the heart of a family band,
Half raised us from earth to that rapturous
 dwelling,
 Described in the Bible that lay on the stand.

3 Ye scenes of tranquillity, long have we parted,
 My hopes almost gone, and my parents no
 more;
In sorrow and sadness I live broken-hearted,
 And wander unknown on a far-distant shore.
Yet how can I doubt my Redeemer's protection,
 Forgetful of gifts from his bountiful hand?
Oh, let me with patience receive his correction,
 And think of the Bible that lay on the stand.

## 391 *P. M.*

HAIL the gospel jubilee,
 Jesus comes to set us free,
Who shed for us his precious blood,
To raise our fallen souls to God;
And since the work of suffering's done,
We'll glory give to God alone.
 Free salvation be our boast,
 Ever mindful what it cost;
 Ever grateful for the prize,
 Let our praises reach the skies.

*Firm united let us be,*
*In the bonds of charity;*
*As a band of brothers joined,*
*Loving God and all mankind.*

Rise, ye heralds of the Lord,
Take the breastplate, shield, and sword;
Against the hosts of hell proclaim
A war in Christ's all conquering name:
Nor fear to gain the victory
When for this glorious liberty
  You on Jesus Christ depend—
  He'll the suffering cause defend;
  Place, oh place in him your trust,
  He's almighty, wise, and just.

    *Firm united brethren stand,*
    *Firm, an undivided band—*
    *Brethren dear, in Jesus joined,*
    *Filled with all his constant mind.*

Sound, the gospel trumpet sound,
Through the earth's remotest bound;
Let Jesus' name, with loud applause,
Ring through the world his righteous laws:
He gives and rules in mercy mild,
Believe, and be ye reconciled
  To a God of truth and love,
  Sending blessings from above;
  Now is the accepted time,
  Listen every joyful clime.

    *Hail—the gospel jubilee,*
    *Jesus comes to set us free,*
    *He is come no more to bleed—*
    *Free we then shall be indeed.*

Now the Sovereign of the sky
Comes, the troops of hell must fly;
He's the Rock of Ages sure,
And all who to the end endure,
A glorious crown of righteousness
Shall wear in realms of endless bliss:
  There with blood-washed throngs above,
  Wondering at redeeming love,

Evermore we'll shout and sing;
Heaven's palace loud shall ring.

*Firm united, let us go*
*On in Jesus' step below,*
*As a band of brothers joined,*
*And eternal glory find.*

**392**                    *L. M.*

IF life's pleasures charm thee, give them not
    thy heart,
Lest the gift ensnare thee from thy God to part:
    His favor seek, his praises speak,
        Fix here thy hope's foundation;
    Serve him, and he will ever be
        The Rock of thy salvation.

2 If distress befall thee, painful though it be,
    Let not grief appal thee; to thy Saviour flee;
        He, ever near, thy prayer will hear,
            And calm thy perturbation:
        The waves of wo shall ne'er o'erflow
            The Rock of thy salvation.

3 When earth's prospects fail thee, let it not dis-
        tress,
    Better comforts wait thee; Christ will freely
        bless;
        To Jesus flee, thy prop he'll be,
            Thy heavenly consolation:
        For griefs below cannot o'erthrow
            The Rock of thy salvation.

4 Dangers may approach thee, let them not
        alarm,
    Christ will ever watch thee, and protect from
        harm;
        He near thee stands with mighty hands,
            To ward off each temptation:

To Jesus fly, he's ever nigh,
The Rock of thy salvation.

5 Let not death alarm thee, shrink not from his
blow,
For thy God shall arm thee, and victory bestow,
For death shall bring to thee no sting,
The grave no desolation :
'Tis gain to die with Jesus nigh,
The Rock of thy salvation.

## 393 *L. M.*

I'LL try to prove faithful,
  I'll try to prove faithful,
I'll try to prove faithful, faithful, faithful,
Till we all shall meet above.

2 Oh, let us prove faithful,
Till we all shall meet above.

3 We mean to be faithful,
Till we all shall meet above.

4 There'll be no more sinning,
When we all shall meet above.

5 There'll be no more sorrow,
When we all shall meet above.

6 There we shall see Jesus,
When we all shall meet above.

7 There we shall sing praises,
When we all shall meet above.

## 394 *P. M.*

LIFE, let us cherish, while yet the taper
  glows,
And heavenly treasures grasp ere it close.
  In vain we seek for earthly bliss:
  The plants of joy, the fruits of peace,

Can never grow in soil like this :
Place all thy hopes in heaven.

2 Life, let us cherish, while yet the taper glows,
And heavenly treasures grasp ere it close.
Our hearts in vain to riches cling,
Our gems are dim, our gold hath wings,
And, when possessed, no comfort brings:
Lay up thy wealth in heaven.

3 Life let us cherish, while yet the taper glows,
And heavenly treasures grasp ere it close.
Set not thy heart on earthly fame,
Its highest gift's an empty name,
That quickly fades, or ends in shame:
True glory comes from heaven.

## 395

LOVE sounds in her sighs, love flows from her
eyes,
How pensive she utters her moan !
The stone is removed, lost is all that she loved,
Ah, Mary ! ah, Mary ! the Master is gone !

2 But in vain was my care, those perfumes to
prepare,
And attempt to embalm him alone,
Taken hence from my view, what, alas ! can I
do ?
Ah, Mary ! ah, Mary ! the Master is gone !

3 But alas ! 'tis in vain to seek ease from my
pain,
From those bosoms as callous as stone ;
None on earth seem to calm, by sweet sympathy's balm,
A heart full of sighs, for the Master that's
gone.

4 Hallelujahs arise! Oh, assist me, ye skies,
    And rejoice with a mortal who mourned!
Hence, sorrow! hence, care! to the winds with
      despair!
Rabboni, Rabboni, the Master's returned!

## 396               *8s, 7s.*

L O! the gospel ship is sailing,
    Bound for Canaan's peaceful shore;
All who wish to sail for glory,
    Come, and welcome, rich and poor.

    *Glory! glory! hallelujah!*
      *All her sailors loudly cry;*
    *While the blissful port of glory*
      *Opens to each faithful eye.*

2 Thousands she has safely landed,
    Far beyond this mortal shore:
Thousands still are sailing in her,
    Yet there's room for thousands more.

3 Richly laden with provisions—
    Want her sailors never know;
Gospel grace and every blessing
    From her noble Pilot flow.

4 Sails well filled with heavenly breezes,
    Swiftly waft the ship along,
All her company rejoicing;
    "Glory!" bursts from every tongue.

5 Do not fear the ship will founder,
    Though the foaming billows roar;
Jesus Christ will safely guide her
    To her destined, happy shore.

6 Foes may try to overturn her,
    But their efforts will be vain;
Guided by so great a Captain,
    Sail she must across the main.
    25

7 Waft along this noble vessel,
    All ye gales of gospel grace,
Bearing all her faithful sailors
    To their heavenly landing-place.

8 Come, poor sinners, be converted;
    Sail with us o'er life's rough sea,
And with us you will be happy,
    Happy in eternity.

## 397        *P. M.*

LET all men rejoice, by Jesus restored;
  We lift up our voice, and call him our Lord;
His joy is to bless us, and free us from thrall,
From all that oppresses, he rescues us all.

2 Him Prophet, and King, and Priest we pro-
    claim,
We triumph and sing of Jesus' name;
Poor idiots he teaches to show forth his praise,
And tell of the riches of Jesus' grace.

3 No matter how dull the scholar whom he
Takes into his school, and gives him to see;
A wonderful fashion of teaching he hath,
And wise to salvation, he makes us through
    faith.

4 The wayfaring men, though fools, shall not
    stray,
His method so plain, so easy the way;
The simplest believer his promise may prove,
And drink of the river of Jesus' love.

5 Yet not many wise his summons obey,
And great ones despise so vulgar a way;
And strong ones will never their helplessness
    own,
Or stoop to find favor through mercy alone.

6 And therefore our God the outcasts hath chose,
  His righteousness showed to heathens like us !
When wise ones rejected his offers of grace,
His goodness selected the foolish and base.

7 To baffle the wise, and noble, and strong,
He bade us arise, an impotent throng :
Poor ignorant wretches, we gladly embrace
A Prophet who teaches salvation by grace.

8 Poor outcasts of men, whose souls are despised,
And left with disdain, by Jesus are prized ;
His gracious creation in us he makes known,
And brings us salvation, and calls us his own.

## 398

MY Bible leads to glory,
  My Bible leads to glory,
My Bible leads to glory,
  Ye followers of the Lamb.

> *Sing on, pray on,*
>   *Ye followers of Immanuel.*
> *Sing on, pray on,*
>   *Ye followers of the Lamb.*

2 Religion makes me happy.

3 King Jesus is my captain.

4 I long to see my Saviour.

5 Then farewell, sin and sorrow.

## 399

MY Christian friends, weep not for me,
  When I am gone ;
And when my lowly grave you see,
  Oh, do not mourn ;
But praise the Lord, I'm freed from pain
  And life's rough storm ;

And pray that we may meet again
    When I am gone.

2 Plant ye some wild-flowers on my tomb,
    When I am gone;
That they may there in silence bloom,
    O'er your loved one;
Entwine a chaplet round my head,
    And often come
And view where sleep the early dead,
    When I am gone.

3 And oft, my friends, in after years,
    When I am gone,
When memory opes the fount of tears,
    Sing ye this song;
And know that though I mouldering lie,
    'Twill not be long
Till we shall meet in yonder sky,
    When I am gone.

## 400    *C. M.*

NOW, brethren, to your homes repair,
    And as you pass along,
Employ your hearts in humble prayer,
    And raise the cheerful song.

2 Praise God, whose mercies brought you here,
    Whose goodness keeps you still;
Whose grace with joy your souls can cheer,
    Whose power subdues your will.

3 Praise him for what your ears have heard,
    For what your eyes have seen;
Praise him for what has here occurred,
    For all you feel within.

4 Improve the strength you here have gained,
    To do his holy will:

Improve the knowledge here attained,
To love and serve him still.

5 Let not the world have cause to say,
You served your God for naught;
But grow in grace from day to day,
As you have here been taught.

6 To friends and neighbors all around,
Oh, let your graces shine;
In ways of holiness abound,
And live a life divine.

7 And now, my Christian friends, adieu,
May Jesus with you dwell;
May grace and peace abide with you:
"So now, dear friends, farewell."

8 Farewell, and to your homes repair,
And as you pass along;
Employ your hearts in humble prayer,
And raise the cheerful song.

## 401 *P. M.*

O CHRISTIAN! will you go with me?
I'm bound fair Canaan's land to see!

*For I'm going home, I'm going home,*
*I'm going home, to die no more!*

2 Our Jesus on the cross did die,
And then he went to reign on high.

3 Our Jesus said, Poor sinner, come,
And from my side no longer roam.

4 The heavenly doors wide open stand,
Up yonder in my Father's land.

5 I'll never leave the union band
Until I reach that happy land.

6 I do believe, without a doubt,
That Christians have a right to shout.

## 402      *P. M.*

OF all religions that are found,
Whose forms do lead their subjects round,
In all this earthly region;
There is one better than the rest,
Which properly is called the best;
And that is pure religion.

2 To visit widows with relief,
And save the fatherless from grief,
In time of their affliction;
And then, against temptations hurled,
To keep unspotted from the world,
Is real pure religion.

3 There's many people who profess
To have religion, more or less,
And talk of sins forgiven;
Who say they walk the heavenly road,
And say they feel the love of God,
And think they're heirs of heaven.

4 But if they gratify their pride,
And will be covetous beside,
And pattern after sinners;
To set their hearts on things below,
And talk as other worldlings do,
'Tis only vain religion.

5 But thanks to God, there are a few,
Who good sincerity do show,
To follow after Jesus:
They joyfully forsake their pride,
And lay their vanities aside,
For the sake of pure religion.

6 They bring their thoughts to judgment now,
 And thus they make their actions bow
   To Jesus their Redeemer ;
 They know, if they're defiled with sin,
 And if they have not Christ within,
   'Twill not be pure religion.

7 All these who count all things as loss,
 And willingly take up the cross,
   To gain a heavenly mansion,
 Although by sinners they're despised,
 They're precious in the Saviour's eyes,
   For they have pure religion.

8 Professors say we are too strict,
 And some good things they contradict,
   Which strike against the worldling:
 And now because we live to God,
 There's many call us very odd,
   Despising pure religion.

9 But while we walk this heavenly road,
 This way of truth which leads to God,
   In which we find such freedom ;
 We'll bear reproach for Jesus' name,
 Endure the cross, despise the shame,
   For the sake of pure religion.

10 Although for Christ we suffer loss,
  We find such virtue in the cross,
    The beauty of his kingdom :
  Oh, let us count all things but loss,
  And like the dung, or as the dross,
    For the sake of pure religion.

# 403

OH say, can you see by the truth's holy light,
 What the fathers once hailed, in the world's
   early being,

When for sin, o'er our race, hung the mantle of
    night—
  When God, for our weal, was in mercy de-
    creeing?
The banner unfurled which shall conquer the
    world,
When sin shall be vanquished—to darkness be
    hurled:
Oh, the cross is that banner, and long may it
    wave,
Till Jesus lead captive both death and the
    grave.

2 'Twas but dimly perceived through the dark-
    ness that reigned,
  And man seemed enchanted in slumbers re-
    posing;
But the prophets their message of mercy pro-
    claimed,
  The banner of peace though obscurely dis-
    closing:
Oft it seemed to unfurl o'er the clouds as they
    rolled,
And the day brightly dawned by the prophets
    foretold;
When the blood-stainéd banner in triumph
    shall wave
Over earth and the sea, over death and the
    grave.

3 Now where is the foe that so vauntingly swore
  By the gods whom he worshipped, that dark-
    ness should rule us;
No home should await us where angels adore,
  But death and the grave should together con-
    trol us?
He has trembled with fear, and will flee in
    despair,

Like the lion the archers have chased to his
    lair;
And our banner in triumph continues to wave,
And triumph it must over death and the grave.

4 Thus will it be ever while Christians shall
    stand
  Near the cross, and remember their high
    destination:
Bless'd with victory and peace, this invincible
    band
  Shall shout when the Lord has renewed all
    creation!
For conquer they must, as their cause is most
    just,
And this is their motto, *"In God is our trust."*
Oh, their banner in glory, in triumph shall
    wave,
When lost is the power of death and the grave.

# 404

OH! weep not for the joys that fade
  Like evening lights away—
For hopes that, like the stars decayed,
  Have left thy mortal day;
For clouds of sorrow will depart,
  And brilliant skies be given;
And though on earth the tear may start,
Yet bliss awaits the holy heart
  Amid the bowers of heaven.

2 Oh! weep not for the friends that pass
  Into the lonesome grave,
As breezes sweep the withered grass
  Along the restless wave;
For though thy pleasures may depart,
  And darksome days be given,—
And lonely though on earth thou art,

Yet bliss awaits the holy heart
When friends rejoin in heaven.

## 405 *P. M.*

OH! give me the flowers that never decay,
  The treasures in heaven that pass not away!
All flowers in this valley of sorrow shall die,
And our riches make wings, and away from us
    fly.

2 Vain man, in the bloom of his health and his
      joys,
Clings fondly to earth and its perishing toys,
Forgetting that beauty will swiftly decay,
And that riches make wings and fly quickly
    away.

3 Go, buy thee new lands and enlarge thy estate,
And write thy proud name with the wealthy
      and great;
But if thou shalt fail of a treasure in heaven,
All thy wealth to the winds shall be rapidly
    given.

4 Go, enter the mart where the merchant men
      meet,
Get rich, and retire to some rural retreat;
Ere happiness comes, comes the season to die;
Quickly then will thy riches all vanish and fly.

5 Go, sit with the mighty in purple and gold,
Thy mansions be stately, thy treasures untold;
But soon shalt thou dwell in the damp house
      of clay,
While thy riches make wings to themselves,
    and away.

6 Oh! give me the flowers that droop not nor die!
A treasure up yonder!—a home in the sky!

Where beautiful things in their beauty still stay,
And where riches ne'er fly from the blessed
    away.

**406**          *2 8s & 4 7s.*

PRECIOUS Bible! what a treasure
    Does the word of God afford!
All I want for life or pleasure,
    Food and medicine, shield and sword,
Let the world account me poor;
Having this, I want no more.

2 Food to which the world's a stranger,
    Here my hungry soul enjoys;
Of excess there is no danger,
    Though it fills, it never cloys;
On a dying Christ I feed,
He is meat and drink indeed!

3 When my faith is faint and sickly,
    Or when Satan wounds my mind,
Cordials to revive me quickly,
    Healing medicine here I find;
To the promises I flee,
Each affords a remedy.

4 In the hour of dark temptation,
    Satan cannot make me yield,
For the word of consolation
    Is to me a mighty shield;
While the Scripture truths are sure,
From his malice I'm secure.

5 Vain his threats to overcome me,
    When I take the Spirit's sword;
Then with ease I drive him from me,
    Satan trembles at the word;
'Tis a sword for conquest made,
Keen the edge, and strong the blade.

6 Shall I envy then the miser
   Doting on his golden store?
Sure I am, or should be, wiser;
   I am rich, 'tis he is poor.
Jesus gives me in his word
Food and medicine, shield and sword.

## 407

RISE—rise—free from thy mourning,
   Light—light—breaks from the sky,
See—see—bright the day dawning,
   Jesus is risen on high.
            Rise—rise—rise—rise—
            Jesus is risen on high.

2 Come—come—sing to the Saviour,
   Love—love—beams from his eye,
Haste—haste—share in his favor,
   Worship the Saviour on high.
            Come—come—come—come—
            Worship the Saviour on high.

3 Praise—praise—yield him with gladness,
   Earth—earth—banish thy gloom;
Where—death—where is thy sadness,
   Jesus returns from the tomb.
            Praise—praise—praise—praise—
            Jesus returns from the tomb.

4 Hail—hail—children adore thee,
   Here—here—anthems we give,
There—there—dwelling in glory,
   Love in thy life we receive.
            Hail—hail—hail—hail—
            Love in thy life we'll receive.

## 408                    P. M.

RELIGION makes me happy,
   Oh, don't you want to go?

I have no time to stay with you,
  I cannot tarry long.

> *Oh, I cannot tarry long,*
> *I cannot tarry long,*
> *I have no time to stay with you,*
> *I cannot tarry long.*

2 I feel the fire now burning.

3 Farewell to all my trials.

4 Oh, soon I'll see my Jesus.

5 With him I'll rise to glory.

6 Christians, don't get weary.

7 You soon will reach the harbor.

## 409 *P. M.*

RELIGION makes us happy,
  Religion makes us happy,
Religion makes us happy,
  We're on our way.

> *Good news gone to Canaan,*
> *Good news gone to Canaan,*
> *Good news gone to Canaan,*
> *We're on our way.*

2 My Saviour says be happy.

3 My sister says she's happy.

4 My brother says he's happy.

5 Ye wretched, come be happy.

6 The mourner may be happy.

7 Oh, soon we'll all be happy.

## 410 *8 lines, 8s & 7s.*

SWEET the moments, rich in blessing,
  Which before the cross I spend!

Life and health and peace possessing
　From the sinner's dying Friend.
Here I'll sit forever, viewing
　Mercy's streams, in streams of blood:
Precious drops! my soul bedewing,
　Plead and claim my peace with God.

2 Truly blessed is this station,
　Low before his cross to lie,
While I see divine compassion
　Floating in his languid eye.
Here it is I find my heaven,
　While upon the Lamb I gaze,
Here I see my sins forgiven,
　Lost in wonder, love, and praise.

3 Love and grief my heart dividing,
　With my tears his feet I'll bathe;
Constant still in faith abiding,
　Life deriving from his death,
May I still enjoy this feeling,
　In all needs to Jesus go;
Prove his wounds each day more healing,
　And himself more fully know.

## 411　*C. M.*

SWEET muse, descend and bless the shade,
　And bless the evening grove!
Business and noise and day are fled,
　And every care but love.

2 'Tis no mean beauty of the ground
　That hath enslaved my eyes;
I faint beneath a nobler wound,
　Nor love below the skies.

3 Jesus has all my powers possessed,
　My hopes, my fears, my joys;
He, the dear sovereign of my breast,
　Shall still command my voice.

4 Some of the fairest choirs above,
  Shall flock around my song,
With joy to hear the name they love
  Sound from a mortal tongue.

5 His charms shall make my numbers flow,
  And hold the falling flood,
While silence sits on every bough,
  And bends the list'ning wood.

6 I'll carve my passion on the bark,
  And every wounded tree
Shall droop, and bear some mystic mark,
  That Jesus died for me.

7 The swains shall wonder, when they read,
  Inscribed on all the grove,
That Heav'n himself came down and bled,
  To win a mortal's love.

# 412

STOOP down, my thoughts that used to rise,
  Converse awhile with death;
Think how a gasping mortal lies,
  And pants away his breath.

2 His quivering lip hangs feebly down,
  His pulse is faint and few,
Then speechless, with a doleful groan,
  He bids the world adieu.

3 But oh, the soul, that never dies,
  At once it leaves the clay!
Ye thoughts, pursue it where it flies,
  And track its wondrous way.

4 Up to the courts where angels dwell,
  It mounts triumphing there,
Or devils plunge it down to hell
  In infinite despair.

5 And must my body faint and die?
    And must this soul remove?
Oh, for some guardian angel nigh,
    To bear it safe above!

6 Jesus, to thy dear faithful hand
    My trembling soul I trust;
And my flesh waits for the command,
    To crumble into dust.

## 413        *P. M.*

TRUST thou not in worldly pleasures,
    Trust thou not in earthly fame,
Trust thou not in glittering treasures—
    Trust in God's eternal name!
In the hour of keenest sorrow,
    In the hour of keenest wo,
Thou canst never hope to borrow
    Comfort from those joys below.

2 Fear thou not a world of folly,
    Fear thou not the scoffer's sneer;
Fear Jehovah, wise and holy,
    (For 'tis wisdom thus to fear:)
Then thy faith shall be augmented,
    And thy heart increase in love;
And thy soul shall rest contented,
    Confident in strength above.

3 And should dangerous snares beset thee,
    Trouble meet thee everywhere,
Fear the Lord; he'll ne'er forget thee,
    He will break the cruel snare.
For his fear is perfect pleasure,
    And his confidence is joy;
'Twill secure thy soul a treasure,
    Which the world can ne'er destroy.

## 414 *P. M.*

THIS world is all a fleeting show,
  For man's probation given;
The smiles of joy, the tears of wo,
Deceitful shine, deceitful flow,
  There's nothing true but Heaven.

2 And false the light of glory's plume,
    As fading hues of even;
  And love, and hope, and beauty's bloom,
  Are blossoms gathered for the tomb,
    There's nothing bright but Heaven.

3 Poor wanderers of a stormy day!
    From wave to wave we're driven,
  And fancy's flash and reason's ray
  Serve but to light our troubled way;
    There's nothing calm but Heaven.

4 And where's the light, held out to cheer
    This heart with anguish riven?
  Affliction's sigh and sorrow's tear
  Have never found a refuge here,
    There's nothing kind but Heaven.

5 In vain do mortals sigh for bliss,
    Without their sins forgiven;
  True pleasure, everlasting peace,
  Are only found in God's free grace;
    There's nothing good as Heaven.

6 From those who walk in wisdom's ways,
    Corroding fears are driven;
  They're washed in Christ's atoning blood,
  Enjoy communion with their God,
    And find their way to Heaven.
    26

**415**　　　*C. M.*

THERE'S not a tint that paints the rose,
　Or decks the lily fair,
Or streaks the humblest flower that grows,
　But Heaven has placed it there.

2 There's not of grass a single blade,
　　Or leaf of lowliest mien,
Where heavenly skill is not displayed,
　　And heavenly wisdom seen.

3 There's not a star whose twinkling light
　　Illumes the distant earth,
And cheers the solemn gloom of night,
　　But Heaven gave it birth.

4 There's not a place in earth's vast round,
　　In ocean's deep, or air,
Where skill and wisdom are not found,—
　　For God is everywhere.

**416**　　　*8s & 7s.*

THERE is a spot to me more dear
　Than native vale or mountain;
A spot for which affection's tear
　Springs grateful from its fountain:
'Tis not where kindred souls abound,
　Though that is almost heaven;
But where I first my Saviour found,
　And felt my sins forgiven.

2 Hard was my toil to reach the shore,
　　Long tossed upon the ocean;
Above me was the thunder's roar,
　　Beneath the wave's commotion;
Darkly the pall of night was thrown
　　Around me, faint with terror:
In that dark hour how did my groan
　　Ascend for years of error!

3 Sinking and panting as for breath,
    I knew not help was near me;
And cried, "Oh! save me, Lord, from death,
    Immortal Jesus, hear me."
Then quick as thought I felt him mine,
    My Saviour stood before me,
I saw his brightness round me shine,
    And shouted, "GLORY! GLORY!"

4 O sacred hour! O hallowed spot!
    Where love divine first found me;
Wherever falls my distant lot,
    My heart shall linger round thee;
And when from earth I rise to soar
    Up to my home in heaven,
Down will I cast my eyes once more,
    Where I was first forgiven.

## 417 *C. M.*

THIS sacred spot, O Lord, to thee
    We consecrate by prayer;
Thy power and goodness may we see
    Displayed in mercy here.

2 While we prepare and clear the ground,
    O Lord, our hearts prepare;
And while we pitch our tents around,
    Lord, spread thy glory there.

3 Erect thy banners, heavenly King,
    As we the stand erect;
May preachers thy salvation bring,
    And souls to thee direct.

4 Didst thou of old thine Israel's camp
    With clouds of glory crown?
By day a cloud, by night a lamp!
    Thus here, O Lord, come down.

5 Now, Lord, before our longing eyes,
　　Thy glory here reveal,
And let us from the lofty skies
　　Thy sacred influence feel.

6 May angels round this chosen spot
　　Encamp by night and day;
May each in order fill his lot,
　　To preach, and praise, and pray.

## 418 *C. M.*

TUNE.—*Carrier Dove.*

THIS book is all that's left me now;
　　Tears will unbidden start—
With faltering lip and throbbing brow,
　　I press it to my heart.
For many generations past,
　　Here is our family tree:
My mother's hand this Bible clasped—
　　She, dying, gave it me.

2 Ah! well do I remember those
　　Whose names these records bear—
Who round the hearth-stone used to close
　　After the evening prayer,
And speak of what these pages said,
　　In tones my heart would thrill;
Though they are with the silent dead,
　　Here are they living still.

3 My father read this holy book
　　To brothers, sisters dear:
How calm was my poor mother's look,
　　Who loved God's word to hear!
Her angel face—I see it yet!
　　What thronging mem'ries come!
Again that little group is met
　　Within the halls of home.

4 Thou truest friend man ever knew,
 Thy constancy I've tried;
Where all were false I've found thee true,
 My counselor and guide!
The mines of earth no treasures give ,
 That could this volume buy;
In teaching me the way to live,
 It taught me how to die.

## 419

TELL me, brothers, will you meet me?
 Tell me, brothers, will you meet me?
Tell me, brothers, will you meet me,
 On Canaan's happy shore?

   *Glory, glory, hallelujah!*
   *Glory, glory, hallelujah!*
   *Glory, glory, hallelujah!*
   *Forever, evermore.*

2 Yes, by the grace of God, I'll meet you,
 On Canaan's happy shore.

3 Say, young converts, will you meet me?
 On Canaan's happy shore?

4 Yes, by the grace of God, we'll meet you,
 On Canaan's happy shore.

5 Heart-broken sinner, will you meet me?
 On Canaan's happy shore?

6 How can a sinner ever meet you?
 On Canaan's happy shore?

7 Jesus will pardon, if you ask him,
 In earnest faith and prayer.

8 Then, by the grace of God, I'll meet you,
 On Canaan's happy shore.

WITHIN the tented grove,
  The followers of the Lamb
Are met to sing his love,
  And glorify his name:
Believers, let your prayers ascend
To him who is the sinner's friend.

2 The Lord of hosts is here—
  His banner floats on high,
He lends a listening ear
  To catch the feeblest cry:
It will prevail, ye need not fear,
If uttered from a heart sincere.

3 Send every vain desire,
  Each trifling thought, away,
And no unhallowed fire
  Upon the altar lay;
Let holy zeal and humble love
In every Christian bosom move.

4 Oh, let the fervent prayer
  Like incense sweetly rise,
And on its pinions bear
  Our offering to the skies;
Through every bosom let it thrill,
And every heart with rapture fill.

5 Save, Lord! on thee we call,
  Oh, save a guilty race—
We at thy footstool fall,
  To seek thy heavenly grace;
Mercy to sinners freely give,
And bid them now repent and live.

**421**

WHAT is life? 'tis but a vapor;
  Soon it vanishes away;

Life is but a dying taper;
  Oh, my soul, why wish to stay?
Why not spread thy wings, and fly
Straight to yonder world of joy?

2 See that glory, how resplendent!
    Brighter far than fancy paints;
There, in majesty transcendent,
    Jesus reigns, the King of saints:
Spread thy wings, my soul, and fly
Straight to yonder world of joy.

3 Joyful crowds his throne surrounding,
    Sing with rapture of his love;
Through the heavens his praises sounding,
    Filling all the courts above:
Spread thy wings, my soul, and fly
Straight to yonder world of joy.

4 Go and share his people's glory,
    'Mid the ransomed crowd appear;
Thine's a joyful, wondrous story,
    One that angels love to hear:
Spread thy wings, my soul, and fly
Straight to yonder world of joy.

## 422

WHEN shall we all meet again?
  When shall we all meet again?
Oft shall glowing hope expire,
Oft shall wearied love retire,
    Oft shall death and sorrow reign,
    Ere we all shall meet again.

2 Though in distant lands we sigh,
Parched beneath the burning sky;
Though the deep between us rolls,
Friendship shall unite our souls,
    And in heaven's wide domain,
    There shall we all meet again.

3 When the dreams of life are fled,
When its wasted lamps are dead,
When in cold oblivion's shade,
Beauty, wealth, and fame are laid;
Where immortal spirits reign,
There may we all meet again.

## 423

WHERE'ER we meet, you always say,
What's the news?
Pray what's the order of the day?
What's the news?
Oh, I have got good news to tell!
My Saviour hath done all things well,
And triumphed over death and hell;
That's the news!

2 The Lamb was slain on Calvary;
That's the news!
To set a world of sinners free;
That's the news!
'Twas there his precious blood was shed,
'Twas there he bowed his sacred head;
But now he's risen from the dead;
That's the news!

3 To heaven above the Conqueror's gone;
That's the news!
He's passed triumphant to his throne;
That's the news!
And on that throne he will remain,
Until, as Judge, he comes again,
Attended by a dazzling train;
That's the news!

4 His work's reviving all around—
That's the news!
And many have redemption found—
That's the news!

And since their souls have caught the flame,
They shout Hosanna to his name;
And all around they spread his fame;
    That's the news!

5 The Lord has pardoned all my sin;
    That's the news!
I feel the witness now within;
    That's the news!
And since he took my sins away,
And taught me how to watch and pray,
I'm happy now from day to day;
    That's the news!

6 And Christ the Lord can save you now;
    That's the news!
Your sinful heart he can renew;
    That's the news!
This moment, if for sins you grieve,
This moment, if you do believe,
A full acquittal you'll receive;
    That's the news!

7 And now, if any one should say,
    What's the news?
Oh, tell them you've begun to pray!
    That's the news!
That you have joined the conquering band,
And now with joy, at God's command,
You're marching to the better land;
    That's the news!

**424**        *7s.*

WHEN our Lord was crucified,
    Two transgressors with him died,
One, with vile, blaspheming tongue,
Scoffed at Jesus as he hung.

2 Thus he spent his wicked breath,
In the very jaws of death,

Perished—as too many do—
With the Saviour in his view.

3 But the other, moved by grace,
Saw the danger of his case,
And, by faith, embraced his Lord,
Whom the scribes and priests abhorred.

4 "Lord," he prays, "remember me,
When in glory thou shalt be."
"Soon with me," the Lord replies,
"Thou shalt be in paradise."

5 This was wondrous grace indeed,
Grace bestowed in time of need;
Sinners, trust in Jesus' name,
You will find him still the same.

6 Oh, beware of unbelief!
Think upon the hardened thief;
If the gospel you disdain,
Christ for you hath died in vain.

# INDEX.